OF BLOOD
AND TIDES

Dear Sarah,

Hope you're
enjoying the story!

Also By Camilla Tracy

Of Threads and Oceans

Of Flowers and Cyclones

Of Blood and Tides

https://geni.us/CamillaTracynewsletter

Or contact me directly at Camilla@camillatracy.com

CAMILLA TRACY

OF
BLOOD
AND
TIDES

THREADS OF MAGIC
BOOK 3

Camilla Tracy

Published by Pudel Threads Publishing

First Printing 2023

Tracy, Camilla, author

Of Blood and Tides / Threads of Magic: Book Three

ISBN (paperback) 978-1-7380086-7-4

eISBN 978-1-7380086-6-7

Under a Federal Liberal government, Library and Archives Canada no longer provides Cataloguing in Publication (CIP) data for independently published books.

Technical Credits:

Cover Image: MiblArt

Editor: Bobbi Beatty of Silver Scroll Services, Calgary, Alberta

Proofreader: Lorna Stuber - Editor, Proofreader, Writer, Okotoks, Alberta

Created with Atticus

For my sister, Jessica.

PROLOGUE

T ARIQ

Three days.

Alexius the dragon had whispered those three words in Tariq's head just as Thali had disappeared with her new dragon friend and protector through a mirror. Ever since his boyhood, Tariq had wished to live among dragons, pegasi, and the creatures in the tapestries and books in his father's library. Never had he thought his childhood fantasies would come true. But there he'd been the other day, conversing with a dragon telepathically.

Now, Tariq was on his way back home after hiding in the forest of his kingdom for a few days. He'd needed to give Thali an excuse to disappear without suspicion, so he'd disappeared into his childhood treehouse deep in the forest. His family and staff knew he wasn't to be disturbed there. Bree had taken the brunt of whatever fallout had resulted from his disappearance, supposedly, with Thali. His darling Bree was too good for him. She had probably smoothed things over with Thali's betrothed, her golden prince Elric, with a single cup of tea.

Tariq paused at the crest of the hill where the trees started to thin out. "Home," he said with a sigh as he gazed upon the shimmering shapes that were the outline of his palace. Even though he'd only been gone three days, he felt a shift in the world. Maybe it was because of his magic that he could sense it. He'd wanted so badly to show Thali his magic ever since he'd used his mind to make a leaf move when they were kids, but his father had forbidden it. He had instructed Tariq to only reveal his weather magic if Thali revealed her own magic first—but to be careful. Magic hadn't existed in Adanek for centuries, and the people would be frightened. Tariq had always suspected Thali's magic was with animals, but when she'd explained it to him initially, she'd described it as threads of magic connecting her to animals. That made sense to him. His magic was like wind to him; hers was like threads.

He'd started vibrating when Thali had finally told him about her magic. He'd sensed its strength when she'd visited this last time. She'd developed her magic much farther and faster than he had. It had taken him years to learn to control wind currents, and there was still a limit to his abilities.

Tariq swallowed as he strode back into the palace. He nodded to a guard as he snuck back in through a quieter, less-used entrance, one Thali could also have snuck through without much notice or fanfare. He hoped she would show up today; he couldn't justify staying in the woods any longer. Alexius had said three days, and three days it had been.

Tariq silently made his way across the cool stone floors, moving from gem-encrusted statue to gem-encrusted alcove on his way to his rooms, careful to stay on the plush gold rugs. Finally reaching his destination unseen, he slipped inside and closed the heavy stone door, hoping Thali would come back before anyone could notice he'd returned alone.

CHAPTER ONE
THALI

A s THALI AND ALEXIUS walked through the thick fog, the ground alternately soft and hard beneath their feet, she felt the effort of each step as if she were fighting through water. Thali had just leaped through a magical doorway in Tariq's bedroom and was starting to have doubts the farther she and Alexius ventured into this numbing place in search of her brother—the brother she'd thought was dead. Did Alexius really know how to get to her brother? Where were they going? Was her brother actually dead after all? What if they were traveling to an afterlife? And why hadn't Alexius brought her to her brother before? What had he been waiting for? The questions came at her furiously.

Alexius hadn't let go of her during their trek so far, and she was grateful for that. The fog was so thick she couldn't see anything past her own nose, so she was trusting him and his dragon senses on their journey. Though the air was thick with moisture, she couldn't smell the salt of the ocean anymore as she could at Tariq's palace. She listened to the deafening silence as closely as she could; all that filled her ears was muted, stuffy quiet, and she felt Alexius's tension in the warm, dry hand that grasped hers tightly.

Just as she thought about reaching out into the white abyss with her mental threads, her magic, to see what they could detect, Alexius spoke in her thoughts. *We'll be there shortly, so keep your threads wound tightly on their spools. And one more thing, Thali. They don't know I can talk to you telepathically, so let's keep it that way for now.*

Thali gave Alexius's hand a squeeze in confirmation.

They walked on for what, to Thali, felt like another ten minutes. She kept her breathing calm as her mind spun out a hundred more questions.

Suddenly, Alexius stopped. He crouched and placed Thali's hand on the edge of an archway, then took her other hand and put it on his shoulder. In her mind, he whispered, *Duck*, so she did as he bid and ducked her head, sensing as she did that they had entered a tunnel. They inched their way through the cool stone tunnel in silence. When they stepped through another archway, Thali shot her arm over her face to cover her eyes as sudden brightness blinded her.

Gone was the fog, and at her feet was smooth white stone. As her eyes adjusted to the brightness of their new location, she realized they were at one end of a wide stone bridge. On the other side of the bridge towered a faded, once-white, gray castle. It looked to be made of a single piece of stone rather than of many stones. Arched doorways had been carved out along the bottom, and battlements had been hewn into the top row. Oddly, while the dense fog surrounded the small castle on all sides, the castle seemed to be holding the fog off, forcing it to hover just yards away.

Thali looked at Alexius, confused. Nothing about this place shouted "afterlife." This looked too ... well, nice, despite the menacing feel of the fog and the dullness of the castle. Thali had the distinct feeling that this building, this area, had once been beautiful. So, if this wasn't the afterlife, then where was she? Was her brother a prisoner here? She didn't understand.

Shaking her head, she followed Alexius as he stepped onto the bridge. As they hurried along its length, their boots clicked and clacked on the stone, barely echoing before the fog absorbed the sound. Thali worked to keep stride with Alexius as she looked around her.

Remember, I will keep you safe. No matter what happens, I have made an oath that I will keep.

Thali nodded at Alexius's reassurance.

They approached sun-bleached, faded blue doors, and before Alexius could knock, the doors opened to reveal a hallway and a grand staircase in multitudinous shades of white and light gray. After a first tenuous step across the threshold, the pair continued down the hall until Alexius suddenly turned right and stopped, making Thali crash into his back. Looming before them was another set of doors, which opened from the inside to reveal a cozy room, cozier than the facade or the hall. A gray-and-white checkered floor was flanked by soaring white walls, a coal-black fireplace set into the middle wall boasted a roaring fire, and a set of plush, plum-purple couches huddled by the fireplace.

A slender man rose from the depths of one couch as the doors opened, his familiar dark brown hair a little longer than the last time she'd seen it. When his gray eyes met hers, Thali froze, his name also frozen on her lips.

"Rou." The tentative smile grew on his face, and in three long strides, he reached her, arms open wide.

"Rommy." She squeezed him back tightly, tears running down her cheeks as she felt the dampness drip off her chin.

He pulled away, grasped both her hands, and led his sister to the plum couches, where they sat down next to each other.

"Rou, there's much I need to tell you."

"Rommy. You're alive." Thali cupped his face, then his shoulders. He was really here, alive. "We all thought you were dead. Why are you here? Why didn't you come home?"

Rommy looked down, his square jaw resting on his chest as he slowly took a deep breath, as if he had to focus on that one task. "Something happened on my last trip, Thali. I can't go home," he murmured. "I have to live here now."

"Rommy, are you a prisoner?" Thali whispered. She noticed the new creases around his eyes, the sharpness of his jaw, the hollowness of his cheeks.

"No, Rou, I'm not. But I can't go back."

"Why?" Thali asked.

Rommy looked away and swallowed.

Why did it seem painful for him to tell her what kept him here? Thali looked around, trying a new tactic. "What is this place?" She shivered at the monotone stone surrounding them despite the roaring fire.

"It's my new home, Thali." Rommy looked up, at once hopeful and homesick. The loneliness oozed from his face, the shadows under his eyes telling a truth he didn't need to say. "Rou, I'll explain everything, I promise. But first, I want to introduce you to some of my friends."

Thali glanced at the doors as they opened again. Alexius stood there, now in the company of three others. They were all impossibly beautiful but had strangely bright hair and eyes.

"This is Xerus ..." Thali's brother, Rommy, motioned to the tallest. The stranger was even slimmer than him and had a sharp nose, the same emerald eyes as Alexius, and long, cobalt-blue hair elegantly tied back.

"... and Jaxon ..." This time, Rommy pointed to a figure as wide as a human could ever be, with shoulders broader than any blacksmith or farmer; short, orange hair; and again, the same emerald-green eyes as Alexius.

"... and Aexie." Rommy nodded to the third: a woman. Her short green hair was angled sharply and stylishly—and exactly matched her green eyes.

They must be Alexius's siblings, Thali concluded. Each wore different clothes but all in various tones of gray. Xerus sported a more formal coat with tails, Jaxon looked like he'd come from weapons practice in a loose shirt and pants, and Aexie had chosen a form-fitting, ankle-length dress. Alexius looked small standing next to his three siblings.

When Thali turned to Alexius, she noticed his expression was grim, his lips drawn into a thin line, and Thali knew in that moment he didn't trust his siblings. She tried not to narrow her eyes as she wondered whether one of *them* had tricked her into letting mythical creatures into the world back when she'd taken her first final exam at school.

"Rou, Xerus and his family have been most generous, saving my life and providing for me here," Rommy explained. He stood and Thali heard his breathing come heavier just from standing.

Each sibling bowed a head to her before exiting, Alexius only waiting a beat longer than the others before leaving her alone with her brother.

When she turned back to Rommy, tea and a small bowl of ramen sat in front of her.

"Hungry, Rou?" he asked.

The gurgle in her stomach gave her away, and she gladly ate as her brother began his tale.

"I wanted to marry Rania, Rou. You must have guessed I would at least try." Thali nodded. "I had gone to propose, but her father was hesitant. I thought he would refuse me, so I got angry and I left. I was planning to come back, but I needed a day or two at sea to sort out my next plan to win her hand."

Thali opened her mouth to speak, but Rommy raised a hand, forestalling her words. "Unfortunately, I didn't realize the storm was as bad as it was. We were tossed around like toys, and half my crew was thrown overboard. Then, my ship capsized, and I couldn't figure out which way was up. I thought I was drowning. I woke up here. Xerus had found me and taken me in. He'd saved my life, but he'd had to use a lot of magic to save me. I'm mostly made of magic now, so I can't survive in your world anymore. I have to stay here." He looked away sadly. "Xerus is kind, and we get along superbly. I told him about your talents, Thali, and he sent Alexius to you. The world, your world, is changing, and I wanted to make sure you would be safe."

Thali stopped mid-slurp. She put the bowl down and took her brother's hands in hers. "You told Xerus about me? When?"

"Xerus is trustworthy, Rou. He saved me. He lets me look out into your world sometimes. And when I saw magical creatures roaming your school's woods, I pleaded with him to send you some protection."

Still suspicious, Thali narrowed her eyes. "And what does Xerus want in return for my protection?"

"He doesn't want anything. Xerus's family just wants peace. Your wild magic, the way you communicate with living creatures with your mental threads, was causing a lot of disruption."

Thali stopped to think for a beat, but as she looked at her brother, she knew there was no one she trusted more. Sustained by magic as he was or not, she hadn't yet encountered any reason to doubt him. She nodded. "Thank you for sending me help." Something was still wrong though. Thali could feel it. Rommy didn't quite seem himself, but he was her brother. If there was one person she trusted most in all the worlds, it was him. She wondered whether he truly believed the words he said and if he had been misled. Picking up her bowl of noodles, Thali filed the information away for later and changed the subject. "Rommy, Mom and Dad are worried sick. You need to show them you're all right."

"I can't do that, Rou. I won't," he said. A shadow passed over his features.

"But why, Rommy? What happened?"

"I told Papa what I wanted to do." He didn't look at his sister as he spoke. "I thought, of all people, he would understand. After all, he stole Mom from that prince, and he was just a common merchant then."

"He didn't understand?"

Rommy looked surprised at her question. He glanced down quickly. "No, Rou, he didn't." He focused on his own wringing hands as he continued. "He told me Rania would have to marry a royal. Her father was already negotiating with other royals in other lands."

"I don't believe it." Thali was stunned.

"I didn't either." Rommy's voice was full of sadness. "I'm sorry I didn't tell you where I was going." He reached absentmindedly for the oyster shell hanging on his chest.

Thali had thought it was still in her father's office. The backside of the shell was facing her. Her brother didn't move to fix it but instead stroked it with a finger. Thali's own fingers itched to turn it back around, but she clenched her fingers instead. Then Rommy cupped Thali's face, as if he didn't quite believe she was really there.

"What are you going to do now? What do you do here?" Thali's heart broke thinking of how lonely her brother must be.

"I help Xerus. I advise him about human behavior mostly. We're trying to find a way to get all the magical animals through the portal and back into this land."

"Wait, that's where I am?"

"Yes, sorry, Rou. I forgot to mention. Welcome to Etciel, the land of magic."

"Is Xerus the king or something here?"

"Xerus is the crown prince. His father, the king, is missing. Xerus has taken over his father's duties until they can find and bring the king back."

"So this is a royal castle?"

"I'm afraid it's not much right now. I've been assured it once teemed with the colors of all the creatures around it before, well, before you opened the portal and let them out." A small smile appeared. "There are some pretty amazing sights here. I'll show you sometime." But then sadness replaced his weak smile once more. "Thali, I've seen glimpses of your life since Alexius joined that school. Are you sure you want to marry Elric? Are you sure you want to be a princess?"

Thali nodded. She had indeed decided that after much thought but was glad she wouldn't have to fill her brother in on everything that had happened to her. She was also relieved she clearly wasn't going to be scolded for falling for a prince of thieves. What saddened her though was realizing her own brother wouldn't be able to attend her wedding.

Her brother read her mind, as always. "Tariq is a good man. He can take my place at your wedding. Thank him for me, will you?"

Thali nodded. She was happy to be with her brother, to know he was here and alive, but something about the entire situation was starting to bug her, and she couldn't figure out what it was.

"You have to leave now." Rommy sounded sad, as if a timer had gone off in his head.

"Why? I just got here. Alexius said we had three days."

"Rou, time moves differently here. Two days have already passed in your world. You have to go back now."

"Can I come back?" Thali asked. They hadn't had nearly enough time together.

"Yes. Please do. There's still so much I need to tell you. But only you. Xerus has said only you are allowed to visit."

Thali nodded. A soft knock revealed Alexius at the door, and Thali embraced her brother, wishing she could bring him back with her.

"Rou, don't tell Mom and Dad I'm alive, all right? They wouldn't understand."

"Are you sure?" Thali asked into her brother's shoulder.

Rommy pulled back and nodded. Thali's brows furrowed as she looked into his sad eyes, and she nodded again and waved before heading out the door and back down the hallway with Alexius. They traveled in silence, Thali following Alexius, holding onto his shoulder, as they retraced their steps back through the fog.

She knew she'd been lied to. But she couldn't figure out if Rommy was lying to protect her, if Xerus was holding her brother hostage and had some kind of spell over him, or if Xerus had just plain lied to Rommy. She had many questions and no answers.

Alexius hadn't spoken since they'd left Rommy. Once out of the castle, they'd trekked mutely back into the fog until Alexius had slowed to a stop before a dirt wall. The journey had felt a lot faster than their first hike to the castle had been. Then, Alexius had touched the low dirt wall, and a rectangle had appeared in the air just above the ground, swirling like porridge being stirred with a spoon. At his indication, Thali had crawled through and arrived in her rooms in Bulstan, Tariq's kingdom, where she was immediately flattened to the ground by an exuberant tiger and a dog. Once her animals were satisfied, Thali flopped down on a nearby chair, overwhelmed by thoughts and feelings and suspicions. Alexius crawled through then and returned the mirror to its solid state.

Alexius pulled a chair up to Thali's. "You have questions."

She looked up at him. "Do you trust your siblings?"

"No."

"Is Xerus bad?"

"No. Of all of them, he's the one I'd trust the most."

Thali was really confused. She absentmindedly pulled at Ana's curly fur and waited for Alexius to elaborate. Why wouldn't he trust his own siblings? But Alexius's lips remained firmly shut, and Thali knew there was no way to force answers from a dragon. Her head spun as she sat back. She would have to mull it over and ask strategic questions later.

Then Elric drifted into her mind. Her eyes widened and she sprang up. Without saying anything to Alexius, Thali asked her animals to stay and hurried over to the painting of a beach landscape and slid it aside. Tariq had taught her about the tunnel system within Bulstan when they were kids. She crawled in, pushing the door inward and letting Alexius follow silently. A couple turns later, she stopped short at another small door. She felt the surface for the short rope she knew would be there and pulled it toward her, pausing and listening to the ruckus beyond the painting she hid behind.

"What do you mean, you left first?!" Elric yelled.

"She's fully capable of handling herself," Tariq replied calmly. Thali recognized the worry in his voice but only because she'd known him so long.

Thali swung the painting to the side and crawled out, Alexius right behind her.

Elric's eyes bulged with surprise, then relief, as his betrothed popped out of the painting. "Thali. You're safe." Elric rushed over to her, and clearly not caring at all who was present, pressed his lips urgently to hers before kissing her cheeks and hands.

Thali looked beyond Elric to see Tariq's shoulders relax.

"Elric, Tari, there's a lot I have to tell you," Thali said once Elric had released her.

Elric ushered her to a white velvet couch, and they all took a seat. He didn't let go of her hands as they sat down. For once, Thali didn't mind the attention. Once they were all settled, she wove a bubble around them and took a deep breath. She would need help to figure this puzzle out.

"Tari, Elric, my brother's alive. He's in some magical world, Alexius's world. I'm not sure if he's being held hostage or if he's even truly himself. He seemed ... different. He told me he almost died at sea, but Alexius's brother saved him. The problem is, Rommy says he can't come back to this world because there's not enough magic here to sustain him. I guess it took a lot of magic to save his life." Thali thought it sounded even crazier when she said it out loud.

A shadow crossed Tariq's and Elric's faces, but neither one said anything.

"Do your parents know?" Tariq whispered.

Thali shook her head. "I'm not supposed to tell them." Then, she thought about what her brother had said about her father. It contradicted what she knew of her father, but she wasn't sure who to believe.

"And what do you have to say about all this?" Elric turned to Alexius.

Alexius had been silent till then. "I was not present during their conversation."

Tariq now turned to him, too. "Surely, you must have some insight."

"I cannot say." Alexius looked like he was struggling with something.

"You cannot, or you will not?" Tariq asked.

"I cannot," Alexius said.

Tariq leaned closer to Alexius until their faces were an inch apart. "Someone has some kind of gag order on you." Tariq eyed Alexius and nodded only slightly when he got the answer he was looking for. "So, what *can* you do?"

"I am to protect the lady and teach her to use her magic."

Elric jumped in. "Can we trust what we say around you?"

"When we're in here, you can," Alexius said as he pointed a finger up and around them.

"In this room?" Elric asked.

"No, in Thali's bubble," Tariq said, sitting back down, still watching Alexius.

Elric looked from Thali to Alexius and back, waiting for further explanation.

"Thali sees magic as threads, and I've been teaching her to use it for more than just connecting with animals. She's woven a bubble around us now, so our conversation remains private," Alexius explained.

"What else does this bubble protect us from?" Elric asked.

Thali answered first. "Only the flow of magic. Nothing physical."

"And you knew?" Elric turned on Tariq.

"She told me earlier. And I know that look on her face, like she's concentrating on the air around her, so I knew she'd created a bubble," Tariq lied.

He'd told Thali he could feel the air stop moving around them when she'd first formed a bubble with him, but apparently, he wasn't about to reveal his secret to Elric. Thali wasn't pleased Tariq didn't trust Elric enough to tell him, but it wasn't her secret to tell, so she played along.

"To clarify, Thali, you were not with Tariq these past three days out on some spiritual retreat in a treehouse?" Elric stood and crossed his arms, staring Thali down.

Thali couldn't help but laugh. "Really, Tariq, a spiritual retreat in a treehouse?"

"You said you'd do that with me next time you were here, anyway." Tariq waved her off.

Thali gripped Elric's hands and said, "I'm sorry I didn't tell you, Elric, but I didn't have time. Alexius said we had to go right then. You have to understand ... he's my brother." Thali felt guilt crushing her insides.

Elric sighed. "It's all right, Thali. If Tariq didn't go with you, I assume you weren't allowed to take anyone with you. As much as I would have protested, at least you're back in one piece. Next time, will you promise to at least leave me a note?"

Thali nodded. Elric brushed her cheek with his hand, and she leaned into it. She wondered if she'd be able to keep the promise. She hoped so. Elric was an only child, so she knew he didn't understand the bond she had with her brother—or with Tariq for that matter. There was always just that little bit of jealousy. Everyone was his adversary. Thali was almost glad her brother and Elric would never meet. She suspected someone would come out bleeding.

"Well, Thali, I think you should go get ready for dinner. Now that they surely know I've returned, our families will be expecting us." Tariq interrupted Elric and Thali's moment.

Thali glared at Tariq while Elric offered Thali his arm. "May I have the honor of escorting you to your rooms?" He flashed her one of his dazzling smiles, and Thali couldn't help but melt.

She stood and curtsied, taking Elric's arm as Tariq rolled his eyes at them as they left his rooms.

They walked a while in comfortable silence before Elric patted her arm. "Thali, I know you had a life before you ever met me. I know there are people in your acquaintance that will continually astound me, but I'd rather hear about them from you than have to piece together whatever information I can find. I love you. I trust you. But you need to trust me, too."

Thali nodded, letting go of the fear that he was going to scold her and instead, tucking herself inside his arm, holding him—her ray of sunshine—as close to her as she could. "I promise I'll try. How were your trials?"

Elric laughed. "I cleaned the palace sculptures with a toothbrush, I mucked out all the royal stables, and I polished the entire armory."

Thali looked up, surprised. Bulstan's armory was extensive.

"Oh, I know." Elric flexed his hand as if remembering how sore it was. "But I think I passed your uncle's tests." He grinned and Thali returned it as she squeezed him. Elric leaned over to kiss the top of her head.

Thali chose the simplest dress she could from the new closet Bree had installed in her rooms. Still, even magnificently dressed, she was strangely nervous about seeing her parents and having to lie about her brother.

A knock on her door brought her back to the present.

"Come in." Thali tucked a strand of her hair behind her ear and checked to ensure the fancy hairstyle her lady had created wouldn't fall apart before she rushed out of her dressing room.

"Daughter! You look beautiful." Her father opened his arms as he walked into her sitting room.

"Papa!" Thali smiled. She had expected Elric to escort her to dinner but was happy to see her father. She ran to embrace him, but he grabbed her hands before she could reach around him.

"A lady mustn't show so much enthusiasm." A twinkle in his eyes told her he wasn't truly scolding her. He bent to kiss the tops of her hands. "Plus, that dress doesn't look like it's meant to stretch for hugs. I will, however, take a kiss."

Thali smiled. She leaned up and kissed her father on the cheek as he took her arm in his elbow and escorted her out of her rooms.

"Come on." Her father held the door open for Indi and Ana, who bounded ahead of them. Thali stroked Bardo, who was draped around her neck, as she thought again of what Rommy had said about their father discouraging him. It sounded unlike their father.

"Where's Mother?" Thali asked as they glided down the hallway.

"Well, Mupto is lavishing his attention on her to try and get a better deal for the gems he wants to sell us. I thought I'd come and bring you to dinner. Tell me, how was the retreat in the trees?" Her father looked at her with a single raised eyebrow.

"It was ... good. Nice. Uneventful." Thali felt heat rise to her face as she lied.

"You're going to have to do better than that at supper time. Maybe I'll ask Tariq first." Her father's mischievous glint told Thali he'd keep her secret. "You should take Elric the next time you and Tariq go on an adventure. The prince was awfully mopey the entire time you were gone."

Thali nodded. She stepped on the edge of her skirts and was glad her father's strong arm halted her headlong pitch to the ground. Regaining her composure and balance, Thali took a deep breath as they paused before entering the banquet hall for supper. She reminded her animals to be on their best behavior.

"He's a good man, your prince," her father said so faintly she barely heard him as they watched Elric head their way.

"I know, Papa."

"But now I know it, too." Her father smiled, turning then to greet Elric.

When they were all seated, Thali watched her parents interact from her seat at Tariq's right. Elric sat on her other side, Bree on Tariq's other side and next to the king. To the king's left was her mother and then her father. Thali wondered if her father had really been capable of refusing to support Rommy when he'd told their father of his plans to ask for Rania's hand in marriage. Yet, when Thali had been a kid, her father had always been harsher on her brother than on her. Not unfairly so, but with higher expectations and less coddling than she'd received. Her father had always been sweet and generous and soft to her. He was a jovial person in general. Even when a deal was going badly, he laughed it off and made the best of it. It was her mother who was harder on people, staring them down or leaping into defensive mode. It was always her father who lightened the mood in the room.

Their dinner was filled with joy and laughter, though Lady Jinhua turned her head away as the king, better known to them all as Mupto, fed Indi and Ana straight from the table. They had abandoned Thali the moment they had entered the room to rest their heads on Mupto's shoulders, and he happily showered them with chunks of meat. By the time dinner was coming to an end, Thali realized she was disappointed to have hardly seen Rania during her stay in Bulstan. Tariq's sister never came to supper for being too ill. Thali would have liked to talk to her about Rommy's tale.

After dinner, Elric escorted her back to her rooms. "You've been awfully quiet this entire night," he commented as he sat beside her in her sitting room. He had taken off his jacket, folded it neatly, and draped it on the arm of the couch so they could enjoy some tea together. Indi tried to wedge herself between them from behind the couch one body part at a time, while Ana took up her own soporific nap on another seat cushion. Even Bardo lay on the table, snuggled up against the teapot.

Thali smiled to see her animals so comfortable with Elric before she frowned. "My brother said something that's been bothering me. He said my father discouraged him when he told him his plan to ask for Rania's hand in marriage."

"Oh? And you don't think your father would have?"

Thali pressed her lips together. "I suppose he isn't exactly fond of royalty. Even when I told him about you, he wasn't excited, nor was my mother, but Rommy and Rania have loved each other since they were ten. Everyone knew. Everyone expected them to get married."

"Wait, your parents don't want you marrying me?"

"Oh." Thali looked down as she realized what had escaped her mouth. Unable to look at Elric's face, she tried to explain. "Well, they just know how much duty and responsibility comes with marrying into a royal family. They're worried for me. On a positive note, my father told me today that he likes you."

"Oh?" Elric threw himself into the back of the couch and burst into laughter, startling Indi, who turned and went to bed.

"What? What's so funny?" Thali was confused.

"You keep me on my toes, Thali. That's all. I've been avoiding young ladies and parents pushing their children on me since I was thirteen. Then when I finally find my queen, she's the only one with a reluctant family."

Thali smiled. She kicked off her shoes and tucked her feet under her skirts before cuddling under Elric's arm.

They sat in silence for a few minutes before Elric spoke. "Thali, what happened to Tariq's mother?" Elric asked after some silence.

Thali's vision blurred even now as she thought of it. "She was a lot like Rania, well the old Rania from before Rommy's shipwreck, beautiful, shy, demure in public. But she loved playing tricks on people. You would have really liked the queen. She was like you in the way that people were entranced by her. She was like a beacon that drew everyone near. Tariq adored her. I adored her. She and my mother were close friends, too. My mother was a lot more lighthearted around her, quicker to laugh, more carefree."

Elric produced a handkerchief from a pocket for Thali as tears rolled down her face. He rested a cheek on her head, holding her close as she continued. "I wasn't here when it happened, but we came for the funeral. All they know is there was an accident. She loved animals. She was working with a horse when he reared up and kicked her in the head. Tariq and Rania weren't allowed near the horses for years after that. Even now, the king refuses to ride horses."

"Did you ... talk to the horse?" Elric whispered into her hair as he ran his fingers through the strands.

"I did. Well, not talk, but connected with. That's how only I know what happened, but I didn't tell anyone. The poor horse felt terrible. A loud noise startled him, and he was young and didn't realize how long his legs were. He loved the queen as much as anyone."

"They didn't destroy the horse?"

Thali sat up. "It wasn't his fault."

"I know, but sometimes when people are angry, they make bad choices. They need to blame something, make someone pay."

"No, the king never really blamed anyone or anything. He was just immensely sad. The queen was her own person, always independent. Even if he'd known the horse would hurt her, there was no stopping the queen when she wanted to do something."

"So much for shy and demure?"

"In public, she was the perfect lady, but in her own home, she was her own person."

"She sounds a lot like you."

Thali snorted. "Perfect lady? Umm ... no."

"Your own classmates admire you. Respect you too. Haven't you noticed more girls signing up as merchants in the last year?"

Thali snorted as she stood up to turn and look at him, rebuttal filling her stormy eyes.

Elric pulled Thali back down next to him on the couch. "It's true. You have a lot more influence than you realize. You're going to make a wonderful queen."

Thali turned her face into Elric's chest and couldn't stifle the laughter that followed when she thought of herself in a pink dress and a golden crown atop her head. She started to snort yet again, she was laughing so hard.

"What's so funny?" Elric looked down at Thali, who had dissolved into a fit of laugher against his chest.

Breathing deliberately to calm herself down, she told Elric about the image she'd envisioned of her as a princess.

"The crown is silver, not gold. And you don't have to wear pink, you know," Elric retorted, looking down at Thali, who had finally calmed herself down. He reached under her chin, bringing her lips to his own. All thoughts of pink dresses and gold or silver crowns disappeared.

CHAPTER TWO

T HALI HAD PROMISED SHE'D go for a ride with Tariq the next morning, after weapons and combat practice. Though her tiger, dog, and snake had joined Thali in Bulstan, Arabelle, Thali's horse, didn't travel by sea very well, so Thali rode an unfamiliar horse. She missed her equine friend. She was happy to ride Bulstani horses, though. They were all pride-filled, magnificent midnight horses with long wavy manes. She barely needed to connect with them as they were already tuned into people. Once they were both astride, Tariq signaled for Lari, his hawk, to fly out ahead of them. Ana and Indi followed in pursuit.

As they rode to their favorite tree in the jungle, they slowed when Thali held up her hand. She always felt better in the wild, surrounded by animals, but sensed a few threads approaching. Indi stiffened and eyed the path ahead while Thali called Ana closer and brought her horse next to Tariq's on the narrow path. Tariq tensed but didn't reach for his sword. The guards behind them did, but Tariq stayed them with a raised hand. Lari landed on his hand as two baby tiger cubs tumbled onto the path ahead as they played. The mother tiger leaped onto the path. Thali sent the mother tiger feelings of calm and stillness. Indi and the other female tiger looked at each other for a few minutes before the mother tiger picked up one cub, turned, and loped off, the other cub following dutifully behind as they left the path and wandered farther into the foliage. Thali could feel Indi's fond acknowledgment of her fellow species and a curiosity at watching the two little cubs. In another breath, the jungle resumed its normal chatter.

Tariq and Thali arrived at their favorite tree and climbed up to the very top, where they could see most of the land around them. Indi climbed up without issue, and Tariq gave Ana a boost. Bardo wrapped himself more tightly around Thali's wrist for the journey, and Lari settled into the branches above them. Thali grinned at being surrounded by her animals. "At least it's too crowded up here for anyone else now," she said pointedly, glancing down at the guards below as the animals spread out on the platform she and Tariq had built in the tree as children.

Tariq didn't reply but rather jumped right into what was bothering him. "Lili, I don't have a good feeling about all this business with your brother. I know he's your brother, so I won't waste my breath saying you shouldn't go there again. But ..."

"I know, Tari, I feel it too. Something's not right there, and I can't help but feel like Rommy's gotten himself involved in something bigger than he realizes."

They were quiet a moment, watching as a bird soared high up in the air. It was a comfortable silence, the kind that exists only between two people whose bond is so close there's no need to speak.

"Lili, what happened with the other fellow?"

Thali's knuckles turned white as she gripped the branch and swallowed. "What other fellow?"

Tariq looked directly at her now and lowered his voice. They hadn't intended to bring guards with them, but being the crown prince of one kingdom and the future princess of another meant they had no less than six guards on the ground, and neither wanted them all to overhear.

"The Prince of Thieves," Tariq mouthed.

Something clenched around her heart as she whispered, "He told me he wasn't good enough for me. That I couldn't do what I needed to while connected to him."

"What else?"

"What do you mean?" She looked at her best friend.

"Lili, you told me all of that in your letter. Was there someone else involved? Someone like an oracle?" Tariq paused, his brows furrowed. "Lili, was there a prophecy?"

Thali was glad for her strong grip and having nestled herself into the tree. Her hands froze as her heart stopped momentarily. Four years ago, oracles had existed only in stories, and now it seemed everyone had encountered one. "How did you know?"

Tariq sighed and slumped his shoulders. "An oracle said you couldn't be together, is that it?" Then he repeated the words that haunted Thali's many dreams and reverberated in her mind:

> *"Centuries locked away,*
> *Legends await the one*
> *To bring the worlds together,*
> *A queen to weave*
> *The future of humans and creatures."*

Unable to open her eyes, Thali whispered, "I don't recognize the last two lines."

Tariq sighed, putting his head in his hands. "I was hoping it wasn't you. When I first suspected your talent with animals, it occurred to me you might be the one the prophecy spoke of, but I'd hoped I was wrong."

"Tari, why didn't you ever tell me?" Thali suddenly felt like the whole world was in on a secret she had only gotten a peek of.

"Tell you what? I wasn't allowed to. You know how oracles and prophecies are. If it happened, it happened. There was no way I'd be able to know for sure until it did."

"And now?"

"My father made you a lady of this court for many reasons, Thali. You have our protection and our help."

They fell silent again. Even the air seemed heavy with all there was to think about and sort through.

Then, Thali smiled. "Remember the first time we climbed up here?"

Tariq smiled back. "Bree kept yelling that we'd break our necks. I was so scared, but there was no way I was going to let you climb higher than me."

Thali laughed. "I was terrified, too. I wanted to prove I was just as brave as you."

"You are. Braver even. But I'll always be here for you," Tariq said.

After a few heartbeats, Tariq asked, "Lili, have you ever considered Alexius ..."

"For what?" She had a feeling she didn't like where Tariq was going with this.

"As a lover." Tari wiggled his eyebrows.

"What?!" In a panic, Thali sent her threads out to wrap a bubble around them magically so Alexius wouldn't hear this conversation.

"You have a lot in common. And is this—" Tariq pulled at the collar of his shirt and motioned at the air around them, "—necessary?"

"He's a dragon, and he's connected to me, in here." Thali pointed to her temple. Her cheeks became as hot as fire as she thought of how mortifying it would be if Alexius did hear this conversation. "And not every male I know has to be in love with me."

"I know. I'm just exploring the possibilities."

"I'm engaged."

"Not married."

Thali put her face in her hands. "Tariq, why can't things be simple? Why is it men are all so ..." Thali waved her hand to let him think what was too embarrassing to say out loud. She turned instead to picking invisible fleas from Indi's fur.

"Hey. I was joking. Alexius has great respect for you. But he certainly doesn't look at you like Elric does." Tariq snorted.

"Good. I'm glad. Because I don't know how to turn down a dragon."

Tariq laughed at that. "But just because you're only noticing it now doesn't mean you haven't had male attention before."

"What do you mean?"

"You've been surrounded by about a thousand protective male figures your whole life. Every time your ship was docked, your crew glared at anyone who dared a glance your way. Crab is one of the largest men I've ever seen, and he's by your side every time you walk into a market—when he's with you, that is. And even here, we've had to rearrange some guards because *I* don't want anyone ogling you either."

Thali was stunned. "You're being ridiculous."

"Oh really? Take Assam, for example. He was your guard when you were here last time. Do you remember him?"

"Yes, he was always helpful and kind. He smiled a lot and often offered his assistance."

"Because he had a crush on you! I reassigned him to town for the duration of your time here because of the way he looked at your rear end."

"What? Why would he be looking at my rear end? Was there something on it?" Thali asked in earnest.

Tariq slapped his own face, running his hand downward in exasperation, "I have no words for your naivete, so I'm not even going to try."

Thali was confused but glad to leave the subject behind them. She decided she didn't want to know what she didn't know anyway and changed the subject to reminiscing about more of their childhood exploits.

CHAPTER THREE
ELRIC

ELRIC HAD INSISTED ALEXIUS and Thali practice magic in his rooms to avoid suspicion, but they were starting to feel a little small and cramped. Tariq had also started to attend her lessons with Alexius, though there wasn't much to see since most of Thali's practicing took place in her mind. Most of the time, Alexius asked her to weave certain shapes with her threads or ask some critters to perform tasks while simultaneously observing other animals in their daily life. It was clearly a lot to focus on because Elric always saw beads of sweat covering her forehead, but Thali took it in stride. She said she was strengthening her ability and diversity with each lesson and that she could follow fifty animals of varying species and distances at the same time now.

Today, Alexius did something different. "Your Highness," he said.

Both Elric and Tariq turned to him, putting their books down in their laps. Thali pressed her lips together, stifling a laugh.

"My apologies, Highnesses. Prince Tariq, is there a place we may practice outdoors? Somewhere we can see the ocean?" Alexius asked.

"Yes, of course. We can go to The Point," Tariq said.

After Thali whispered a few words to her animals to stay put, all four rode west into the forest, nine guards trailing them as they made their way toward a grassy clearing that jutted out into the ocean. After tying up their horses to the branches, Thali and Tariq raced to the farthest point of the cliff before quickly disappearing below the ground. Worried, Elric ran over and realized there were stairs carved into the cliff. Following them, he soon discovered the stairs curved back out along the cliff's side, then ended abruptly at an expansive cave chiseled out of the rock face. It looked as if a giant had taken a bite out of the side of the cliff. It was brighter inside than he'd expected; it was a cozy, private space surrounded by ocean. A sitting area filled much of the space, with heavy waxed cushions gathered in the middle of the flat gray floor and lamps set along a low bench etched in the back wall. Thali and Tariq moved in unison as they went to each lamp and lit them with a match, their backs to the open ocean. They looked at each other before dropping their lit match in a bowl on either side of the cave's opening. Flames raced up and across the ceiling to a central point above the multicolor plushness of cushions and then spread along other spokes across the room. The entire room glowed then, a warm light keeping the cool ocean winds at bay.

"This is amazing," Alexius breathed as he appeared at the opening. He even seemed a little surprised to find such a comfortable spot in such an unlikely place. Thali grabbed a couple of the oversized cushions and dragged them closer to the mouth of the cave where she would have ocean on both sides of her, and Alexius joined her.

Elric strode over to where Thali and Alexius were setting up near the cave's edge. He had to take a step back. The roaring of the waves, the humid mist from the ocean soaking his face and shirt, and endless open seas staring back at him were overwhelming.

"It's beautiful, isn't it? It's like being on the ocean." Thali took a deep breath, closing her eyes blissfully.

"It's incredible." Elric put his hands on her shoulders. He didn't understand, but he was happy for her. Guilt crept into his gut though, as palace life would tear her far away from this.

A cough made Elric turn to look at Alexius, who sat waiting to start his next lesson with Thali.

"Right. My apologies, Alexius," Elric said.

"Your Highness." Alexius nodded, and Elric returned to the other colorful cushions in the middle of the room where Tariq was sprawled, head back, likely listening to the roar of the ocean as it echoed along the surfaces of the cave. Elric sat down, cross-legged, watching as

Alexius and Thali sat next to each other, cross-legged as well, eyes closed and concentrating on something Elric couldn't see or be a part of.

"When did you know?" Tariq asked suddenly. Elric was surprised he could hear him clearly over the crashing waves.

"What do you mean?" Elric asked, still wondering how they could hear each other. Looking around though, he realized perhaps the cushions had been placed specifically in this spot because the acoustics allowed them to speak normally and still hear each other despite the ocean echoing around them.

Tariq looked over, a smile on his face as if he held a secret. "I mean, when did you know you loved her?" Tariq's eyes flicked to Thali's back before returning to Elric's face. Elric wondered if Thali could hear them.

Elric watched Thali's back for a full minute before replying. "I think I fell in love with her the moment I saw her. She was arguing with her instructor, so passionate about her point that she didn't even see me walking in the same space, even with the crowd that was following me. I'd heard her arguing before she even turned the corner and ran right into me, shoulder first. If I hadn't had that warning and braced myself, she might have knocked me over."

"Love at first sight?" Tariq asked.

"I said, I *think*. I *knew* I loved her when I first danced with her. By then, I'd watched her spar, and it was beautiful. But it was the way she treated everyone in her class: It doesn't matter to her whether they're nobility or common. They're all equal in her eyes."

"Huh. Well, speaking of sparring, would you care to spar with me tomorrow morning?" Tariq asked.

Elric sensed the change in Tariq. He sighed. He'd faced her father, her secondary father figure, and a whole ship full of paternal protectors. Now, he had to face her adoptive brother. But he smiled as he thought of all the people who loved Thali without her probably even realizing it.

"Of course, Tariq, I'll spar with you. Just return me to my kingdom in one piece, please."

"You haven't had an easy time with her family, have you?"

Elric shook his head, remembering the bruises that had come with boarding her family's ship. He'd been shoved *by accident* more times than he could count and been watched like a hawk.

A sharp cry interrupted them, and they jumped up to see Thali hugging her knees, shaking.

They ran to her. Alexius put a hand on her shoulder.

"What happened?" Tariq and Elric demanded together. Thali was sobbing into her knees, curled into a rocking ball, but she pointed to the ocean.

Tariq and Elric looked up to see a boat on a patch of ocean filled with red in the distance. A glint caught their eyes, and Tariq disappeared back up the stairs while Elric sat down on the cold wet floor, gathering Thali into his lap and holding her tight.

"We were practicing the number of minds she could touch and see. I'm always scanning for magical creatures, but I never thought to check for humans, too." Elric looked up to see even Alexius looked startled. "The whaler didn't realize she had a baby."

Elric's heart broke in two. He couldn't imagine what Thali was feeling.

"She was with both the mother and the baby when it happened," Alexius whispered, flapping his elbows as he shuddered. Alexius turned away from Elric and Thali, looking to the ocean instead. Thali and Elric sat there, Thali's sobs turning into quiet tears as she buried herself into Elric's chest.

"I felt it, Elric. I felt the mother's panic and anger as the boat came upon her. She was shielding her baby. And then the baby got confused when her mother wouldn't keep swimming with her, and her heart started breaking when she realized her mother wasn't responding. I can't even describe it properly."

Elric sat and stroked Thali's hair. He kissed the top of her head, wrapping himself around her in an effort to protect her from the world in that moment.

"Thali, I know you're hurting, but you can help the baby." Alexius's voice was a whisper.

"Maybe she should be done for today." Elric stared meaningfully at Alexius.

They all looked up to see a small fleet of ships—Tariq's Royal Navy, Elric assumed—chasing the whaling ship as it left a wake of red behind it.

Thali

I can't, Alexius. Thali burrowed into Elric. Maybe the pain would subside if she could burrow into her sunshine.

Alexius's voice piped up in her mind. *I know it hurts, but you can do something about this. Find it a family. Bring them to her. Convince them to take care of her.*

Knowing he was right, knowing she could help, she carefully retreated into her mind with Elric's arms still around her. Shakily, she opened the door to that part of her mind and cringed at first, afraid of the feelings she would encounter through that doorway. She reached out carefully along the hundreds of strands she could see, looking for a periwinkle-blue one, a whale of the same species. Thali searched far into the ocean, surprised at the increase in her range, and finally found a traveling pod. She sent a feeling of worry down their threads, showed them the stranded, orphaned baby, and compelled them to care.

Be careful. Not too forcefully.

She deserves a family.

Thali pushed feelings of need to take the baby in down the threads then. She didn't care if they wanted to or not, so she pushed anyway and compelled them to swim toward the baby, but from the opposite side so they wouldn't run into the whaler. For a brief moment though, she considered getting them to sink the whaling ship.

She willed them blindly into the area, forgetting to think of what else the blood might attract. Thali was so set on bringing the whale pod to the baby, she didn't sense the other whales coming in from the baby's other side until it was too late. As her whales found and surrounded the baby, a large pod of orcas arrived to investigate the blood that had been spilled. The whaling boat was now surrounded by the Royal Navy in the distance and being guided back to shore, having been forced to cut their whale carcass loose. But the orcas didn't focus on the already dead and floating whale. Instead, they homed in on the whale pod directly in front of them, who had been foolish enough to have unwittingly put themselves near shallow water on their way to the baby.

Thali reached out to the orcas, but the horror of her own mistake upset her to the point where it was difficult to focus. The orcas were already in a frenzy for the kill they were about to achieve.

Elric's grip tightened around her as he looked up when the whales called out. A muscle twitched as Alexius clenched and unclenched his teeth.

Thali was desperate to prevent the massacre. Instead of sending images or feelings, she grabbed hold of the threads in her mind that were orca and simply shouted in her mind, *LEAVE NOW!*

They cried out and turned tail to flee, abandoning everything. The effort to keep her mind divided so she could keep the pod of periwinkle whales calm and still send the orcas off urgently was exhausting, so once she'd made sure the orcas were far enough away, she released her hold on the threads, passing out in Elric's arms.

CHAPTER FOUR

WHEN THALI CAME TO, she was staring up into Bree's face. Her tiger was stretched out along one side of Thali, her dog blanketed her legs, and even Bardo came into focus as he rested like a necklace around Bree's neck. At first, Thali thought the sound of crashing waves was in her head, but then she realized she was still in the cave. Her skin was misted with salt, the wind was whipping her hair, and her face was moist with the spray of the saltwater crashing underneath the cave's entrance. With her torso sunk deep in the plush cushions, she felt the cool hard rock only under her legs. The air smelled humid and earthy. Bree was dabbing a cool cloth on her forehead.

"What ...?" Thali tried to sit up. Bree hushed her and helped her to sit, Indi shifting to prop Thali up from behind.

"Boys are so inconsiderate," Bree said, patting Thali's hand. Worry creased Bree's brow, but in her beautiful blue dress and matching light-blue breeches, she looked like the subject of a painting as she kneeled next to Thali.

Thali blinked, then looked beyond Bree to Elric, Tariq, and Alexius. All three were quietly pacing, arms loaded with foodstuffs and dishes, from the stairs to the cushioned area in the middle of the cave where two benches had been moved together to form a square table.

"Tariq alerted the navy as soon as he'd realized what you'd seen, and they've caught the poaching whaler. They came to get me next, and I decided we'd have a little picnic here tonight," Bree said cheerily.

Thali shook her head and immediately regretted the action. Bree pressed a cup of tea to her lips. Thali took a sip without thinking and clamped her lips together the moment she realized it was the disgusting mix her mother had sent to reenergize her.

Bree covered her mouth to hide a delicate laugh. "Sorry. I should have warned you."

Thali swallowed. "How do you do it?" she asked, trying to take her mind off the contents of the cup as she prepared herself to gulp the rest of the vile liquid down.

Bree raised her eyebrows.

Feeling the hot liquid flow through her, Thali sat up a little more on her own. "You rode here, with all this food I assume, they're not fighting, and they're all quietly working away without even cracking jokes."

"Thali, they're worried about you. Their behavior has nothing to do with me," Bree said.

Thali could see Elric sneaking glances at her, trying very hard not to come over to her.

"I told them it only took one person to dab a forehead, and you'd be famished when you woke up, so they had best have dinner ready." Bree squared her shoulders. Then, she leaned down to whisper in Thali's ear. "I almost had to break up a fight between Elric and Tariq, though. Elric wanted to take you back to see a healer, and Tariq insisted you stay here to rest." Bree's eyes glinted with mischief.

Thali gulped down the rest of the disgusting tea, rushing to place a sugar cube that Bree handed her on her tongue to chase down the taste. She could feel her energy returning. She'd be sore tomorrow, but her arms and legs didn't feel as much like dead weight anymore.

Alexius came over to them. "Ladies?" He bowed and moved to help Thali up.

Elric glared at Alexius and ran over to hover around them as Alexius and Bree guided Thali carefully to the low table. Elric immediately sat down next to Thali, pushing Alexius aside so he had to sit across from her. As Bree and Tariq settled down to the feast they'd brought, Thali looked up to see Alexius's grim face. Her animals adjusted themselves to surround her and keep her warm, though Bardo still adorned Bree's neck.

I'm sorry, Thali, Alexius whispered in her mind as quietly as a passing thought. *I'll be more watchful of what's going on around us next time.*

Thali shuddered at the memory of what had happened, of the feelings that had coursed through her. She thought of the catastrophe she'd almost created in her blind desire to make things right.

I'm sorry I let my emotions get away from me.

Alexius gave the smallest nod.

Elric took hold of her hand, and his lips grazed the top of her knuckles. "Are you sure you're feeling all right? I'd feel better if you saw a healer."

Thali smiled at Elric. "I'm feeling much better now. Just tired. This is normal when I overextend myself."

Elric eyed her carefully. Tariq seemed to scan her, but Thali smiled to reassure him. Thereafter, Tariq and Bree kept the conversation light to cheer her up, though Thali was quiet until they had all finished their dinner, bellies full and sipping mint tea.

"Bree, can I assume you know everything Tariq knows?" Thali asked.

Bree looked to Tariq, who looked down, his cheeks turning pink.

"I'm sorry I didn't tell you myself, Bree," Thali said. Bree smiled and shrugged her shoulders.

"I can feel you all want to ask me privately, but instead of having to tell you all the same answer four times, can I just tell you all now?" Thali had felt them all scanning her, watching her closely, trying to decipher for themselves how she was, whether she would crack like an egg, or if she needed more time.

One by one they nodded, so she continued. "I let my emotions cloud my judgment today. I brought those whales closer to shore, to the baby, without caution, and it almost cost them all their lives. When that calf … when that calf's mother died, I was connected to them both and I felt what happened to them. It's not the first time I've been connected to something when they died, but it doesn't happen often, and not usually violently. One reason I hid these powers before was so I could turn a blind eye to that suffering. But I know now that as I continue to develop them, this won't be the last time."

They were all quiet. Thali suddenly didn't know if she'd done the right thing by bringing this out into the open.

Bree cleared her throat with a small cough. "Thali. I'm sure I speak for all of us. We all love you. You don't have to go through this alone. You have all of us here with you. Whatever you need, we're here."

Thali felt a lump rise in her throat as she stared back at all the faces waiting for her response. She'd always felt alone, sure that anyone who knew about her gifts would reject and hate her. Yet, here were four people who knew and loved her anyway. Indi and Ana bumped her hands. Garen's face floated into her head, but she pushed it away, burying it deep.

"Thali … I'm sorry I suggested using your powers for war. I can't imagine how it would feel, and I don't want to see you like that ever again." Elric spoke clearly, but he hung his head in shame. He almost looked like he was waiting for someone to slap him.

Thali moved to cover his hand with hers. "It's okay. You have a kingdom to think of. I'm glad you think of your people and your kingdom. But I'm glad to hear you say those words, too." She looked at the others around the table, her gaze finally resting on Alexius. "I don't want to ever have to demand something from them again."

Alexius nodded. He'd been stoically quiet all night, contemplative. It worried Thali that Alexius had been able to do so little when it had all happened. She depended on him so much as a teacher, she often forgot he didn't have her abilities and might not be able to fix all her mistakes.

Bree, ever the diplomat, broke the tension as she turned to Alexius. "So ... you're a dragon. I see you like the short ribs, but what do you eat when you're in dragon form?"

"Oh ... well, you know, mostly cows and sheep, the odd castle or village here and there." Alexius grinned, his ever-pointy teeth showing, and they all laughed. The atmosphere thankfully lightened and became more jovial then.

Rather than ride back late that evening, they decided to sleep at The Point that night. The princes set up a tent Bree had brought for the men at the top of the cliff, and Thali and Bree piled all the cushions together inside the cave to make themselves a luxurious bed. With the heat of a tiger and dog, they huddled together and talked until they fell asleep mid-sentence, glad to catch up and to have each other to lean on. Two female guards slept on the edge of the cavern, and a small army of guards kept watch above with the two princes and the dragon.

CHAPTER FIVE

T HE NEXT MORNING, THE king sent them breakfast along with a note to hurry back for the celebrations that evening. The ride back was uneventful, with the last two miles a horse race that Thali obviously won, with Tariq a close second and Elric third. Alexius, the consummate gentleman, rode at a slower pace with Bree, who refused to join their foolish race because if they all broke their necks, someone would need to rule all their lands.

They arrived just in time for combat practice, and Thali was glad to throw her aching body into familiar work, though she wasn't excited for the physical beating she'd take.

Once they'd all started their own drills, Thali and Tariq joining Lady Jinhua and Crab in their drills, Thali did not miss the nod between her mother and Amali, one of Thali's two personal guards. Thali would have rolled her eyes at her mother's traditional beliefs if she'd had the energy. That nod made it clear her mother had given explicit instructions for their male and female sleeping arrangements.

The morning passed quickly as it took almost all Thali's energy to focus on the task at hand and not perform so badly that her mother or Crab assigned her more drills. What Thali loved most about combat practice in Bulstan was that everyone was welcome. The participants were sorted by skill, so it never mattered whether you were from the village or the palace; only skills differentiated individuals here.

Thali stood aside after many rounds, thankful to have made it through without additional drills thus far hoping she'd get lucky and be done for the morning. She was watching her mother spar against Tariq for a third round when Elric joined her.

Thali turned to him. "You done?"

He was about to put an arm around her, but as more eyes turned to them, he quickly turned it into a wide-armed stretch and let his arms fall back to his side. "Nope. I'm just warmed up." He turned and pulled the leather string from her hair to tie back his own golden curls before mutely watching the two most elegant and fierce fighters Thali had ever seen.

"Wait, you don't mean to tell me you're sparring with Tariq?" Thali spun around to face Elric, mouth agape.

He pressed his lips together, raised his eyebrows, and nodded.

"He's going to pulverize you," Thali said matter-of-factly.

"I know." Elric offered a halfhearted smile.

"Then why?"

"Because he asked. And I won't turn down a chance to learn from the best." He grinned his best confident smile.

Thali rolled her eyes. "I hope you like being bruised and battered." She took a moment to wonder why Tariq would have challenged Elric in combat.

Lady Jinhua and Tariq hugged then, signaling the end of their session. Elric made his way over to Tariq, way too happy to be humiliated.

Bree walked up to take Elric's place next to Thali and said, "Tariq wants to send his own Bulstani guards with you back to Adanek."

Thali turned around to face Bree, shocked, "But why?"

"You're becoming quite prominent. And popular. He wants to make sure you're safe. It'd put his mind at ease, and mine." Bree tried to offer her an apologetic smile.

"And when was he going to ask me what I thought?"

Bree shrugged. "I'm sure he was getting to it."

Elric and Tariq began stalking each other, slowly moving in a circular dance of sorts. Tariq tried a few halfhearted hits with his staff, and Elric tossed them aside. Though suspicion showed on Elric's face at first, Tariq put on a good show, feigning fatigue from four rounds and a late evening. Eventually, the suspicion in Elric's face was replaced with focus.

Thali watched as Tariq started laying out his plan. She'd seen this routine before. He pretended to slip, landing a hit seemingly by accident on Elric. That revived Elric's suspicion. Everyone in the training ring was now gathered around them, watching the two princes face off.

"Great, he's toying with him." Thali rolled her eyes even as she tensed when their words reached her ears.

"So, why did you want to spar with me, anyway?" Elric suddenly asked.

"I'd like to send four guards back with you to guard Lady Routhalia," Tariq said, using her full name for the benefit of their audience.

"Is that it?" Elric asked as he tried to jab and swing his staff around to land a hit on Tariq's ribs.

Tariq dodged the hit and swung his own staff behind his back to land on the now unprotected side of Elric's ribcage.

"Oof," was all Elric managed as he cringed at the hit. "If that was all, I'd be glad for it."

Tariq straightened suddenly. "Really?"

Taking the prince's sudden surprise as an opportunity, Elric swung his staff just above Tariq's hips. The *thunk* against pure muscle was audible, and Elric's dismay at his victory registered on his face. He struggled to contain it though and continued their conversation. "Of course. She is a lady of your court. Bulstan's combat training is obviously much more thorough than ours, and I trust you feel as I do about Lady Routhalia's well-being."

"Great!" Tariq stuck his hand out to shake Elric's, ending their little match abruptly.

Her blood was singing in her ears as Thali grabbed Bree's staff and stomped over to the two princes.

"And *who* was going to ask *me* what *I* thought?" Thali whacked them both at the same time, throwing Bree's staff at Elric while whacking Tariq with her own.

When they both turned to her, Elric looked guilty, but Thali didn't care. "How dare you talk about me as if I was an inanimate thing to be protected. I am quite capable!" Thali made quick work of Elric by sweeping his feet from under him. He landed harshly on his bottom, stunned at how quick Thali had moved. Thali turned her attention to Tariq.

"We have been best friends since before we could talk, and you didn't even think to ask *me* what I thought of having even *more* guards than I already like to have?!" Thali and Tariq spun around each other, the *clack, clack, clack* of their staffs increasing in speed.

"Lili, I thought you'd prefer it."

"You didn't say '*instead*,' you said, '*in addition*.'" Thali was losing her temper and she was enjoying it.

Tariq met each of her strikes evenly. Though they were close in skill, Tariq was still the better fighter. He let her taunt him and work her anger out.

"You all think I'm completely incapable of handling myself, even though I've been handling myself just fine since long before I ever met Elric!"

"She has a point, dear!" Bree called from the side, trying to hide a wide smile behind a fan.

Thali's mother looked on, trying to smother her own smirk.

Thali noticed Tariq had been leaning into the side Elric had hit, and she suspected Tariq had taken quite a few hits on the opposite side in his previous rounds. So she took her time, her staff flying in different directions. When she finally found her opportunity, she swung as hard as she could into his right side. Tariq doubled over, winded from the repeated hits on the same side. Thali took her chance and knocked him to the ground.

"The next time you want to interfere in my life, maybe you should BOTH think of talking to ME FIRST." Thali threw the staff at Elric, who hadn't bothered to get up off the ground, then turned around and stormed through the crowd of onlookers. Bree followed her, trying to school her smug face into a more demure expression.

CHAPTER SIX

THALI AND BREE WALKED to the female bathing pools deep underneath the palace, where Bree led her to the private pools reserved for the royal family. Thali kept her towel wrapped around her as she stepped into the pool and sat on the carved rock bench, tucking the corner of her soaked towel under her arm. Bulstan had access to hot mineral springs they'd siphoned in to mix with cool water to create baths beneath the palace. The minerals were said to keep skin young and supple, and the women of the island attributed their youthful, glowing skin to them.

Bree, not being nearly as shy as Thali, folded her towel on a nearby table before stepping into the pool. It wasn't large, since it was only for female royals, but the round, dark-gray slate was the perfect backdrop for Lady Ambrene's golden-brown skin. The small pool's bench ringing the inside edge could fit up to eight people. Though it had been naturally etched out of the rock, King Shikji had had images of mermaids and fish inlaid into the rock in gold leaf and gems placed strategically to help light the room. They made the pools glow in spectacular contrast with the dark rock, shimmering gold, and dancing squares of light.

Bree sat on the bench and leaned back to rest her elbows on the sides, tilting her head back to rest on the rock behind her. Thali, still stewing about the audacity of the princes, readjusted her towel as she tucked her arms into her body.

"You're face will freeze like that," Bree teased loftily to the air above her.

Thali exhaled, letting her grimace melt. "How do you do it? You've known you were going to be a princess since you were five. The expectations, the talking above you, over you, about you. Sometimes I feel like a piece of land to be acquired and protected."

"They mean well." Bree opened her eyes, still staring at the ceiling. "Thali." She lowered her head and looked into Thali's eyes. "You're not like most girls." She paused. "Not in a bad way, but most girls would do anything to become royalty."

Thali had loosened up enough to hang her own elbows off the edge of the pool, though she was still worried her towel might come undone.

Bree continued. "Being a queen is the most powerful position a woman can aspire to—at least that's what we've been taught. It's only the few and far between that want something else. Your mother is already different from most in that she didn't choose what most girls dream of. She decided to follow other dreams, harder dreams. And you're an apple off the same tree. You're going to have to cut the princes a break. They're so used to the other kind of girl, the one who only wants pretty things and political warfare."

"And you, Bree? What do you want?" Thali asked into the air as she finally relaxed enough to unfold her limbs like Bree and stare up at the ceiling.

"I love Tariq. I want what he wants. Maybe it's because we were raised together. But we have the same ideas about the people and this island and where we want to be within all of it and the world. But don't get me wrong, I love the pretty things. I wish you'd love them a little more, but I suppose I can love them enough for the both of us." She smiled then as Thali glanced briefly at her before breathing deeply and letting her head fall back again, eyes closed.

"I don't really know how I'm supposed to fit in as a princess. And I can't even imagine myself as a queen."

Bree chuckled. "I can. I've always thought you'd make a good queen if you didn't have one foot in the ocean. I still do."

"Thanks, Bree." Thali thought her friend was being generous. "How do you know what to do and not to do?"

"Each royal family is different. You'll have to ask Elric, but you'll probably both want to strive for the same vision. Elric chose you for a reason. And the formal stuff is only the dressing, not the important work. You have time to learn. If the king and queen approve of you, they'll want you to succeed, so I'm sure they'll arrange a teacher. Oh, and if in doubt, smile and cast your eyes downward."

Thali laughed at that. She was fully relaxed now as she looked up at the ceiling, arms resting along the edges of the pool, her legs floating toward the middle. She let her fingers dip into a tiny puddle of cold water in a groove in the slate floor. Bree sighed, then slowly reached across and grabbed Thali's towel, pulling it away from Thali so she rolled over like meat on a spit. Bree threw the towel with a loud *splat* against the far wall.

"Bree!"

"Thali, you're beautiful and your skin is never going to soak up what it needs if you keep it cloistered in a towel." Bree rolled her eyes and settled back into her reclined position. After a few moments, after Thali had returned to floating, Bree changed the subject. "So Thali, tell me, what are other boys like? I've been engaged since I was five. I'm going to have to live my romantic dalliances vicariously through you."

Thali couldn't help but giggle as she recounted the little she knew, such as how Ban had been sweet and kind at first, then become barnacle excrement. She had an easier time than she'd thought she would telling Bree of how she'd overheard him telling another turd-for-brains that Thali had wanted Ban in her bed but that he wouldn't because of what he'd seen *"down there."*

Bree tutted at her.

"What?" Thali asked.

"You rejected Ban, so he was trying to save his pride to avoid becoming an outcast. Yes, it's deplorable and inexcusable, but he was trying to save face in front of his friends. Add in that you are definitely unattainable now and I'm sure he's still secretly in love with you, and it's no wonder he behaved so abominably," she said.

"You think everyone is in love with everyone," Thali said. She couldn't imagine the glares she and Ban always exchanged could be anything other than hostility.

"Maybe. It's a lovelier way to think than thinking everyone hates each other," Bree said.

They were quiet for a time before Thali moved on to describing all the latest fashions to Bree from what she could remember of Mia's latest work. Mia had been Thali's lady's maid and dear friend since childhood. They'd even gone to trade school together, though Thali had taken merchanting and Mia had taken the seamstress route.

When the girls returned from the mineral pools, they found Tariq and Elric pacing the hall in front of their rooms, each still wearing their dirty combat clothes.

Tariq went to Bree first and kissed her hand, dropping to his knees and putting his forehead on her hands as they whispered quietly to each other. Elric ran up to Thali and gathered Thali's hands together in his. She didn't soften. He glanced at Tariq then before dropping to his own knees and bringing her hands to his lips. He kissed her fingers, her palms, and the insides of her wrists before looking up again. So enthusiastic was he in covering her hands completely in his kisses that Thali's anger melted away and she giggled. Elric's head shot up and that brilliant smile that was her own personal sunshine lit up his face.

"Will you forgive me?" His raised eyebrows and his wide, hopeful eyes made him look like a sad puppy.

Thali sighed, nodding her head.

Elric jumped up, his kisses now moving up both her arms until she was gasping in between her fits of giggles. Suddenly he stopped, standing inches from her. "I'm an idiot, Thali. Your safety is my first priority, and though I've lived with guards my whole life, I'm sorry I didn't consult you first. I can appreciate how difficult all these changes are for you, and I'll strive in the future to make sure you feel included in decisions that affect you. And ... and I love you." He flashed a shy, brilliant smile that made Thali smile.

"Thank you, Elric, I'm grateful you're concerned with my safety. I love you, too." She gave Elric a peck on the lips.

"Great. Now, Prince Elric, maybe you would be so kind as to walk me back to my rooms and help me pick out which of my shiniest jewels I ought to wear tonight?" Bree had come over and taken Elric's arm so Thali and Tariq could have a moment alone. Whenever Elric acted impulsively in Bulstan, Thali knew it was usually Tariq that made him do so, so Thali's fury was mainly aimed at her best friend.

When Bree and Elric were out of earshot, Tariq turned to Thali. "I suppose I can't just lick your arms and make sad puppy eyes at you and you'll forgive me?"

Thali crossed her arms, leaned back on one leg, and stared at him.

Tariq sat down on a beautiful divan edging the corridor. Scrubbing his hands up and down his face, he said, "Lili, I'm sorry. I know you hate having guards, but I don't think you realize how important you are, to me and Bree, to your family. I mean look, your family has friends in all the world's courts, you've had three suitors in as many years—two of whom are princes—and now you're about to become the princess of one of the most powerful kingdoms in the world? Need I mention you have a dragon for your teacher, the magical portal you opened, and the brother you have living on the other side of that?" Tariq put his head in his hands, his elbows resting on his knees. He stayed there, looking defeated.

Thali knew he was trying to figure out how to express himself properly and recognized a new level of stress in Tariq she'd rarely seen before. She sighed, then sat on the floor facing Tariq, leaving just a few feet between them. Then, she spun around to face the far wall, lay on her back, and shimmied toward Tariq so her face was directly between his boots. It was reminiscent of how Thali used to always climb a tree branch higher than him and then hang upside down while they talked.

"Tari, I know you feel responsible for me. And I understand you're worried. I'll admit I don't really know what I've gotten myself into. I can understand why you tried to go around me and appeal to Elric about the guards, but don't do it again. Whatever this future brings me, you are *my* best friend. If you really want me to take those guards with me, I will. I won't like it, but I'll do it if it's what you really want."

Tariq's whole body sighed as his relief became evident.

"On one condition though." Thali's words made him stiffen again. Tariq raised one eyebrow, his face flushed, whether from stress, upset, or exertion though, Thali wasn't quite sure. "Next time you come visit, bring Bree please?"

Tariq grinned. "I'll have to convince my father to let both his future monarchs go, but consider it done." He moved his feet closer together, Thali's head squished between them. "I really am sorry, Thali. I felt terrible going behind your back, but I just ... I want so badly to ensure your safety, and I feel like my hands are tied sometimes. I love my people and my island, but the downside to that is I can't go on your adventures with you. I'm always so far away from you. I feel like you're getting caught up in this ... thing, this imminent war between human and creature, and I won't be able to help you. And that prophecy gives me a bad feeling about it all."

Thali bunched her lips together, making a ridiculous fish face at him. "Maybe you won't always be physically there with me, but I'm going to need your advice."

"And you'll always have it. But it'll always be delayed and just a little too late."

Thali's eyes widened and she suddenly sat upright, smashing her fore-head into Tariq's nose. "Oh, sorry. Are you alright?"

"I'll live." Tariq mumbled as tears sprang from his eyes and he covered his nose with his hand.

"Ok. Good, come on." Thali jumped up and grabbed Tariq's wrist, dragging him back to her rooms.

Alexius, I'm bringing Tariq. Meet me in my rooms.

When they burst into her rooms, Alexius looked at Tariq with surprise. His hand still covered his bleeding nose.

"Not that it's any of my business, but was it necessary to break his nose?" Alexius glanced between Tariq and Thali.

"Oh, that, no, it wasn't like that. It was an accident. Anyway, Alexius, do you think—wait ..." Thali threw up her threads and weaved them around the trio. "Alexius, do you think, you know, the way you and I talk to each other up here ..." Thali pointed to her temple. "... well, do you think that would work over longer distances, and with other people?"

Alexius huffed in a very nonhuman way as he thought it over. "It might be easier to send images down the line, like you do with animals. As you get stronger, you might improve to the point where you can use words. But it's worth a try. You must be careful, though. Anyone you let into that part of you has equal access to you."

Tariq had finally recovered enough that he let his hand fall to his side. "Lili, I thought you couldn't communicate with people magically."

"I can't send suggestions to people, but I can sense them. And lately, I can see their threads, like a cobweb you catch at certain angles. But yours is brighter than the others. Yours and Bree's. Alexius thought it might be because of your magic. If you'll let me, I want to move your thread into the forward part of my thoughts. Then, maybe even with the distance, I'll be able to send you letters by looking at them or reading them."

"Is it going to hurt like my nose does?" Tariq rubbed his nose. He'd need to see a healer before tonight's festivities.

Thali shook her head, sat down, and took a few breaths before she loosened the weave on the imaginary door she'd created in her mind to separate everyone else from her. There, Tariq's golden thread shimmered just enough for her to be able to see it. She gently nudged it toward the door, and taking a deep breath, nudged it through next to Alexius's thread.

Once there, she closed the door again so nothing else could get in. Then she quickly thought of something random, letting the thought drift over the gold thread toward him.

"Purple pineapples?" Tariq looked at Thali, puzzled.

"It worked!" Thali jumped up from the couch she was sitting on. "What was it like?"

"It was strange. I knew it was you because it sounded like you, without actually hearing your voice, but the thought was just suddenly in my brain like it had just occurred to me."

"Interesting." Alexius sounded contemplative.

Tariq continued. "I feel it like I feel the air currents moving around me. It was like a breeze drifting into my mind, and it was a thought that ... that *felt* like you."

Thali squirmed with excitement. "Try to send something back to me."

"Try an image of something," Alexius suggested. "Thali thinks in images easier than in words or sounds."

Tariq went over to Thali's desk, picked up a pen, and wrote something. With his back to her, he concentrated. Thali felt the golden thread waver.

"Eight," Thali said, "with a smiley face in the top loop."

Tariq turned around, showing her the piece of paper. A huge grin filled his face. "I wonder what the range is like."

Suddenly, a light knock sounded, and Thali's sitting room doors opened. A light-blue dress swished in, the person underneath completely hidden by the yards of fabric in her arms. Thali thought for a second maybe it was Mia under the fabric. She missed her other best friend. Then all at once, Thali remembered to undo the magical sphere she'd created around the trio, hoping the servant hadn't noticed anything amiss.

"Looks like we'd better get going." Tariq was as giddy as a toddler with candy as he and Alexius left Thali's rooms. Then Thali received a picture of a doorknob. Then a sculpture in the hall. Then a flower from a vase farther down the hall. She wove a mental sleeve for Tariq's thread as he bombarded her with images. They stayed strong even as he continued to get farther and farther away.

Thali shook her head and blinked, looking at the blue dress. A note was pinned to it:

Inspired by Mia. Took some liberties with this one.
-Bree

More ladies entered and Thali wondered at the liberties Bree had taken as the ladies worked to get the dress on her. A shimmery mesh fabric peeked out of slits in sleeves that draped down in large panels to her wrists. But the bodice was snug as a corset. It was particularly tight right under her chest, pushing her cleavage up and out as though her breasts were being served on a platter. Thali was grateful for the shirt she wore under the dress that would essentially hold her cleavage in. From just under her chest, the dress flared out over her hips, with a silver-and-purple embroidered trim lining the slits in the sides, and indigo tights covering her legs beneath shimmered like the spaces between her sleeves. Thali looked at herself in the mirror. She wasn't sure what to think. But Bree knew fashion better than she did, so Thali shrugged and let the ladies Bree had sent do her hair. The corset didn't allow for Thali to conceal her daggers, but she kept the ones strapped to her legs and across her lower back under the dress. And she left one more dagger on: the one Isaia—her classmate and captain—had made for her. It stayed strapped to her hip on top of the dress. As capable as the Bulstani were, Tariq would throw a fit if he caught her unprepared.

The evening's festivities were in celebration of the royal family's foreign guests. Thali, her family, and Elric would be leaving in a couple days and Mupto liked his celebrations. Thali checked herself in the mirror before leaving her rooms, hoping as she did that they would serve her favorite honey-covered pastries.

Chapter Seven

S HE MET HER MOTHER, father, and Elric in the hall at the doors to the main ballroom. The doors were made of an impossibly heavy, creamy-white stone, and always surprised Thali with how they swung so easily. Perhaps it was a testament to the strength of the Bulstani. Whatever the secret, she and Elric had been informed that King Shikji, Tariq, his sister, Rania, and Bree were already inside. Her guards and Elric's—formally dressed but looking as they always did, ready for anything—flanked the couple. Thali noticed her new, additional guards were Nasir and Khadija. She recognized them from practice that morning; they were both skilled and often sparred with Tariq.

Tariq had been pestering her down their new link since the day before, so Thali had ignored him by wrapping her own thread in a ball around his thread in her mind after he'd started sending her images of Bree's bosom. She could sense him sending more and more images down the link, but she'd had enough of his silliness. Every once in a while, she needed some time to think her own thoughts. She was chatting with Elric when their guards pushed the doors open.

Apparently, the doors were also good at insulating sound. The royal couple and their guards stood in the doorway, staring at the chaos. The entire room was in disarray, and four griffins stalked toward the royal table. Chairs were overturned and all other guests had already fled. Thali grabbed the two knives she'd strapped to her thighs and scanned the room for Tariq. Mupto, Rania, and Bree were hiding behind the raised table reserved for the royal family. Dishes were strewn all over the floor as the table had been pushed over to give the family a shielding wall. They'd also toppled the massive throne chairs to create even more of a barrier between them and the griffins.

Alexius had shown her what griffins looked like before, but to see them in person was still a shock. They looked like huge lions in body, but with a shimmering golden-orange coat. And instead of a furry face and muzzle, fur morphed into feathers to become the giant face of a hawk. The animals were bigger than any lion she'd ever seen, maybe two to three times the size of her Indi.

Thali and Elric's guards closed in around them as the couple watched the royal family's guards and Tariq being cornered by a single griffin.

"We want the girl." The voice was quiet but strong and rang through the hall in a low-pitched echo. The griffins took their time approaching the royal family. Without thinking, Thali bolted from the protection of her guards, counting on them to follow her. Nasir and her mother were the only two quick enough to pursue her. The royal family was without guards, and no matter how good the family's combat skills were, they were overpowered. One griffin was dangerous, three was a slaughter. But Thali knew they could escape through a secret door behind them; she just had to get there. Only she could do it because Tariq was busy with his guards defending themselves against a griffin who had snarled them into a corner.

Don't do anything stupid, Tariq. She opened her link to Tariq and thought along the thread in her brain as she slid across the floor before leaping over the table and royal dais, Nasir following suit. The griffins hadn't slowed or increased their pace, but they showed their teeth as if grinning as they continued their approach.

"Nasir, the candle on the wall directly behind us, grab hold of it and slide the handle down the wall and to the right. A door will open. Get the king and the princesses out through there. Once you're in the tunnel, go straight, and at every intersection, pick the middle path. After three intersections, go left, and you'll end up in my chambers. Keep them safe, and we'll deal with this." Thali placed herself in front of the royals.

Newly assigned Nasir hesitated a moment before nodding and running with the royal family to the wall. Bree put a hand on her shoulder in thanks before glancing at Tariq and bringing up the rear with her own dagger in hand.

Thali leaped onto the overturned furniture.

Her mother stood to her side, keeping the other griffins from closing in on her. "Thali, have you fought these creatures before?"

"Not quite," Thali said. She waved her arms, hoping to draw all the griffins' attention away from Tariq and the guards while she waited for Alexius. She sent what she saw down the turquoise line to Alexius.

Coming was all she heard from Alexius.

The griffins all stared at her, their orange, glowing threads banging at the door in her mind. They wanted to control her, and she wasn't about to let that happen.

Lili, can you hear me? Tariq's voice was in her brain. She nodded ever so slightly. *This cat thing, I think it's a griffin. Body of a lion, head of a hawk. I don't think this one wants to hurt us though. He's here to keep us in one spot.*

Thali nodded. *Please stopper your amazement. It would just as likely slice you in half with a single claw.*

I know, but ... but a griffin! I can hardly believe my eyes, Tariq sent back.

Thali's attention was pulled away then.

"Will you come willingly, girl, or should we start killing your friends one by one until you change your mind?"

Khadija and Thali's father edged their way to her side as well. She wished they would have exited with Elric and his guards.

"Ranulf, I'm supposed to jump into the fight, and you're supposed to stay safe, remember?" Thali's mother squeezed out between gritted teeth.

"We already lost a son. I won't lose a daughter, too," her father said.

Tariq's guards had wedged him to the back of their group and built a wall with chairs. Now, the griffin faced twelve guards standing between him and the crown prince of Bulstan.

Thankfully, Elric's guards had carried him out of the room the way they'd come in, even though he'd been kicking and screaming and trying to get back to Thali. It was ingrained in them to get their prince out of danger, and Thali was grateful Elric was safe.

The griffins padded closer and closer to her, their gait relaxed as they swung their hips and rolled their shoulders.

Thali let out a breath when she saw Elric, Mupto, Rania, and Bree were safely out of harm's way. She hoped these griffins were the only ones on the grounds and she hadn't sent them into yet more danger.

"What do you want with me?" Thali shouted.

"We want to bring you back to our master. He has a special interest in you."

Thali bit her tongue. Her secret. Did they know?

"Who is your master?" Thali asked.

"You will find out soon enough," the griffin said.

A crack and a tinkle of glass was her only warning before the ceiling above Thali crashed down, and a red dragon dropped down in front of her. Thali's shoulders dropped in relief. Thali, her parents, and Khadija dove for cover behind the table as the dragon's wings unfolded to block the griffins from sight. A great shriek came from the dragon's maw before he snapped the head off one griffin and turned to the other two. He breathed fire, first shooting out bright orange flames that slowly turned to white and then blue. Only when the flames turned blue did the griffins back up, careful not to let the fire touch them.

Thali tried to remember what she could of griffins from Alexius's lesson. They were fireproof except for the hottest flames, and those were blue. The two griffins snarled and growled. One leaped up, pushing off the side column to get around Alexius the dragon, but the dragon snapped him in half in his jaws in mid-air.

The third griffin, apparently the smartest of the bunch, was backed into the corner opposite Tariq. "You're a traitor," he growled before the dragon turned him to ash.

The fourth and last griffin that had been cornering Tariq leaped suddenly to sink his claws into the dragon's extended wing, beak open and ready to tear into flesh. But his eyes widened in mid-air as a spear appeared through his middle, red blossoming on his side. His eyes rolled back, and he dropped harmlessly to the floor. Tariq grinned from his position behind his twelve guards, arm still in the air.

The dragon nodded once before leaping up into the air through the destroyed ceiling.

Tariq rushed over to Thali, and his guards surrounded them.

"Thali, are you all right?" Tariq asked.

Thali nodded. "And you?" As her eyes roved over him, his did the same.

Tariq nodded back. Then, everyone ran for the doors and back to Thali's rooms to check on the others. As she burst through the doors, she noticed how crowded it looked with so many people stuffed into the sitting room. Elric was the first to run up to her and wrap his arms around her before glaring at his guards. Tariq emerged to stand behind her, and Bree ran into Tariq's arms. Together, they faced King Shikji, sitting beside his daughter on the sofa. The king would want an explanation.

The king, who had been holding Rania's trembling hands, stood, and the whole room fell silent.

There was a soft knock on the door, and it opened to reveal his captain of the guard. Once bade to enter, he reported, "They entered through the prison sewers and avoided the hallways by climbing through the ceiling. Given the lateness of the day, there weren't many people around to hear anything unusual. But the rest of the palace is unharmed and none the wiser."

The king nodded in acknowledgment of this information and said, "Leave us." As the captain did so, Mupto nodded to Thali's mother and father to stay and instructed a guard to gently lead Rania back to her rooms. In her weakened constitution, she looked close to fainting. "The rest of you," Mupto began, "please, if you would, join me in my rooms. It seems we have much to discuss."

As the door of the king's personal suite closed and Thali and Elric, Thali's parents, and Tariq and Bree were finally alone with the king, his expression softened. They were far less crowded now, and food and tea had been brought to calm their nerves. King Shikji turned to Lady Jinhua and Lord Ranulf and said, "I understand why you didn't, but I wish you'd trusted me with the knowledge of Thali's gifts."

Lord Ranulf pulled his mouth taut, and Lady Jinhua looked ready to leap into battle and fight her way out, one hand on the hilt of the dagger at her hip. Her expression and stance only eased when Mupto sighed and sat down, raising his hands, palms up, to show he meant no harm. "Child, come here." He nodded at Thali.

She went and knelt before Tariq's father, who held out one hand. She glanced at the array of jewels adorning his fingers and bent her head to kiss a barren space.

"I assume your prince knows?" he asked. Elric stood stoically to the side but gave a quick nod.

"Jin, Nulf," the king continued, "you probably ought to sit down. I've a long story to tell you."

As they all sat, uninterrupted for the longest time Thali could ever remember, Mupto told the story of how his family had been charged with guarding a gateway connecting an ancient magical world and theirs. There were four such gates in the human world, and at each was a family on either side, charged with the same duty. Many centuries ago, a human had cast a terrible spell taking magic away from all humans, and because magic thrives on magic, the magical creatures in the human world started to die. As such, they willingly returned to their own world, one filled with magic.

"This story has been passed down through the generations in our family. Along with it is a prophecy:

Centuries locked away,
Legends await the one
To bring the worlds together,
A queen to weave
The future of humans and creatures."

Thali tried to calm her nerves as she heard the words again.

Mupto continued. "The last verse predicts that someone will one day be born with the gifts necessary to bring magical creatures back into the human world peacefully, to bring magic back into this world once the time is right." He looked up at everyone, searching their faces for a reaction. Finally, his gaze fell upon Thali. He leaned over and placed his hand on hers, where it rested in her lap. "Now is that time."

Thali's parents looked meaningfully at each other, that one look saying they'd suspected as much. Tariq nodded and Elric looked scared. Thali herself simply gulped and bit her lip, waiting for judgment and accusation. When none came, only smiles of solidarity, she finally let out the breath she'd been holding.

The little group spent the rest of the evening in the king's suite, the only interruption being Alexius's arrival at Thali's request. The king was honored to meet the red dragon—in his human form of course—and offered to give him Bulstani titles so he could be acknowledged in the human world, but Alexius kindly turned him down.

"I have enough land to care for, but thank you for your generosity," Alexius said. Thali made a note to ask him later about his estate and wondered which world it was in.

It was late in the evening before Alexius, Elric, and Thali were finally alone in her rooms. Suddenly, Elric strode over and punched Alexius in the face.

"Elric!" Thali exclaimed.

"What happened today, dragon?" Elric shoved his face right into Alexius's. "I thought you were constantly vigilant, keeping the magical creatures away?!"

Alexius snarled a warning at Elric. Despite his smaller human stature, he clearly wasn't intimidated by the blond prince. "Tread carefully, princeling." He gave one last low growl. "They must have snuck through my protective barriers from below somehow."

"The sewers," Thali explained. "Mupto's guards found a sewer grate destroyed." She sat down and rubbed her temples.

But that didn't satisfy Elric. "I thought we were in agreement that her safety is paramount. Isn't it your duty to protect her from magical creatures?"

"I handled it. There's not a scratch on her." Alexius's words came out on a growl, his lips pulling back animalistically, showing off all his pointy canines. "And where were you, princeling?" Alexius had drawn himself up, elbows out. Apparently, he didn't appreciate insults.

"My guards are too jumpy for their own good." He turned and looked at Thali. "I fought them the whole time to get back to you. But they wouldn't budge. They've been trained their whole lives to protect me, and until we're married, their first priority is me. That's the protocol." Elric deflated as he sank onto the couch.

Thali slid her hand under his, intertwining their fingers. "I'm glad you stayed safe, Elric, I couldn't stand it if something happened to you."

Elric gave a hollow laugh. "I'm pretty sure that's what *I'm* supposed to say."

Thali's brows knit together; she'd never heard Elric talk like this before. He seemed utterly defeated, completely at odds with his usual enthusiastic, optimistic self. "Elric, what's really bothering you?" Thali ignored Alexius for the time being and focused solely on Elric, scanning his face, his body language.

He ran a hand through his wavy golden hair. "Thali, I … I've been preparing my whole life to become king. I've imagined my future queen, and you've surpassed all my possible expectations and desires. But this whole magical world, I … I know nothing of it and I'm completely unprepared. It's like studying for a test your whole life only to suddenly find out you've been studying the wrong thing."

"I'm new to magic too, Elric. We'll figure it out together. Plus, it's better to know about it now than to find out when you sit down to write that test."

Elric offered up a small smile at that. He seemed to return to himself a bit as he brought Thali's hand to his lips.

"And Alexius, how can we prepare? What can we do so we're not surprised like that again in the future?" Thali turned her attention to the now-thoughtful Alexius.

"I need to visit your brother." He furrowed his brow; he'd been taken by surprise and clearly wasn't pleased about it.

"I'm coming with you." Thali sat up.

"No, you're not. I need to speak with my family too, and they will not be forthcoming if you're there," Alexius said.

"And what if we're attacked again while you're gone?" Elric piped up.

"I'll only be gone a few hours. I can travel much quicker alone. Thali can hold the magical barriers for the short time I'm away."

"How *do* you get back and forth anyway?" Thali asked.

"As guardians of the gate, my family has certain ... privileges," Alexius said.

Thali nodded, confident that she could indeed maintain the magical barrier around the palace. Alexius had showed her weeks ago how to create small barriers and how to hold an existing barrier. Even though she could only create a small one, she knew she could hold the one he'd created for a day on her own, though she'd have to concentrate.

Without another word, Alexius marched over to the peacock-blue papered wall across from him, waved his hand, and stepped through the shimmering doorway that appeared, leaving Thali and Elric alone.

CHAPTER EIGHT

A SMALL SIGH ESCAPED Elric, breaking the silence that had filled the room once they'd finally been left alone.

Thali tried to lighten his mood. "All things considered, you know, without griffins and magical worlds and me disappearing for a couple days, have you had a good time here? Well, and besides Tariq giving you a hard time?"

Elric smiled. "It's beautiful here. I can see why you love it so much. I'll be glad to be home though. Familiar territory and all. Though I'm not looking forward to the trip back." He made a face.

"You did not just say that. The ocean is a close, personal friend of mine, and he is offended by your comment."

"He?"

Thali shrugged. "Why not? Ships are shes, so why can't the ocean be a he?"

"You sure have a lot of protective males surrounding you, Lady Routhalia."

Now Thali made a face at him. "I grew up around men. They make more sense to me than most women."

Elric laughed. "You are one unique lady, Thali. I can't wait to see the changes you'll make among the women at court."

Thali squirmed. The thought of having to face a court full of ladies was scarier than the griffins they'd faced today.

"They won't give you a hard time. I'll make sure of it. But I can't wait to see them scramble to find leather vests so they can imitate your style." Elric grinned.

Thali laughed, trying to imagine dozens of fine court ladies wearing leather vests over their pretty silk-and-lace dresses. She felt her cheeks heat at the thought and lowered her head.

Before she could look up, Elric placed his fingers under her chin and pressed his lips to hers.

A cough interrupted them then and they leaped away from each other. When they looked up, they discovered Alexius standing there, his red hair mussed, but otherwise looking none the worse for wear.

Elric coughed, likely buying himself a moment to recover. "That was quicker than expected, Alexius."

"I did not want to tarry. Lady Routhalia, Your Royal Highness, may I introduce to you my older sister, Aexie?" The air next to Alexius shimmered and suddenly, the woman Thali had met when she had visited Rommy appeared. The imposing woman was tall and thin, with impossible curves and now shoulder-length, emerald-green hair, a perfect match for the unmistakable green eyes Alexius shared. She wore dark-brown tights and a green tunic that hugged her in all the right places such that the outfit looked more feminine than a gown ever could.

Thali turned to see Elric's jaw hanging open at Alexius's counterpart. Alexius, while beautiful, had at least dampened his beauty, but his sister obviously liked the attention given how she flaunted everything she could. Thali smirked as Elric finally noticed she was staring at him staring at Aexie. She knew women looked at Elric, but he rarely reacted. Seeing his usual cool self get tripped up tickled her. Elric coughed, turning a bright shade of red.

"Pleased to see you again, Lady Routhalia, and pleased meet you, Your Highness." Aexie gave a quick curtsy. Her voice was a little higher than Thali would have expected, musical and beautiful. Thali half expected her to giggle after every other word. She looked to Alexius for an explanation.

"I brought Aexie back with me to help. Your strength is growing, and it will be easier for me to focus solely on your training if Aexie can focus on your protection."

Thali's eyebrows rose as she caught Elric again staring at the beautiful female dragon. She had to admit, though, that even she was fighting the urge to stare at her.

"Aexie, that's enough," Alexius said under his breath.

"Just having some fun while I can," Aexie replied, a pout on her very pink lips.

Elric shook his head, making Thali wonder what exactly Aexie was capable of.

Alexius must have known what she was thinking because he said, "Aexie can conceal herself and control her appearance. However, she has been forbidden to enter anyone's minds while she's in this world." Alexius clenched his jaw as he looked to his older sister.

She stuck a tongue out at him as her image flickered, and she turned into a bear, arms still crossed, tongue still out.

Thali laughed. Elric shook his head again when Aexie disappeared beside Alexius.

Can we trust her? Thali asked Alexius in her mind.

For now, yes. But if you're unsure of anything, ask this way. She doesn't know we're connected. While she can detect magic like a shark detects blood, she will not be able to detect this method of communication.

Suddenly, Thali grinned. She called on the other thread secured in the front of her brain seconds before a knock sounded at her door. Tariq and Bree entered immediately thereafter.

"We thought we'd check in before turning in for the night," Bree managed diplomatically.

Thali nodded at Alexius and Aexie reappeared. The red dragon introduced his sister once again. "Your Highness, Lady Ambrene, may I introduce you to my sister, Aexie?"

Aexie dipped into a curtsy again, and Bree smacked Tariq in the arm before moving past him to greet the female dragon. Thali noticed Bree sashayed into the room and flicked on the ultimate mask of a courtly lady: radiant, beautiful, and welcoming.

"My lady." Aexie curtsied so low, her knee touched the floor as Bree approached.

"Thali, however shall we welcome a female dragon to our lands?" Tariq asked, finally picking his own jaw off the floor and approaching the newest dragon. He bowed his head at Aexie. "And when did you arrive?"

Seeming to sense the sudden edge in Tariq's voice, Alexius jumped in. "Your Highness, I've brought Aexie to help me protect Lady Routhalia. My sister will focus on our concealment and protection so I may focus on training."

Tariq didn't look pleased but nodded. *How much do you trust Alexius?*

Thali heard Tariq's voice in her head clear as day. *I trust him enough*, was all Thali sent back.

Because the way I see it, he brought another powerful magical creature into this world through the gate my family guards as easily as if he'd walked into this room from the hall.

Thali nodded ever so slightly and noticed Bree had been occupying the two dragons in conversation. Elric sat on the couch, watching all that was going on and listening to the conversation Bree and the two dragons were having.

Thali couldn't help but yawn then. Thankfully, the others took that as their cue and said their goodbyes.

You can tell if she's in the room if you look for the thread, Alexius sent as he bowed and left Thali, his sister walking behind him before disappearing. Thali took a moment to note what her thread looked like as she stalked gracefully down the hallway. Her thread was a glittery turquoise like Alexius's, but with more glitter than turquoise.

"We still on for tomorrow morning?" Tariq asked on his way out. Thali nodded.

Elric lingered again. He smiled at her, then glanced down. She tried to shove down the butterflies fluttering in her stomach as he took a few steps toward her. Thali was all too aware of how close they were. She could smell him, like warm sunshine in a grassy meadow.

"And I assume I'm not invited to whatever you and Tariq are up to tomorrow morning?"

Thali smiled; she was always surprised to hear jealousy in Elric's voice. "It's a little tradition we do before I leave." Thali stared at the narrow space between her and Elric.

"Oh?" Elric brushed his hand up her arm, and it took all of Thali's energy to keep that narrow space between them.

"We ride out to The Point, and we talk about our plans until we can see each other again. Then, we toss some flower petals into the ocean breeze. It's our way of saying goodbye and reassuring ourselves we'll see each other again."

Elric's lips were less than an inch away from hers. She still had a hard time believing this golden god was in love with her and jealous of her friends. Thali closed the gap, throwing caution to the wind. Her heart started to hammer in her chest as she ran her hands up his chest to wrap around his neck. He wrapped his arms around her waist, running a hand through her dark-brown hair. It was like drinking in sunshine.

The warmth and the heat chased away all her problems, leaving them to cower in the corner as Elric's sun beams kept them at bay.

He pulled away suddenly.

"I should leave." His breath was ragged, and Thali grinned at the molten color of his green eyes as flecks of light danced in the inner edges.

Elric held her hands, kissing each one. "I love you," he said as he walked backward to her doors and quietly left.

Thali bit her lower lip, still tasting her own personal sunshine on them as she dove into her bed among her tiger and her dog and fell asleep dreaming of sunny meadows and churning green eyes.

CHAPTER NINE

THE NEXT MORNING, THALI woke with a jolt. It was departure day. While she was sad to leave Bulstan, it was a blissful morning because today she would be excused from combat practice. She stretched out in her bed before her nose alerted her to something sweet nearby. She followed her nose to her sitting rooms, where Elric was waiting with coffee and an assortment of pastries.

"Can't ride on an empty stomach." Elric grinned widely. He had probably had less sleep than she had, and he still looked refreshed and blindingly handsome. "Are you still wearing the same clothes from last night?" he asked as he bent down to pour a precious cup of coffee for Thali.

As she sat on the sofa in her rumpled clothes, she replied, "Yes." She rubbed her bleary eyes.

He piled a small plate with pastries and handed them to her before sitting across from her. Thali blinked and sipped her coffee, staring at her golden prince.

"Do I have something on my face?" Elric suddenly brushed his face with his hands.

"I'm enjoying the view." Thali grinned into her mug of coffee, breathing in the aroma and feeling her blood stir.

Elric grinned, moved to sit next to her, and planted a kiss on her forehead.

"What are *you* going to do this morning?" Thali drank a blissful sip of coffee and let the hot liquid slide down her throat.

"I'm going to combat practice. Then, I was hoping to accompany you on your tour of the barns when you get back with Tariq."

Without opening her eyes, Thali nodded. She was still enjoying her coffee, feeling the warmth of it spreading through her limbs.

Elric moved closer and put an arm around Thali's shoulders as she leaned into him. This was a quiet moment she could stay in forever. She breathed out a sigh, then took another sip of coffee and felt it rush through her body as she sat in the comfort of her prince's arm.

Thali went to take another long sip of coffee only to have to tip the cup upside down as she searched for the last drop. She frowned as she removed the cup from her face.

"Don't worry, I have more." Elric leaned forward and grabbed the carafe from the tray. Even on Bulstan, coffee was only available in small quantities. Elric must be sharing his own portion.

"Did I ever tell you that I love you?" Thali asked.

Elric grinned. "If all it takes is coffee, I'll fill the whole garden with coffee plants." Elric carefully poured every last drop into her cup.

"It won't grow in Adanek," Thali said as she hugged the cup closer to her.

"Ah, then I will find a way to make sure you have enough of a supply so you can drink to your heart's content!" Elric placed the carafe back on the table.

Thali smiled as she took another sip. She got shaky if she had too much, but she didn't want to spoil Elric's gesture. Just then, her animals finally deemed it time to wake up and padded into the room. The tiger and dog were never chipper in the morning, but Ana sat before her, and Bardo curled up on the dog's head. Thali often wondered if they communicated with each other through her bond with them because what dog lets a snake sit on their head?

Bardo though, was most active in the morning, and he slid off Ana then. He slithered right up Thali's leg and arm, then around her shoulder, about to dive right into her coffee.

"Bardo wait ..." Thali started to say when Elric's hands swooped in above her cup and scooped Bardo up.

"I've got him," Elric said as his hands moved one over the other to let Bardo continue on his little slithering burst. Indi and Ana stretched out on the couch opposite them, and Bardo finally slowed when Elric placed him in a sunny patch on a cushion.

"Don't say I've never saved you," Elric grinned.

Thali laughed.

Thali grit her teeth as she and Tariq rode out in the bitter wind to The Point. They rode in silence, Thali monitoring her horse's breathing. As they neared the ocean, Thali pulled her scarf tighter around her face as the rain hit them so hard, it felt like they were swimming. The bright, sunny dawn had darkened to a cold, wet morning. When they approached the cliff, their horses slowed to a walk, sinking their heads low to brace against the wind and rain pelting them in the face. Thali was completely soaked through as they dismounted and led their horses to a shelter on one side of the clearing. Their guards followed, glad to be able to huddle in the shelter as Thali and Tariq bent their heads into the wind while they traversed across the clearing to the steps leading down to The Point.

The stairs were protected against the worst of the wind, but the friends gripped the inner rail carefully, dreading the thought of having to swim in the icy waters. When they arrived at the entrance, they shrugged off their cloaks and scarves. They hung them up near the lanterns with overly optimistic hopes their attire might dry before it came time to leave. Thali grabbed the bowl in the corner of the room, some dry firewood, and a match. She started a fire and turned to raise her eyebrows at Tariq, who gladly complied by creating the ultimate air flow for the fire. Finally, they huddled around the fire, dragging the cushions closer and trying to absorb the heat into their bones to stop their teeth from chattering. Instead of lighting the entire room, they sat around the fire bowl.

Once they were warm enough to control their shivering, they looked out into the icy wind whipping the edges of the cave. Thali knew Tariq was keeping the wind at bay to help them stay warm and dry.

"So, Lili, what do you think you're going to do in the next year?" Tariq asked.

"I'm going to finish my last year at school. And plan a wedding—or maybe that's not up to me? Who plans royal weddings, anyway? And you better be in Adanek by the end of the year because that's when I'm getting married." Thali looked at the ring on her finger.

"Oh, I'll be there. Bree too. My father might even come. I still can't believe you're going to get married before me. You've known Elric for what, two years?"

"We can't all find our soulmates at the age of five," Thali teased, making a face at him.

Tariq reclined into his cushion, crossing one leg over the other knee. "Lili, Elric's a good man, but are you absolutely sure you want to do this?"

Thali stared at the fire as she took a couple breaths to calm her mind. "Be plain with me, Tari. What are you getting at?"

"Lili, Elric is a prince. He will one day be king. And no matter what, you will always come second. His kingdom will always come first. Plus, you'll always be second in command. I just always imagined you being first. Not second. Either your brother would have shared leadership of your father's fleets, or you'd branch out and command your own fleets. Simply because it's such an independent lifestyle, I always thought you'd take up a life at sea."

"Me too." Thali said it softly as she thought of the life she had imagined for herself since she'd been able to imagine a future. Until two years ago when she'd thought her brother had died. Still, he couldn't come back to this world. Yet, she hadn't spent as much time as she maybe should have thinking about what her future next to Elric would be like.

"Are you sure you love him?" Tariq asked.

"Yes," Thali said.

"And you're sure you want to be a queen?"

Thali could feel his eyes carefully watching her face. "No. I don't know. It's not something I've given much thought to." She thought of Bree and how perfectly suited she seemed to be in each situation, always so diplomatic and standing proudly at Tariq's side. She thought of Elric's mother, elegant and commanding, yet always hovering a step behind her husband.

"Lili, I'm not saying you won't be a good queen. I know you'll be a great queen. But is that what you want?"

"I want Elric. I need Elric." She thought of the dark place she'd been in when Garen, her first and truest love, had left her heart in pieces after an oracle had said Thali was destined to save the world but couldn't do it with Garen at her side. Then, she thought of the field of sunflowers Elric had arranged on her birthday. Elric was her steady and unwavering light. Her life was all happiness and laughter with him. She couldn't go back to the bleakness of before.

Looking thoughtful, Tariq kept quiet. Thali knew Tariq doubted them, but she was happy now. She loved Elric. That would have to be enough for Tariq.

"So ... what do you want as a wedding present?" Tariq grinned.

Thali knew then he didn't doubt her love, didn't doubt her ability to be a good queen. He was just worried about how much of herself she would pour into the world and the toll it might take on her.

Thali grinned. "Hmm ... well, it's supposed to be ridiculous, right? How about a palace like yours?"

"Done," he replied without missing a beat. "Do you want it in blue or purple?"

"Purple! With gold trim and diamond windows!" Thali exclaimed. She couldn't help but grin at the extravagance.

"Done!" Tariq announced proudly as if he were making a royal decree.

"So ... when are *you* getting married?" Thali asked.

Tariq smiled. "Well, now that you're getting married next year, Bree and I figured we might get married a year after you. Then you'll *have* to come visit us."

"Have you really set a date?!"

Tariq grinned and said, "Bree is going to hurt me now that I've told you before she had a chance to, but yes."

"Congratulations, Tari! Your father approves?"

"He suggested it."

Thali jumped up to hug her best friend.

"Now, I have another important question. Will you stand up there with me?" Tariq asked.

"Of course!" Thali couldn't help but squeeze her friend tighter. "Bree is going to skin you alive, isn't she?"

Tariq laughed and let Thali go. "She's been bargaining with me since last year about whose side you should stand on."

"Ha, well you can tell her you asked first after I've left the country." Thali crossed her ankles.

"Coward," Tariq said.

"I'm not about to get on Bree's bad side."

"But I'm the one entering matrimony with her!"

"Then you'll have a lifetime to make it up to her." Thali grinned, imagining how Bree would react to the news. "So, what else does this next year have in store for you?"

"Well, most of the trade for the season is done with your father leaving tomorrow. We're keeping a close eye on the gate, and we have some other delegations coming to visit," Tariq said.

"Who are you sending with me as my guards?"

"Nasir, Khadija, Naseem, and Jaida."

"Four?"

"Two at a time. Two to relieve."

"Wait, you're sending them as full-time guards?"

"Yes. Thali, you won't recognize a threat until it's close, too close. And at court, you'll never know who you can trust. Trust my four. You know each of them; they volunteered, and they know about your magic and can be trusted. Moreso than even Elric's guards."

Thali rolled her eyes. Was it too late to choose a life at sea? She'd have five guards following her around now, full time.

"I wonder if I can convince Elric to go down to two guards. Then there will be four instead of five."

Tariq laughed. "Maybe."

They chatted and enjoyed each other's company a bit longer before Tariq reached into his trouser pocket and pulled a handful of light-pink flower petals from a pouch. Thali stared at them for a long while before pushing off her cushion and taking half the handful. These were Tariq's mother's favorite flower. When she'd died and Thali and her family had come to visit next, Thali had found an angry Tariq in his mother's gardens, bashing and stomping all the flowers. Even then, she'd known her friend was hurting and hugged him fiercely. Even when he'd started to pummel her, she'd held on. He'd finally broken down crying and couldn't even look at the shredded flowers strewn around them. When he'd fallen asleep and his guards had carried him back to his bed, Thali had stayed behind and swept up the mess. She'd picked out all the petals and at dawn had climbed into the tree by Tariq's window and let the petals fly away on a passing breeze. Tariq had spotted her, and ever since then, it was their way of reaffirming their friendship, of wishing each other luck, and saying they loved each other.

As they stood at the edge of the cave, facing the ferocity of the storm, they slowly opened their hands and Tariq's gifts allowed the petals to soar into the ocean. They stood watching them float through the air until they had to squint to see the last dots of pink be swallowed up by the storm.

As they started to dress themselves in their heavy cloaks and scarves in preparation to venture back outside, Thali raised her eyebrows at Tariq. "Why don't you do something about this as we ride back?"

"Not all the guards know. And I'm not supposed to be quite so blatantly obvious." Tariq shrugged into his cloak.

"Shame." Thali wrapped her scarf around her face as they headed up the stairs. She noticed the rain and wind didn't hit them until they surfaced at ground level this time though.

They rode in silence with the shrieking wind pulling at their hoods, and Thali was glad she always maintained the waxy layer of her cloak to keep out the wet.

When they arrived at the barns, the rest of the horses were all inside, snug and cozy in their stalls. Elric was sitting on a straw bale, reading a book by candlelight, when the heavy door slid open to reveal a dripping, shivering Thali, Tariq, and their guards. Elric put his book down and joined the rush of stable hands as they all went to bring the wet horses into the stables and get them warm and dry and safely back in their stalls.

Elric took the cloaks Tariq and Thali shrugged off and stretched them over some straw bales. Thali and Tariq first rubbed their hands together to warm them up, then as the horses were put away, jumped up and down to heat their bodies.

"I've brought hot melted chocolate and spice!" Bree announced as she appeared around the corner at the far end with a basketful of goodies.

The four friends gathered in a nearby corner, and Bree poured four steaming cups of hot liquid chocolate. She'd even brought sweet almond cookies to go with them. They enjoyed a little picnic right there as the stable hands continued caring for the horses.

When the stable hands finished their work and disappeared, Tariq went to find the royal horse master to close and lock the barns so they could be assured they were the only ones in the stables. After the queen's death, Thali had snuck into the barn to touch on the minds of all the horses serving the royal family. She had only been able to show them that Tariq, Rania, Bree, and Mupto were safe, but she'd at least been able to impress upon the horses how it important it was for them to protect the family. Since then, every year, she'd snuck into the barns in the middle of the night once each visit. Tariq had followed her once, and now it was part of their tradition. He'd listened to her when she'd said which horse would be better suited to which task, and he'd never questioned the information because she'd made a show of touching each horse, running her hands along its body and muscles.

This tradition, Thali realized, would be a lot easier now that Tariq and Bree knew what she was doing, and she didn't have to disguise it. Her strength had also grown to the extent that she could now remain where she was and touch on each individual horse thread to determine how they were feeling.

She closed her eyes to better see the images they sent her, and she said aloud which horses were happy and which weren't, and even which had a bellyache. She told her friends which horses didn't like their jobs and what they would prefer to do. Bree wrote it all down.

When she was done, Tariq unlocked the barn doors and they departed, leaving him to chat with the royal horse master. Bree took Thali's arm, giving Elric the basket of leftovers as they traveled along the underground tunnel back to the palace without having to go above in the bad weather. Bree hung onto Thali the rest of the way.

Back in the palace, Thali and Bree settled on Bree's incredibly plushy couches.

"He asked you already, didn't he?" Bree asked as she poured them each a cup of tea.

"Don't be too mad at him." Thali raised her hands as a peace offering.

"I knew I should have asked you last night." Bree sighed dramatically. "Will you walk with me down the aisle?"

"Really?" Thali sat up.

"My parents are long gone, and I have no other family, just Tariq, Mupto, Rania, and you," Bree said.

"Of course," Thali said. She thought that might actually be a fairer way to show her affiliation with both sides. Leave it to Bree to come up with the best balance.

Bree nodded and handed her a cookie. They chatted until supper about the books they'd been reading. Supper was quiet; both families were cheery but saddened at the coming departure. The next time they would see each other would probably be at Thali and Elric's wedding.

The next morning, the storm had abated, and the sky was clear as Tariq, Bree, and King Shikji walked their guests to their ships. They stopped at the same circle of sand in front of the docks as they had when the royal family had greeted Elric, Thali, and her family upon their arrival. Thali stood at the end of the line as they hugged and shook hands and said their goodbyes.

"I've sent an entire three extra trunks with you on your journey back." Bree's eyes sparkled with mischief.

"Three?! Bree, you really don't need to do that." Thali smiled at her friend. She peeled Bardo from around Bree's neck. She was his favorite person and stuck to her most of the time they were in Bulstan. Thali secretly vowed to imitate her friend when she was finally presented at court. *What would Bree do?* would be her new mantra. She would strive to be half as graceful and ladylike as Lady Ambrene.

"My dear, you always have a home here. I'll be sending you some gifts later in the year." Mupto kissed Thali's hand, and her eyes filled with tears she had to choke down. She only managed to squeeze her sort-of uncle extra tightly as she hugged him.

Her parents were already headed for their ship as Elric waited patiently a distance away when she said her goodbyes to Tariq.

"Whenever you need me," Tariq said.

"And even when I don't." Thali stuck her tongue out. She hated goodbyes and would cry if she were to think too much about it.

They hugged and Thali took in the moment before letting go and turning so he wouldn't see her tears. Then, she took Elric's arm and shooed Indi and Ana along. She didn't turn back until she was almost at the ship. Tariq and his family were still waving from where they stood on the sand. She would miss them terribly.

CHAPTER TEN

E LRIC CARRIED TWO CUPS of water across the deck and managed to dodge an elbow directed at him without spilling a drop as he made his way to where Thali stood near the bow.

Thali leaned along the rail, soaking in the endless, open ocean.

"Water?" Elric asked as he handed her a cup.

"Thanks," Thali said. She took it and drained half of it.

"Are they being nicer to you?" Thali asked as she glanced to the side where the crew was coiling rope.

"Some, yes. I'm getting better at dodging, too." Elric smiled. Even when getting picked on, he was still filled with joy.

"I think you helping to wax and mop the deck is helping," Thali said.

"I will scrape the planks free of algae if that's what it takes," Elric said.

Thali grinned and said, "Don't say that too loudly. They'll take all the help they can get for that task."

"Hey, what are you two talking about up here?" Mouse jumped in between them, forcing them to separate as he leaned up against the railing with them.

"We're talking about how nice it is that Elric helps clean the deck in the mornings, Mouse," Thali said.

"I thought I heard the words 'scraping' and 'algae'?" Chip sidled up to Thali's other side.

"You misheard." Thali raised her eyebrows in a challenge.

Chip held her gaze for a minute before ruffling her hair. "Fine, but host a feast for us when you're a royal, will you? I want to fill my belly and see the shiny inside of the palace."

"Done," Elric said.

Chip glanced at him as if he'd just appeared but nodded. "I need an extra set of hands with the nets. You up for it, princeling?"

"Of course," Elric said as he put his cup on a nearby crate. He followed Chip away to the other side of the bow, and to his credit, didn't once look back at Thali.

Thali sighed as she watched Chip and Elric.

"I always thought I'd join *your* crew eventually. At least help you get settled with your own crew one day." Mouse still rested against the railing next to her.

"I know. I hoped for that too for so long."

"You'll make a great queen though."

"I hope I will."

"You will," Mouse said. They watched in silence for a time as Chip made Elric fold the nets one way and then the other way.

"Might be crazy, but there's a shift in the world, Thali. And I keep getting the feeling you're a big part of it. Be safe and don't be too brave, all right?" Mouse looked at her sternly.

Thali nodded. She wondered what Mouse knew. He had always been a quieter, more perceptive member of her little family.

"And don't forget about us." Mouse ruffled her hair too before the wind caught it and threw it around some more.

Thali grinned and slipped an arm under his to hug him. "I'll never forget my family." Thali looked up just in time to see Mouse swallow the emotion bubbling up in his throat as it did in hers.

CHAPTER ELEVEN

"I HATE THAT YOU have to go back to the palace. I feel like we barely got to be alone together," Thali said. They had disembarked from her parents' ship and were heading for her school. Indi and Ana bounded ahead of them.

"Actually ..." Elric began.

Thali's eyes grew wide. She'd thought Elric was just walking her back to her rooms before heading off to the palace. "What? Tell me. You don't have to be back for another week?"

"Longer."

They stopped in the middle of a walkway on school grounds. "Here, why don't I show you?" Elric motioned to a path in the forest behind her building. He took her hand and led her to a quiet manor in the forest unused by the school. Thali had originally stumbled upon it during her walks with her animals, but it had always been frozen in time, with a layer of dust and vines to prove it. Now, throngs of people streamed in and out, most in military dress, but Thali recognized the royal livery of the kingdom's messengers streaming in and out.

"What is this?" Thali turned to Elric.

His eyes shone with glee, and he smiled his smile just for her. "Well, I thought since you were going to be here for another year—and I couldn't stand to be so far away for a whole year—and there's much we have to do to get ready for the wedding that, well ... I thought I'd temporarily relocate."

Elric rubbed the back of his neck as the workers rushed in and out of the old building. "Maybe I should have asked you first? I mean, I'm moving in practically next door, but ..."

"You did all this, for me?" Thali watched as the building buzzed with activity like a hive and its stones shone with the cleanliness of many hours spent scrubbing in preparation for royal habitation. Thali knew Elric was all about big gestures and he had never been afraid to show her how he felt, but this was overwhelming. The amount of effort and the number of people, all relocated so he could spend his measly free hours with her, touched her deeply.

Elric blushed. "Is it all right? We don't have to see each other all the time if that's not what you want. I know you have your own friends and schoolwork and stuff. I just thought ... well, I wanted to be closer to you."

Tears filled Thali's eyes. "Elric, I can't believe you did all this for me."

Relief flooding his face, Elric took her hands. "I'll do all this and more for as long as you'll have me."

Thali wanted to roll her eyes at the ridiculous statement, not quite believing his words, but couldn't help but try to push back the abyss of love threatening to overwhelm her. Suddenly, a noise made Thali turn toward the tree line.

"Whoa. Did the palace move while we were away?" Daylor, who seemed to have become even broader since she'd seen him last, came striding out of the forest, Tilton, looking like the slender gentleman he was, close behind him. Indi and Ana ran up to Thali's fellow merchant students and friends. Ana threw herself at their feet looking for belly rubs, and Indi rubbed her face and chin on them as she purred. The boys obliged with vigorous scratches and pets. Thali smiled as she watched her friends greet her animals.

Elric coughed. "I decided to relocate for the rest of the year."

Thali pressed her lips together as she watched Elric's polite, charming mask drop over his annoyance. She ran up to her friends and swept them up in a hug, scattering her animals.

"We were coming to see if you'd returned yet and saw you heading into the forest. Sorry if we interrupted." Tilton, ever the diplomat, bowed to Prince Elric. Daylor followed suit after Tilton gave him a nudge.

Just then, a liveried messenger made a beeline for them.

"I guess I've been spotted." Elric sighed and turned back to the others. "Dinner tonight, Thali?"

Daylor opened his mouth to speak but quickly shut it again.

"Actually, we have this tradition for the first night's dinner ..." Thali said, her words dropping off because she hated to disappoint Elric. "How about dinner tomorrow night?"

Elric nodded and smiled, though the smile didn't quite reach his eyes.

The messenger arrived. "Your Highness." He bowed low to Elric. "My lady." He bowed again, almost as low as the first time, and even nodded his head at Daylor and Tilton. "Sirs."

Thali was taken aback at the special treatment.

"We will leave you to your affairs, Your Highness." Daylor imitated a court drawl and a deep bow before throwing his arm around Thali's shoulders and steering her back to the forest path. Tilton shrugged his shoulders in apology and bowed again before following the pair.

Thali waved at Elric as she let Daylor pull her back into the forest toward the school. Ana and Indi had already taken off into the trees, and Tilton caught up to Thali and Daylor just as they crossed the tree line. When she glanced over her shoulder one last time, she saw Elric staring at their backs as the messenger tried his best to herd the prince into the building to tend to the many waiting people.

Daylor and Tilton escorted her as far as her door before letting a squealing Mia take over. Thali, too, was excited to see her friend, but no one could match the enthusiasm Mia could express. Tilton and Daylor dashed outside before their eardrums broke. Even Indi and Ana went straight to Thali's room.

Thali spent the afternoon regaling Mia with all that had happened on the Island of Bulstan. She focused especially on all the fashions Lady Ambrene had worn or spoken of but edited out all the magical parts. And though it pained her, she didn't tell Mia about her visit with Rommy. Enough people already knew too much, and Thali worried about what kind of danger it might put them all in.

As the sun sank that day, Thali and Mia welcomed all their friends into their suddenly cramped common rooms. Their little group had grown over the last couple years. Daylor and Tilton came in with trays and trays of food they'd taken from the dining hall, and more people and food arrived with each knock on the door. Soon, there was food piled on food as everyone covered every available surface. Thali had to lock Indi and Ana in her bedroom so they wouldn't eat everything in sight.

Somehow, all Thali's fellow third-years were gathered in her rooms, along with many second-years and even a couple first-years who had been drawn by the sound and smell of food. They caught up with each other about their happenings over the holidays, though it was mostly the third-years dominating the conversation. The second-years tried to absorb all they could, and the first-years were just grateful to be there.

Thali sidled up to Tilton. "Hey, have you seen Kesla? I would have thought she'd be here tonight, too." Almost all the other merchant students were here, but she hadn't seen Kesla or her cousin, Ari, Thali's other close merchant friend. Daylor, Tilton, Isaia—the creator of Thali's most coveted dagger—and Ari had all taken their first final exam together at sea two years ago, and Isaia had nearly died.

Tilton put down the roll that had been halfway to his mouth and looked down at his plate instead. "She died last month. Some beast attacked her family's farm while she was home helping with the harvest, and it killed her parents and her. Her brother was in town running errands and came back to find them shredded to pieces."

Thali's eyes grew wide as her heart sank. "That's terrible. What happened?"

"They don't know. No one saw. The thing was big though, and Kesla's brother thinks it came from the sky because there were no tracks leading on or off their property."

Immediately, Thali thought of a griffin and the gashes she'd seen in Joren's torso that night he'd run into them. Garen's brother and leader of his own thieving family had been trying to learn what was attacking the animals when he'd been hurt.

"I hope whatever it was doesn't come here. It would have a feast, what with the village *and* the school," Tilton said.

Thali tried to smile and lighten the mood. "Master Aloysius would take it down with a single spear."

They fell into silence when they realized someone must have picked up a piece of their conversation, the room eventually filling with whispers of who had been killed over the school break. One downside to her family's travels was missing out on local news, and Thali wished she would have known about Kesla earlier. Thali's eyes landed on Ari, and a weight lifted off her chest. As her gaze continued to sweep over the room, she took note of exactly who was absent and sent a silent prayer they were just elsewhere, not wiped out of existence like Kesla.

Alexius caught her eye. He was halfway across the room, chatting with his fellow second-years. *I can't shield the whole world, though I wish I could.*

Thali nodded. She needed air. The cramped space felt at the same time empty and overwhelming, as though it would swallow her whole. She made her way to her bedroom, and when her animals looked up, went to scratch their heads before climbing out her window to the roof. She sat there quietly, enjoying the first tendrils of winter starting to chill the air around her. Taking a deep breath, Thali thought momentarily of the wickedly smart Kesla. She'd thrown knives like an expert in last year's exams, showing a control Thali had only ever seen bettered by Ari. Thali thought back over the last two years and how much had changed within that short time.

"Have you saved the world yet?" The voice squeezed her heart like a vise, and she had to focus on breathing slowly in and out before she could turn around.

Silent as ever in his soft black boots, he stepped into the moonlight, and the achingly familiar outline that haunted the shadows of her heart appeared. Garen stood just two feet away from her. She studied him from the side, the angles of his square jaw, the shadows under his eyes. Those had darkened since she'd last seen him. His eyes drew her in like the ocean on a stormy night. Even in the dark, she could see the glint of mirth there though. She hoped that never disappeared.

"How have you been?" Thali managed to squeak out far more smoothly than she'd thought.

"Outside the village, we've had plenty of attacks, apparently by big beasts, winged ones, invisible ones even. It's happening in other parts of the world, too. It's becoming dangerous to be in any open field or meadow. Up north by Henrik's territory has the most casualties. Their people have to keep to their stone buildings to stay safe."

Thali swallowed, unsure of how much conversation she'd be able to muster when her heart thundered in her chest and her blood pounded through her body. She took a deep breath and turned away. She thought of her aunt and her fellow student who hadn't returned, who wouldn't have the opportunity to see another sunrise. Garen sat down near her, but far enough away that she couldn't feel the heat of his body next to hers.

"I feel like everyone is telling me to take the helm, but I have no idea what to do there," Thali whispered.

Garen chuckled. She felt him taking his own turn to study her. He was careful to keep his distance though, not to tempt either of them. "You'll figure it out. I believe in you. Whatever darkness is coming, you and the sunshine prince will lead us out of it." His voice cracked at the end of the last word.

"He's taking so much in so calmly. I keep expecting him to snap or yell or even faint from disbelief. But he just furrows his brows and accepts it and then recalculates." It felt strange but nice at the same time to be talking about Elric with Garen.

"He's a good man." Thali barely caught the clench of his jaws as he said it. "You're worth the world, Routhalia, and he knows it. At least he's smart, too."

Thali turned to look at Garen, wanting to say something but not knowing what. What they'd had, she knew, was over. The thrumming of her heart wasn't the same as it had been before. Their relationship had been so secret, so intimate, so powerful, she wasn't sure it had actually happened. Elric was so different, so open, it was hard to call the two relationships by the same name.

"When the time comes, we'll be ready to stand with you. If you need us, you know how to get hold of us." Garen rose silently and melted into the shadows.

His departure was like a spear to the heart. She didn't know what would have been better, his presence or continued absence, but Thali sat there a while longer, wondering if she'd dreamed the encounter. Not feeling like she could go back to a crowded room, she crossed the roof quietly and leaped onto the tree before shimmying down it and following the path through the woods. She practiced seeing through other animals in the forest as she made her way to the manor Elric had commandeered. She walked right up to the front doors, and despite the late hour, people were still milling in and out. But no one stopped her. The guards she passed only nodded as she walked by.

She followed the streams of people into the building and found the concentration of guards highest outside a door at the end of the hall.

After she raised an eyebrow at one of the guards, he bowed and opened the door for her.

Amid bookshelves already lined with tomes and a large oak desk, Elric sat signing some papers, his brow furrowed as he read them over again. His staff whizzed in and out of the room, and a side door was propped open, allowing runners access as they narrowly avoided running into each other. Thali quietly made her way to an armchair next to the fireplace and curled her legs beneath her. She enjoyed watching Elric work. He was in his element, reading this and that, writing a letter here and there, or signing this or that before sending it off. A couple runners had glanced at her as they'd entered the room, but Thali had put her finger to her lips and they'd nodded.

For the first time in a long time, Thali enjoyed not being the center of the attention. She just melted into the decor and watched Elric confidently going about his work.

She must have fallen asleep because she woke up with a blanket around her. The fire was starting to die down, but when she glanced up, Elric was still hard at work, brow furrowed as he wrote a letter before handing it off to a waiting runner. Still curled up in her armchair, Thali felt immensely cozy and fell back to sleep.

The next time she woke, Thali felt a warm, muscled body carrying her up the stairs. She tucked her head under Elric's chin and wrapped her arms around his neck in her drowsiness.

The next morning, she woke with a start, sitting bolt upright, unsure of where she was. The bed was an ivory cloud of softness. The four muted lilac posters were ornately carved, and the walls around her were a matching lavender. Violet furniture rimmed with gold filled the remaining space. Her tiger's groan brought her attention back to the fluffy bed then. Indi and Ana were somehow there, sprawled on the bed, refusing to acknowledge the morning as usual.

Then, Thali remembered where she was and how she'd gotten there. She raised an eyebrow at her tiger and dog, wondering how they had arrived. Bardo was wide awake as he dropped from a poster onto her pillow and slithered up her arm and around her wrist to his favorite spot.

Indi decided it was indeed morning and time to wake up; she stretched with a low bow, butt high in the air, letting a yowl of sleepiness escape her mouth as she turned to the couch at the foot of the bed.

A figure sat on the couch. His outfit was all mussed from sleeping in clothes not meant to be slept in. Even disheveled, Thali was awestruck by Elric's beauty. He sat up taller and stretched his arms wide, the muscles under his shirt highlighting his wide torso.

"When did you know I was there?" Thali asked. She tried desperately to comb her hair down before he turned and saw her.

Elric yawned, then peered at her over the back of the couch. "The moment you came in."

Thali pouted. "Then why didn't you say anything?"

Elric shrugged. "I figured you needed some quiet time since you snuck out of a party and all."

"Were you spying on me?" Thali asked.

"No. But I could hear it from here," Elric said.

"Reconsidering your neighbors?" Thali asked with a grin.

"Never." His own grin widened, and Thali's heart melted.

Thali looked around at all the purple. "Is this your bedroom?"

"No, it's yours." Elric looked sheepish as he too looked around. "You can redecorate if you want."

"Oh no, it's fine." She looked around again at all the golden accents in the purple furniture offset by white. "I can't imagine a couch is a comfortable place to sleep though, Your Highness." Thali raised an eyebrow.

"Well, after Indi and Ana waltzed through the front door and up the stairs to find you, I wondered if something was wrong and wanted to stay close in case there was."

She smiled and tilted her head. "Is charm part of your royal training too?"

"Why of course." Elric dipped into a low bow with his torso. His hair stood up at odd angles, and it made her feel warm and fuzzy inside.

Thali's eyes suddenly went wide, and she glanced out the window at the sun. She shrieked and jumped out of bed.

"What's wrong?" Elric jumped up.

"I have Combat class!" Thali leaped up and was happy to find she was in the same clothes she'd arrived in. She dashed out of the bed and right up to Elric, giving him a quick peck on the cheek before running out the door, down the stairs, out of the manor, and across the forest at a full run with her tiger and dog right behind her. She sent Ana and Indi back to her room as she continued running for the combat field.

When she arrived, Master Aloysius made a point of checking the time on the sundial behind him before looking at her pointedly. Daylor looked like he was having a tough time keeping a straight face, and Alexius sidled up to her. *Interesting night?*

Not really.

Good.

"All right, lassie, lad, come 'ere and demonstrate the drills for the first-years. The rest of ya seconds and thirds, start with the first drills, and work yer way up to the most recent ones ya remember. And if any of ya forget the last one we did, I'll throw yer sorry behinds in with the firsts."

Thali groaned as she and Alexius started to demonstrate the drill. After they'd shown the youngsters twice, the first-years started stumbling around them in imitation as Master Aloysius nodded at Alexius and Thali and told them to go through the last set of drills.

Thali was at least grateful to have practiced them over the break and had even added more to them. Afterward, she and Alexius started sparring.

Where did you learn to fight? Thali asked.

My brothers, then trial and error. Jax is the best fighter among us. He trained us as my uncles and aunts trained him. I'm old, remember?

Did anyone worry when I left the party?

Your guards did. Alexius's face stayed serious.

Thali faltered a moment, getting a whack on the shoulder from Alexius as a reward.

I sent them to the manor to look for you. Nasir returned when they confirmed you were there.

Thank you, Thali said.

What did the thief prince want?

Thali cringed. *I'm not completely sure.*

She could feel the next question Alexius wanted to ask, one she wanted to avoid. She closed the mental door and dedicated her attention solely to their sparring. Alexius took the hint and didn't press her. He just followed her lead and continued sparring until class was over. They emerged from combat sweaty and out of breath, but happily so.

That night, after a long first day of classes, Thali let Mia convince her to wear a dress for her evening with Elric. She regretted it the moment she stepped into the forest with Indi and Ana and fell out of her fine silk shoes when one foot got caught in a tree root. Her efforts to remain upright sent mud splashing up to soak her ankles and skirts.

"Shall I—" Stefan started to say, his arms outstretched, but Thali raised a hand to stop him from offering to carry her through the woods.

"Don't even ... I would rather face a hoard of bandits than be carried through the woods," Thali muttered. "Bandit" made her heart twist as she thought of Fletch and Ilya, Garen's second and third men. She shook her head to clear it and pushed on.

She asked Indi to walk in front of her so the tiger could find the dry spots on the forest floor. It was in that painstaking, zig-zag fashion that she managed to keep from adding any additional mud splatters to her outfit while carefully picking her way through the dark woods. After a longer than anticipated trek, Thali emerged from the woods into the glowing light of the brightly lit manor. As soon as she appeared, the guards all turned to her, never mind her own five guards who had been trying their hardest to trail her at a respectable distance, even though she had trod so slowly they'd continued to have to stop and wait for her.

As she reached the beautifully manicured lawns and approached the manor's front doors, Elric came bursting out and almost ran her over. At the last second, he registered her presence and dodged to the side, grabbing hold of her arms to steady her—and him.

"Always running into you." He smiled and she smiled back. "I was coming to get you. Did you walk through the woods? At night?"

"I think my five guards, tiger, and dog can keep me safe. Plus, I have a few tricks up my sleeves," Thali said, showing him the knife under her arm. Ana huffed as if offended before she trotted into the manor without waiting for them.

"I don't know how you could keep anything in those sleeves." Elric grinned. "Have I mentioned how breathtakingly beautiful you look?"

Now it was Thali's turn to grin.

Nasir coughed. "Perhaps we could bring this inside?"

"Weather not agreeing with you, Nasir?" Thali teased her guard. Nasir was still getting used to the chilly temperatures of her kingdom's winter, and Thali couldn't resist having a little fun at his expense. She chuckled as she watched his cheeks turn pink.

Elric offered Thali his arm and they entered the manor, where Elric gave her a proper tour of his temporary abode. Though she'd already spent a night in "her" rooms, she hadn't really noticed the decor, so he even showed off the rooms he'd designed for her. He made a point of saying she was welcome at any time. They made quite the pair strolling through the house, with Ana leading the way and Indi trailing behind them as they went from room to room. Staff plastered themselves against the wall like tapestries as they passed.

"Elric, I have a proposal for you," Thali said.

"I thought I already did that." Elric raised his eyebrows and grinned.

Thali grinned too, but she didn't lose her nerve. "Elric, the school has guards, your royal guards have created a perimeter at the school, and I am a fully capable warrior in my own right; therefore, I think my personal guard can be reduced to three, one from Tari and two of your own." She stuck her chin out, hoping he'd come back with a counteroffer instead of a clear no.

Which he did. "Four."

"Four is a bad number in my mother's culture. The word, when spoken, is the same as the word 'death.' Having only three guards on duty at a time will allow the others more rest and give the Bulstani guards more opportunity to adjust to the culture and the climate here." Thali glanced at Nasir, who still had a pink tinge to him as he warmed up.

Elric sucked on his top front teeth momentarily before responding. "I will say yes to three if you will agree to wear three dresses a week for at least three hours at a time and agree to attend the lessons I have arranged without complaint."

Thali's eyebrow shot up. She hadn't expected another counteroffer. She pouted her lips, knowing better than to make a deal without knowing all the details. "What lessons?"

"Lessons about what's expected of someone about to become a member of the royal family, things like how and what to do when, what is appropriate when, how princesses and queens behave in particular situations, what's appropriate, your duties once we're married, the differing roles of your staff, and such."

"Do I have to attend those specifically wearing a dress?" Thali asked.

"No. And they'll only take about an hour every day."

An hour every day seemed like overkill for such piddly details, but if it meant she could reduce her security detail, then she'd endure it.

"Deal," Thali said, sticking out her hand.

"Good, you start tomorrow. After your other classes, someone will come to you in your common rooms. Have you thought about what you'd like to do for the wedding?" Elric asked.

"Do I have much choice? I assumed it was already planned." Thali waved at the air to indicate the manor they were currently standing in.

"A bit perhaps, but you can still choose some things. What did you picture when you imagined your wedding?"

Thali smiled and a dreamy look flashed across her face. "I imagined it at sea, on the bow of a ship."

"Well, that might be a little difficult. What else?" Elric asked.

"Honestly, not much else. I never really gave it much thought," Thali said as she realized she was going to have an opulent wedding. She picked at Indi's fur, picking out a clump of who-knew-what from between her shoulder blades.

"I thought that's what most little girls did: plan their wedding and put their dolls through numerous wedding ceremonies."

"Not this little girl." Thali pointed at herself. "I didn't have dolls. I had rats, snakes, and an octopus. And knots to tie or letters and languages to learn."

Elric grinned. "It's never going to be boring with you, is it?"

"I hope not." Thali looked down. She again didn't feel worthy of such affection. "So, what is it you do here as prince and all?" she asked, wanting to change the subject. Thinking about planning a wedding and moving into a palace was starting to overwhelm her.

"You mean what was I doing last night with all those runners darting back and forth?" Elric glanced at the office he had occupied and that was probably requiring more and more of his attention.

Thali nodded.

"Well, I've taken over Adanek's armies. The generals all report to me now. Usually, it's border reports and status reports on neighboring countries and such since we're mostly at peace right now. But lately, with all the magical creatures around, we've seen an increase in attacks. Unprovoked ones. At the moment, we're trying to figure out what's doing it, why they're doing it, and what they want, if there's a pattern to it at all."

"Have you asked Alexius?" Thali asked.

"I was actually hoping you would." Elric looked around. They were still alone in the vast dining room. "You know, you'll have to ask Alexius to either join your personal guard or take up a position close to you to continue your lessons with him."

"I know." She waved a hand. "How many outposts does the kingdom have?" This was the part she found fascinating.

"Eighty-seven, but they all report to a main outpost, which filters down to a few runners coming and going. I used to end up getting about twenty reports a day, with some only reporting in once in a week. But with all the activity lately, I've asked for daily reports."

"And what else are you responsible for?"

"Well, I have my correspondence with various committees where I represent the palace. My father handles trade though, and he's excited for you to get involved. We're actually hoping you'll take over the trade committee. Father also oversees citizen affairs, land disputes, things like that. My mother takes care of court disputes, but I think I'll start taking on some of the more local disputes and affairs here eventually."

"Is there anything I can do to help now, before we get married?" Thali asked. She didn't know how any of those roles could be handled by a single person, or even two people. Running a kingdom sounded like a lot of work for just three people.

"I'll ask if there is. But there will be lots for you to do next year, when we move back to the palace, so maybe you should just enjoy your freedom while you have it," Elric suggested.

Thali swallowed; she'd been purposely avoiding thinking of moving to a landlocked palace. She focused instead of turning her hands this way and that as Bardo slid from one hand to the other, then around and back again.

"Just focus on school, lessons with Alexius, and princess lessons," Elric said. "There's time for you to learn the rest."

Thali laughed at the new term. Never in her wildest dreams had she ever thought she'd be taking "princess lessons." Elric grinned, covered her hand with his, and squeezed. Maybe she *would* be all right with Elric there to help her.

CHAPTER TWELVE

I T WAS WEEKS LATER when Thali woke early, and after letting her animals run through the woods and giving them some breakfast, she wrote Mia a note and headed over to the manor. Elric had made her promise to keep this whole day for him, and she was excited at the prospect of spending more time with him. As she neared the manor, she noticed quite a buzz around it. Many more people than usual dashed in and out, so Thali slipped through the main doors and went straight to Elric's study to see what was going on. She had been hoping for a quiet day together, but either that hadn't been the plan or Elric had unexpectedly gotten very busy.

Thali knocked on the door before opening it, and Elric beamed his bright smile at her when he saw who had come in.

"Ah. There you are." Elric stood and came around his desk to hug her and give her a peck on the lips. She tried to pull him in for a longer kiss, and it worked for a moment, but then he pulled away.

"Have you eaten yet?" he asked.

Elric looked nervous. He'd run his hands through his golden hair at least three times since she walked in. "What's the matter?" she asked.

Elric led her to a side table flanked by two chairs and filled with a small mountain of pastries. He went to close the doors and briefly stuck his head outside as he did so. Thali hoped he was telling his staff not to let anyone disturb them. That done, he sat opposite her, poured her some coffee, and offered her a plate so she could help herself to the pastries. Thali waved the plate away though because she had already grabbed a particularly sugary pastry with her fingers.

After Elric had opened and closed his mouth repeatedly as if he was trying to find the best way to say something, Thali narrowed her eyes. She was starting to worry she'd done something wrong.

"Sera says your princess lessons are going very well." He ran his hands through his hair again.

"All I'm learning about is court history. And we've had a couple etiquette classes. I feel like I have so much more to learn still," Thali said. She stuffed another pastry in her mouth and then felt a little guilty considering she wasn't following her etiquette lessons at all. Maybe that was the problem?

Elric exhaled, his shoulders dropping as he rushed to say the words. "I was going to surprise you and then I thought this morning it might not be a good idea to surprise you when you're connected to all the animals all the time and—."

"I don't like surprises, you're right." Thali spun the tiered plates before her and noticed they contained all her favorites. She took another and stuffed it in her mouth as she turned back to Elric. "What's the surprise?"

"Sera thought you might be ready, so I planned a party for this afternoon, a picnic where you could meet some of the other nobles from court." Elric pushed all the words out at once. Thali's eyes widened.

So far, she had been quite isolated from the nobles living at court. She'd only visited a few times and living and having the ceremony here at the manor—as they'd recently decided—had meant she wouldn't spend any time at the palace among the other nobles until after her wedding.

"I thought, since you wouldn't really be at the palace until after the wedding, I'd invite them here. I only invited my friends and a few others around our age though. It's a half a day's ride, and they all left this morning. They'll arrive for a picnic lunch on the front lawn, and then they'll leave. What do you think of an isolated first dip into palace life?" Elric cringed a bit as he asked. This time his hand stayed frozen midway through running it through his hair as he watched her expression.

Thali shoved another pastry in her mouth to give her a moment to think so her temper wouldn't react first. *What would Bree do?* she thought logically instead. Thali supposed she would have to meet the nobles eventually. She'd survived going to school with peers her own age despite being terrified of that, so could the nobles her age really be any different?

"All right." Thali licked her lips and then took a large gulp of coffee, enjoying how it seared her throat on the way down, calming her nerves. "So ... it's to be a picnic on the front lawn?" She swallowed and put her wants aside as Elric's face brightened. This was for the palace, and Thali could tell this was important to Elric. She wanted to help him run the kingdom and that came with responsibilities. One of those was getting along with the other nobles. She took a deep breath as Elric ran through his plan.

An hour later, Thali was dressed in an overly fluffy dress. She'd been scrubbed clean, placed in a pink dress of the latest fashion, and had her hair styled according to court trends. The dress was much more delicate than anything she was used to wearing. Thali was worried she'd rip it simply from standing up too fast.

Mia, thankfully, had been there to help her put it on. She looked at Thali one last time and scrunched her face.

"What?" Thali asked.

"It just doesn't look like you."

"I know. But this is a time for me to fit in, not stand out," Thali said.

"My dearest friend, I hate to break it to you, but wearing wool and walking on all fours does not make you a sheep." Mia pulled one of Thali's curls down and flipped it out so it stretched to frame Thali's face.

"A little better." Mia winked at her.

Thali and Elric stood at the top of the outer manor stairs as the carriages started to pull up the drive. Thali swallowed, trying to imagine how Bree might stand and smile, and Elric squeezed her hand as the first carriage stopped and three ladies and two gentlemen stepped out and joined them.

"Your Highness, what an honor to be invited to this party," the first gentleman said. He was tall and blond but had polished wood-brown eyes that ignored Thali for a moment too long. "My lady, it's a pleasure to finally meet our future princess. Lord Tarint, at your service."

Thali smiled and murmured her thanks as the man bowed over her hand and pressed his lips to her knuckles. Thali had never been happier to be wearing gloves.

"My lady, I have heard so much about you. I feel like I know you already." A brunette woman came right up to her, grasping her shoulders and air-kissing each cheek.

"I'm sorry. I am at a loss of knowing you," Thali said.

"I am Lady Gabrielle. But you'll discover eventually who my secret informant is," she said. She was certainly incredibly pretty, and alongside Lord Tarint, seemed to lead the others.

Thali couldn't remember all the names of the other ladies and gentlemen she was being introduced to. Some seemed just genteel, while others were sharp-eyed. She gulped. *There are only twelve of them, and it is only for a couple hours*, she kept telling herself. She would survive.

After the introductions were complete, Thali realized there was something familiar about Lady Gabrielle, who had remained close. Her yellow dress hugged her in all the right places and was perhaps more revealing than was fashionable. Her brown eyes reminded Thali of someone, but she couldn't figure out who.

Elric finally rejoined Thali, and it seemed Lady Gabrielle's smile shone brighter. "Gabrielle, Tarint, are you hungry?" Elric asked as he put a hand on Thali's lower back.

"We're famished, Your Highness. Thank you for putting this party together," Gabrielle said. "I cannot believe how you've managed in such a quaint place as this."

Why did that sound like an insult to Thali's ears? Elric smiled and nodded. But it wasn't his court smile; it was a genuine smile. Had he not seen her words as an insult?

Thali followed as Elric led her to the front lawns, where blankets and a long, low table had been placed. Soft, colorful pillows served as seats, and umbrellas had been planted into the ground to protect the guests from the sun.

Thali looked around and whispered, "It's beautiful."

"I'm glad you like it," Elric said. He turned to her and the sparkle in his eyes made her heart swell. She could do this, for him.

"Nothing like the afternoon teas at Lady Carbello's," Lady Gabrielle was saying behind Thali as the mob of nobles followed the oddly familiar lady.

Elric and Thali sat at the head of the table, but it was obvious to Thali it was Lady Gabrielle who held everyone's attention. She sat herself and Lord Tarint at the middle of the table, and everyone's attention was on them. Though they periodically glanced at Elric for cues, it was Lady Gabrielle who led them.

"Lady Routhalia, you must tell us how you managed to capture the heart of His Highness," Lady Gabrielle eventually said.

Thali swallowed. She tried to think but didn't want to take too long to answer. Bree would offer something polite and nondescript. Thali smiled what she thought was a court smile and replied, "I fear I cannot tell you what I have no knowledge of."

"How shy of you to keep your secrets to yourself. Elric, you did not tell us, last you visited the palace, that your fiancée is shy." Lady Gabrielle fanned herself.

Thali wondered if she'd misstepped with her words. Maybe she should have told them a story. Yet, she didn't want to tell this group anything because she felt like cornered prey.

Thankfully, the food was brought out on massive platters just then, and Thali was glad for something to do. But remembering that ladies did not scarf down food, she held her breath and waited. When Elric nodded, absorbed in conversation with the lord at his side, she slowly moved her hand to the platter in front of her.

A lady should not reach. Sera's words echoed in her head. That meant Thali had three options within arm's length: a scone, a fruit tart, and a cookie. Her hand froze as she was about to grab the fruit tart. *Consider how easy it is to eat. A lady should not shove things into her mouth.* Disappointed, Thali grabbed the scone at the last second and brought it back to her plate. Elric grabbed the cookie and Thali groaned inwardly. A scone was the worst choice. It was just a biscuit with fruit. Maybe adding jam and butter would give her something to do though. She looked up to see the others were all politely taking one thing at a time. Scones were popular. Cookies, too. Some of the gentlemen took a tart or two, but most of the tarts were still on the platters. Why have something hard to eat on a platter at all then? *These rules are silly*, she thought.

Thali broke a piece of her scone off and grasped her butter knife. At least she didn't have to share her butter and jam. They each had their own tiny dishes of the condiments. Just as she was about to dip her knife into the butter, someone called her name.

"Lady Routhalia, we have rarely seen you at court. I think I can count perhaps two times before today. What kept your family so entertained as to never present you?" Lady Gabrielle asked.

It seemed like an innocent question, but Thali put her knife down and folded her hands in her lap as she remembered to sit up straight. She swallowed yet again with nerves, not because she had anything in her mouth. "My family is always busy with their business. I have not often stayed in one place for longer than a month over the course of my life. We usually spend only a week or less in most places," Thali explained.

"You must tell us something of the world beyond then!" Lady Gabrielle smiled brightly. Too brightly.

"There is too much to convey in a single sentence or even a story." Thali flipped her butter knife in her hand. She wished it was a real knife and wondered what would happen if she threw it at Lady Gabrielle.

"Oh come, there must be one at least. One story of the dangerous people you've come across on your travels? Something exciting?" Lady Gabrielle pushed her. Thali purposely placed the butter knife back on the table and placed her hands together, squeezing them tightly under the table. Apparently, she wouldn't be eating.

She looked around at all the faces watching her. Thali knew this was the moment they would decide what kind of queen she might make. She wasn't sure what kind of story they wanted to hear, what story would highlight herself best. Bree would tell a story with children, something delightful and fun and light ...

"Well, there was one time in Cerisa—" Thali began.

"Oh, it must have been nice to return to your people," Lady Gabrielle said.

The words felt like a spear to Thali's heart. Lady Gabrielle's people were here. Thali though, had never fit in in Cerisa, and though she'd thought she was fitting in here, now ...

"You know, last year when that darling Prince Feng of Cerisa came to visit, I ran into him in the hallway. My shoe had broken not two steps before, and he was kind enough to get down and assist me with my shoe, then help me return to my rooms. We had a lovely conversation on the way." Lady Gabrielle slid Thali a sidelong glance and chills ran down her spine as she remembered how ill-behaved Feng had been when he had visited. Knowing he had no high opinion of her, Thali now wondered what he'd told Lady Gabrielle and what rumors were floating around the palace as a result.

As Lady Gabrielle turned to some of the other ladies, Thali considered getting up and leaving. Brushing Indi in her room in the spring was a preferred task to this. Oh, she missed her animals. Elric had thought it best to leave them in her rooms so as not to startle the nobles. Thali went to pick up her knife to at least eat something until she saw Lady Gabrielle turn her head in her direction. Thali put the knife back down and Lady Gabrielle turned away.

Fine, Thali thought.

All right there? Alexius, playing a guard for the afternoon, stood just six feet away.

Fine. I hate politics.

I'm not very good at it either.

You must be better than me. You've at least had hundreds more years to practice. Suddenly, Thali had an idea.

Alexius, will you pretend you see something at the manor and then come over and whisper in my ear?

Out of the corner of her eye, she saw Alexius look over at the manor. She called Indi and Ana to her and asked Bardo to please come along with Indi.

Alexius strode over and whispered in her ear, "I don't know what you're trying to accomplish with this."

Thali schooled her expression. "Thank you," she said out loud.

Everyone turned to her, even Elric, who had gone to the other side of the table to add more of his friends to his conversation—everyone that is, except her.

Thali turned to look at the manor as a crash interrupted the conversation before a tiger and dog came running toward the gathering.

Some of the ladies gasped and backed up to the far end of the table.

Indi and Ana ran to Thali. Indi rubbed her leg, tearing a slit in her skirts, and Ana sat at her other side, leaning in as Thali pet her.

"Please," Thali said as she placed a hand in front of Indi's mouth, aware that Indi was in full view of everyone. Even Elric had paused his conversation to watch with curiosity. Indi opened her mouth and Bardo slid out onto Thali's hand. She let Bardo slither up her arm and settle around her neck.

Gasps encircled the table and a couple ladies squealed. Thali couldn't bear to see the disappointment in Elric's eyes, so she avoided looking at him at all. "If you'll excuse me." Thali stood and turned. She whirled back around, grabbed three fruit tarts, and walked back to the manor with her animals in tow. Never mind what Bree would do. She couldn't stand these people. She popped each fruit tart completely into her mouth as she marched back, her animals trotting along with her.

Once back in the manor, Thali ripped off her dress and scrubbed her face free of the paints. With each layer she peeled off, she felt more and more relaxed and more and more herself. If this was an example of life at the palace, of the court's expectations of her, she wondered if she could ask to live in a hut in the woods behind the palace instead. She slid into trousers and a shirt and left out the back door before Elric had a chance to come back. Racing to the woods with her animals, she worked off her anger with every step, thinking her guards would just have to keep up with her. After she'd calmed a bit, she wondered if it was a warm enough day that her friends might be at the lake swimming. It would be a nice walk either way.

It was dark and the carriages were gone by the time she slipped back into the manor. Thali wondered how mad Elric was as she stopped at the kitchen to feed Indi, Ana, and Bardo before ushering them all back to her rooms. She passed Elric's study and kept walking, gently closing her door and hoping she could just go to bed.

But the moment Thali had finished changing her clothes, a soft knock on the door before it opened had her turning around.

Elric leaned up against the door frame. "So, that was you trying?"

The anger that Thali had walked off earlier spiked immediately. "Your friends are awful." She clenched her jaw so she wouldn't say worse.

Elric looked offended. "You didn't even give them a chance. You spent what, five minutes with them?" He stomped into the room, slamming the door behind him.

His anger only stoked hers further.

"I didn't give *them* a chance? They didn't even let me eat. And everything they said was an insult, especially that Lady Gabrielle. There wasn't a single drop of sincerity in the lot."

Elric started to pace. "Were we at the same lunch? *You* are the outsider. They were being their usual selves. I heard Gabrielle ask you questions to draw you into the conversation."

"Only to interrupt any answer I gave with a slap to the face!" It was Thali's turn to pace. Indi and Ana were tired enough that they lay on the bed, but Bardo started getting irritated too and slid along her arms and shoulders.

Elric stopped his pacing, dropping his shoulders and running both his hands through his golden hair. "Thali, in a year's time, they will be your constant companions. You should have given them a chance to get to know you. I want to make this as easy for you as possible."

Thali's anger boiled to the point where she started to see red. Elric sounded as if he was scolding a small child for the third time. She took a deep breath in and out before she answered, "I thought I was marrying you. Not the nobles at court." Then she went to the bed, gathered the clothes she'd brought for tomorrow morning, and stormed out. Her animals got up and flanked her, pushing Elric out of the way. Thali didn't let her tears fall until she was running through the forest, back to her rooms.

Elric had always been on her side. He'd always seen her point of view once she'd explained it. Why hadn't he seen his supposed friends' barbed words and mannerisms?

Thali didn't care to look behind her as her guards ran with her, and she was grateful when she returned to her rooms that Mia was asleep. Sneaking quietly into her bedroom and letting her animals lay on top of her, she cried herself to sleep. Would palace life really be just more of this?

CHAPTER THIRTEEN

E VERY EVENING, THALI WOULD walk through the forest to a big clearing north of the school grounds between Thali's building and the prince's manor. There, Alexius would join her. She would send two of her guards to scout the perimeter, allowing only Nasir—who always had night shift now—to remain within the meadow. He had been the only guard to have seen her abilities for himself during the griffin attack in Bulstan, so he was the only one allowed to be present during Alexius's lessons. Though Thali knew the others were aware of or must suspect her abilities, they weren't commenting or asking about them yet.

The meadow was surrounded by tall trees, and unless something flew out of the clearing, it was completely hidden from view. Tonight, Thali was tired. With the extra classes and lessons, she was rarely in her own rooms long enough to do anything but sleep and scrawl out assignments in the late hours of the night.

"Alexius, when are we going to reach out to magical animals?" Thali asked out loud. Aexie was with them, controlling the bubble to keep them hidden from unexpected activity in the meadow.

"You'll be ready soon. We're still working on a way to make it possible without compromising your safety or Lanchor's."

"Why don't you practice on me?" Aexie suddenly appeared, sitting on a nearby boulder three feet away from Thali.

"Are you sure?" Thali was practically salivating at the opportunity. She could feel her abilities growing and wanted desperately to flex those muscles and test them.

Alexius narrowed his eyes. *Strengthen your own walls first.* "Let's meditate first."

So Alexius and Thali sat to meditate, Thali checking and prodding the walls in her mind as Alexius's thread started moving in her foremind. It was strange to have him with her in her own mind.

Here. Add more thread here, he thought. He showed her a couple other places before getting her to seal the door for now. Finally, he had her build a wall between her and the familiar threads she kept in a corner of her mind: those of Alexius, Indi, Ana, Bardo, Arabelle, and Tariq.

She could theoretically take hold of them, so make sure if she gets in here, there's nothing for her to see or do.

Why don't you trust your own sister?

I'll explain it another day. Dragon siblings are not like human ones. Anything you see is what she wants you to see.

Thali finished the wall and felt Alexius building his own little wall on the other side to protect Tariq, her animals, and himself.

Alexius and Thali finally opened their eyes. Alexius always started a lesson with a lecture. "All right, magical minds are much more complicated. They'll have a natural wall for you to have to push through, especially sentient ones who know how to close their minds to prodding magic. When you reach for Aexie, set up your own walls around the thread reaching out to make sure nothing slips by you. Then, try to find a crack in her wall."

Thali wove walls as she extended her thread toward Aexie's mind. She had felt Aexie's glittery thread before, and now Thali allowed her threads to join with it. As she slid up the glittery thread, Thali let her own thread weave into the glittery one until she saw herself from where Aexie was sitting. Thali realized she could see what Aexie was seeing. Aexie then closed her eyes and showed her a memory. Thali felt it before she saw it, the pure joy and happiness. It was of Aexie the child and Alexius the child playing in the snow. They were grabbing large pieces of bark, then running and sliding down the side of a mountain together. They raced each other faster and faster, dodging trees and rocks until they were about to fly off a cliff. Then, as the sled flew into the air, both popped into dragon form and flew into the sky, doing loops before flying back to the top of the mountain to do it all again.

Thali suddenly realized she wasn't seeing the memory from Aexie's or Alexius's perspective and wondered whose eyes was she looking out of. She looked down and saw she was standing on a mountain platform that jutted out high above the snow.

Aexie gasped and immediately sent a wall of stone to snap down on the thread connecting them, snapping Thali's thread and making it spring back into Thali's mind. She recoiled as if she'd been slapped and shook her head. She opened her eyes to ground herself and found that she was sitting in the meadow with Alexius. It was dark out now, so they couldn't see each other beyond the glint in their eyes.

"Who are you?" Thali turned to look at Aexie.

"Aexie, what did you show her?" Alexius chimed in.

"Us, sledding, through *his* eyes," Aexie said quietly in the dark.

Alexius sighed. "My family has the ability to gift each other with memories from one another. You saw one of my father's favorite memories of Aexie and I."

"Where is your father now?" Thali remembered something Rommy had mentioned. Was it that their father was lost or missing?

Alexius and Aexie exchanged a glance before Aexie replied, "We don't know." She cut her words off as if her voice had broken and that was all she could manage. After a moment of silence, she turned to Alexius and continued. "She's very strong. One of those threads wove right through the middle of my magic."

He nodded. "That's enough for tonight, Thali. You'll be mentally exhausted tomorrow."

They stood and returned to Thali's building. As they walked, Thali turned to Aexie and asked, "Where do you sleep? If you're invisible, surely you must sleep somewhere hidden, keep your stuff somewhere?"

"There's a spare room next to Alexius's."

Thali nodded. In the last few days, she had almost forgotten about Aexie because she was completely undetectable with sight alone. Thali made a mental note to check her mind's threads more often to see if the female dragon was skulking around.

After they'd said their good nights and parted ways, Thali entered her room, the day's exhaustion catching up with her with every step. She only barely made it to her bed and patted her animals before diving in and falling fast asleep.

CHAPTER FOURTEEN

"**U**P, UP, UP. I have your dress for the ball," Mia announced, pointing at the low stool in the middle of the room the moment her friend walked in the door.

Thali groaned. The Founders Ball. All first years and children of founding members had to attend. All the other students usually went as well, but it was optional for them.

"What color this year?" Thali grumbled.

"Emerald green, to match Elric's eyes." Mia fluttered her eyelashes at her.

Thali groaned, still unsure of where she stood with him. But, with the last of her day's energy, she let Mia poke and prod her with pins and needles as she adjusted where necessary. Mia didn't allow any mirrors when she was working, so Thali had no idea how it looked. Her friend even went as far as blindfolding Thali this time so she couldn't see the dress at all. After a time, she fed off Mia's energy and they were soon chatting as they always did.

Thali secretly loved being fussed over by Mia. And as much as she had hated balls at first, she did have fun dancing all night, and if she was truly honest with herself, she liked the attention she received when she walked into a room wearing one of Mia's master creations. She was proud of her friend and proud to show off her unique work. Thali was tempted to peek through the blindfold to see what Mia had dreamed up this time, but Mia was quick to fix her blindfold whenever it slipped.

There was a knock on the door, and Mia went to answer it. "You're Highness, welcome!"

Thali heard Elric's quick intake of breath when he saw her. "Mia, that dress is incredible. Thali, you look even more beautiful than a ..."

"I'll stop you right there," Mia said. "She's wearing a blindfold because it's a surprise. Don't you dare give anything away. She only knows the color."

"Understood," Elric said before going mute.

Mia guided Thali, still blindfolded, into her own room and helped her change out of the dress. Thali returned to their common rooms in a loose shirt and pants and without the blindfold to find Elric disheveled. He was still unbelievably handsome, but his shirt was untucked, and he looked as if he'd run there. He stood looking out her window, playing with the fingers of the gloves he held in his hand. They hadn't spoken much since their fight, but Elric had brushed it under the rug and pretended like nothing had happened in the few moments they had seen each other.

"Elric, is everything all right?" She scanned his body now, looking for any injuries she might not have seen on first glance. Was he still angry with her?

"I'm fine. I came over right away because I thought you might want to see it. I've sent a messenger to Alexius, too. In the northern forest earlier tonight, my soldiers finally took down a griffin. They've brought it to the manor."

Thali's eyes almost bulged out of her head. She nodded.

"It's not a pretty sight, so if you don't think you can handle it, we're hoping to catch a live one soon," Elric said as he watched her closely.

"No, I want to go. I've never been queasy at the sight of blood."

Elric nodded. Thali grabbed a coat and asked her animals to stay with Mia as she followed Elric out the door. She felt guilty for not bringing her animals, but from Elric's disheveled look, she knew the manor must be busy with people flowing in and out. Plus she didn't know how they might react to a dead griffin.

Elric took Thali's hand as they strode through the forest. She sighed with relief. Maybe things were still okay with them despite their fight. Besides, she was glad to feel the warmth and appreciated the contact as she mentally prepared herself to see a corpse. She'd come across plenty of animals that had already passed in the forest, but a life snuffed still brought sadness.

As they emerged from the forest, Alexius was standing by the door, waiting for them. Thali did a quick check in her mind and saw Aexie was there, too.

Elric nodded to Alexius, who bowed to Elric and Thali. They took the stairs down to the lower level, and Thali shivered at the cold of the stone walls. When they stopped at a door with three guards, Elric turned to Thali. "Are you sure?"

Thali nodded.

The guard opened the door and they walked into a brightly lit room. Candles placed in front of shiny silver dishes all around the room made it almost as bright as day in the stone room. A massive wooden table lay in the middle, and upon that was the body. Its back paws drooped over the edge. The room was otherwise bare but for a few chairs lining one wall and a dirt floor.

Thali's brows furrowed, and she felt the familiar sadness of seeing a life that had once been, pull at her heart. She hadn't known this griffin, so it wasn't a great sadness, but she mentally checked for a thread, even a weak one, and found none. He had been gone awhile. Thali rolled up her sleeves and started to examine the griffin. It looked exactly as Alexius had shown her in her mind and like the ones that had attacked the Bulstani royal family, but she reached a hand out to feel the fur and examine the details anyway. It had paws and pads like a lion, but the talons of a falcon armed each toe. Though it also had a muscular set of shoulders and hindquarters, when she looked closer, she noticed one back leg was less muscular than the other. And upon closer inspection of its paws, it was obvious the talons had grown longer in that paw than the others from lack of use.

"Leave us," Elric said. The guards jumped to obey, leaving only Elric, Thali, and Alexius visibly hovering around the dead griffin.

Thali continued to circle the lion-falcon. She marveled at how seamlessly the transition from lion body to falcon head seemed. The transition from fur to feathers was nothing short of beautiful, with its golden-tan fur fluffiest at the base of the neck. From there, each strand of fur branched out and transitioned into golden feathers. She carefully examined the creature's head, being gentle as she took in each aspect of its eyes, beak, and ears. The beak itself was astonishing. It looked like it was pure gold. Thali didn't ignore the number of marks all over its body but took it as a sign of how difficult it had been to take down the griffin. "He was injured. Before the fight, he wasn't using his right hind leg fully."

Alexius had done a similar circle around the body and nodded his agreement, his jaw clenched.

"How do you know so much?" Elric looked at Thali with amazement and pride.

Thali shrugged. "I had to find ways to explain what I knew to others, so I learned to inspect the injured animals to find the reasons that explained what they were showing me."

Elric, not caring who was there, or where they were, took hold of Thali's shoulders and kissed her cheek. "You are the most amazing person I've ever met." Thali felt heat rise in her cheeks, surprised at the show of affection. Part of her had to stop herself from checking behind her to see who Elric was smiling so brilliantly for.

It was then Thali noticed Alexius wasn't quite as calm as she was. She turned her attention to him, and she could feel the anger and inner conflict boiling in Alexius. He was as close to rage as she'd ever felt him be.

"What happened?" Alexius tensed his jaw tight as he squeezed those words out as calmly as he could.

Elric noticed his change, too. "Three griffins attacked a village in the forest north of here. It was unprovoked, as all the attacks have been. It was lucky the army was nearby and that they saw the smoke and fire and heard the screams. They managed to chase two off and bring this one down. He didn't flee like the other two."

"His name is Gabol. And he was my friend," Alexius said quietly.

The door to the room was still closed, and Thali felt Aexie creating a bubble around them so they wouldn't be overheard and she wouldn't be seen as she appeared, kneeling on the table, her head hanging and one hand on the griffin's side.

"Oh, Gabol, what did you do?" Tears streaked down her face, dampening the griffin's golden fur.

Alexius clenched his fists, but Thali could feel the anger wasn't directed at her or Elric. She could also feel his sadness and anger and frustration roll down his thread, so she stayed quiet and let him speak.

"Gabol and I trained together a long time ago. In the magical world, we were in what you might call an army together. We patrolled together and were sent to mediate disputes or apprehend criminals. He was one of my unit of twelve. After father went ... missing, I had to return home to help my siblings. But Gabol stayed with the unit." His eyes suddenly lost their fire and grief washed through him. He almost stumbled, but Thali had felt it along the thread and caught her friend, tucking herself under his arm to bolster him.

"Why was he attacking a village?" Elric looked confused.

"I don't know. Gabol had a good heart. He was valiant and coura-
geous. He would have given you a hard time, Thali, but he too
would have died for you after meeting you just once," Alexius said.

"Was he protecting someone or something maybe?" Elric asked.

"Maybe." Alexius looked up to meet the prince's eyes, clearly
struggling with something. Thali could see Alexius's internal battle.
He wanted so badly to say something but didn't—or couldn't.

Thali tried to ask Alexius through their connection, but Alexius
wouldn't answer. He gently pushed a mental door into place, and
she didn't push through. Instead, she helped him to a chair leaning
up against the wall and Alexius slumped into it, putting his head in
his hands.

Elric, trying to stay as diplomatic as possible, continued trying to
come up with plausible reasons that might have caused Gabol to be
present at the attack. "Could he have been trying to feed himself?"

"Gabol wouldn't eat intelligent animals," Alexius replied softly.

"So, could there be another reason he was there?" Elric asked.

Alexius didn't reply.

"Wait, you said he was part of your unit, in the military. Who's in
charge of that?" Thali asked.

"My brother, Xerus, used to," Alexius said.

"And now?" Thali asked.

"I don't know," Alexius said.

"Aexie, do you know?" It seemed Elric had caught Thali's line of
thought.

Aexie pressed her lips together and shook her head.

They all stared in silence at Gabol, who was covered in wounds. Finally, after minutes of silence, Elric whispered, "What is the custom in your world?"

Aexie looked up. "We burn them as high up as we can, so they have less distance to travel to the afterworld above."

"I will arrange it. Thali and I will leave you two to grieve your friend. Spend as much time as you'd like here," Elric said solemnly.

Thali felt Aexie thin her bubble to let them through, and Elric took Thali's hand as they left the room and closed the door. She felt the bubble close after them. Elric relayed some instructions softly to the guards and then guided Thali to his study.

There, after more quiet words, the study emptied of guards and runners, leaving Thali and Elric alone and sitting by the fireplace.

"Thali, can you ..." Elric motioned above and around them. Thali nodded and wove her threads around them in a bubble. She nodded when it was done. "Thali, how much do you trust Alexius?"

"I trust him to keep me safe, to teach me," Thali said. She still hadn't quite figured out what he was keeping from her though.

Elric paused a moment, then nodded. "How much do you trust Aexie?"

Thali shook her head. "Not much. Alexius even told me not to."

Elric chewed on his bottom lip. His gaze flicked briefly to Thali and then back to the fire. "I think we need to be careful how much we trust Alexius and Aexie. Especially Aexie."

Thali frowned. "Alexius has done nothing but help me. He even risked his life to help me." But Thali didn't feel as convinced as she sounded.

"There's something they aren't telling us. We don't know if they're working for someone else or what their intentions are."

Thali nodded. But she felt guilty being suspicious of someone who had given her so much.

Then she had an idea. As soon as he was ready, she would ask Alexius to take her to her brother, Rommy. Maybe he would have more insight as to who controlled the army now if it wasn't Xerus. Or perhaps Xerus had changed, and maybe he was still silently running the army, using another dragon as camouflage. Not only was Rommy better at reading people and situations, but he would also have a better idea of what was going on given he was there with the dragons everyday.

Thali shivered involuntarily and Elric came over, picked her up from her chair, and sat in it himself before holding her close. They stayed like that for a long while, just breathing each other in, enjoying the closeness and the heat of the fire.

"I'm sorry about the fight we had," Elric whispered quietly. "I know these changes are nothing like what you wanted for yourself and that you're doing everything for me, for the kingdom. I love you," he murmured in her ear.

"I love you too," she said into his sternum. She had tucked her head into his neck, under his chin. They stayed there a moment, breathing each other in.

"I promise you, whatever's coming, we'll get through it together," Elric said.

Thali wasn't sure of anything anymore, so she just snuggled closer to her personal ray of sunshine, hoping it'd burn everything bad away.

They had fallen asleep in the chair together, so when Alexius knocked on the door, they startled awake. The door opened just as Thali climbed out of Elric's lap and into her own chair. Alexius came over and sat down on the arm of Thali's chair.

She looked up at him. *Are you all right?*

I will be.

She checked for Aexie and sensed her standing by the fireplace. *I want to visit my brother,* Thali said into Alexius's mind.

Do you want to go tonight?

I can go later, when you're feeling up to it.

We can go whenever you want, but you'll need to book two days of time here if you want to have any kind of conversation.

Thali thought about her classes and her promise to Mia to spend time together. *How about the day after tomorrow?*

That should be fine.

"Ready to go back?" Alexius said aloud.

Thali nodded, looking as if she was about to fall back to sleep in the chair. Elric stood, clearly about to offer to escort her back himself.

"It's fine, Elric. I'll have Nasir and Alexius with me."

Elric opened his mouth, looking ready to object, but Thali shot him a pointed look and he nodded slowly.

The walk back to her rooms was quiet. As Alexius stopped at the door of her building, she said, "I'm very sorry about your friend, Alexius." She couldn't bear to look at his face so turned instead and went inside. Mia was asleep when she came in and Thali quietly greeted her animals before climbing into bed herself. She wasn't as tired now that she was in bed, and she glanced at the window and the desk drawer that would have long ago held a scrap of parchment with a meeting place and time or words of encouragement from Garen. She thought of how long ago that felt, yet it had been less than two years ago. She hoped he was doing well—not too well, but well.

Thali fell asleep to the soft snores of her tiger and dog, waking up only once in the night when Indi's tail landed in her mouth.

CHAPTER FIFTEEN

"READY?" ALEXIUS AND AEXIE joined Thali in her room in Elric's manor. It was a little cramped with three people, a tiger, a dog, and a snake. It was fortunate Elric was busy again and had said goodbye earlier.

"One second." Thali shooed Indi and Ana to the adjoining room. Elric would take care of them for the next two days. Only he knew she was going to visit her brother. She'd tried to send Tariq word by looking at a picture and sending it along their thread, but she never did receive confirmation that he'd received the message. Mia thought she was going to stay at Elric's overnight so they could go out for an early-morning ride and then share a late dinner. Thali didn't want Mia to worry, so she'd told her friend not to expect her back for a couple days.

Thali turned back to the dragons and nodded. Alexius waved a hand at the wall and a door appeared. Aexie hugged her brother before stepping aside. She was to remain behind to hold the protective barrier. Thali was surprised when Aexie hugged her too before turning invisible.

Thali and Alexius stepped through the door and walked down the same long foggy hallway. Again, Thali had to keep a hand on Alexius' shoulder as they walked because she couldn't see anything besides fog.

How can you tell where we're going?

I use my magic. You could, too. Send a thread out from your feet and follow it along the floor. The thread should show you where it dips, becomes steps, or hits a wall so you have to turn.

Thali sent out a mental thread, not far away, and was surprised to find it was just like Alexius had said. She could follow the ground by allowing her thread to flow like water away from her. She felt any dips or steps or turns through her thread first before they came upon them.

You see magic as threads, but magic grounds itself in its connection with other living things. You also hold a certain reserve of it yourself. It's how you can weave a bubble around yourself to protect your privacy.

Thali nodded but then felt stupid as he obviously couldn't see her nodding her head when he couldn't even see her in the fog.

It felt like they arrived at another door quicker this time than they had the first time. This time, they had come to a white marble door, and when they opened it, Thali realized they were already inside the white stone palace. They stepped out into a closet and then into the main hall where the room in which she'd discovered her brother was. They approached that door again, and Alexius paused for a full two seconds before opening it and signaling Thali to go through first.

To her surprise, Alexius did not follow. When Thali walked in, she found her brother sitting on the couch, pouring over the pages of a book.

"Rou!" He shut his book and rose to greet his sister. Thali immediately noticed her brother had lost weight, and the shadows under his eyes were darker than before. His whole face lit up when he saw her though, and he rushed to hug her. His clothes hung loose, and she could tell he'd lost muscle mass. His embrace wasn't the solid ribcage-crushing hug she remembered.

"Rommy, are you all right?" Thali pulled away to get a better look at her brother.

"Yes, I'm fine. I've been working hard for Xerus lately, and long days and late nights in libraries make me look like this," he replied, pulling his jacket tighter around himself.

"Are you allowed to go outside? Do you still do your drills?" Thali asked.

"Is that a challenge, little sister?" Rommy's grin and raised eyebrow relaxed her. This was the big brother she knew.

"Maybe." Thali grinned.

"I'd still kick your sorry bum all the way back to the human realm." Rommy pulled back to see her response.

"Oh? I don't know, brother. I've been training every day with Alexius, and Tariq sends me new drills all the time. Not to mention, Crab's cousin is my Combat teacher, so you know, I've gotten pretty sharp."

Rommy reached out to poke Thali under the collarbone. He paused and raised an eyebrow. Then, he poked her in the arm, a grin following. Finally, he poked her in the belly and his grin widened. "You *have* been hard at work with your drills."

"So, what do you say, *big* brother? Up for a little spar?"

"How long do you have?"

"Two days," Thali said.

Rommy smiled, looking over Thali's shoulder. "Maybe next time. We don't have much time left if you only took two days in the human realm."

Thali was comforted by her brother's teasing. "Rommy, who leads the armies here?"

"Xerus," Rommy said.

"Are you sure? Alexius didn't think so. And do you trust Xerus?" Thali lowered her voice to a whisper.

"Yes, I'm sure, Thali, and I do. He saved my life. I told you last time. He only wants to return peace to both realms. He's trying to bring the magical animals back into this realm."

"We found a friend of Alexius's, a griffin. Elric's army killed him because the griffins were attacking a village. Why would they attack a village?"

"I don't know, Rou. Maybe they got hungry." Rommy looked like he was thinking about something else.

"Rommy, what if they didn't? Would there be any other reason for griffins to attack a village of people?"

Rommy stopped to think, moving to sit on the couch. "I only know a little about griffins. Maybe they felt offended by a villager? I've heard they're easily offended. And they're vicious when they're avenging a slight."

Thali joined him and sat down on the couch opposite him. "That makes sense. Do you know what offends them? I could tell Elric and he could send his army out to make sure no one else provokes them." She decided to ask Alexius too so she could make a list for Elric.

Rommy stared into the air for a few minutes before replying. "It could be something else. The lack of magic in your world is said to cause magical animals to lose their sanity." He jerked his head up as if he'd heard a bell she couldn't. "Rou Rou. You have to go back now. By the time you get back, two days in your world will have passed."

"But the griffins? Do you know? Can you find out? Can you send me word once you do?" Time always cut their visits too short, and Thali felt like she always had more questions than answers. "It's your world, too," she murmured as she rose and gave her brother one last hug before heading for the door.

"I'll ask Rus and Jax about the griffins, Rou. I'll have a list for you next time you come see me. And if you stay longer next time, I'll even kick your sorry butt in combat." The familiar glint of mischief filled his eyes as Thali looked back again at her brother before slipping out the white marble door to find Alexius standing in the hallway.

He raised an eyebrow at her in question and she nodded. He opened the door they'd come through and they traveled through the fog tunnel back to her rooms at Elric's manor. This time though, she put her hand on his shoulder and let him guide her down the halls. Thali was still thinking about her brother. Each encounter seemed short, and this one had felt odd. She went over each moment and the conversation with a fine-toothed comb, hoping to glean more information by reviewing all the things her brother had said, the way he'd said it, or the way his body had moved as he'd said it.

They climbed through the other door, Aexie popping into existence as Thali stepped through. Alexius closed the door, and it melded back into a wall.

"How did it go? Did you see Jax and Rus?" Aexie asked Alexius.

Alexius nodded. "Only briefly. They're doing all right. They miss you of course." Aexie only nodded. Then she turned to Thali. "And did you get what you wanted?"

"I think so." Thali was careful not to reveal too much in case Aexie went running back to her brother to tell him everything Rommy had told her. "If you'll excuse me, I'm going to go talk to Elric."

At Alexius's nod, Thali left Alexius and Aexie to catch up while she went to find Elric. She went to his study and he sprang up, lighting up like the sun peeking through a cloud at the sight of her.

"You're back!" He leaped over his desk and the stacks of paper and ran to her. He looked her over briefly, then crushed his lips to hers. Thali let his sunshine flood through her. Her visit with her brother had only filled her with more worry. This moment was only a reprieve, but she always felt like she could take on the world with Elric by her side.

He finally pulled away. He wiggled his finger up and around in between them. Thali understood and wrapped them in her thread bubble.

"So, did you ask your brother who leads the armies now?"

"He said Xerus does. And he says he trusts Xerus completely. He also mentioned griffins are easily offended, so perhaps someone in that town offended them and they attacked in response. Of course ... um, it also seems they could be losing their sanity."

A crease appeared between Elric's brows. "They're easily offended? Really? Or they're going crazy ... hmm .... What do *you* think?"

"I don't know what to think anymore, Elric. It sounds like it makes sense. I'll ask Alexius, but I do remember him saying griffins are fierce and protective and think themselves the noblest of creatures."

"So you think someone offended them?"

"Well, besides Alexius and Aexie, only my brother would have had actual experience with them." Thali shrugged. When had she had to start questioning her friends and loved ones? She decided she didn't want to think about it for a while. "How long was I gone?"

"Two days. It's about suppertime here now. You'll have class in the morning. Will I have the honor of your company for supper?" Elric asked.

Thali grinned. "The honor would be all mine." She dipped into a formal curtsy.

Elric smiled and said, "You've been practicing."

Thali laughed and hooked her arm in Elric's before dissolving their little magic bubble as he guided her down the hall to the dining room. Instead of sitting at opposite ends of the table, Thali sat to Elric's right and Alexius joined them, sitting next to Thali.

Once all the food was served and they were alone, Thali turned to Alexius. "Alexius, could Gabol and his friends have been offended by someone in the village? Are griffins easily offended?"

A flash of something crossed Alexius's face for a moment before his mask of politeness returned. "Is that what your brother said?"

Why did Thali feel like Alexius was buying himself time? She nodded, turning her full attention to him.

"Then that must be what happened. He has had more experience lately than I have with my brother's efforts."

Thali stared at Alexius. He looked pained. She'd ask him more when they were alone. She searched in her mind and felt Aexie sitting next to Alexius, so she let the subject go for the night and just enjoyed her dinner with Elric.

They finished the meal with Elric sharing the news of the land over the last two days. Afterward, Alexius and Aexie waited ahead by the treeline for Thali to say goodnight to Elric.

"I feel cheated of the two days you were supposed to have spent with me," Elric whispered.

"I'm sorry, Elric. I didn't mean to throw you into the middle of this," Thali said.

Elric drew back sharply. "Hey, I didn't mean it like that. I'm honored to be on the inside of all this secrecy. I mean, I wish I'd actually spent those moments with you. Every moment with you is like breath for my soul, for my life."

Thali heated at the declaration and looked at the ground. She wasn't used to such open and flattering words—and wasn't sure if she believed them. She dared a glance up only to see Elric's grin.

"You are beautiful." He kissed her forehead. "You are intelligent." He kissed her eyelid, "You are strong." He kissed her cheek. "You are kind." He kissed her jawline. "You take my breath away." He kissed her neck, right behind her ear. "And I can't wait to marry you." His voice hummed on her neck, and she sighed into his shoulder, glad for his arms around her holding her up.

A cough interrupted them. "Excuse me, Your Highness. A captain is in your study, waiting to report." A messenger, whose face was beet red, stood two feet from them, nervously staring at his shoes.

"I would growl at him to go away, but I don't think that would be fair," Elric murmured into her neck.

Thali tilted her head up and reached for his lips with her own. He kissed her gently, longingly, letting his lips linger on hers.

The messenger coughed again. Thali and Elric were forehead to forehead.

"See you tomorrow night?" Thali whispered. Now *she* felt cheated of their two days together.

"Sooner. I'll see you in my dreams tonight," Elric said. Thali tried to hide her smile in his shoulder before pulling away from him. She smiled like an idiot as she joined Alexius and a hidden Aexie at the edge of the forest. Her three guards trailed them and tried to pretend they hadn't all blushed at the farewell they'd witnessed.

Once she was safely in her rooms, one guard posted outside the common room's door, she said good night to Alexius, hoping he'd loop back later in the night to talk with her.

Chapter Sixteen

U NFORTUNATELY, ALEXIUS NEVER CAME back that night. Thali didn't see him until the next morning at combat practice. They sparred as usual and as soon as they were done, Alexius left her to talk with some other second-years.

"You two have a fight?" Daylor came up to Thali. Tilton soon joined them after he had finished his last sparring match.

"Not that I know of." Thali's brow furrowed, trying to figure out whether she'd offended Alexius in some way.

"Thali, what can you tell me about sculptures from the south in the ten minutes before our next class?" Daylor asked as he threw an arm over her shoulder.

Thali grinned. "What happened to studying?"

He shrugged. "It's like the blind leading the blind without you."

"Our study group has devolved to dirty jokes and push-up contests," Tilton added.

Thali laughed. "I'm surprised you want me back!"

"Thali, we miss you." Tilton stopped, turning to face Thali. "We know you've got a lot going on, and if you need our help ..." Tilton shrugged, smiling.

Thali was struck with how handsome Tilton was now. She remembered him in their first year, awkward and gangly. But now, he was tall and slender and had filled out in all the right places.

"Tilton. When did you get so handsome?" Thali asked out loud, making Tilton blush.

"Hey, don't you already have a prince you're betrothed to?" Daylor clapped both Tilton and Thali on the shoulders. He folded Tilton into his other side, scooping them into his own walking rhythm as they made their way to class.

"So ... southern sculptures ..." Daylor looked expectantly at Thali.

She smiled, realizing she missed her friends. She launched into the fastest explanation she could about the most typical sculptures found in the south and their purposes as they walked up the hill to their next class.

Thali joined her classmates for a little study group before she was supposed to meet Elric for supper. Anytime Thali showed up, all the merchanting students in her year seemed to make an appearance. They went over what they were currently learning, but Thali's biggest headache was sorting out all the right and wrong information Master Brown had given them. This year, unlike in previous years, he was quite knowledgeable in the topics he was teaching, but the way he had grouped them all together and was presenting them made things more confusing than they had to be. She didn't mind correcting Master Brown though because he'd always hated her.

Earlier today even, he had reminded her she wasn't allowed to speak in his class, using a ruler to smack her table the moment her mouth opened. So now, maybe she wanted revenge, or maybe she cared enough about her fellow classmates that she didn't want them all to get killed because of his misinformation, but she started from scratch and explained the different tribes in the south and how to tell them apart. Then, she spoke of their customs as merchants, things like what to do with water or how to trade or gain their favor. She even taught her classmates some of the phrases she'd had to speak as a child to impress some chiefs.

Then, she shared the story of the matriarchal tribe where her father and brother had been caged and guarded while she and her mother had negotiated their deals, yet when it came time to present their deals, the men had to do it. The leaders of that tribe judged foreigners based on how they treated women and how they dealt with their matriarchy.

"So, how do we know if we're talking to the tribe with female leaders versus the one with the canoe ritual if we inadvertently come across them? They both live in the same kinds of tents, right?" Daylor sagged on the desk, his head held up only by his hands.

"The tents do look similar. They're made of leaves and resemble giant barrels with a low, flat, conical roof. But the women who send their children out in a canoe don't wear tops, and the women of the matriarchal tribe wear brown robes with painted rings here." Thali pointed to her sleeves. "More rings mean higher status. The chieftess has about twelve rings usually, in bright colors."

"No shirts!" Bannick's eyes were wide. "Can I live there?"

Thali rolled her eyes. While she accepted that Ban would be part of her time at school, and her punching him in the teeth had made her feel really good, she'd chosen to mostly ignore him. It had taken until their third year, but he was no longer afraid to show his less gentlemanly side. He guffawed now with some of his cronies.

"If you lived there, you'd be castrated. It's considered a terrible offense to look too long at another tribesman's wife," Thali muttered. Tilton, Daylor, and Ari choked on their laughter.

Ban and his cronies scooped up their books and left.

The remaining students sighed. Thali looked at her fellow third years, hardly believing this was their final year together. After this year, they'd all start their apprenticeships with various merchant families. That made a lump form in Thali's throat. She still couldn't believe her position—the one her father had promised her after a three-year delay—wouldn't be hers anymore. Her father had promised her a bigger ship of her own and longer routes when she finished school. Now she was going further inland instead of taking to the ocean. Though she was going to ask Daylor and Tilton to join her royal staff, and Mia, of course, she wondered if they'd give up their chance to be merchants and see the world. She also wondered if any of her other classmates would want to live in the castle instead of going to sea. On the other hand, she knew who she'd recommend her father take under his wing. Ari would make a wonderful captain. She felt a pang in her heart imagining Ari on her beautiful ship, at the helm instead of her.

"I can't believe this is our last year together," Daylor said.

Tilton looked up from his texts. "It feels like just yesterday when we all stumbled into that dining hall, trying to figure out who Thali was and what imperial silk was."

"We all know what we'll be doing this time next year, or at least that we'll be doing something on a ship. But Thali, do you know where you'll be?" Ari asked.

Thali tried to smile but only managed a halfhearted one. "I'll be at the palace, welcoming foreign royalty probably. Hopefully managing the kingdom's trade ..." she trailed off, but not wanting to kill the cheery mood, she narrowed her eyes. "So, you all better be on your best behavior, or I'll raise all your taxes!" She jokingly pointed to them all.

"No way!" Daylor leaped up and tackled Thali, throwing her up onto a shoulder. Pretty soon, their whole group had doubled up and were playing a game of chicken, wrestling each other while on another's shoulders. Thali managed to shove Ari off Tilton before he tripped Daylor and Thali went down. Thali's guards had stepped closer, obviously unsure of the protocol with such a physical game. They looked relieved when the game ended.

Once the students had recovered from the fit of giggles that had them rolling on the floor, they went their own ways to supper. Only Daylor and Tilton walked Thali back to her rooms, ignoring the three guards trailing her.

"Daylor, Tilton ... I was wondering if—please feel free to say no—but I was wondering if you'd like to come to the palace with me next year?" Thali looked at her hands, unable to face their rejection.

Daylor and Tilton stopped at her door. They loomed over her, fully grown into their six-foot something frames. Thali opened her door and welcomed them in with a raised eyebrow. In they walked, looking a little dumbfounded in their stunned state. Daylor linked his hands together, arms behind his head, as he settled in a chair nearby, and Tilton fell into a chair.

"Like I said, you don't have to. And if you want a position with my father instead, he said himself he'd love to have you both. But ... I was wondering ... I mean, I'd be honored if you'd be part of my staff." She cringed at that word. She wanted to crawl under a rock.

"What positions would you like us to fill?" Tilton asked gently.

"Anything you like. Something close to me. I don't know anyone at the palace. Or at court. I'd love to have you both close to me. Mia is coming. She's decided she'd like to be my first lady."

"Thali, we aren't nobility," Tilton said.

"I don't care," Thali said.

Daylor and Tilton looked at each other. She could tell through their silent exchanges they were thinking it through.

It was Daylor who finally turned to her. "I'd love to, Thali. It would be my honor to serve the future queen of Adanek." He rose and offered a low bow. It wasn't comical or mocking, but a true, heartfelt bow. For a moment, Thali saw Daylor the man, grown up and serious.

"As would I, Lady Routhalia, future Queen of Adanek." Tilton offered a bow like Daylor, and Thali's vision blurred as her eyes filled with tears.

"Ohh ... Daylor, Tilton. I'm so glad you said yes." She jumped up and hugged them both, crying into their shoulders as they held each other tightly.

"Well, that's not very queenly." Mia poked her head out of her room.

"Get in here," Thali said, and Mia strode into their group hug.

For the first time, Thali knew whatever her future held at the palace, she'd at least have her friends with her.

When she arrived for her dinner with Elric that night, Thali came upon a beautiful ivory-colored wood table taking up most of the space in the dining room. Every edge was carved with ornate dips and swirls. Even the high-backed chairs in the same ivory-colored wood were etched with whorls, but plush purple velvet on the seat, back, and arms softened the imposing look.

Thali let out a breath in awe. "This is new," she said.

"Do you like it?" Elric asked.

"It's beautiful. I didn't know you were redecorating," Thali said.

He shrugged. "Well, I was thinking we could keep this manor. It could be ours. It's close to the ocean and close to the palace so we could get away for few days and still get back quickly. It's even closer to your family's lands than the palace is," Elric said.

Thali's jaw dropped, "Really?"

"I was going to give it to you as a wedding present. But then I thought you might want some say in how it's decorated."

Thali was speechless. This was as extravagant a present as she could ever possibly have imagined—besides her ship. The thought of her ship reminded her of how her brother could never again be in this world, and it tugged at something in her heart.

"So?" Elric's green eyes sparkled; he was about to burst into his usual sunniness.

"I love it." Thali forced a smile and threw her arms around him, pressing her lips into his. She could have gotten lost in his kiss and his embrace, but her stomach let out a growl of protest and she pulled away. "I missed lunch."

"Then we better get you fed." He led her to the table. Thali sat down and examined the wood, marveling at the color and the way the grain squiggled like a line drawn in the sand.

Elric was grinning like a fool when she finally looked up, her examination having been interrupted by a soup bowl being placed on the spot she had been staring at.

"What kind of wood is this?" Thali asked.

"I'm not sure. I think it was a gift from the prince of the Northern East. I'll find out for you if you like," Elric said.

Thali nodded. It reminded her of the wood from the Northern East, but it was lighter than she'd seen, and its grain was darker than usual. Turning her attention back to Elric, it was her turn to grin. "I asked Daylor and Tilton to join me at the palace next year."

"Oh? What positions are they taking?" Elric looked up with genuine curiosity. He had encouraged her to surround herself with familiar faces next year when the palace would be new to her.

"I'm not sure. We didn't really go into the details." Thali felt like the wind under her sails had suddenly disappeared.

Elric pursed his lips. "How about personal secretary for one?"

"Perhaps. When do I have to decide by?"

"Probably before the final exam. Are they going to finish classes like you?"

"I assume so. But who knows, they might go to the palace with me and hate it. I wouldn't begrudge them for leaving." Thali gulped, realizing in less than a year, she would be living at the palace ... as a princess.

Elric nodded. "I'll make a list of the people you need to hire and some possible candidates already at the palace."

"That would be helpful. Thank you." Thali suddenly felt overwhelmed.

Elric reached out to cover her hand with his. "I know it's all strange and new and overwhelming, but I promise I'll help you navigate it. Then it's about putting the right people in the right places. It'll make your job a lot easier."

Thali focused on breathing. She felt like she was at the edge of an abyss, standing on crumbling rock. "Elric, there's much I need to learn. And I feel like I don't even know all that my role is going to involve." Thali tried to calm her racing heart as she looked up at Elric's emerald eyes.

"Aren't your lessons with Sera going well?"

"They are, but so far, all I've done is memorize which houses are noble, their histories, and who married who. I've learned when I can walk next to you, when I can or can't stand up at what party or table, and when or when I can't leave a room. I know nothing of my future role, if I even have one beyond being your arm candy."

Elric pushed his chair back and reached for her hand. Thali rose, ignoring the untouched soup despite her stomach's protest, and went to Elric. He pulled her into his lap and circled his arms around her as she burrowed into his chest.

"I know it must be overwhelming. You're learning in just a short time what I've had a lifetime to learn." Thali curled up into his lap, feeling ever so small. Elric put his chin over her head, tucking her into him.

"Ultimately, you are their princess, court protocol be damned. While my mother adheres to the protocol, she's never been one to punish someone for not following it. I wanted you to learn all the rules so you can choose which ones to break. You'll know how to fit in when and if you want to."

Thali laughed. "Elric, I've never fit in. Ever."

"You fit in right here." Elric cooed. Readjusting his arms around her to give her a squeeze, he added, "You're right though. You don't fit in. You lead. I can't wait to take you back to the palace to meet everyone."

"Why?"

"Court is incredibly dull. You're going to liven it up and really throw all those stuffy court ladies and lords for a loop."

"I'm not sure that's encouraging."

"I'll be right there with you. How about if I promise to thrash anyone you want me to?"

Thali laughed. "Wouldn't there be consequences?"

"Father and Mother adore you. They wouldn't reprimand me for defending your honor. I am, after all, the Crown Prince of Adanek," Elric said. They were quiet for a few minutes as they thought. Thali wanted to enjoy this quiet moment with Elric, but all she could think of were all the responsibilities she expected to have but didn't know about.

"Elric, what exactly does a princess do?" Thali asked.

"What do you mean?" Elric asked.

"I mean, as a princess, I wake up in the morning, then what?" Thali began before pulling back far enough to look at him.

"Well, I think a lot of that will be up to you. So, how about I tell you what I do?" Elric asked. She curled back into his body and nodded her head against his chest as she tucked her head under his chin.

"Well, after I wake up in the morning, usually my secretary gives me a summary of anything happening locally, nationally, and internationally I should be aware of. Then, I'll eat breakfast and look over the correspondence I've received, often starting with those from outside Adanek, so they can be replied to and sent before lunch. The messengers appreciate being able to get home sooner. Then, I attend a meeting or two before lunch, though sometimes one *is* a lunch meeting. Next, I squeeze in a lesson with the captain of the royal guard before I attend two more meetings and move on to paperwork or specific meetings with people who have requested an audience with me. Supper I typically spend with my parents. That was my mother's one request of my father, that we all dine together when we're in the same city. Afterward, I attend to my remaining paperwork, which is mostly reading, signing, and responding to reports until I fall asleep on a stack or I can't keep my eyes open. That's unless, of course, I'm with you." Elric winked.

"Wow. That seems like a lot of work. What kind of meetings do you have?"

"Well, much of it is redundant since my father is also at many of the meetings. I'm just there to learn, but in the last few years, I've taken over a fair-sized chunk of the paperwork from my father with regards to our army and guard. He oversees most of the trade issues and foreign politics, and he sees to the people, too. Every Monday morning, he holds an open audience, where anyone in the kingdom is allowed to line up and request his advice or judgment in the case of a dispute. My mother handles most of the agricultural and infrastructure aspects, but she's always in attendance with my father most Monday mornings."

"And is all that stuff you do, or that your mother and father do, normally done by just one person?" Thali asked.

"Well, my father told me once he used to delegate more when it was just him, before my mother and I came into his life. He generally just received updates from those he'd appointed to run specific offices. But now that he has my mother and I, he likes to keep it in the family, to keep the country's management personal. And despite giving my mother full responsibility for agriculture and infrastructure, he still sits in on an agriculture meeting with Mother occasionally, just so he knows what's going on." He paused and craned his neck to look at Thali's face. "Do you remember when I said my father was hoping you'd take over trade and foreign affairs?"

"What ...?" Thali began, but then she remembered Elric had brought it up once, but it hadn't really registered at the time. Now that it had, she was surprised they already had plans for her.

"You're Lady Routhalia of Densria, famous merchant daughter, and now with an education to match. I think you'd be like a fish in water leading trade and foreign affairs."

"I'm still learning when I'm allowed to get up from the dinner table when there's a guest from the southern lands versus the southern isles."

Elric pursed his lips. "That might be true, but I've watched you with Prince Tariq and his family. I've heard you talk about various foreign nobility and royalty like they're old family friends. I think you'll be the best thing to ever happen to our foreign-affairs committee."

Thali thought about her acquaintances around the world. Her family's fame as merchants often did open the doors of many important people in other lands. Her father was such a big, jovial personality and her mother was so beautiful, they often found themselves dining in palaces. It also just so happened that most children of the royal families she knew were either hers or Rommy's age. Thali's eyes grew wide as a realization hit her. "Elric, I'm going to have to invite a lot of people to our wedding."

"Was that a surprise to you?" He pulled away to look at her stunned face.

"No, I mean like a lot, a lot of foreign families, royals even."

"I figured so. Your family is famous for a good reason. I fully expected our wedding to be the international event of the decade." Elric grinned.

Was he enjoying the realization she had just come to? Thali wondered.

"Why do you think my mother's been hiring an army to organize the wedding? Oh, that reminds me, the official royal wedding planner is coming here to meet us tomorrow."

"I thought I would just be showing up at our wedding."

"Hey, that's what I'm supposed to do." Elric stuck his lips out in a fake pout.

"No really, I assumed since it was a royal wedding, there wouldn't be anything for me to decide."

Elric tilted his head, confusion evident in his eyes momentarily as he considered her words. "Well, I suppose some of it is already decided given protocols and traditions. But there's still lots for us to decide. Or so I hear. Father said it would be easiest to nod and smile and give you whatever you want."

"But I don't know what I want. What about you? What do you want in our wedding?"

Elric took a deep breath in and a deep breath out as he watched her closely. "I want to stand in front of all our friends and family and marry the woman I love. The woman who loves this kingdom almost as much as I do."

Thali smiled and then nuzzled into Elric again, readjusting her legs. She had always fit when Garen held her. Surprised that Garen had popped into her mind, she quickly shoved him back out. She focused instead on watching Elric trying to eat his soup over her. That effort was comically unsuccessful, so he settled for dipping his bread in it and giving it to her instead.

Eventually, bowing to her stomach's wishes, Thali went back to her own chair, and they finished their supper in peaceful, quiet contemplation. As the moon rose high in the sky and the hour got late, they said their goodnights. Thali briefly thought about staying at the manor, but her room at school was much closer to the Combat class she had to get to in the morning. As she walked through the forest, her ever-present guards trailing her, Thali couldn't help but feel weighed down with thoughts of her future and her past.

CHAPTER SEVENTEEN

T HALI STROLLED THROUGH THE forest, trailing her hands along the deciduous tree trunks and smiling as a squirrel leaped from one tree to another. She stopped to breathe in the fresh, crisp air and watch a lone bat head out in search of breakfast as daylight eased into twilight. As they approached the edge of the meadow, Indi yowled with displeasure before Thali let her and Ana run around a bit in the open space, even if it was only for a few minutes. Even Bardo slithered to a rock to sun himself. She only had time to take her beloved animal friends out to relieve themselves this morning and needed to figure out when she could take them out for a real run next. With her busy schedule lately, it had been far too long since she'd given her animals free rein in the forest. And she could use some free time, too. Suddenly, she had another important thought.

Alexius, can we talk alone tonight?

Yes.

While she'd already known he was keeping things from her, and he had told her there were some things he couldn't say, it troubled Thali that he had been keeping his distance lately. They only saw each other in class and during her nightly magic lesson. She wondered if there was something besides the prophecy and the open gate between the worlds that was bothering him.

Once back in her room, she saw a note from Mia saying she'd be out late sorting thread at the seamstress building. Thali was glad. Even though Mia knew of and accepted her talents, Thali knew they made Mia uneasy. And when she was in a good mood, she always had a thousand questions that would interrupt her lesson with Alexius. Thali wandered into her bedroom and saw another note, this one in the little basket she kept for the messenger bats outside her window. Opening one fold, she read,

Lili,
I've only been getting fragmented images from you.
Please write me.
-T

She unfolded it further and Tariq's note went on to tell her about what was currently going on in his kingdom, but there was nothing of importance. His letter made her think of the bond now linking her to Tariq. She thought about different ways she might be able to strengthen the line and send messages through consistently.

A knock sounded at the common-room door, and Indi raised her head. Ana let out a sigh as she changed positions on the bed.

"Come in!" Thali yelled so they could hear. Nasir opened the door to let Alexius in, then positioned himself just inside the door. From her bed, Thali checked her threads for any sign of Aexie, and when she found none, motioned for Alexius to join her in her room.

Alexius shuffled in and sat on a chair. Indi padded over and put her head in his lap. After consistently showing up with meat for two weeks, Alexius had won Indi over. He pet her face, tracing a line from her nose up between her eyes and across the top of her head to her ears with his thumbs, which she seemed to thoroughly enjoy. Thali sat cross-legged on her bed and scratched Ana between her ears. Why did she suddenly feel awkward? Feeling fidgety, she tucked her hands into the folds behind her knees, then clasped her hands in her lap, then started to play with the ring on her left hand.

I'm sorry to put you ill at ease.

It's not your fault, Thali said automatically.

It is. And I'm sorry for it. There are certain things I ... I cannot tell you. And I fear it's pushed us apart. It was just easier to stay away as often as I could.

Finally, Thali settled her hands on her knees and looked right at him. At least they were talking. *Why can't you tell me?*

Alexius shook his head as if a fly was near.

Is it a dragon thing?

Alexius nodded. Thali read tension in his face. He was straining against something.

And you're bound by something that won't let you say certain things?

Alexius nodded again. *You should know my first priority is your safety. That supersedes everything. Whatever I can or can't tell you, I will always put that first.*

Can you tell me why your brother, Xerus, is so interested in my safety?

Alexius shook his head. Thali recognized the pained frustration building in Alexius's face.

Dragons aren't always known to be loyal creatures, so there are ways to either force a dragon to be loyal or to allow a dragon to pledge their loyalty completely.

Thali's eyes widened. To be able to force a dragon to comply ...

The cost is great. If another creature was to find the way to force a dragon to comply, the controller would only live another ten years. If a dragon was to pledge their loyalty, their life would become permanently tied to that creature's. If that creature were to die, the dragon would also die within the next year.

"That's ... who would—or could—ever ask that of a dragon? Who would do that?" Thali asked out loud.

Alexius tapped his head to remind Thali of the safest way for them to converse.

As I said, the cost is great, so it doesn't happen often.

And dragons can enslave other dragons?

Alexius nodded. Thali's thoughts spun straight to Xerus. Xerus must have tricked his siblings into serving him, and perhaps he'd even forced Alexius to hide things from her.

Is there a way to set you free?

Alexius shook his head, drooping his chin to his chest as if he was becoming very tired.

Will you let me know if there's anything I can do to help you?

Alexius nodded. He looked up and gave her a halfhearted smile. *You know, I wasn't pleased to get this assignment at first. I didn't like the prospect of babysitting and teaching a human with wild magic. But you've impressed me. I'm proud to call you a friend.*

And I you. Thali smiled at Alexius. She trusted Alexius, even though she wasn't sure if he could be considered completely trustworthy if he was doing someone else's bidding. *Can I ask you something ... personal?*

You may ask. I may not answer, though I have nothing to truly hide.

Do dragons ... court each other? Fall in love? Have partners?

Alexius sat up straighter. He touched a gold band on his left wrist. *We do. We each have one bonded mate. Sometimes it takes centuries to find them, and ... well, the time you have with them varies.*

Have you found your mate?

I found my mate a long time ago. Alexius swallowed, a muscle in his jaw flexing. *She died. Xerus is also mated. Jaxon and Aexie have not met theirs yet.*

I'm sorry. What happened?

This is something I do not wish to talk about.

Thali saw the hurt and guilt cross Alexius's face and cringed. Even if whatever it was had happened a long time ago, it was still fresh in his mind.

I'm sorry for your loss.

Alexius offered her a small smile. *She would have loved you. She was very free-spirited.*

Thali smiled to think of a free-spirited dragon, the exact opposite of Alexius.

Will you tell me more about her?

Alexius smiled a little.

Brixelle was beautiful. I used to fly to visit her using any excuse I could. And she would put me to work the moment I landed. Then, because I'm a hard worker, we'd be done early, so we'd fly through the clouds, just talking. She'd disappear sometimes and come back with flowers for me, or a tasty snack.

Alexius's smile turned sad. Thali bumped his shoulder with hers and Ana climbed into his lap. He recounted a few more stories for Thali, and they spoke late into the night, Thali wishing she could ease Alexius's grief and free him from both his guilt and his bonds.

CHAPTER EIGHTEEN

T HALI WAS UP LATE the next night, practicing her magic with Alexius. Aexie was away checking on some disturbances nearby, so Thali and Alexius had been working on exploring the other possible aspects of her magic. She was gaining enough strength now that she could use the threads linking her to other animals to make them perform physical, tactile tasks some distance away from her. And once, after weaving a piece of mental fabric with her magical threads, she had even wrapped that invisible fabric around a cup and was able to stop Alexius's magic as he tried to put water in the cup. The moment she tired, Alexius used his magic to freeze the water immediately.

"Do you have specific skills like I do?" Thali asked.

"Dragons are skilled in many things, but manipulating matter is what comes easiest to me," Alexius said. Then he pointed to his temple.

Alexius, someone once mentioned ants might have a single consciousness, so I might be able to communicate with someone far away by using ants.

Alexius raised an eyebrow. *Perhaps ants from the same colony. But I'm not sure about ants as a species.*

That discussion prompted them to find some ants in the forest and separate two groups from the same colony. Thali found it was easy to communicate her desire for her ants to perform a task, but she struggled with how to get them to convey a message to the brethren Alexius had isolated.

Thali got her ants to turn in a circle and spell out the number five. They marched dutifully through each maneuver. But when diving into their consciousness, she couldn't figure out how to determine which ants had been separated. There were too many for her to try communicating with each one, and she realized as she tried seeing through their eyes to identify the ants Alexius had that it was taking too long.

Try to use their other senses, Alexius prodded her.

So, Thali dove into an ant and tried to learn how they lived and what senses they used most. As a result, she learned they used smell to identify their trails and had an especially strong sense of smell to detect the essences they left trailing behind them. She could even "see" the scent they left behind in their wake, and when she focused on it, the trails they had been walking made a map.

Alexius, give me your hand. When he did, Thali focused, picked up one of her ants, and put it on Alexius's hand. She homed in on both the essence that was Alexius's personal brand of sweat and the ant's chemical trail. She could see both clear as day and labeled them "Alexius" in her head. Then, she returned the ant to her group and searched among them for Alexius's scent. This time, it was easy to spot him and the ants with him, so she sent a message through her own ants to march the number five.

And his ants did it.

Five. Good. Try something longer, Alexius urged.

Now that she was connected to the ants and could see the various scents, this time, she didn't even have to send a message to her group. She just sent the message straight to Alexius's group. His ants marched around him, then created the word, "Hi," in cursive as they marched.

I'M TIRED. Thali could think of nothing she wanted more than to go to bed, and now.

Good. Send them an even longer message now.

This time, she struggled with a sentence because the ants had to separate into groups to write out each word. Either that, or she needed more ants.

CAN WE GO HOME?!

Okay, okay. Got it. All right, that's probably enough for tonight. Very interesting though. Next time, we'll have to test your range and find out more about how ant colonies work.

Alexius looked deep in thought as he walked Thali back to her rooms at school, Nasir close behind. Thali was glad for the quiet walk home as her head throbbed from all that effort. This may have been an exciting discovery, but it sure took a physical toll on her.

The next morning, Thali was exhausted. Indi and Ana had come with her last night for her lesson in the forest, and she'd let them run and hunt while she'd toiled. They were tired enough that they opted to stay in bed that morning. Thali thought they had the right idea.

"Thali, are you up yet? You promised ..." Mia sang through the door.

Thali replied with a groan and slid out of her bed onto the floor. The cold floor was motivation enough for her to open her eyes, push herself up into a sitting position, and lean her back against the side of the bed. There, she pulled on a simple shirt and pants, leather vest, and belt. The medallion attached to the belt came loose and clunked to the floor right on Thali's thumb. She yanked her hand to her chest with a yelp before putting her thumb in her mouth.

When the shock of it wore off, Thali picked up the medallion Garen had given her so long ago. It was to stay permanently attached to her belt. She had made a vow that she would always wear it, and she wouldn't be a promise breaker. She rubbed a thumb over the symbol carved into its surface, the edge worn with time. For a while after their breakup, Thali had briefly thought about not wearing it. What would it mean if she chose to wear the medallion once she was married? What did it even mean now when she was betrothed to the Prince of Adanek? At first it had been a promise, a remnant of her first love and maybe even a shred of hope for it in the future. But she'd become fond of it on its own, even after she'd realized that she and Garen, Prince of Thieves, could never be. Every once in a while, she'd spot Fletch—Garen's silent second—who would nod at her, and Ella—Garen's only female captain—who would always wink at her. They too were Thali's family, so this medallion represented more than just Garen. It was part of her now; it meant she had another family. So, she'd decided to keep it with her. These were her people too, now more than ever, and wearing it reminded her of her duty to them.

"Thali! Let's go! I want to get the good stuff!" Mia was more chipper than usual this morning. Thali rallied and hauled herself off the floor, then looked at her tiger and dog to see if they would come with her. Ana groaned and stretched her legs out, while Indi turned her head away, sinking her face into a pillow. Bardo didn't even move.

"Fine. I guess I'll come back for you three later," Thali muttered as she grabbed her coat and opened her door to the common room.

Mia, Daylor, and Tilton stood there, waiting for her.

"Oh. Hi." Thali was surprised she hadn't heard Daylor and Tilton.

"Ready?" Mia asked. She looped her arm around Daylor's elbow, and Tilton offered his arm to Thali. As she stepped out, she noticed her guards were dressed in plain clothing, their weapons barely concealed by their robes and cloaks.

Thali rolled her eyes. "We're not at all conspicuous."

They headed out of the building, down the sloping path to the school's gates, then toward the village and the market. As they made their way into town, Thali's guards dispersed so they could trail their charge less obviously.

She noticed there were more tables today than usual and that there were also a lot more people milling about. "Where did all these people come from?" Thali asked of no one in particular.

Mia had come up beside her, and Daylor leaned around her to explain. "Rumor has spread that Lanchor hasn't been attacked, so all the surrounding farmers and such have made their way here. People are living in tents in the field on the other side of the village."

Thali furrowed her brows. Alexius and Aexie had been vigilant in keeping their perimeter against magical animals up, and the by-product of keeping her safe was keeping those in her proximity safe. She had been glad for it, but now the streets of the village were crowded. Thali wished she would have known about this.

With all the extra people, Thali saw the market wares going for more than what was fair. She knew it was unavoidable though. With more people came more mouths to feed and seemingly fewer products. She made a mental note to write to her father to arrange more supply to this market.

A hulking man waved at her from two aisles over. Dashing away from her group, Thali ducked and wove and ran to the man before jumping into his arms like a gleeful child. "Crab!" she said as he twirled her around.

"Thali. There ya are. Didn't ya get yer pa's note?" Crab asked.

"No, I didn't," Thali said.

"He was hopin' to get yer help today," Crab said.

Her guards and friends finally caught up to them, panting. Her friends greeted Crab, and the guards fanned back out into the crowd.

"I'd love to help! It's been a while and I was thinking to write to Papa about sending more supplies out here."

"He's a step ahead of ya. Ya ain't a princess yet, so let's put ya to work." Crab nodded, eyes glistening as he looked down at Thali. "And yer friends are welcome to work, too. There's a hot meal and payment in it fer 'em."

Tilton and Daylor gladly took him up on his offer, and Mia was already in the back of the stall, checking over the inventory in the wagon. They all spent the day selling the wares Crab had brought from her family's estate, though Mia took a quick break to look for some fabric. Some of the people who recognized her looked a little taken aback to see her on top of a box, selling textiles and pottery and spices. But whatever her guards thought of the situation, they kept quiet and stationed themselves an inconspicuous distance away.

At the end of the day, Thali hopped off the box that had given her a better vantage point and crawled into the wagon. While Mia finished organizing what little was left, Thali handed Crab the money she'd made and sat down on a rug that hadn't been sold, feeling more satisfied than she had in a long while. Daylor and Tilton climbed into the wagon, which was much roomier than it had been that morning.

"Thanks fer all yer help there, lads and lasses. It was mighty kind of ya to step up." Crab shook everyone's hand, and Thali saw the glisten in his eyes after he hugged her.

"That was actually fun," Tilton piped up. He'd taken to textiles like a fish to water and sold almost every bolt of fabric. There were only two left, and Mia had hidden them in the back of the wagon because she wanted to buy them. "Is that what working at markets is always like?" Tilton asked.

Thali nodded. She loved markets because even if the wares or the languages or the cultures were different, they were still all the same.

"It would have been fun," Daylor said, wistfulness tinging his words.

"What do ya mean?" Crab said as he turned back to them and handed Thali's friends their payment for work well done.

"Daylor, Tilton, and Mia are coming to the palace with me next year," Thali explained.

Crab nodded, pursing his lips. "Your father won't be too happy. He just bought three more ships." He grinned then and added, "I'm mighty happy you'll have friends at the palace though."

They had just settled on the floor of the wagon with a pitcher of chilled mint tea, ready to hear the tales Crab had at the ready, when a knock on the side of the wagon made them all jump.

Derk, one of Thali's longtime guards, stuck his head into the back of the wagon. "Excuse me, m'lady, but I believe His Highness is looking for you."

Thali's eyes grew wide as she realized she'd forgotten something.

"Weren't you supposed to meet Elric for lunch today?" Mia rubbed her sore feet.

Thali nodded once and jumped up to rush through the wagon's flap. "Bye, Crab!" She leaped off the wagon and started to run up to the school before being stopped in her tracks as she ran into something warm and solid.

"You know, we could meet without concussions every once in a while." Elric threw his arms out to catch her.

"Elric, I'm *so* sorry. Crab asked for help and then I got completely carried away."

Elric closed his eyes and took a deep breath. Thali watched his jaw clench and unclench. "You do know you're going to be the royal princess of Adanek, yes?"

Thali nodded.

"And as such, selling wares at a market will no longer be ... ethical," Elric opened his eyes and looked at her.

Thali cringed as she looked down. "I know. People could just be buying from me to say they bought from royalty. I'm sorry, and I'm sorry I forgot about lunch." It was a possibility she'd considered, but no one had stopped her. And she really loved working at the market so very much.

Elric sighed and rubbed his hands up and down her arms. "Well, I'm glad you enjoyed yourself. I was productive too and got caught up on some work. I just finished, actually."

"Oh." Thali kicked a loose cobblestone away.

"Care to join me for a walk?"

Thali noticed Elric's shiny, expensive, clean clothes and looked at her own, now coated with a layer of dirt. She spent a minute trying to smooth out and wipe away the dirt before she realized she was just moving it around. When she glanced up at him, he was grinning at her, so she followed Elric as he strode easily toward the river, deeper into town. The guards were more conspicuous now because the streets were emptying as people retired to their homes for the evening. Thali glanced longingly back at the wagon where Crab was regaling her friends with stories from markets he'd been to. Then, she turned back to the candlelit street where Elric had slowed his pace so she could catch up. She felt a pang of sadness at leaving one situation for the other and wondered whether she'd always feel like she was being pulled in two different directions. Two years ago, she would have been listening to Crab's stories, happy after a hard day's labor and for hot food in her belly. Now, she glanced at Elric and his guards nearby. Elric she was excited to see, but the guards and Elric's finery were symbolic of the luxury she'd never wanted.

Elric motioned to her, and she jogged to catch up, asking as she did how his meetings had gone. She only got a few terse words in reply. But when she noticed the movement in the windows of buildings nearby, she suddenly understood Elric's hesitance. They were out in the open with who knew how many ears and eyes on them. Left with nothing they could safely say, she took Elric's elbow in her arm and ambled with him through the village.

Thali wondered where they were going when Elric finally stopped near a wall at the edge of town. He climbed a nearby set of stairs to the top of the wall and looked out. Thali followed him, wondering what he was looking for. When she reached the top stair, Daylor's words from earlier rang through her head.

Past the outermost city wall, in the field normally filled with tall grasses blowing in the wind, was a village of tents. Some were true tents, and some were makeshift, with fabric sewn together, wide slats of wood twined together, or even blankets draped over rickety wagons. The grass had been replaced with a patchwork of hastily constructed shelters as far as the eye could see.

"One of my messengers mentioned the tents when he rode in to report." Elric's brow was furrowed as he looked out at the field of refugees. In Thali's mind, he was either counting the tents or trying to see through them to the families inside.

"What can we do for them?" Thali asked. She wondered if Garen could use some help.

"We can ensure they have the supplies they need, but they won't be able to stay for much longer. It's driving all the prices up, so they'll eventually have to go somewhere else where the prices aren't so high," Elric said.

"But where will they go?" Thali thought of how this area was safe thanks to Alexius and Aexie, of how her family's estate and Elric's palace were also protected. But the dragons couldn't protect the entire kingdom from all the magical animal attacks.

Her heart sank at Elric's next words. They echoed her own thoughts. "The attacks are increasing, Thali." He sounded grim.

"How often?" Thali asked.

"From what I can gather, there's one every day somewhere in the kingdom now." Elric didn't take his eyes off the tents.

"But why?"

He rubbed the back of his head with his hand. "I don't know. We don't know what they want. We don't know how to appease them."

"Have a lot of people ... have a lot of people died?" Thali asked.

"No. Most people are just injured, and that's because they panicked—or because they were trying to be brave. When folks hide in their homes, the animals seem to only run or fly around threateningly, knock a few things over, chase people, and leave."

"Is it only griffins?" Thali asked.

"No. I've heard of basilisks, alcetaurs, hippogriffs, pegasi, the odd multi-headed giant dog, centaurs even. All animals that I grew up thinking existed only in stories."

"Is there a pattern?"

"Not that we can tell."

"And what's the military's plan?"

"I don't know, Thali. We don't have enough soldiers. We're spread thin as it is. We're recruiting and training as many as we can at all our bases, but there's not much we can do at this moment," Elric replied. He was running both his hands through his hair now.

"Is there anything I can do to help?"

"I'm glad you asked." He stilled his hands and turned to look at her over his shoulder. "If we ... if we can catch a live one, could you ... would you come and ask what it wants?"

"Of course," Thali said. She was happy to be able to do something.

"And ... I hate to ask this of you, but could you visit your brother and try to find out why they're doing this?" Elric gazed at her hopefully.

"I will," Thali said.

Elric shook his head then, tousling his blond hair. He turned back to Thali and the stairs. "So, since you missed lunch, how about some dinner?" Elric offered his arm.

Thali gave Elric her biggest smile. She could feel his weariness and wanted to bolster his spirits as much as she could. As she took his arm, she thought she saw a shadow of a silhouette on a nearby rooftop melt into the shadow of a chimney. She wondered what Garen thought of all these people fleeing to Lanchor and if he had any solutions. Then, she wondered whether the ache in her chest when she thought of Garen would ever go away.

CHAPTER NINETEEN

T HE NEXT MORNING, THALI got roped into teaching some of the beginner merchants in Combat class. While she didn't mind helping out, she lamented the time not spent training. She started by guiding them through a specific drill involving twisting your wrist; it wasn't particularly practical but helped increase showiness or general flexibility in the wrist. After she'd demonstrated it for the third time and sent them all off to practice, she made her rounds from person to person, correcting angles and making suggestions to improve their positions.

Ari, a fellow classmate and shipmate who'd experienced the same near-fatal final exam as Thali in their first year, also circled the younger students, helping her. Ari tossed her knives in the air like someone might tuck hair behind their ear. They made a loop in opposite directions before coming together at the end.

"I can't believe we ever looked like this," Ari murmured under her breath. "It's like they don't know the pointy end from the handle."

Thali pressed her lips together to suppress a laugh. Then she yelled, "Sebar! Pointy end down when you twist like that, or you'll take your eye out!"

Ari sighed, and they stood quietly together. The two girls had formed a bond after their ship had been tricked into going to the wrong island for their final exam, where they'd had to solve a dangerous riddle and Thali had inadvertently opened a gate that had let magical creatures into the human world. They still hadn't figured out which teacher had been responsible.

Thali watched Ari's gaze slide to Alexius on the other end of the training field.

"So, Thali, are you and Alexius …" Ari wiggled her eyebrows at her.

Thali's eyes widened. "What? No! Ari, you know Elric and I are engaged."

Ari shrugged. "I know, but you and Alexius are always exchanging glances, and you spend a lot of time together. I dunno, I guess I thought maybe you were having some fun before you settle down."

Thali wanted to be angry, but she could see how Ari had come to that conclusion. She and Alexius were constantly talking to each other in their minds, and with him teaching her magic, they always had to crawl off to some secluded area.

"I assure you, Ari, Alexius and I are just friends. I'm engaged to Elric, and happily so," Thali said, swallowing down the thought that other rumors might be swirling.

Not one big on drama or scandal, Ari shrugged again then and added, "Would you put in a good word for me?"

Thali was taken aback as she looked at Ari again but decidedly did not glance at Alexius. Then, she started to wonder if Alexius courted human women. Did dragons court dragons, or could they court humans? That wasn't something she'd considered before.

Ari interrupted her thoughts. "I know we're as tough as the guys, but Alexius is beautiful."

Thali laughed at that. "Sure, Ari, I'll mention it to him."

"Thanks." Then Ari rushed off to forestall a student from stabbing another by going the wrong direction.

Hey Alexius, do dragons court human women?

Some do. For fun.

Do you?

I thought it'd be too cruel, given my immortality and other form.

Do you have a type? A preference?

Sebar is about to chop off his own foot.

Thali rushed over to Sebar, knocking his sword away from him before he could complete the next rotation. Master Aloysius was crazy to give these students actual swords to practice with. It wasn't lost on Thali though that Alexius hadn't replied to her last question.

Later that night, Thali was allowed to skip her court lessons with Sera to join Elric and meet their official royal wedding planner. After that meeting, she had lessons with Alexius, and after that, Mia had made her promise to stand for her last dress fitting before The Founders Ball.

"Elric! I almost forgot, Founders Ball?" Thali asked as they ate dinner together before their meeting.

Elric laughed as he plopped a potato chunk from the stew he was eating into his mouth. "Is that your way of asking if I'll go with you?"

Recovering, Thali sat up taller. "Well, I assumed an advantage to being engaged was I'd always have a date to fancy balls."

Elric bowed his head as he handed her a basket of rolls to go with her stew. "Mia sent a letter about colors weeks ago. I have my outfit all ready."

Thali let out a breath. "Good. Now, how do royal wedding planners get appointed?" She cut up her next potato, and it was halfway to her mouth when the dining room doors opened suddenly.

"Put that down, my lady! You only have eight months to the wedding! You must start dieting now! Green vegetables and broth only!" A high, nasally voice pierced the room and Thali froze.

A wispy, tall woman with hair like brown polished wood that fell like a curtain to the middle of her back glided into the room. She approached Elric first, who rose to greet her.

"Your Highness, I cannot believe this day has come. I am excited to have the honor of directing your wedding." She took Elric's hand, bowing low, and kissed his fingers.

Thali shoved two potato pieces into her mouth and also rose, but only because she was still stunned as she took in the woman before her. The wedding planner had green eyes like a grassy meadow, a pointed chin, and high cheekbones. She was impossibly thin, her waist corseted to look smaller than Thali's own thigh. Her outfit was almost intriguing, with its form-fitting dusty-pink dress and brass-buttoned jacket in a lighter shade of pink. The jacket reminded Thali of a military jacket.

"Cassandra, it's nice to get to work with you. How is your family?" Elric wore his courtly charming face and smiled politely.

"Oh, Your Highness honors me. My family is doing very well, thank you."

"That's lovely to hear. Cassandra, this is my bride-to-be, Lady Routhalia of Densria."

Cassandra giggled as she turned her attention to Thali. She scurried around the table and bowed low in front of Thali, taking her hands as she rose.

"Now, my dear, there is nothing to worry about. We will get you to your thinnest self possible for the wedding, I promise. I have recipes and tricks like you've never seen. But from now on, you eat only green vegetables and broth. Trust me, you'll be grateful come the day of the wedding."

Thali's eyes went wide, and she sat down with a *thunk* as Cassandra the wedding planner ushered in her assistants, who carried tomes of books, swathes of fabric samples, and boxes of plates. It took about the same amount of time for everything to be brought to their table and their supper cleared out as it did for Thali to regain her composure.

This woman had breezed in informally and no one had stopped her. Thali couldn't believe it, though she figured the planner must work with the royal family all the time for their introductions to have been so casual. Thali was also flabbergasted she'd managed to insult Elric's intended so quickly. Thali had never been a wispy-thin woman like her mother or this woman, but she'd always kept fit and trim. Mia had called her shape hourglass given that her wider hips and wider shoulders showed off her waist. She'd never thought of herself as needing to eat only vegetables and broth.

"Congratulations to the happy couple!" Cassandra exclaimed. Thali had to stop from cringing at the nasally sound of her voice. "What do you envision? What do you want to see? What colors would you like to incorporate? Have you thought of a primary, secondary, and tertiary flower to focus on? Will we have a theme for your wedding? Will there be two parts, the ceremony and the feast afterward? How far away does your farthest wedding invitation have to go? We should get a move on all these things. But first, we can get the invitations done and sent out."

Thali's eyes remained wide, and Elric glanced over only to see Thali's bewildered expression. His barely hidden smirk indicated he was holding back a laugh, but that smirk was suddenly replaced with concern as fear began to overtake her. Indi stalked into the room and put her head under Thali's hand. Ana followed Indi and leaped up into Thali's lap, forcing her head under Thali's other hand.

"Oh my! I'd heard the rumors, but oh my, what a sight they are in real life! Are they well-trained? Will they be in the ceremony? We could have the tiger come in with a wagon full of doves, and the dog could carry the rings and perhaps even a bouquet." Cassandra continued babbling in her high voice, and Thali focused on calming the racing heart threatening to drown her. She hadn't even started to imagine what her wedding would look like. As she'd already told Elric, she'd always imagined a quiet ceremony at sea, on a ship.

"Oh, and the dress, have you ideas about the dress? I can get us appointments with the queen's own dressmaker, but we have to start right away. Really, we should have started months ago, but we'll have to manage. This will be the wedding of the century, so I'm sure they'll make your dress a priority."

That snapped Thali back to reality. "No," she whispered. Then she cleared her throat.

Cassandra shut her mouth abruptly. "Sorry, my dear, I didn't hear you."

Thali stood up then, carefully placing the heavy lap dog on her chair. "No. The wedding dress is already underway. It will be made by my future lady-in-waiting, Amelia Blacksmith. I've always worn her dresses, and this occasion will be no different." Her heart fluttered a moment as she wondered whether Cassandra became more high-pitched when she was angry.

"Good. I'd like to meet her, but if you've got that under control, then all the better for me!" Cassandra smiled, not at all affected by what Thali had thought was a stand against her.

"Cassandra, if you'll excuse us a minute." Elric stood as well, using his commanding voice.

"Of course, Your Highness. I'll go see to the ribbon samples." She bowed deeply, then backed out of the room and shut the doors.

Elric came over and took Thali's hand. The warmth rose up her arm as he held her hand in both of his, rubbing his thumb on the back of her wrist.

"I know Cassandra can seem a bit ... intense. But she has a good heart, and she means well. She's the best party planner Mother's ever found."

"There's ... she's ... a lot."

"I know." Elric raised her hand to his lips and kissed her fingertips. Then, he moved to kiss her knuckles, then the back of her wrist and slowly up her arm until he stood right behind her. He kissed her shoulder, then her neck, and then the tender spot right behind her ear.

Indi huffed a complaint, but Thali finally felt warmth crawling back into her body as Elric put his arms around her and held her tight.

"There's so much to decide, Elric. I know we can't have a simple wedding. But couldn't it be simpler? What even is a tertiary flower? I thought you only had to pick one."

Elric laughed into her neck, and she enjoyed the feeling of his lips on her skin as they stretched into a smile. It made the hairs on the back of her neck tingle.

Before she could spin around to kiss Elric, he extricated himself and stepped around Indi, heading for the doors to the hall. "I have an idea," he said before disappearing.

A minute later, Thali sat back down, squeezing Ana behind her, while Indi curled around her chair. Elric opened the double doors and strode back to his chair. Cassandra came in after him, looking a little sheepish as she nodded to Thali and retreated to a corner. A slender man in a sweeping metallic-green coat, purple shirt, and black pants swept in after her. His skin was dark brown and his black hair long but tied back neatly into a ponytail with a purple ribbon. His brassy-brown eyes looked friendly.

"My first assistant, Taybro. He has a way of bringing forth your wants and imaginations with little effort," Cassandra announced as she took a seat in the corner.

Taybro bowed low to Elric. "Your Highness, it is an absolute honor to have the opportunity to serve you again." His voice was deep and soothing, like honey. At Elric's nod, he turned to Thali. "My lady, it is also an honor to meet the daughter of such an illustrious family and the future princess of this kingdom." He turned his brown eyes on her, and Thali felt her throat dry.

Taybro was the epitome of charm as he smiled brightly at her. She found herself breathing deeply, as though a sudden calm had swept through her body like a wave over a rock on the beach. "My lady, if you'll entertain the idea, I'd like to take you through your own imagination and help you learn what might please you for your upcoming nuptials." He seemed to be waiting for approval, so Thali nodded.

"Very good. Thank you, my lady. Now, please, close your eyes. Imagine if you would, the ocean. It is a beautiful day, the sun is shining, the sky is clear, and all around you is the ocean. Do you have that in mind, my lady?"

Thali nodded absently, imagining one of her favorite sights in all the world.

"Now, my lady, look at the water. What color is it?" Thali looked down in her mind's eye.

"Open your eyes, my lady. Before you is a book of colors. If you could find the one you saw in your mind's eye?"

Thali opened her eyes and flipped through a book of blues. When she found the exact one that stood out to her, she pushed the book back toward Taybro.

"Excellent. This will be the secondary color, the primary color being the royal purple of your family's crest, Your Highness." Taybro bowed his head in Elric's direction. "And with your permission, my lady, I believe this blue here," he flipped a page and pointed at yet another blue, "is the color of your family's crest? This will be the tertiary color."

Thali looked and recognized it as the light sky blue of her family's crest. She nodded.

"Excellent. Now, if you would please close your eyes again. His Highness has mentioned sunflowers are your favorite, so we will make this the primary flower for the wedding. But for the second and third, imagine you are walking in a forest. It is sunny and bright, and you hear the normal animal sounds of squirrels and rodents and deer around you. You walk into a meadow, and it is filled with beautiful little flowers. Can you describe these flowers to me?"

"They're white, small, and shaped like delicate sacs. They hang from the end of the stems."

"Ahh ... the delicate *Cypripedium candidum*, otherwise more commonly known as Queen's Lady's Slippers. Very good choice, my lady. Now, close your eyes again. You are in this meadow filled with little white flowers, but there's another flower there. Something even smaller. Can you describe it to me?"

"It's a small flower with four purple petals. It has a ring of yellow in the middle, around a dark-brown spot. They grow in clusters out of the ground as if they burst through all at once."

"Hmm ... perhaps creeping bluets, or *Houstonia serpyllifolia*. Beautiful choice, my lady." Taybro bowed then. "That will give us plenty to work on for the moment, so I will leave you with Cassandra."

"Thank you," Thali managed as Taybro left. Already, Thali was wishing Taybro was their planner, not Cassandra. That had been relatively easy. But now she was thinking of that meadow and how she'd much rather be there.

Cassandra rose and strode over, giving a brief curtsy. "His Highness tells me you work best with lists. I will leave you with a list of questions I'd like you to answer as specifically as you can. If you answer three a day, that will be plenty for us to work on." Cassandra had reined in her enthusiasm, so despite the grating of her nasally voice, Thali made an effort to smile so she could try to convey her appreciation.

The planner left a stack of parchment on the table as her assistants cleared all the samples away, and she bowed to the royal couple before leaving.

"Better?" Elric asked.

"Much," Thali answered. She reached for the list Cassandra had left. She swallowed but scanned the list. Written as it was like a list of questions, Thali could attack it like she was studying for her classes. "Is this all for me, or are some for you?"

"How about you take first crack, and I'll take second if you come across some you don't know the answer to?"

Thali nodded. "Thank you, Elric." She looked down at her hands, suddenly shy about her inability to handle party planning.

"Hey." He slid his finger under her chin. "We'll do this together. I've had years more experience than you, so don't even dare apologize. You'll get used to it."

Thali wondered if he meant she would be planning many parties in the future or if he meant she would get used the stress of having someone bombarding her with questions. The questions, at least, she didn't mind as long as she had answers.

As Thali left Elric's manor, soon to be their manor, she headed into the forest with Indi and Ana and then turned north. She walked until she was in the meadow where she always had her lessons with Alexius. As she looked around, it reminded her of the other meadow she'd imagined earlier that night, the meadow where she'd hidden with Alexius and where she'd seen an angry Garen come stomping toward her, the light glowing on his dark-brown hair, his dark-blue eyes piercing right through her.

Shall I return another time?

No. Can you teach me to shut you out?

Should I be concerned?

Thali tried a different tactic. *It must be tiring to hear all my thoughts all the time.*

I can shut you out.

Then isn't it fair I learn to do the same?

Yes. I suppose it is. You know how to shove me back to the wall, but you can also build a wall around my thread. Or rather, you can spin a thread around mine. Try it.

Thali sat on the boulder and pulled out a thread to coil it around Alexius's thread.

How far along do I need to go?

Until it's hard to feel me. That should be enough to block me from your random thoughts. But go further and I'll try to push my way through.

Thali imagined her column of thread hardening against the push she could feel was Alexius trying to move down the thread.

Good. That's perfect. Since it seems we're working on blocking tonight, we'll work on how to block someone trying to come into your head.

Will it appear like a thread to me? Or like smoke—like Tariq's—or whatever way that person's magic appears?

All of the above. It might appear as something different, or the highly skilled might try to make it look like your own magic to trick you into connecting with it. Connecting with animals around this area has been safe because no magical animals can seize hold of them with the barrier protecting them. But someone else with your ability, or another kind of magic even, will be able to enter your mind through the mind of another animal when you don't have the benefit of a magical barrier. Be careful and always stay on your guard.

That made Thali think of a time when she wouldn't be with Alexius.

Alexius, will you come with me to the palace next year? You can have whatever role you want officially, but I think I'd like you with me.

Alexius stepped aside and swept Thali a grand bow. *The honor would be all mine.*

Alexius was all business as he continued, now poking and prodding at Thali's mind from different angles so Thali had to either deflect or bring a shield or wall up against him.

It was late when they walked back to her rooms, Alexius always walking her to her door as her guard before saying good evening. He warned her that from now on, he and Aexie would try to sneak up on her mind at all times of the day, so she ought to be ready and always on alert. The real world outside their bubble would be similar, so they would start practicing.

Mia was already asleep when Thali opened the door, and she breathed a guilty sigh of relief. *At least I can get some sleep tonight. No silly dress fittings or school gossip.*

CHAPTER TWENTY

T HALI BARELY PAID ATTENTION to her classes, impatient as she was for school to be done for the day, just as many of the merchant students were. Her birthday had dawned unusually warm, and they were all antsy and dying to dive into the lake they'd found in their first year. Every leg in the room bounced and every hand fidgeted as Master Kelcian reviewed the details and advantages and disadvantages to the different sizes of vessels commonly used by merchants. Eventually, he took one last look around the room, glanced at the clock, and sighed. He silently waved the class out, letting all the third-years out early to enjoy their celebration.

Off they all ran, whooping and hollering all the way to the lake. Startled birds took flight and frightened animals ran for cover, but Thali sent them happy, calming thoughts. Finally reaching their special lake and dumping their book bags by the trees, they peeled off their boots and leather vests and coats.

Stefan cleared his throat as Thali jumped up and down on one foot while pulling a boot off.

"Is something the matter, Stefan? Do guards not swim?" Thali looked up, falling against the tree trunk as she struggled with her boot.

"We cannot secure the lake, my lady. And I'm not sure how appropriate it is for you to be swimming with other gentlemen," Stefan said.

Thali dropped her foot, finally freeing it from the boot. Stefan had never spoken directly about what she should and shouldn't do, so it came as a surprise to hear him voice his opinion on her propriety.

"Thali, get in here! I need you on my team! Milo has Alexius!" Daylor shouted as she spoke with her four guards.

"And what do you think?" Thali turned to Amali, Derk, and Khadija.

Amali and Derk looked at their feet. Khadija was the only one to answer. "My job is to protect you. My opinion is not necessary for me to perform my duty." She watched as a muscle in Stefan's jaw flexed.

Thali rolled her eyes. She could feel the sweat dripping down her spine as the day got hotter with every passing moment. She stood with her hand on her hip, lips pursed for a moment, wondering whether she was blindly heading into some kind of scandal. "Thank you, Stefan, for offering your advice in this matter, but I am not yet a princess and these gentlemen *and ladies* are my friends and not unknown to Elric."

She quickly peeled off her other boot and then decided to leave her canvas vest on. Surely that would suffice for propriety's sake. Shaking off her coat, she ran over to the lake to join her friends. Thali didn't turn back to see her guards' faces, and though she hoped Elric wouldn't actually be mad at her, she knew this might be one of her last opportunities to act freely. Feeling the cage walls starting to come down, she leaped free of them and into the lake, splashing all her friends. She climbed onto Daylor's wide shoulders, ready to take on any contenders in a water wrestling match. She wrestled with Tilton then Ari, and eventually some first- and second-years as they came to join the fun after class. They were all thoroughly soaked and tired when the sun started to descend, and they trudged back to school, the warm air drying their clothes until they arrived at the edge of campus once again and headed for their rooms.

Thali stood in the bathing chamber she shared with Mia, combing out her long brown hair. She was surprised her friends had all forgotten her birthday, though she didn't really mind as she enjoyed not being the center of attention for once, and this afternoon at the lake was now one of her best birthday memories. She'd only wished Elric had been there, but he'd promised her a birthday dinner. With that reminder, she let her hair hang loose to dry and headed for her bedroom.

Mia had been away all day, but she'd left Thali a blueberry muffin in the common room by the windowsill in the morning so Indi and Ana couldn't get to it. As Thali walked into her room now, her attention was caught by the box on her bed. Excited, she ran over, opened it, and pulled out a beautiful sky-blue dress. Her eyes bulged in astonishment at the delicate lace that was the bodice and sleeves, then the full skirts—perfect for twirling, Mia would say. The lacy bodice was embroidered in violet thread; birds and swirls had been artfully sewn on the skirts to look as though they were in flight. As Thali trailed her fingertips along the delicate threads, Ana snuck up behind her. She jumped about a foot in the air when Ana suddenly ran her tongue up Thali's wet leg, licking the moisture from the bath off her legs.

"Ana!" Thali chastised, to which Ana replied by licking her leg once again before trotting to the bed and jumping up on it.

Snapping up the dress so the dog wouldn't wrinkle it, Thali turned and pressed it to her toweled self as she looked in the mirror. When she turned back around, she couldn't help but laugh. Indi was standing, with all four of her giant tiger paws, in the box Thali's dress had been in and was contemplating sitting down. Looking up as if she'd been caught red-handed, Indi sank down onto her haunches, filling the little box with her giant tiger butt.

"Well, I'm glad to know the two of you will be entertained tonight." Thali pulled the curtains over her windows before putting on the simple but exquisite dress. She took a moment to stroke Bardo along his head as he lay on her desk around the lamp. Opening her curtains when she was done, she had the distinct feeling she was being watched and peered out into the dark forest outside. She shrugged before jumping back to brush her hair, realizing she was going to be late if Elric showed up on time, which he always did. In her hurry, she didn't see the pair of dark-blue eyes watching her from a tree branch level with her window.

Garen

Had she looked, really looked, she would have seen him. She should have felt he was near, and at the same time, he knew he should have stayed away. But it was her birthday, and he couldn't help but think of her today. He couldn't help but come see her, wish her well from afar. It ripped his heart apart anew, but if she was happy, then he would be happy for her. He swallowed down the emotion threatening to overwhelm him and climbed down out of the tree. Taking a few deep breaths to steady himself, he strode through the tree line back into town and slid right back into his role as Prince of Thieves as he made his way to his merry court. In his little tavern, his family awaited him and would help him forget what day it was. And they didn't let him down. The place was raucous with laughter as he stepped in: Folks were extra loud, extra jubilant, extra drunk. He swallowed as he put the last brick in place around his heart and sat down, taking the ale placed in front of him and downing the entire thing in seconds.

Thali

As she finished the braid—because truly, that was the only thing she could do with her hair herself that wouldn't make a folly of the dress—Thali felt a tingle along her skin, and she looked out the open window into the dark trees again. Her forehead creased as she dove into her threads to see if she could figure out if someone had been watching her. Her heart did a flip-flop to think who it might be, who part of her hoped it would be. She thought she saw movement in the trees, but when she opened her window, all she saw was a light-blue ribbon. Thali redid her hair, weaving the ribbon in this time, and couldn't decide whether Mia had left it and it had flown out the window, or if it had been left by someone else. Thali swallowed, chastising herself for thinking of another man and absentmindedly touching the ribbon in her hair and the ring on her finger.

A knock on her common-room door interrupted her thoughts as they started to drift. As she left her bedroom, Stefan opened the door and Elric waltzed in with a massive bouquet of sunflowers. "I hope you're not disappointed by the lack of flowers this year." Elric bowed low over her hand as he brought his lips to them.

Thali giggled at the memory of having every surface in her common room covered in sunflowers. Even the practice field for Combat class had been surrounded by sunflowers that year.

"No. I'm glad there are sunflowers left for other people this year." She took the flowers and grabbed a jar to put them in water before they left.

"You look beautiful. That's quite the dress."

"Thank you. From Mia, as always." She did a little twirl and Elric caught her hand as she twirled right into his chest.

"You'd be beautiful in a potato sack." He kissed her, his soft lips gently pressing hers. Thali could feel the heat rise in her cheeks as she let out a little giggle.

"I don't know if they make potato sacks you can wear." Thali smiled.

"That's next year's birthday present then." Elric grinned his sunshine smile and produced a box from his inside jacket pocket. "Speaking of birthday presents."

Thali raised her eyebrow as she took the beautiful, flat velvet box. Her merchant eyes knew this was a box that typically held necklaces.

She pulled at the ribbon and let it drop to the ground, then snapped the lid open. Inside was a necklace of amethyst jewels, worthy only of royalty.

"Elric, this is too much."

He held firm. "It was my grandmother's. And it's not too much. You're going to be a princess. I'm just adding to your collection."

"It's beautiful," Thali said. She looked at her wrist where she'd placed the bracelet he'd given her last year. It wasn't the same stone but matched perfectly.

"May I?" Elric reached to take the necklace and fasten it around her neck.

"Thank you." The moment felt surreal, wearing such an extravagant necklace. But while she felt the heavy weight of the gems, that same weight comforted her.

Elric offered her another brilliant grin. "Ready?"

As they left her rooms, Stefan looked down, not making eye contact with her. Thali wondered if he felt embarrassed about speaking out earlier.

As they ambled to the doors, Thali leaned in closer to Elric. "Would you be angry with me if I told you all the merchant students and I went to the lake this afternoon for a swim?"

"Perhaps if you were naked," Elric said.

Thali blushed, "No. We wore shirts and pants, and I even kept my vest on."

"I wish I'd been there to join you, but no, I trust you. And I trust there were both male and female merchant students present?"

"Absolutely. We've all been dying to get to the lake for a swim. And today was so warm, we were practically buzzing with anticipation."

"Daylor and Tilton were there?"

"Yes."

"Did you abandon your guards?"

"No. But they advised me not to go in. They couldn't secure the lake."

"I'd prefer you swam in the lake on the palace grounds, but no, it doesn't anger me. Our deal was for you to enjoy your days at school."

"Good. I'm glad." Thali took Elric's hand then. They'd come upon a carriage outside the door, and he handed her into it. She wondered momentarily what had motivated Stefan to suggest the impropriety.

Elric followed her in, and as he sat opposite her, she asked, "Really? A carriage for the short ride to your manor?"

"*Our* manor. And I couldn't bear to ruin your dress. Or scratch my stunning boots." Elric smirked.

"Well, I guess we can't have anything scratching your boots then." Thali smirked back. She could tell Elric was in a really good mood, and it was infectious. Her own smile broadened.

The short carriage ride ended and when the door opened, Thali was surprised to see his staff all wearing the formal livery of the manor staff.

"Please tell me you had a foreign dignitary come today, and all this formality isn't for my birthday?" Thali waited for Elric to exit first before reaching out and placing her hand in what she assumed was Elric's hand. As she descended the carriage steps, she suddenly recognized the familiar calluses on the hand she'd grown up holding.

Thali turned and stumbled into her father's arms. "Papa!" She threw her arms around her father's neck, and he wrapped her up in his usual bear hug.

When he let her go, she saw her mother standing next to him and went to embrace her, too. Elric stood behind them, grinning like a fool. "But … how? I thought you were in the south?"

"Surprise! We're not!" Lord Ranulf's eyes twinkled with glee.

Elric appeared at her side again. "Surprised?"

"Yes, thank you. This is the best birthday present I could ever ask for!" She gave Elric a kiss on the cheek.

"Well, let's not let dinner get cold." Elric offered his elbow again and Thali took it, grasping her mother's hand with her free hand, not wanting to let her go and not quite believing they were actually here.

Her head was bent in conversation with her mother as they walked when the doors to Elric's manor opened and a great roar of "Surprise!" blasted Thali nearly back out the door.

She stood stunned and blinking, looking at all the faces around her. It looked like every single student was there, more than just her merchanting peers. Even Crab was there, and Master Aloysius.

"Did you really think they all forgot?" Elric whispered in her ear.

Thali turned and threw her arms around Elric, kissing him soundly on the mouth, and the crowd cheered again.

As she let Elric—who had turned pink—go, Mia ran up to her. "That dress looks exactly how I thought it would on you. Happy birthday, Thali. It killed me to avoid you all day! What you must have thought of me!"

"Now it all makes sense!" Thali hugged her best friend. Mia wouldn't have been able to keep this from her if she'd seen her today. Thali smiled broadly, aware the crowd was watching her.

Thali let herself be guided in and hugged all the friends she had known for the last three years, even the ones she'd met only a few months ago. She was amazed to see every single person from earlier at the lake and was even more surprised that no one had let the secret slip out.

Daylor and Tilton were impeccably dressed and assigned themselves as her tail, making sure all her adoring fans got a few moments with her. It was a full hour before Thali even made it to the dining room, which had been rearranged to house mountains of food on its many tables. She wasn't at all surprised to find her mother and father there waiting, her father popping something in his mouth between every other sentence. Thali went over and placed herself between them, hoping the crowd of people wouldn't see where she'd gone. As much as she enjoyed her friends and classmates, she was tired of the smiling and polite conversation she'd kept up.

Thali wasn't able to hide for long, though. Elric ushered her to the living room and to a high, wing-backed, cushioned chair sitting atop a box, much like a throne. Her eyes went wide, and she suddenly felt panic rise as she looked at all the expectant faces. Then, Thali felt Alexius's thread in her mind. He sent her a wave of calm she was ever so grateful for.

"I know your classmates have a tradition of performing for your birthday, so let the show begin!" Elric threw his arms out.

As she sat, Elric took a seat at the edge of her box, and everyone settled in beside and behind her. Group by group jumped up to perform a silly little something for her. She couldn't help but let her mind drift back to a year ago, when her friends had put on a little party for her, and she'd laughed more than she could ever remember. Tonight, she smiled like she was supposed to, but it was for their benefit. The school was safe, but in the opulence of the manor, she watched some of her classmates shift uncomfortably. Looking around the room, she was reminded of who wasn't here, of who had died from animal attacks. As Thali sat there among all the decadence, she began to feel tonight was frivolous, and sudden anger that all these people didn't know the threats they faced welled up in her.

The village was overpopulated, and magical animals were attacking throughout the kingdom; people were dying and no one did anything about it. Did the people in this room even know about it? They must. She thought of Kesla, of the girl who wasn't here because she'd been killed by a magical creature. And no one knew why, not really. Thali felt like they were all sitting ducks, waiting for Xerus, Alexius's oldest brother, to make his next move.

Thali smiled until her face hurt, unable to let her friends down, despite the rising anger in her. She was honored they'd come together for her, and loved seeing her parents, but felt a burning need to see her brother.

It was late when most of the party guests finally left. Her mother and father had to leave early in the morning to actually get to the south, so they left first. Thali hugged them for a long time before letting them go, sad they'd gotten to see so little of each other. It was for that reason that she pushed the kernel of suspicion about her father aside when she remembered how Rommy had said their father had doubted him.

Eventually, only Daylor, Tilton, Mia, Alexius, Elric, and the guards remained with Thali in the manor as the sun started peeking through the windows. They had gathered on the couches, talking and enjoying the temporary carefree company. When Daylor, Tilton, Alexius, and Mia finally rose to leave, Thali asked Alexius in her mind to loop back to the manor.

When the door had closed and the manor was thankfully empty, minus the staff and guards, Elric walked her to her own chambers upstairs.

"Elric, I'd like to go visit my brother," Thali said.

Elric swallowed and gave her a tight smile as he nodded. "I'll bring Ana, Indi, and Bardo to the manor tomorrow and say I'm keeping you busy."

She nodded and he smiled softly, telling her to sleep well as he closed her door. He left her and returned to his study to finish some paperwork.

Alexius was in Thali's chambers when she closed the door. "I'd like to see my brother."

Alexius gave a little nod as Aexie appeared. "Happy birthday, Thali!" she said, embracing her as Alexius rolled up his sleeves. Thali was again surprised by Aexie's hug.

"Would you like to change your clothes first?" Alexius asked.

Thali shook her head. She hadn't wanted to be rude to her friends, but she'd wasted enough time tonight already. Suddenly, she felt such an urgency to see her brother that she couldn't be bothered with her outfit.

Alexius walked over to the wall and drew an outline of a small door with his finger. The door appeared piece by piece as he drew it. When he was done, they pushed it open, and he offered Thali a hand as they walked through.

They took precisely the same journey as they had the last two times, walking through more thick fog. Thali felt anxious; this time, it felt like it was taking much longer. Finally, they arrived at a familiar door and after pushing through it, they walked into the hall and came upon her brother. He stared at them as they oriented themselves.

"Rou!" Rommy's voice was filled with glee as he rushed over to her and embraced her. "Come, come and join me."

He led her through the same double doors to the same checkered study with the plum-purple couches. She noticed again Alexius did not follow them. She'd have to ask Alexius what he did while she visited her brother.

On this visit though, on the iron table between the couches was a little purple box with a silver bow.

"Happy birthday, little sister." Rommy pushed the box toward her. As he did, Thali had to suppress a gasp at how Rommy's hand had aged. His joints bulged, and his skin was ashen, cracked, and wrinkled. She put her hand on the box but looked up at her brother's face.

The circles under his eyes were dark, even bruised, as if he'd been punched in both eyes. His cheeks were drawn, his skin looked paper thin, and his complexion was tinted a strange tinge of gray that matched the room.

"Rommy. Are you all right? You look terrible."

He smiled at her weakly. "Yes. I'm fine, Thali. I've been experimenting with some magic, and it's taken more out of me than I expected. I'm all right. Please, open your present. Tell me all about your birthday party!"

She opened the little box and was shocked to see a silver ring inset with an amethyst. It matched the necklace Elric had given her perfectly. "Rommy. It matches it exactly. How did you know?"

"Remember, I told you Xerus lets me look into your world every once in a while. I saw what the prince was going to give you, so I couldn't resist completing the set."

"It's beautiful. Thank you, Rommy." She slid it on her right hand and then went to sit next to Rommy.

"Rommy, you really don't look well. Can't one of the dragons help with your experiments?"

Rommy shook his head, "I need to do them to myself. I'm the only human here, after all. You know how I like to push myself. The attacks have been more frequent lately, and I'm trying to figure out why they keep happening. I was hoping to have some kind of answer for you, but I'm glad to see you on your birthday." He offered her a grin, but Thali's brow creased with worry at her brother's current health.

"Take a rest, Rommy, or you'll be too weak to help."

Rommy laughed full heartedly, recognizing the words Crab had always said to them. "And how is old Crab?"

"He's great. You should have seen him with his cousin last night, Rommy. They wrestled each other, and it was an epic battle. I think together they could destroy a castle if they weren't careful."

Rommy laughed, and it turned into a coughing fit. Thali put a hand on his back, feeling his spine poke through the layers of his fine clothing.

"Rommy. Don't you have anything to eat here?" Thali's concern returned.

"Yes, we have fine food. You know how time can run away with me when I'm focused. Don't be too concerned for me. I want for nothing here. I'm only sorry I don't have anything of import for you yet. Magical beasts are tricky creatures."

"No. Don't worry about that, focus on you. I want to see you healthy again. You still owe me a sparring match." Thali smiled kindly. On the inside, she wanted to find Xerus and demand answers.

"Oh, Rou, you've grown up so much. I wish I could be there for your wedding day." Her brother looked at her engagement ring and put a hand on her shoulder. She barely registered the weight of it. Suddenly, her need to know what the eldest dragon's ulterior motive, what his next move would be, didn't seem nearly so important anymore.

"Oh, Rommy, I wish you could too." Thali meant that with her whole heart. She'd looked up to her brother since the day she'd been born, and she couldn't help but be saddened by the fact that he wouldn't be able to celebrate the big day with her.

"Well, you have to get going. Your prince will be worried." Rommy looked wistful, as if he wanted to say something more but was holding back.

He rose and led Thali to the door. He pushed it open for her, and Alexius was already there waiting for her, door in the wall open for them.

"Be safe, Rou," Rommy said.

Before she could look back at Rommy to say goodbye, the door was already closed; her brother had returned to his study.

Thali didn't feel as dazed as she had the other times as she walked through the fog with her hand on Alexius's shoulder.

She took advantage of the opportunity and asked, *Alexius, what do you do while I'm talking with my brother?*

I check on my brothers.

Does the visit seem as short for you as it does for me?

I would assume so. Though I wouldn't know directly.

Before they knew it, they were back in Thali's chambers in the manor, and Thali jumped at the banging on her door.

"Thali, let me in. Please." Elric banged on the door a few more times.

She ran to the door and swung it open. "What? What's wrong?"

The look of relief that crossed Elric's face soothed her thundering heart some, but she was still wondering what was going on.

"I've been knocking on your door all morning. I thought you'd already be back." Indi and Ana came charging in and enveloped Thali.

Once they calmed, Thali sighed, inviting Elric into the room, where an awkward-looking Alexius and Aexie stood by the window.

"I told you I went to see my brother," Thali said, feeling annoyance bubbling up and guilt for not getting answers as she cast her eyes downward.

"I know. I just—" Elric's whole body relaxed. He put his arms around her, and she shrugged them off.

"Time doesn't work there like it does here," Thali said.

"I was just worried," Elric said, his hands up defensively. He took a deep breath and Thali felt her annoyance dissipate.

"I'm sorry I panicked. I should have realized. How is your brother?"

"Terrible. He looks unwell. He's working so hard to try and figure out why the attacks keep happening and a solution for them."

"He's a good man," Elric said as he approached her again. This time, Thali let him embrace her and he held her tightly and she rested her head on his shoulder.

A cough made Thali and Elric jump apart. Alexius's jaw was tight as he said, "We will leave you now. I'll see you tomorrow morning, Thali."

She left Elric's side and threw her arms around Alexius. "Thank you for all your help."

He stayed stiff as she hugged him. "The honor is mine," was all he said before turning on his heel and leaving.

Thali searched in her mind for him, but he had blocked her out. She wondered what had made him angry so suddenly.

After Alexius and Aexie had gone, Elric raised an eyebrow at Thali. She shrugged as she picked Bardo up from the corner of the table. He slithered around her hand as she stared after Alexius. She really did wish she knew what that had been all about.

Chapter Twenty-One

T HE NEXT MORNING, THALI was happy to see Alexius had returned to his normal self as they sparred. They were using staffs this week, and Thali was excited because the staff was her favorite weapon and the one she trained with the most. Alexius had such different moves sometimes that she would stop and ask him to show her the new move before trying it out herself. They were in a world unto themselves when they were in Combat class, and even Master Aloysius never interrupted them. Thali couldn't help but smile as she settled into the rhythmic *clack, clack, clack* of two wooden staffs striking each other. Strike, move, block, the actions settled Thali's soul. It made her realize how important training was to her. At times, Thali would even convince Nasir to train with her in the evenings when she couldn't sleep. The warriors from Bulstan were the world's most talented, and she wanted to take advantage of the opportunity.

How have you been? Thali asked along her thread with Alexius.

Well, thank you. He started to prod her mental barriers. Thali felt sweat break out on her forehead.

Are dragons more conservative? Thali asked.

What do you mean? Alexius asked.

I mean, do dragons wait until marriage to kiss and stuff? Thali patched a hole Alexius had snuck through.

No. Our society seems to be more open-minded than yours. Why?

You seem to interrupt Elric and me ... often.

Thali almost managed to land a blow on Alexius' shoulder. She stood stunned for a moment.

I apologize, Thali. Aexie is more open with her sexuality. I was quite shy when I met my mate, so we were quite conservative. I don't mean to put that on you. Alexius bowed his head.

"It's all right, Alexius. As long as we're all right?"

Alexius gave her a small smile then. "We're definitely all right, Thali."

Global Culture class became a little more interesting for Thali when they started to explore the various legends told by different cultures, and it was a nice refresher for her. It enticed her to pour herself into any literature she could find about magical animals, and she was at times rewarded with tiny tidbits like when she came across the story that explained the differences between the hippogriff and the griffin.

In class, the other students paid close attention to Master Brown because the tales were fascinating, though Thali knew his stories weren't all accurate. He certainly liked to add his own flourishes and even went so far as to whisper as he spoke at times, making a big performance of it. She thought Master Brown might be enjoying the attention a little too much, but she didn't want to give him any excuse to pay more attention to her. It was griffins that were attacking people beyond her protective bubble, so everyone wanted to hear everything they could about them, and when he ran out of griffin stories, he told stories of other magical creatures. At least classes were a little less boring now.

The weeks flew by, and between wedding plans, school classes, princess classes, and classes with Alexius, Thali's life was a blur. There was just no time to worry about the griffin attacks or even to go see Rommy, as much as that all bothered her.

Suddenly, it was time for the final exams. Thali was excited when she found out she would be a captain, and a big part of her was thrilled to finally be commanding her own ship with her own crew. It was finally her year. Only third-years could be captains. She chose Ari as her first mate and Alexius as her second so Ari would have a better chance at getting a job with Thali's father. Plus, as her first mate, Ari was responsible for navigation, which was another big reason Thali had chosen her. She'd always had a knack for reading maps.

This year, the school had changed the format of the exams again, just as they had the year before. Either the teachers were still working the kinks out of the exam procedures, or they thought the exams were still not safe enough. So, a week beforehand, the school publicly announced that the students would be sailing to Toad Island. There were four places to dock around the island. The fastest ship would get the closest dock, and the last ship would have to go all the way around to the other side of the island. Each year would perform their challenges simultaneously, as opposed to the previous year when each year had done so one by one. The first ship to return with successfully completed tasks would gain extra points.

Thali assigned Ari to map out a path to Toad Island and to check the currents on the way to the other three docks in case something happened and they needed to use the other docks instead. The rest of her crew was to review their knowledge from all their classes so they could get through their challenges as quickly as possible.

Elric had thankfully excused Thali from her princess classes in the last week so she could focus on her exam. She was elbow deep in books about the ships the school had made available so she'd know everything there was to know about her ship: the way it moved, the way it had been built, and why it had been built that way. Most importantly, she needed to know everything about their negative aspects so she could be prepared for anything.

Master Kelcian now had assistant instructors—merchant graduates—and each ship was assigned one to monitor the students' ship-handling skills and score them based upon their efficiency and knowledge. The assistant would be allowed to ask any question with regards to the ship or the plan at any time of any student. It made Thali nervous that they wouldn't meet their assistant until the day of their departure.

Each crew's navigational plans, lists of provisions, and manifests all had to be approved by their instructors before they would be allowed to leave, and they would draw numbers out of a hat the day before to determine which ship they would sail and the order in which they would leave the dock. The students would only have access to their ship to double-check everything the day before departure. As an added security measure, an observer ship would sail with them with an instructor and a team of healers on board in case of emergency. With each year and each final exam, the fledgling school was learning which safety precautions were warranted. Thali would have rolled her eyes at them in her first year, but after the last two exams, she respected the school's decision. There was always an incident of varying degree. Even though they were only sailing about a day away, anything could happen.

Given the short distance, if the crews left first thing in the morning, they could feasibly get to the island by nightfall. They were to sleep on the ship and then start the exam on the island the next morning. Thali, however, was confident they could get there before nightfall and be better rested than the other teams.

Thali was oozing excitement the morning they were to learn which ships they would sail and which order they were to depart in. The chosen captains gathered in Master Kelcian's cramped little office to watch the draw.

"Welcome, captains." Master Kelcian had eight pieces of paper on the table before him. He wrote the name of each ship on four of them, and then the numbers one to four on the others. Thali looked around the room. She was sure Daylor and the two other captains, Aleena and Jer, felt the tension in the room just as keenly as she did, even though just the other day they'd all been laughing and joking with each other as they'd studied their ships together.

But Thali enjoyed the buzz of excitement and tension in the room. She was giddy with anticipation of finally having her adventure and hoped to leave her mark before she left school. As she sat fidgeting in her chair, it felt like the instructor was purposely taking his time just to increase the suspense.

Master Kelcian folded each piece of paper with a ship name on it in half, then in half again, and popped it into an old sailor's cap on his desk. He stirred the four pieces of paper and then offered it to the first captain to have arrived at his office that morning.

Because Thali had spent the last week studying all the school's ships, she knew one was badly weighted to one side. Another she'd been on last year, so she knew it was relatively fast as long as they didn't weigh it down too much. And she'd seen the third ship list quite dangerously, making her wonder if the rudder was bent, so it was the last one that she hoped to get. It was the oldest, but it was the ship she'd ended up taking command of in her first year when her captain had been critically injured in an attack by a magical creature she'd never seen before, a leviathan. It was also the most solidly built ship. It was slow to change direction, but it had been made well and she was confident she could guide it quickly.

Aleena's face lit up when she read the word on the paper. "*Excellence*," she said.

Thali was relieved. The *Excellence* looked like the fastest ship at first glance, but the crew would have to be careful not to weigh it down too much.

Daylor was next. They'd studied the ships together and he knew everything she knew, except he was hoping for the one with a bent rudder. He'd said he knew what the problem was, so he could fix it. That made it something he could control. He knit his brows together in anticipation and reached his hand in to pick a piece of paper. "*Knowledge.*" It wasn't the one he'd wanted. This ship was weighted to one side. Thali, though, thought it would be easier to control the weight in the ship than hope a rudder could be fixed by tomorrow.

Then, it was Thali's turn. She held her breath as she reached into the cap and took the paper to the left. She unfolded it and breathed out a sigh. "*Integrity*," she said. It was the ship she'd wanted. It was older but solid.

Jer too looked happy about his pick as he took the last paper. "*Honesty,*" he announced. Thali wondered if he knew the rudder was bent. He'd find out soon enough, and maybe it would cost him time.

Next, Master Kelcian folded the numbered pieces of paper and put them in the cap. He twirled his finger around in it a few times to mix them up, then did it again in reverse order.

This time, Jer picked first. "Three," he ground out through gritted teeth.

Thali reached in, picking the one farthest away from her. "Two." She exhaled. Leaving second was better than leaving fourth.

Daylor grinned and his eyes lit up when he opened his paper. "One."

Thali watched Aleena's shoulders sink. "Four," she confirmed as she showed everyone the number on the paper. Master Kelcian wrote all the results down in his book.

"Safe journey." He nodded to them before opening his door and disappearing down the hall. The captains wouldn't meet their assistant instructors until they got to their ships, so they didn't waste any time hurrying out, Aleena and Jer jogging to meet up with their crew. All the merchant students had gathered by the dock in their groups, waiting for their captains to give them their ship assignments.

Once they'd left the school though, Thali and Daylor took their time walking down the pier. "Do you think Jer knows his ship has a broken rudder?" Daylor asked.

"Hopefully not. Then it'll take him longer to get out," Thali replied.

"And what about Aleena's ship? If she puts too much weight in it, it'll move like a snail." Thali nodded, so he asked, " You got what you wanted, right?"

"Sure did," she said. "Let me know how it goes with that starboard list and if you need any advice."

Daylor nodded and they parted ways as they approached their crews. It felt strange but also really good to stand with the people she'd come to know so well in the last few years and call them her crew.

From all her years on her parents' ships, Thali knew she'd have to emit authority right from her first word if she wanted to earn her crew's respect. "We have the *Integrity*," she told them as she stood as tall as she could, "and we're leaving second. You all know the plan, so let's go check out our ship." Thali marched off in the direction of the *Integrity*.

Thali had assigned each crew member a specific item to inspect. She'd decided not to share her knowledge of the ship because she'd wanted to both ascertain their skills and have them unwittingly double-check her work.

As they approached their ship, Thali couldn't help but smile when she saw a familiar head of white-blond hair.

He bowed low as Thali approached. "Lady Routhalia."

"Isaia." Thali ignored his bow and embraced him. "It's really good to see you."

"As it is you. It's an honor to be on the same ship."

"Wait, you're our assistant instructor?"

He nodded. "Your father and mother send their regards."

"But ..." Thali started.

"All the assistants work for your family, so ..." Isaia shrugged. "Don't think I'll be going easy on you. We have specific things to look for and grade you on." Isaia looked down at the papers in front of him.

Isaia, her captain on their near-fatal final exam in her first year, had been working for her parents since he'd finished school. And he'd been doing very well from what her father had said. He was hoping to move Isaia to captain of his own ship in the next three years.

Thali nodded back. Isaia trailed her as she boarded the ship and began supervising her crew as they dispersed to perform their tasks. When she came upon Ban and one of the first-years snickering, she stared at them menacingly and they stopped short. They hurriedly got back to work before Thali could open her mouth. She had tried to trade Ban with someone from another ship, but it had turned out that was against the school rules. She would just have to keep an eye on him.

"My lady—" Isaia began.

"Isaia, I've literally had my hand inside your leg, so please, call me Thali." When their ship had been attacked and Isaia injured, it had been Thali and Jethro who'd saved his life when everyone else had been in shock.

Isaia turned pink and relaxed a little. "Thali then, at some point on this journey, I wonder if I might have a private audience with you."

Thali raised an eyebrow and stared sidelong at Isaia. She wondered if he wanted to talk about their brush with the leviathan, about how she'd had to take command in Isaia's place to get them back safely.

"You know, Jethro is the one who saved you. I didn't do much. He's the healer."

"You saved me from that monster. It was your medicines, your hand holding my leg together, and you who returned us safely from an island everyone thought didn't exist. People still don't believe me when I say I've been there. But if we *didn't* go there, then where did we go?"

Thali felt her cheeks heat at Isaia's words. She had simply done what had to be done. "Well, no time like the present. Follow me." She turned and nodded to Ban, who'd been trying his hardest not to look like he was listening in, and said, "I'll be in my quarters." Unfortunately, as a fellow third-year, she'd had to make him her lookout, but she'd hoped he'd stay in the crow's nest the entire time. They'd been assigned together since their first year, just as everyone else had, so her plan was to ignore him as much as she could. As she walked past, her gaze caught on Ban's new leather boots, which were far too nice to be worn on board. She shook her head then and pushed the thought away. She didn't even like Ban, so why should she warn him his boots would be ruined at sea?

She descended to her captain's quarters, where her maps were spread out on a low wooden table, and Ari was checking her navigational calculations for the fifth time.

"Captain." Ari stood up straight at Thali's arrival, then nodded as she left the room, closing the door behind her.

When they'd been left alone, Thali said, "Isaia, you and I are friends. Please, speak plainly with me." Thali wanted to put Isaia at ease.

"Thali, first of all, thank you for the private audience. Second, I owe you a life debt. I would not be alive today had it not been for you."

Thali nodded as her fingers ran along her best dagger strapped to her side: His family had gifted it to her for having saved his life. It had been handmade by the best sword makers, who just happened to be his family. Isaia had mentioned this on many occasions, and her cheeks burned from the discomfort of being the recipient of such an honor.

"I'd once hoped to serve your ship when you finished school and returned to your father's business. But when I heard of your engagement, I realized I'd like to apply to join your guard next year. It would be my honor to serve as your personal guard, and I hope you'll accept me," Isaia said.

Thali scrubbed her hands up and down the length of her face, groaning quietly. She had hoped not to think of princess things on this journey.

When she looked back up, Isaia looked alarmed.

"I'm sorry. Isaia. I mean no disrespect. Of course, I'd be honored if you joined my royal guard if that's what you'd like—but only if that's *really* what you want. I'm groaning because my father is going to be most unhappy to learn how many of his finest employees I'm taking with me to my new home."

Isaia looked relieved. "I think he's quite proud, if I may say so."

"Proud, maybe, but still grumpy because this school promised that this was a great way to expand his business, yet here I am taking some of the most qualified merchants with me to the palace next year."

Isaia couldn't help but smile as he bowed again. As he turned to leave, Thali said, "Isaia, wait."

He froze and turned back to her. "Yes, Thali?"

"While you're on board, you should spar with Alexius. I'm curious to watch that."

"Of course," Isaia bowed, not quite hiding his smile.

Thali left her quarters just moments after Isaia had gone. She passed her own three guards—Stefan, Amali, and Derk— in the hall and couldn't resist saying, "You'll have another recruit next year."

"Oh?" Stefan raised an eyebrow.

"Isaia wishes to join my guard next year."

"Ah." Stefan smiled and nodded. The Quinto family was as famous as hers as sword makers and fighters. No doubt Stefan was glad to have such a famed fighter personally asking to join her guard. The rest of Isaia's family was already part of the royal guard in some way.

Thali took the long route back above deck, walking below deck to check the ship herself even though her crew already had. When she did return to the helm, her crew was lined up and ready to report on what they'd found. As she'd expected, the ship was older, but well built. They'd found some spots of moisture they'd have to take care of, but nothing of great concern.

The inspection done, Thali sent her crew to prepare to leave in the morning. She gave the order for everyone to be on board and at their stations, with their things put away, by the time the sun was just full on the horizon. Alexius was her second, but besides their lessons and continued discussions about the creature attacks—which were still increasing in occurrence—they hadn't spoken at length with the busyness of the last few months.

"Have time for a sparring session?" Thali asked as she offered him a staff. They stood alone on the deck, but the limited space of the deck would add an element of challenge they didn't usually experience. Plus, she knew that any warrior may be verbally more forthcoming while they were sparring. Thali felt like it might be her last chance to get some answers.

They started gently, Thali feeling the tension leave her own shoulders as they settled into the rhythm. *Will Aexie be joining us onboard?*

No, she's going to stay to hold up the barrier.

Thali was quiet as she thought of how best to approach Alexius. Eventually, she decided to just be direct. *Alexius, you've been avoiding me this last while. Have I done something to offend you?*

No.

Do you miss your brothers?

Yes.

Do you miss Etciel?

Yes.

Thali was perplexed. She'd never known Alexius to give her single-word replies. *Are you happy?* Thali's staff hit the mast when Alexius stepped away and didn't return a blow.

No, he said before moving to strike her again.

Do you want to return to Etciel? Return to your brothers?

No. Alexius's lips were a tight line as he tossed the staff at Thali—who caught it—turned on his heel, and stormed off.

Their session had been so quick that Thali could still hear the rest of the crew all babbling excitedly as they strolled down the dock on their way to their own beds one last time.

Thali wanted to go after him. But he'd never lied to her, so if she hadn't offended him, then was he maybe frustrated with Xerus? It was clear that he wouldn't be forthcoming with answers anytime soon.

"Ready?" Ari poked her head out of the captain's quarters.

Thali nodded, then spent a few hours with Ari going over the navigational charts and discussing how their particular ship would travel best. Thali was debating water currents with Ari when a knock on her open door interrupted them.

They both jumped and turned, Ari immediately sinking to a low bow.

"Elric!" Thali said. She was a little annoyed that he'd overshadowed her moment and brought princess things back to everyone's mind.

"Permission to enter, Captain?" Elric smiled.

"Of course." Thali forced a grin and Ari mumbled something and backed out of the room.

"Ari, wait. We'll have time to figure out the currents for the way back on the way there. Just assign someone to keep their eye on them while we're sailing that way."

"Yes, Captain." Ari nodded, clearly trying to hide her smile at the excitement they both felt at beginning their journey.

"Good night then, Ari. I'll see you tomorrow morning," Thali said.

"Good night, Captain." Ari dipped her head again before leaving and closing the door behind her.

Thali listened to the shuffle of feet and imagined a half a dozen guards standing in the cramped hallway outside her door trying to make enough room for Ari to walk by.

"How many guards came with you?" Thali asked.

"Only five," Elric said.

Thali and Elric looked at the closed door concealing the tight hallway as a muffled "Oomph!" made them laugh.

"How do you feel?" Elric asked.

"Ready, excited, and I want to check the coordinates once more," Thali said.

Elric grinned, watching as Thali scanned her papers again. She was checking the angles for the millionth time when she saw a small, square, purple box blocking her next angle. Thali looked up.

"Open it." Elric grinned as he looked from her to the box.

Thali couldn't help herself as she took the palm-sized box in her hand and popped the top open. Reaching inside, she pulled out a round silver compass. On the top was inscribed, "So you can always find your way home." She clicked it open and saw the beautifully etched interior where "N," "S," "E," and "W" had been inlaid in its face.

"It's beautiful, thank you." Thali smiled at him, and he stepped closer, pressing his lips to hers.

"Can I walk you back with a detour for supper?" Elric asked.

Thali really wanted to check her maps again, but she swallowed the words and nodded. She turned back to look over her quarters one more time before leading Elric back above deck and to the dock. She was a little surprised to see a dozen royal guards on deck and a half dozen more on the dock. "I thought you said five. Is all this really necessary?"

"It is," he said seriously. "Precious cargo and all." He grinned as he brought her hand to his lips. Thali could only see his profile in the setting sun. A flutter of nervousness rose as she thought of what her life might look like in a month's time. After she returned from her exam, it would only be a few weeks before their wedding and then they would move to the palace. Seeing all those guards made Thali wonder just how many were at the palace. She was already starting to feel smothered, and she hadn't even moved there yet. She blinked and pushed it all away, deep in her mind. Thali wanted to focus on her exam. Even though it might not mean anything for her career anymore, it would for her classmates, and it would be her last opportunity to captain a crew on the open sea.

CHAPTER TWENTY-TWO

A S THALI SAT DOWN for dinner with Elric, she was bubbling with excitement about her trip as captain. She was telling him all the little details about their ship and their journey and her crew when they were suddenly interrupted by a guard, who came rushing into their dining room with a messenger.

The messenger started to whisper in Elric's ear and Thali watched closely, trying and failing to read his lips from where she sat. Elric, watching her, suddenly put his hand up.

"Speak plainly. Lady Routhalia is welcome to hear this information," Elric said.

"Yes, Your Highness. There was another griffin attack southwest of here. Five villagers died, but they've caught one of the griffins alive, sir. They're bringing him back here now."

Both Thali and Elric's eyes went wide.

"When will they arrive?" the prince asked.

"Within the hour, Your Highness."

Elric nodded to the guard. "Bring him straight to the dungeons below." The guard nodded in reply and turned on his heel to deliver the order. "Elric turned his attention back to the messenger. "Is he injured?"

"I do not believe so. But I left as soon as they caught him." The messenger's eyes darted between Thali and Elric.

"All right. Thank you. Go get some supper and rest before you write your report," Elric said.

The messenger bowed and left.

Elric turned to Thali. "How much do you trust Alexius?"

"With my life. And you won't be able to get that griffin here without he and Aexie knowing, anyway. The griffin might not even be able to enter the barrier. I'm not sure what kind of protections they've put up."

Elric nodded at that. "Should I dispatch a messenger to fetch him?"

Thali shook her head. She reached into her mind and found Alexius's thread.

Are you available?

Of course.

There was another griffin attack in the southwest. They captured one and are bringing him to Elric's manor. Can they get through the wards? And can you come?

They will now, and I'm on my way.

She let go of his thread and found Elric watching her. "It takes you less and less focus to do that now."

Thali shrugged. "He'll be here in a bit. We better go."

They hurried to the dungeon so the rest of the household wouldn't be alerted to Aexie's presence.

Elric paced the length of the hallway in the dark while Thali sat on the cold stone steps as they waited. Alexius appeared in the stairwell in minutes, and Aexie popped into existence right after. Thali had noticed her thread before she even appeared with a frown on her lips and her brow creased.

Aexie was with me.

Thali nodded, too anxious to deal with Aexie just then. Fortunately, the doors at the end of the dark hallway creaked open, and a dozen guards filed in carrying a large cage between them. Aexie popped back out of sight, and Elric told the guards to move the cage into the cell nearest him and then to leave. Once they had, Aexie reappeared and she stood with Alexius, rooted to the spot watching the griffin.

"Do either of you know him?" Elric asked.

"Her. I've seen her before, but I don't know her personally," Aexie said. "Her name is Ayelle."

The griffin was laying calmly in her cage, looking at them with her bright-green eyes, taking them all in. When no one spoke, she said, "So this is where you two are." Her eyes flitted from Alexius to Aexie, her gaze remaining there, making Thali wonder whether Aexie knew her better than she had said.

"Why did you attack the village?" Elric asked, finally recovering from his surprise that the griffin could talk.

The griffin, in the cramped space of the cage, let out a roar that looked strange coming out of a hooked beak.

"What is your goal?" Elric asked.

Another roar echoed off the stone walls. Thali covered her ears with her hands. "The whole kingdom is going to know she's here," Thali said.

"How about you give me a hand then?" Elric asked, annoyance lacing his words.

"No. I'll do it. Thali's not ready." Alexius stepped forward. He took a step toward the griffin, and Thali felt a pull on the thread that was Alexius.

I've put a wall up to protect you, Alexius told Thali. *She doesn't need to know about your abilities. But you can observe. Don't try to push in.*

Thali concentrated. She set up her own walls, ready to slam them down if necessary, and traveled along his thread to see the images he sent down the line as he probed the griffin's mind.

Intense, burning heat forced Thali to stumble backward. Taking a deep breath to steady herself, she focused harder. Flames engulfing homes, people screaming, and children crying filled her mind as the griffin's memories played out around her. As the griffin, she walked along a dirt pathway, stepping slowly, and passed human corpse after human corpse, nudging them into the fires surrounding every home. Sadness. She felt so much sadness. The Thali part of her mind wondered at that.

She gulped as the image changed. She, the griffin, was running in the forest, stalking the scent of fear as a man raced through the trees, eventually tiring and slowing, stumbling even from time to time as his energy gave out. She slowed to a walk and prowled along, relishing the sound of the cracking twigs. More and more twigs snapped as the man tired. She didn't need to see him to know where he was.

"Look closer, Thali," Alexius growled, struggling to even get the words out.

She briefly realized Elric was standing next to her now, his arm wrapped around her shoulder as she trembled. She concentrated harder and let the next image wash over her.

Thali was back in the burning village. The smoke and smell of burned flesh stung her nostrils, but she pushed on, the soft dirt under her paws oddly cool as she passed between two blazing fires. The screams were quieter now, but ahead of her was a toddler. A small boy in rags held the tatters of a half-stitched rabbit. The boy sucked on its ear as tears filled his eyes. In the memory, the Thali that was the griffin approached the boy slowly, and the Thali that was her true self felt dread creep up her spine as the griffin neared the toddler. Wanting to close her eyes and flee the memory before she experienced what she knew must be coming, she held her breath and whimpered.

But then she suddenly dipped her head, the griffin touching her forehead to the little boy's chest as he stood frozen. A few heartbeats later, a small hand reached out and touched her chin, stroking the feathers. Thali felt the packed earth beneath her chest and belly then as the griffin first knelt, then stretched out on the ground. The boy disappeared briefly before Thali felt him scramble onto her back, just behind her shoulders. He held on to some fur with one hand, his other hand still hugging the rabbit, its ear still in his mouth.

And then she was running, smoothly speeding over the forest floor, putting more and more distance between her and the flames. She scented humans in a house not far away and ran toward it. But just a few giant, griffin strides from the house, she suddenly felt as if someone had struck her in the head. Pain exploded in her mind. The boy flew off her back and landed in the dirt just feet from the house. He started to cry, but when she looked up and saw lit candles dancing in the windows, she rose and turned, her head still exploding with throbbing pain, and ran back to the village.

Thali came back into her own mind then, shaking her head and wondering what was going on. "I don't understand."

"Thali, what did you see?" Alexius asked.

Before Thali answered, she looked at the griffin with her actual eyes, oddly seeing only fear and what looked to Thali like regret and sadness. "Destruction, fire, death. The griffins set the village on fire. She chased a man in the woods, intent on killing him. But then she rescued a little boy and took him to a home in the woods before the pain ..."

She turned to look at Alexius and Aexie, who now looked grim as they silently returned her gaze. Alexius looked frustrated, as if he was again trying to tell her something but his mouth wouldn't open. Finally, he closed his eyes and let his shoulders sag.

As Elric held her tight, Thali felt herself slump, spent from the memory. She realized she was trembling and soaked with sweat.

"Let's go upstairs," Elric said. He turned and guided Thali to the door. The two dragons followed.

"Wait."

They all turned back to the griffin.

"I'm sorry. I never wanted to ... I wouldn't have chosen this ..." She choked the words out. "We're not like this, truly ..."

Even with her hawklike eyes, Thali could see this griffin was broken. By what or whom, she wanted to find out. She nodded, almost imperceptibly.

"Let's go upstairs." Elric nudged Thali to the door. No one spoke on the way back up the stairs to the manor and its warmth.

They all gathered in Elric's study. He sent two of his guards to watch the griffin, then after requesting blankets, dismissed everyone but the three allies—four once they were alone.

Standing next to the fire roaring in the hearth, Thali finally stopped trembling. She gladly accepted the steaming cup of melted chocolate but was too tired to ask Elric where he'd gotten it. Hot chocolate was a second favorite of hers next to coffee.

"The griffin is not herself." Alexius struggled to get the words out, clearly unable to say more.

Elric tried another tactic. "Just nod if what I say is correct. One, she can't tell us who sent her."

Aexie and Alexius nodded silently.

Elric pressed on. "She can't tell us why."

They nodded again.

"And even her mind is protected against you?" Elric asked finally.

Alexius nodded. "I only kept seeing the first two memories over and over again." He turned to Thali. "That third one only appeared once."

"Someone knows about me, that we'd find her and try to enter her mind," Thali said.

"Many magical creatures can enter minds, Thali," Aexie said.

Elric glanced out the window and sighed. "Thali, you're going to have to get going soon if you want to make it to your exam on time."

Thali glanced at the window and realized light had started to fill the sky. She had completely forgotten about her final exam. Groaning, she savored the last of her hot chocolate, knowing there would be no sleep for her tonight.

Aexie finally piped up. "I'll keep an eye on the griffin."

Elric nodded to her, and Thali realized Aexie was more perceptive than she let on. He was sending a few dozen guards with Thali on a separate ship to ensure her safety, so he'd be a little lacking in security while she was gone. He would need Aexie's help.

A knock on the door made them all turn. "We'll have to figure all this out when you get back," Elric said before turning to open the door. A tiny wisp of a woman rolled a cart laden with coffee and pastries into the room.

Sighs filled the room as coffee was poured. On a night like this, hot chocolate just wasn't enough. No one spoke for many moments as they appreciated the hot liquid warming their limbs and recharging them.

"If you don't want to, or feel you can't, take this exam right now, I can get you out of it." Elric sat on the arm of the chair Thali had draped herself in. She would have to leave in the next few minutes.

"No, I want to go. I'm no beginner. I'll be fine." She couldn't let her crew down. While her future may be secured, most of the rest of the students still had school to finish and lives to live, their futures unknown and unsecured. This might also be her last opportunity to travel freely, so she wasn't about to give it up.

"You're sure?" Elric asked. Thali nodded, so he continued. "I sent someone to grab your bag from your room. It should be at the front door."

"Thank you." Thali turned her head up to him and when their lips brushed, Thali tasted the chocolate on them.

"You've been hoarding the chocolate for yourself, haven't you?" Thali asked.

Elric grinned. "You'll have to find out when you get back."

"Captain, we have to go now." Alexius had been talking with his sister in the corner of the room while she'd chatted with Elric, but now he stood with a hand on the doorknob.

Thali turned her coffee cup upside down, letting the last drops fall onto her tongue. She pushed herself out of her chair, threw her arms around Elric, and kissed him thoroughly. Then she straightened her spine and strode out the door Alexius held open for her. She put on her captain persona, marched to the front door, and grabbed her bag. But when the guard opened the front door, Indi and Ana were sitting patiently on the front step. Bardo pulled himself up from his position around Indi's neck.

Smiling at them, she dropped her bag, kneeled, and scratched and kissed each head in turn. Then, she sent them images of her ship and sailing, but they had already known she was leaving when they'd seen her bag. She always used the same bag for that reason. After leaning over and giving them each a warm hug, Thali told them not to go into the basement and that they were to stay out of trouble. Elric would take care of them. Then, she showed them where Elric was and let them run past her to his study. Elric blew her a kiss from the open study door before being bowled over by the tiger and dog. Thali took one last look at the three pieces of her heart before turning back to the open door, picking up her bag, and heading out the door.

Releasing her sadness at leaving her loves, she instead let in her excitement for her adventure and ran the last bit to the dock. If her crew had followed her orders, she and Alexius would be the last ones aboard the ship. They had plenty of time before they were allowed to leave, but still, Thali, as captain, liked to be there first.

Daylor was boarding his own ship when she arrived. When he spotted her, he paused and waited for her. "May the best captain win." He grinned at her and suddenly, she, Tilton—who'd appeared seemingly out of nowhere—and Daylor were locked in a group hug before she could back away. Not that she wanted to.

"See you on the island." Thali waved to them as she headed for her own ship, now focused on the task ahead. The griffin would have to wait until she returned.

"Race you there!" Daylor grinned again before becoming all business the moment he stepped foot on his deck. His crew was already on board and preparing to leave.

"Captain on deck!" Alexius shouted as Thali boarded her own ship.

Her crew too was at their stations, wax at their feet as they stood at attention to greet their captain.

"Trying to get extra points already, I see." Thali grinned as she looked at every one of her crew members. They all grinned back at her, and she knew she'd made the right decision in coming. Even with everything going on, she couldn't let her crew down. "Well, back to work, mates!" She grabbed a spare block of wax and started on a bare spot that hadn't been worked on yet.

What felt like only minutes later, with all top surfaces freshly waxed, she and the crew stood in position, anxiously awaiting the moment they'd be given permission to depart. Finally, Isaia boarded and gave Thali a nod as he made his way to join her at the helm.

"Prepare for launch!" Thali yelled. Immediately, everyone dove into the maneuvers they'd been practicing these last few months. It was like watching a smoothly oiled machine. They all moved efficiently and calmly—but quickly. In just a few minutes, they were gliding toward the open sea without a hitch.

"Well done," Isaia said with a nod.

"Thank you."

Ari came and made some adjustments to ensure their most efficient route to Toad Island. Normally, this would be when the captain handed over the helm and direction to their first mate or navigator, but it was only a day's sail to the island, and Thali wanted to get there as fast as possible. She wasn't taking any chances with Isaia watching. Besides, she wasn't sure when she'd next get an opportunity to sail.

She corrected the ship's course at Ari's request before her first mate darted back to her map, rechecking that they were indeed on the fastest, most correct route to the island. Thali spotted Daylor's ship in the near distance and knew they could overcome them by the afternoon if they could just hit the right ocean current. Glancing behind her, she saw the next ship was struggling to leave the dock. She almost felt bad for them, but it would leave more room for her to maneuver should she need to.

The morning was tense as everyone felt the gravity of Isaia's presence. All their futures hinged on his assessment. Isaia had always been stern looking, and though Thali knew he was kinder and fairer than people assumed, his white-blond hair and steel-blue eyes only hardened his usually stern countenance and put her crew on edge.

"Isaia, how's your family?" she asked.

"They're doing well," he said as he surveyed the deck.

Her crew was getting jittery. Thali switched tactics. "I saw this blade once that had been fashioned in two pieces instead of one. Then they'd put tar in the middle of it, hoping to ease the metal's flexibility. What do you think?"

Isaia laughed. "That it was foolish to fabricate it in two pieces. One piece would lend much more strength and flexibility, the same way a shorter blade of grass can't bend much, but a longer one can." Thali followed the conversation but eyed her crew as she did. Thankfully, she achieved the effect she'd been hoping for. She felt her crew exhale as Isaia grew more animated as he discussed blade smithing. He even visibly relaxed as he went into the details of a one- versus a two-piece sword and the effects of tar on a blade. It was her turn to breathe a sigh of relief then.

CHAPTER TWENTY-THREE

T HAT AFTERNOON, THEY SAILED alongside Daylor's ship. Just then, something in the water caught Thali's eye. "Angle the ship starboard," she said.

Ari's brow creased. "But that's not what we planned."

Thali raised her eyebrows. "Trust me."

Ari nodded—though she looked a little perturbed—and did as bid, then watched as they took a wider approach to the island.

Isaia perked up at the change, and as their ship picked up speed on the new current and was carried swiftly past Daylor's, he and Ari both turned to Thali.

"How did you do that?" Ari asked, looking from her map to Thali to the ocean beyond and back to her papers.

"A whale just passed by. We tailed him to take advantage of the slipstream. Basically, we borrowed his momentum temporarily."

"How did you know there was a whale?" Isaia asked.

"The way the water folded in on itself." Thali pointed off to the side of the ship where the whale had veered off. They were on their own again now, but their ship had moved ahead of Daylor's. They would make it to the dock first unless something unforeseen occurred.

Ari and Isaia both squinted and stared into the ocean.

Thali was proud she had known that even without using her gifts. It was an observation she'd made as a child from knowing where the whales were by using her threads, but this time she'd used only her experience rather than her magical abilities.

By cutting ahead of Daylor's ship, and with Ari's careful study of maps and ocean currents, the *Integrity* did indeed make their dock first. The sun was at their backs as they glided up to it, six members of the crew ready to hop off, ropes coiled in hand to guide the ship in. Daylor's ship, the *Honesty*, veered to the side to navigate their way to the second dock.

Once the ship was tied off, Thali leaped off the ship herself to check the job her crew had done and was pleased to see they'd all been paying close attention and had done an excellent job with the knots. She turned, smiling at her crew. "Great job everyone! Now, let's pull out the fishing poles, catch ourselves some supper, and go to bed early. Anyone wanting to review their knowledge for the goods or culture tests can gather in the galley after supper."

This year, no one was allowed to leave their ship until the next morning. But that didn't stop Thali from trying her hardest to see what she could make out of the territory around her, ignoring the fleet of guards Elric had sent that had pulled up next to them.

The ship full of instructors had already docked nearby, and little blobs of light bounced along the foot of the mountain as they wound their way inland even as the sun was starting to set. Thali guessed they were double-checking the exam set ups. She looked west to find Daylor's ship, knowing he'd be docking now in the second berth. Her ship and his were fortunately closest to the exam sites, and her crew would get to head for their exams first. The other teams would have to wait for their own turn to leave.

As her own crew hung their legs off the dock, their fishing poles out in front of them, she wondered what challenges they would face tomorrow. Though she knew the first-, second-, and third-years would all undertake their challenges simultaneously, she didn't know if each student would be tested individually or as a team given there were three students of each year on her crew. All she knew is she would not be allowed to leave until all their crew members had completed their challenges and were back on board.

"Captain! I've got one!"

Thali was ripped from her thoughts at the exclamation, and she spun around—only to be slapped in the face with a fish.

"Oh, turtle turds! I'm sorry, Captain!" Nareena, a first-year, froze, the pole in her hands and a fish now swinging back toward Thali.

Thali dodged the swinging fish and said, "It's okay, Nareena," even as she used her sleeve to wipe her face. She scrunched her nose at the slime on the back of her hand after she wiped her cheek.

Isaia grabbed the fish and took care of it while Thali swallowed her grief at the thread that dissolved in her head. *Thank you,* she thought silently.

She headed for the back of the ship, leaving her crew to their fishing. She needed a moment.

Death is a part of life, Alexius said into her mind.

Says the dragon of undetermined age.

If we do not fish, the population will get out of control, eventually killing themselves off.

I know. I have a harder time adjusting to it here though.

You should put your wall up the entire time we're here and keep it up. I won't be able to follow you into your challenges tomorrow. It'll be good practice.

Thali nodded and returned to her quarters. Derk stopped outside her door while the other three followed her into her quarters. She stopped in the middle of the tight space and turned around. "I'd like some privacy," she said.

Stefan nodded, and the three left. Before they could say anything further, Thali rushed over and closed the door in their faces. Her guards would just have to stay vigilant from the hallway.

Thali climbed onto her bed and crossed her legs. Breathing in and out, she tried to relax. She missed her tiger, snake, and dog, who always calmed her. Instead, she focused on her breathing. Inhale, exhale. Thali tried hard to meditate but found her thoughts racing in many different directions. She felt like her life, her sense of self, was fragmented into so many different pieces that didn't fit together. Daylor, Tilton, Ari, and all her classmates knew her as a captain and a merchant's daughter, but also as their friend; they knew what made her laugh, what made her temper flare, and what made her tick.

Elric knew her seemingly better than she knew herself and made her swoon with his brightness, generosity, and fairness. Alexius knew her magically; he was in her thoughts and though he probably knew more than he let on, he was kind enough not to comment. Mia knew her as friend and sister, and Tariq and Bree knew her as sister.

But who was she, really? Merchant? Daughter? Captain? Princess? Savior of worlds? She felt responsible for this crew, she felt responsible for her friends' and family's happiness, and she felt responsible for the kingdom's well-being. More than anything, she felt responsible for having unleashed magical creatures into the world and every attack, every death was her fault. Yet she had no idea what to do about it. She wasn't strong enough to take on even one griffin, let alone a whole herd of deadly, magical animals.

And in a secret, tiny, hidden place in her heart, she held Garen's memory; she wished he was still in her life. He had made everything seem easier and more fun. No problem was ever too big, too grand, to be conquered. He would have been able to knit all these different pieces together. She smiled at the thought. Garen would probably have made her put all the pieces back together herself, and when she did it, she would have wondered why it had ever caused her such heartache to begin with.

Thali wondered for a moment what Garen was doing, whether he was happy. She hoped so.

She let her mind wander where it may before finally giving up on a peaceful end to her meditation. She opened her eyes and flung her door open. Amali, Derk, Khadija, and Stefan snapped to attention when she walked out. Realizing she'd been rude before, she tried to offer them a smile. "Hungry?"

They smiled back and she led them to the galley. As she rounded a corner, her eyes flew open wide when she saw the unmistakable silver-blond hair of Isaia entangled in the embrace of the darker-skinned Ari just as the door to her room closed.

Thali stopped dead. "Did you know?" She glanced at her guards.

Most shook their heads, but Stefan looked down at his feet. Thali made a note to always ask Stefan about gossip. He seemed to know everything that went on. She shook her head and continued to the galley.

The crew had managed to catch half a dozen enormous fish, so they had the pleasure of indulging themselves that evening. She noticed Ari had joined them rather quickly, Isaia a few minutes later. After their bellies were full, the crew speculated about what the challenges would be, which turned into a review of all the things they'd all learned. Thali was happy to be the center of the discussions given her extensive knowledge.

As the sun sank behind the horizon, she brought the discussions to an end, ordered the first watch to their posts, and called it an early night for the rest of the crew before heading to bed herself, anxious for the next morning.

Chapter Twenty-Four

S HE FELT LIKE SHE'D just closed her eyes when she woke, the sun's first rays shining over the horizon and right in her eyes. Donning her usual layers and weapons before heading to the galley to grab some breakfast, she hurried to join her crew on the dock. They were to wait on the dock for an instructor to arrive and escort them inland. Thali and her crew waited eagerly at the very end of the dock, many bouncing from foot to foot trying to keep warm in the early-morning chill. From what she could see just ahead, each year would run through a different archway, labeled with their year, into fenced-off areas to their first challenge.

Finally, they saw Master Aloysius striding toward them. He looked them over, nodded in approval, and stopped in front of them. "Here's how it works. Ya may work in teams, but there be individual components that each of ya will haf to do by yerself." He squinted in the bright sun.

"All right, remove your weapons and pile 'em here." The instructor pointed at his feet.

They all groaned and stripped their weapons off. Ari pulled off six daggers, and Thali couldn't help but grin as she pulled the same number off herself. Once everyone was done, Master Aloysius nodded at Thali. "All of 'em." Thali slumped her shoulders and peeled off the knives strapped to the insides of her boots, and a few other crew members followed suit. Master Aloysius eyed her a moment, and she knew anyone else would have physically checked her for more weapons. Thali was never without a weapon, and she still had three concealed.

Master Aloysius nodded. "Ya may start."

"Good luck, everyone. I expect your swift return tonight!" Thali yelled as her crew stampeded through their respective archways. Her guards followed her as far as the archways and stopped there. She'd been informed as they'd waited on the dock that the royal guards from the ship following her had already combed through the challenges and considered them closed and secured. Thali could go in without a shadow.

She picked up on her crew's excitement then and ran with Ari and Ban as they headed for the rightmost archway. Running through it, Thali looked around at all the greenery surrounding them. Their running was slowed by the sand, but the palm trees and thick vines growing right out of it were beautiful. They spotted a cave ahead of them and ran up to its mouth. Once there, they stopped to catch their breath. Inside, the cave was pitch black and silent.

"Should we tie ourselves together?" Ari asked.

Thali nodded and Ban took out a rope. They each looped themselves into it but gave each other enough slack to be able to spread out quite far. Thali was tied in at the front, Ban in the middle, and Ari at the rear. Thali touched the wall with her right hand and started shuffling into the cave, feeling her way in. Once they were completely in the cave, and blind, she stopped and waited for her eyes to adjust to the black, but it was so dark she still couldn't see anything. She wondered about cheating by using her magic to get a general layout of the area. Alexius had asked her to keep her walls up though, so she decided magic was perhaps not a good option. It would be a bad idea to lead a magical animal into a cave where she couldn't see it anyway.

As she kept following the wall, she ran into something solid. "Oof!"

"Thali, are you all right?" Ari's voice sounded a bit muffled.

"Yes. I'm fine. I ran into something." She felt around and discovered the surface of a table, upon which seemed to be three different objects.

"There are three objects here." Ban and Ari followed the rope to join Thali, and she helped them put each of their hands on an object, so they could feel it and try to discern what it was. Thali had felt all three objects. They felt like vases but were shorter. All three objects were also exactly the same and had identical triangular shapes protruding from one side. Then, Thali had an idea. She brought one object to her nose.

"Smell it!" Thali's voice was slowly becoming swallowed by the cave as if something was muffling it, and she had to yell her words though her classmates were right beside her.

"This one! It's made of cedar!" Ari yelled.

Thali barely heard her. "I think there's something in the air muffling our sound!" Thali yelled back. She felt the heaviness of the void she yelled into and knew that trying to clear it, or stop it somehow, would all be for nought. That did lead her to realize they were to find the true object of value out of the three without the use of sight or sound.

Thali put her object down because its texture felt like ordinary stone. Then, she followed her rope to Ban and gently took the object out of his hand. She was sure it was clay, so she put it on the table. Finally, she went to Ari, put her hands around her first mate's over the object, and moved it to Ari's chest to indicate that object had to come with them. Something was now sucking the sound right from their mouths, so they'd have to rely on touch to communicate. Thali made her way back to the front of the rope and continued to feel her way along the wall.

She was better prepared for the next table she came across and suspected they had to identify three unique objects from three different tables. Because cedar was one of the most valuable materials, she knew this was their goods test. But the instructors had made the challenge immensely harder by taking away their sight and sound. Her trio of third-years would have to know everything about various goods to get through this challenge.

On the second table were another three vases. She gathered them all together on the table and pulled Ban and Ari closer to her so they stood huddled. They each took a vase, and Thali hoped they were doing as she was, feeling all the way around them. Her vase felt cool and hard to the touch. It felt like a rock polished smooth. Bringing her vase to her nose, she sniffed it, but it didn't have any kind of smell. Holding it in her left hand, she used the pads of her fingertips to flit over the surface, trying to feel for any anomalies and felt only a circle.

Suddenly, Thali felt a hand crawling up the rope toward her. It was Ban. He took her vase from her grasp, and she let him, but kept one hand on his elbow to keep track of him. She couldn't see or hear what he was doing, but she hoped he was sniffing it as she had. Then, he grabbed her hand, put the vase back in it, and placed his hands atop hers. This was the one to keep then.

Confused, she felt Ban move away and assumed he was telling Ari he'd found the second object. Why this one? Thali lifted the vase to her face and could now smell a slight saltiness that she'd missed the first time. She stretched her tongue out tentatively. As soon as she licked it, she tasted the saltiness and realized this vase must be completely carved out of salt rock.

A tug of the rope was her signal to go on. She put her vase in her bag and then continued feeling her way along the wall with her hands, looking for the third table. A few steps farther on, Thali came upon the third table. She grabbed the rope and gave it a shake so Ban knew she had stopped. Tension on the rope told her he was coming closer. As he gripped the rope at her waist, she felt another hand following the rope to her other side. Ari was positioning herself next to Thali too.

Thali patted lightly around the table. She found a vase that was by far the smallest of all. As she slid her fingers over its surface, she felt the protruding shape of a star on one side. Continuing her tactile exploration from bottom to top, she startled, almost knocking the vase over, when she felt something wet on the rim. She dipped a finger in, pulled it back out, and rubbed her thumb over her finger; it had the same consistency as water. Bringing her finger to her nose, she coughed as strongly scented rose water flooded her senses. Water scented that strongly was valuable, and Thali wondered what the other vases contained.

Ari's hand nudged Thali's, so she reached over and gently dipped a finger into Ari's vase. Thali felt the thick stickiness and the viscosity of this liquid immediately. Rubbing it with her thumb again, she determined it was indeed tacky and sticky, thicker than water, but not grainy. Carefully, Thali sniffed it before bringing it to her mouth and testing it with her tongue. It was honey. Licking the rest of it off her finger, she tried to determine whether it was a special kind of honey or if it was just plain honey. To her, it tasted like plain honey. Thali carefully put her hands around Ari's over the vase and guided the vase to the table. Then she patted Ari's hands, hoping her friend would know to just wait there.

When Ari didn't move, Thali knew her message had been received, so she sidestepped over to Ban and gently patted his arm to determine his position. Pausing a moment to realize he was a lot more muscled than she'd given him credit for, and feeling the revulsion of having to touch him, she inched her way down his arm to his hand. He'd cupped a small vase between his hands, and at her light tap, he held still for her. She slipped a finger over the edge of his vase, too. The liquid was cool to the touch, and when she rubbed her thumb with her finger, the substance felt watery, though she did detect an almost grainy consistency. Thali sniffed it. Seawater. She'd know that smell anywhere. She gently pulled his hands off the vase. Seawater was definitely the least valuable of the three items on this table.

Honey was valuable, but if she was right about the scented water, she knew the scented water would be even more valuable than the honey. Scented water was often distilled to more concentrated forms for perfume. That decision made, she eased over to Ari and slipped her hands off her vase. Then, Thali grasped the rosewater-filled vase with one hand and found Ban with the other. After reaching down to pull his hand up, she put the vase in Ban's hand and squeezed. Once he'd put his other hand over hers and squeezed back, she slid her hand away—glad to be just about done touching Ban—and turned and nudged Ari's elbow to signal it was time to go. Ari felt her way back around Thali and then Ban before Thali continued shuffling along the wall in the darkness, careful to feel the floor ahead step by step.

Suddenly, her toe bumped the edge of a protruding step. She wiggled the rope and felt Ban stop in his tracks. Thali put one foot on the step, and when she realized there were no more steps, it was clear this was more of a platform. She felt the wall in front of her. At chest height was an indentation. It was star shaped, like the ornamentation on the smallest vase Ban currently held. The edges felt like a perfect match, so she gently pulled Ban over and felt for his hands. When she tapped one hand, he pulled it away briefly before bringing it back, vase in hand.

Thali turned, keeping hold of Ban's arm and urging him to follow. She found the platform with her toe again. She stepped up and pulled Ban's arm. He stumbled but landed on the platform with her. When he was steady, she felt for the star with one hand, then took Ban's hand with the other, rubbing it over the star on the vase, then over the star in the wall. Having no choice but to assume he had the idea, she gingerly stepped off the platform, hoping he'd pressed the vase into the wall, fitting the two shapes together like key in a lock.

After taking a deep breath, Thali continued to feel along the wall. When her feet found a second protruding step, she followed the same procedure, searching the wall for an indentation shaped like a triangle or a circle. When she found a triangle hole in the wall, she hopped off the platform and followed the rope past Ban to gently pull Ari over. Thali tapped her hands, signaling, she hoped clearly, for Ari to pull her cedar vase out of her bag. Ari's hands too disappeared momentarily before nudging Thali's once again, the cedar vase between them. Thali guided Ari to the step before putting her hand on the triangle indentation. Ari needed no more instruction. Thali felt her first mate's arms raise and knew Ari had also pressed the two triangle shapes together.

Now, it was her turn. Thali turned and felt her way along the wall, past the first two platforms, until her toe unearthed the third. She climbed onto the platform and let her fingers graze the wall until she discovered a circular hollow. Smiling an invisible smile at her excitement about this challenge, she took her vase from her bag with her other hand and pressed it into the hollow. She pushed hard. Nothing happened.

With a heavy creaking, the ground they stood on started to move. Light poured through a crack in the wall, and the ground beneath them rotated. The wall they were facing slowly slid away, and when it was done moving, they found themselves in a much quieter, softly lit room. The three platforms had been placed on a rotating platform, allowing them to slide into this hidden room. They squinted against the bright light after being in the darkness for so long.

"That was kind of fun," Ban said. His voice echoed and boomed through the room. They had been straining to hear for so long that his voice felt like a punch to the head.

"Sorry," he whispered.

"Ari, yours is cedar, right?" Thali asked.

She nodded.

"Rosewater? The smell is permeating my nose." Ban said, pointing to his vase.

Thali nodded and said, "Salt rock," as she pointed to her own vase. They blinked repeatedly as they tried to adjust to the candlelight reflecting around the room.

After their eyes had adjusted to the light, the trio untied themselves and hopped off the platforms and looked around them. Tables filled the new room, and on each was a weapon and a picture of a crest or flag. There were easily twelve tables arranged in three columns. Thali walked around the room, looking at all the weapons. Each column of tables contained the same category of weapon, but each table consisted of varying types, conditions, and qualities. She assumed they were to each pick a weapon from a column to arm themselves for their next challenge. Ari would of course want knives, and Ban would want a bow and arrow. Thali didn't really care what she ended up with—until she saw that the third column had staffs.

The problem, Thali thought, was that they must have to pick a flag or crest within each column. But at least they could see and speak to each other now, so it should be a lot easier than the challenge they'd just completed.

"Ban, can I smell that scented water again?" At his nod, Thali went over and sniffed the small vase's contents. She was eighty percent sure this particular scented water was from a country in the far east, so she examined all the different flags and crests until her eye fell upon a bright purple, blue, and green one with white triangles. Excited, she turned and said, "Ban, that one there."

Ban nodded and went to the table Thali pointed to. He placed the vase carefully on the table, then picked up an unassuming bow with a quiver full of arrows. He tested the bow and seemed satisfied with it.

That left two columns for Ari and Thali.

"My mother is obsessed with salt crystals. The best ones are from here." Ban walked to a table with a red-and-white flag with an image of a running lion. Crystals were expensive and Thali wondered for a moment how wealthy Ban's family really was.

She shrugged off the thought and put the salt-rock vase on the table before glancing at the staffs on the tables and realizing a few were made of a weaker wood. Some were even partially splintered. Then one, partially buried beneath some of the staffs made of the inferior wood, caught her eye. Thali picked up the staff and tested its weight, then bounced it on the ground to test its density.

Satisfied, Thali looked at the last column of tables as she smelled the bright cedar of Ari's vase. The crest that represented the kingdom cedar was famously from jumped out at her and she hurried over to it. She nodded at Ari, who came over and set the cedar vase on that table. Then, she grabbed a couple knives and spun them in the air. Wordlessly, she nodded as if to acknowledge that they would do.

The trio came together at the other end of the room, where another archway led them down a corridor to their final challenge.

Chapter Twenty-Five

T HE THREE THIRD-YEARS LOOKED at each other, nodded, and followed the corridor until it opened into a bigger chamber. Three doors faced them, and before each door was a raised platform, upon which was a drawing. The leftmost drawing was only a single line, while the middle one depicted a half circle with an arrow. The rightmost drawing was of two knives with short hilts. Ban hurried ahead and climbed on the center platform. As he did, Thali felt the hairs on the back of her neck rise in warning and looked around the chamber. This was only a final exam, so why was she suddenly feeling anxious?

But nothing happened, so Ari jumped up on the rightmost platform. A *click* sounded, but still nothing changed. Thali approached the left platform slowly, trepidation halting her steps. She stopped just before the platform, looking over to Ari and Ban.

"See you back at the ship," Ari said. The quiver in her voice told Thali she also felt nervous about this challenge. But they trusted Master Aloysius, so they had no choice but to continue.

"Hurry up, Thali. Let's get this over with." Ban said as he turned to his door, obviously not feeling the same nerves she and Ari were.

Thali carefully stepped onto her platform. The moment she did, there was a series of clicks before all three doors swung open simultaneously. The trio looked at each other one last time and counted down from three before running off their platforms into their separate chambers at the same time.

Thali ran into her chamber, staff loosely held at her side, anxious to see what their combat challenge would be. She felt the buzz of adrenaline coursing through her veins as she entered a cavernous space, bigger than the one they'd just left. The space was lit by a hole at the top of the cavern; they must be near the surface of the mountain somewhere. The chasm was empty from what Thali could tell, until she saw a red mark in the middle of the room, the sun beaming straight on it. She approached carefully, scanning the walls around her. When she got closer, she crouched and realized the streak of red was blood.

"Finally. I thought I was going to have to wait all day." A voice as smooth as silk that reminded her of crashing waves echoed through the room.

Thali sprang up and spotted a tall, lean man with long golden hair that he wore tied back. It wasn't gold like Elric's but looked as if his hair had been spun from actual gold. His silver eyes shone unnaturally bright in the dim light. He sported a gold coat perfectly tailored for him, along with dark-green pants and golden boots. Everything about him shouted opulence and power. But something about him made her think of Alexius's eldest brother, Xerus. Did they perhaps have the same coats?

"You're a dragon," Thali said.

"Why, you're smart too. That's a lovely surprise." One side of his mouth pulled up in a smirk.

Thali realized this was not part of her final challenge. This was a trap.

"What do you want?" Thali tried to back away toward the door she'd just come through.

"Don't bother. It won't open. I'm smart too." And now he grinned, showing off his pointy teeth.

"What do you want?" Thali wanted to glance up to see if there was any way for her to climb out but resisted because she didn't want to draw his attention there. Instead, she checked her mental barriers for gaps or holes.

"Ahh, I see you want to get right to the good stuff," he said. He hadn't moved in her direction, but Thali stumbled back anyway and fell as if a wave had crashed into her. Shaking her head, she realized the shove had been in her mind and quickly checked her mental wall for damage. She sat up and scrambled to her feet. There was no way she'd physically be able to overpower the dragon. She'd have to outsmart him.

"What ... do you ... want?" Thali asked between breaths as she glanced around the room, searching for inspiration. What should she do?

The dragon-man rocked back onto his right hip, settling his left elbow into his side as he examined his nails.

"You know, when I'm in this form, I miss my talons quite a bit." He focused his attention solely on her as she watched his nails grow into sharp golden talons.

Remaining stationary, Thali squared her shoulders, not wanting to give him the benefit of seeing her scared, whoever *he* was.

"My name is Xenon, by the way. It's a pleasure to finally make your acquaintance, Lady Routhalia." The golden-haired man swept into a low bow. His long fingers now looked unnaturally long, with those golden talons at the tips.

Thali said nothing. She crossed her arms to keep them from shaking and raised a single eyebrow. Despite her fear, she realized Xenon liked to talk, so she would let him until she could find a way out of her current predicament. She thought about reaching out to Alexius, but she was using all her energy to maintain her mental wall and didn't want to risk it. The best she could do was to tug gently on the thread that was Alexius, hoping he would know to come and find her.

The dragon watched her every move, her every muscle twitch. He clearly knew he was pressing up against her mental barrier. He smiled again. "How do you know *I'm* not the good guy? How do you know *you're* not on the wrong side of all this?"

Though he tore his gaze away from her, she could still feel the pressure on the wall inside her head. Still, she didn't reply to his questions.

"Have you met Xerus?" Despite herself, her eyes widened at the mention of Alexius's older brother, which was acknowledgment enough for Xenon.

"He's such a weak creature. I never thought he'd be so useful." Xenon grinned.

Thali wondered what game he was playing. "How do you know Xerus?"

"He is my mate. And no, not the platonic kind." He sauntered along the side of the room, taking his time as he slowly strolled closer to her.

"Ahh, young love." The dragon put his hand under his chin and fluttered his eyelashes at her as he wiggled his talons in her direction. "You see, we met in the air one day. Bumped into each other we did, and from that moment on, I knew. He took a little longer. You know, he almost joined us, but then his daddy got wind of things, and I never saw him again." His smile faltered for the briefest of moments before he grinned again.

"And now, I've taken command of my own little army. And apparently, Xerus has, too." Xenon drew one of his talons along his arm.

Suddenly, Xenon's eyes hardened as he stared at Thali. "Has anyone even told you what you are? Do you even know who's behind everything that's happened since you started school?"

Thali didn't want to respond, but she could feel herself being drawn in by his questions, each one bringing him a step closer to her mental wall.

"And where are your friends?" Xenon smiled, knowing he'd found her weak spot, the way into her mind.

Thali's eyes grew wide as she thought of Ari and Ban and her crew, of Daylor and Tilton and Neera. She thought of the other merchant students on the island, the instructors, the royal guards. There were many people on this island he could burn in a flash if he wanted to. She was glad at least Elric was safely tucked within Aexie's protection.

"What do you think your friends would do if they knew about you? Your magic, your abilities?" Xenon crept along the shadows of the walls, closer and closer to her. "Do you think they'd accept you?" He smirked. "Or would they hate you? All your lies all these years? You're already a more talented merchant than they could ever be. And you're also, oh, the drama, going to be queen one day. Don't you think they'd be right to be afraid of you? To despise you?"

Thali had tried very hard not to think of what Daylor and Tilton might think of her once they knew her secret. She hoped they would be as accepting as Elric, but she didn't know for sure. They had been cautious of her around Indi and Ana.

"Ahh, Elric, your golden prince. How has he handled all this newfound knowledge? The magic? The magical creatures? How he must have been prepared to ascend the throne and then you came along with all these magical creatures. Mean magical creatures too, attacking his people and lands and resources. Do you think he's put two and two together yet? Has he started to blame you yet?"

"He wouldn't blame me. It's not my fault!" Thali insisted between gritted teeth.

"Maybe, maybe not, but are you sure your shining prince isn't crumbling under the pressure? You grew up knowing about your magic, maybe not the depths of it, but at least accepting that a magical world was a possibility. But Elric? He grew up in a normal world, one in which he would one day be king. And now ... now there are forces he has no control over, no way to detect, never mind defend against. Has he asked you to use your magic to defend his people yet? Wouldn't a good king ally themselves with someone useful who could defend his people?"

Thali swallowed. She had refused Elric that once, but what would happen when she saw the suffering first hand? When she was their queen?

His gaze flashed to the middle of her shirt where Garen's medallion hung. She hadn't truly thought she'd need it here, on this island, during her challenge, but a promise was a promise.

"Ah, and the prince of thieves. He left you, didn't he? Abandoned you because you were too much trouble for even his kingdom to take on. If you weren't worth the trouble for him, what makes you think you're worth the trouble for the golden prince?"

The mention of Garen was the last straw, and Thali gasped as she felt her mental wall crack, right before the waves crashed in. Water filled every crevice of her mind, sweeping to overtake as much of it as it could. Thali's eyes went wide as her mind flooded, the water rushing around it, soothing and calming the panic and fear coursing through her neurons. It enveloped her mind and hardened like glass.

When he spoke next, it echoed through her mind like her own voice. *Lady Routhalia, thank you for your cooperation. You have been deemed too dangerous to keep in this game. I'll take it from here.*

Thali both felt like herself and didn't feel like herself, though she couldn't tell what was different. Then she heard it, a loud knocking on the wall behind Xenon at what must have been the exit.

"Open this door this instant! She has been in there too long." She recognized Stefan's voice as a door in the rock across from her popped open. Then, she felt Xenon disappear. Though it felt as if her mind was encased in glass, she could still feel Xenon's invisible presence. It was as if she were both in her body and in Xenon's mind.

The crack of light widened and flooded the room as Stefan, Derk, Khadija, Amali, and a sleepy Nasir rushed in, Master Aloysius right behind them. She saw them run to her body, felt their warmth on her skin as they crowded around her.

"Lady Routhalia, can you hear me?" Stefan's face was only a foot away from hers as her guards knelt on the floor around her. More guards filled the room, setting up a perimeter around her.

"She's still breathing." Amali had brought a mirror to her nose, and Nasir put his ear to her chest, nodding his confirmation.

Khadija and Amali checked her body for injuries. Thali wanted to respond; she tried to speak, then tried to shout she was fine. She was all right. But her lips wouldn't move. Gentle hands poked and prodded her but found no injuries.

"Master Aloysius. Where is the challenger?" Stefan rose and looked around the room.

"He was here. I gave him his instructions and locked him in this room myself." Master Aloysius too looked around the room. "Thali would have taken him in five minutes."

"Captain." A guard brought their attention to the blood smear in the middle of the floor.

Master Aloysius and Stefan went over to look. Thali knew they wouldn't be able to say much of anything. It was simply a smear of blood, but it portended nothing good.

It was disconcerting that Thali could also "see" from where Xenon must still be standing. *He must have the same invisibility talent as Aexie*, she thought. But through his eyes, she saw next to the smear of blood was a black staff and a metal belt.

A guard ran up to Stefan. "Nothing else is out of place, sir. There's nothing else in this room to suggest what happened."

Thali felt Nasir take off his coat and tuck it around her to keep her warm. Then, a wooden pallet was brought in. Her guards gently lifted her up and placed her on it. She wanted to yell at them, "I can walk myself!" She wanted to sit up and walk. But she couldn't. It was infuriatingly frustrating.

Don't worry, I'm sure they'll take good care of your body. And I'll eventually let you go.

What do you want from me? Her voice was small and quiet.

I want you locked up. For now. You could say I'm taking a piece out of the game so the outcome changes. But I won't hurt you.

Thali saw only the sky as her guards carried her out the exit. Bright light blinded her, making her pupils shrink as the light seared the back of her eyeballs.

"Is the captain ok? What happened?" Thali heard Ari trying to get closer to her.

"She's alive but not responding," Stefan said. They started to carry her, and when she smelled the seawater, she knew they'd reached the dock. There, she felt Xenon fly into the air and watched the crowd get smaller and smaller as he rose.

Through Xenon's eyes, she saw Alexius run over to her guards. "What happened?"

Ari filled him in as they walked down the dock.

"Captain!" Isaia rushed over to Stefan.

"Master Quinto." Stefan stopped walking.

"I can sail this ship faster than anyone," Isaia said. "We would be honored to take our captain back to the mainland."

"She'd be safer on our ship," Stefan countered.

"But our ship is smaller. We'll get back faster," Ari said. "Captain Routhalia has trained us all well. We're the fastest crew on this island. We need not remind you we arrived first yesterday, even before you."

Stefan nodded his head then, and the guards carried Thali to her own ship. She was incredibly flattered to hear Isaia and Ari fight for her. She also felt her chest swell with pride at how confident her crew was.

Alexius walked next to her stretcher and kept glancing over Thali. Then, he looked around him at the crowd. "I need to see the room you found her in."

Amali replied, "There's nothing there, I assure you. We found nothing."

"Let him go look," Nasir said. "What could it hurt?" He nodded at Alexius. He was the only guard who knew what Alexius really was.

"We leave immediately," Stefan said.

"I need to see the room." Alexius stayed firm.

"We'll bring him back to school," Daylor piped up. When Xenon's attention was drawn to him, Thali saw that Daylor and Tilton were both pale with worry. They were such good friends, Thali knew they'd do anything they could to help. *Well, Alexius has grown to be a pretty one.* Xenon said in her mind.

"Khadija," Nasir suddenly said. A woman appeared at the edge of Thali's physical vision. "You will go with Lady Routhalia back to the mainland, and no doubt, the prince's manor. I will accompany Master Alexius to the room Lady Routhalia was found in."

The woman nodded and joined the ranks of Thali's personal guard as Thali watched from high above. If Stefan was surprised to see Nasir leave Thali's side, he didn't show it. He just nodded as he and her guard carried her aboard her ship. Isaia took the helm and shouted orders to the crew to get the ship out of the dock and onto the open ocean.

CHAPTER TWENTY-SIX

ALEXIUS

WHEN HE'D TRIED TO connect with Thali through their bond, he'd come up against a hard wall. Dread made his heart drop into his stomach, and he hoped his first suspicions were wrong.

The others had left to take Thali back to Lanchor. Nasir now led the way back to the room they'd found Thali in, Alexius and Tilton following close behind. The island was mostly abandoned now. Thali had been in the room so long the other groups had made it through their challenges and left for home. Only Daylor's ship, the *Honesty*, had remained. He wouldn't leave without his friend. Now, Daylor was on board, ready to go as soon as Alexius arrived.

Alexius knew Tilton and Daylor suspected there was something different about Thali but had left it for her to tell them when she was ready. Alexius also knew they suspected he was different too, that his relationship with her was different. At first, they'd thought the two were romantically involved, but after Alexius purposely started to flirt with other ladies at school right in front of Thali, those suspicions eased. The dragon certainly didn't want to give Elric any reason to end things with Thali. The fate of the world depended too much on his relationship with her.

When Alexius had taken his challenges earlier, Alexius had thought them too easy. Like he often did, he'd had to feign needing time to think before coming to the right answer. Their group had still finished faster than expected, and he'd already been back at the ship when he'd heard Ari and Ban had returned without Thali, that they'd come to get help. Everyone knew there was no way Thali wouldn't have come out first, so if they'd all beaten her out, there must be something wrong.

Now, Alexius followed Nasir as he led them through the door the guards had forced open to get to Thali. As soon as Alexius walked in, he could smell him. He could smell Xenon.

The kingdom of magic was ruled very differently than the human world. In the magical world, some dragons were gifted with the ability to see glimpses into the future, though they only worried about their own families despite many other species sharing the same realm. Each species was responsible for their own survival. However, in recent times, Alexius had heard rumors of the Ancients making a resurgence into current affairs.

Alexius shook his head, shaking away the memories bubbling up.

"I know what happened." He had suspected it as soon as he'd seen her blank stare. Now that he could smell Xenon here, it confirmed his guess.

Nasir turned to Alexius and raised an eyebrow, patiently waiting for him to reveal more.

"There was someone else in here with her. He likely killed the challenger. That smear of blood was for show, so we had some idea of what happened to the challenger. He's entered her mind and has blocked her consciousness from connecting with the rest of her. He's imprisoned her in her own mind."

"You got all that from an empty room?" Daylor appeared in the doorway, leaning on the wall with his arms crossed.

"Aren't you supposed to be with the ship?" Tilton turned and asked.

"They're ready, whenever we are." Daylor shrugged.

"True," Tilton said with a sigh as he turned to Alexius. "We were waiting for Thali to tell us herself, but I think it's time you explained yourselves, Alexius."

Tilton joined Daylor in blocking the doorway. They wanted answers and they weren't leaving until they heard them.

Alexius looked at Thali's friends. He knew they would die for her. He wouldn't have encouraged their friendship had they not been true of heart. They all wanted her to be queen, but better yet, happy.

Alexius sighed. He had hoped she would be the one to tell her friends, but in this circumstance, he supposed he would have to do it. "It's not really my secret to share."

"You're right, it's not your secret to share. Keep quiet," Nasir growled, gripping his sword.

"She can't talk. We want to help, but we have to understand what the problem is before we can even begin to figure out how to do that. Tell us. Please." The last word was more of a whispered plea.

Alexius and Nasir looked at each other. Alexius knew Nasir was just doing his job, protecting his lady. And while Nasir wasn't privy to people's thoughts, Alexius was, and he knew he could trust Daylor and Tilton.

"I can't tell you everything. But I can tell you some. The rest will have to come from her own lips," Alexius finally said. Nasir's shoulders drooped in defeat.

Daylor and Tilton nodded.

"Routhalia has ... higher abilities, things she can do with her mind. I've been training her to help her control and better use those abilities. Someone else obviously knows about them and has trapped her in her own mind so she can't connect to anyone or anything."

"Can she read people's minds?" Tilton asked, genuinely curious.

"No." Alexius shook his head. Tilton and Daylor nodded. They didn't look surprised.

"Well then, if you're done here," Nasir's brow furrowed in concentration, "we should get back to the ship and back to the mainland."

Chapter Twenty-Seven
Thali

Thali felt herself being moved from the ship to her bedroom in Elric's manor without much pomp or circumstance. She assumed they wanted to keep her condition quiet so the entire kingdom didn't find out and panic. The moment she entered the manor, Xenon disappeared from her awareness. Thali was left alone in her own mind. She could only see from her own eyes now. Her lungs breathed and eyes blinked on their own, but that was all. She was trapped in her own body.

Elric arrived in her view suddenly, hair tousled as if he had ridden back in haste. He paled at the sight of her and dropped to his knees by her bedside, grasping her hand. That made her grateful she could at least feel her body. She warmed as his hand held hers, and she tried to let him know she was there. Try as she might though, she couldn't move.

She wanted so badly to grip his hand, to throw her arms around him, to tell him she was all right. But she couldn't. Thali was a prisoner inside her own mind. Now that Xenon had disappeared, she was on her own with no way to reach Elric.

Elric must have sent for palace healers as soon as he'd heard because she saw an unfamiliar woman loom over her. She could still feel Elric's hand holding hers, and the woman moved to Thali's other side, gently putting cold fingers on her wrist. Then, the woman leaned in close to Thali's face—so close she could see the brown flecks in the irises—to examine her eyes before putting a mirror under her nose to monitor her breathing.

"She is alive and in good health. She is simply not connected to her body," the woman declared.

"What does that mean?" Elric sounded hoarse. He must have been yelling at someone, likely demanding answers.

"Something is preventing her mind and her soul from connecting with her body. She is awake but asleep."

"How do we cure her?" he asked.

The woman shook her head sadly, still within Thali's sight. "There is nothing we can do. She will wake when she can."

"We ... we're supposed to be married in three weeks' time. People are arriving from around the world," Elric whispered. Thali felt cool drops of water fall on her hand.

"Your Highness, I will stay with her, but first I need to prepare things to keep her body strong while we wait." Thali was impressed with how calm this woman remained.

"I thought you said there was nothing we could do," Elric said.

"We will need to nourish her body so she has a body to come back to."

Elric swallowed audibly. He nodded to her, and she bowed her way out the door before Elric put his forehead to Thali's warm hand.

"I need you, Thali. Come back to me."

Thali lay there for what seemed like hours. Eventually, Elric and her new caregiver propped her up into a sitting position and slowly tried to dribble broth into her mouth. She could feel the warm liquid run down her throat to her stomach. Her stomach growled at finally being fed. They kept her propped up afterward so the broth wouldn't come back up, and Elric eventually fell asleep on the bed, his head in her hand.

As he slept, the rest of the manor was abuzz. Thali continually felt the draft of the door opening and closing as things were gathered for the healer and, eventually, messengers came to find Elric.

Days passed. Thali wasn't sure how long she'd been in the manor, but she was always wide awake; as far as she could tell, her new condition meant she didn't really need to sleep, which made it hard to track the days beyond the light replacing the dark. Then one day, she heard the window open before feeling a soft breeze that smelled of the trees outside cross her face. Elric was asleep next to her, snoring softly.

Her instincts perked up, and she suddenly wished more than anything that she could turn her head. She felt the bed on her free side dip. Someone took her hand in theirs, and she felt a shock go up her arm that blossomed to fire in her body as Garen leaned over her. He glanced at Elric, his eyes darting down to where he held her hand in his sleep and at the ring that would leave an imprint on his cheek when he woke.

Garen's eyes slid to her face. Thali could see Garen was looking well. He had dark circles under his eyes, but his dark-brown hair looked as attractive as always, tousled as it was from his climb to the window. She didn't know how he'd gotten past the guards now lining the outside of the manor. His blue eyes bore into hers, searching for something, anything, that would tell him how to help her.

"I know you're in there, and I promise I'll help you get out," Garen whispered so softly, it sounded more like a breeze than words.

Elric groaned and Garen's gaze shot immediately to the sleeping figure bent over her hand.

Thali saw the pain that crossed Garen's face before it turned to determination. He turned to stare into her eyes once more before he disappeared from her view, and she felt the bed return to its normal position and the sudden stillness in the air as the breeze disappeared.

Thali screamed in frustration, but it did nothing but echo in her own glass chamber. Elric stayed asleep, and her body hadn't even twitched. Even Xenon didn't give any indication he'd heard her.

Eventually, Thali decided to go over the various alphabets she knew in different languages, then moved on to reviewing different pieces of poetry she'd had to memorize from different cultures and in different languages to pass the time.

The next morning, she was surprised to see Daylor and Tilton, who'd stopped by to see how she was doing and bring the well wishes of her crew and other friends because only those two, plus Mia and Alexius, were allowed to enter her room in the manor. They surprised her with a bunch of sunflowers, then left them in her view when they left. At least when she was sitting up, she could see more than the ceiling. Indi, Ana, and Bardo had been allowed into her room too, and they completely surrounded her much of the time. Indi and Ana both kept a head on her leg or her stomach, pressing their furry warm bodies against hers, and Bardo took up residence in any warm nook on her body.

The days passed in absolute agony as people came and went and they dribbled broth in her mouth several times a day. But Thali was surprised she hadn't seen Alexius.

After a few days, Elric was finally persuaded to leave her room for short periods. The military had pressing matters. They had started to deliver reports in hushed tones in her room, and from what Thali could gather from the little she could hear, the attacks were still happening, once a week now. Daylor and Tilton were now spending hours with her, and they promised Elric they would stay with her while he attended to his most pressing work. It was with reluctance when he left though, and he was never gone long.

CHAPTER TWENTY-EIGHT

E VENTUALLY, ELRIC HAD TO be gone longer and longer, and Mia, Daylor, and Tilton always stayed with Thali for him. One morning, things were different, though Thali still heard the usual group of messengers waiting for Elric outside her doors, and he still reluctantly left her.

On this day, as soon as Elric was gone, Tilton locked the door from the inside, and Daylor moved one of the dressers in front of it.

"Thali, you're going to be all right," Mia said as she stood before her. But when her friend left her field of view, Thali knew something of import was happening.

She felt her heartbeat quicken as she watched Daylor write something on a piece of paper. He raised it to her face, but it was too close until Tilton came over and pushed it farther away so she could read it.

We think we have a solution to bring you back. You have to trust us.

Thali wanted to nod, to move her eyes, to do something, but she was as immobile as she'd always been. She wondered why they'd written it down instead of telling her directly.

Thali felt the familiar draft of a breeze on her arms. Someone must have opened a window. She heard another person enter the room and wondered—panicking—if Garen had come back and if Daylor and Tilton knew about him. Mia sat on the bed next to her then and moved to reshuffle her pillows so Thali could sit up. After Daylor and Tilton had raised her into position, Mia held Thali's hand in both of hers and patted it reassuringly.

Someone sat on the bed on her other side and gently took her hand. She felt familiar calluses as their palm cradled her chin. Thali was alarmed when she saw blood on their hand as it was brought up to her mouth. It seemed they intended for her to drink their blood. She wanted to shut her mouth, clamp down on her lips, and turn her head away, but of course, she couldn't. Daylor stood in front of the dresser, within her eyesight, looking focused, worried, and hopeful. The heel of the unknown hand pressed hard into her lips, and a liquid ran down her throat like icy water. There was no iron tang like she'd expected from the times she'd bitten her cheek, only the taste of cool water from a stream.

The hand disappeared as Daylor pulled a tree root from a purple velvet bag she hadn't seen before. Thali didn't understand until he put it in front of her. It was easily the biggest piece of dried galinka she'd ever seen in her life. She knew a piece like that would be worth entire kingdoms and wondered who possibly could have bought it—or perhaps stolen it. Daylor handed it to Tilton then, who used a flint from his pocket to spark the end of it. Thali watched it catch fire from the bottom and slowly start to burn to the top. The bloody, calloused hand took the top of the root and finally came into her view. She should have known. The calluses. It was Alexius. He clenched his teeth as he held the burning root, the fire licking at the cut in his hand.

Alexius held up another note.

> *Some things we can't say or Xenon will hear, hence the notes. But don't worry. I'm coming to get you, Thali.*

Watching the root burn took less time than she would have thought given its size, but eventually, Alexius was left with only a small disk, charred on the edges.

"We need to help you to chew this." Alexius gently prodded her mouth open, and Mia wiped away the drop of blood Thali could still feel on her lips. Tilton and Mia kneeled on the bed then, opening her mouth as Alexius approached to place the disk in her mouth.

"The left side," Mia said. Alexius nodded and placed it there. She and Tilton were as gentle as they could be as they moved her jaw back and forth to mash the disk of the root between her teeth. It flooded her mouth with a bitter and burned, powdery, ashy taste, and Thali was embarrassed at being made to chew something in her own mouth. "Does she have to be the one to chew it?" Mia asked.

"No." Alexius answered. They fished the pieces of root gently from her mouth and Mia took it between a mortar and pestle to grind it up in front of her. She ground it finely into a paste, adding some water to get it all. Mia was careful to do everything in front of Thali so she saw the whole process, even though she couldn't respond to any of it.

Mia came and kneeled back onto the bed, then nodded at Tilton, who opened Thali's mouth. Taking a finger and dipping it into the paste, Mia ran her finger along the insides of Thali's gums. Then, she dipped her finger back into the paste and gently spread it along her gums inside her lips, along her teeth.

"It's not the first time I've had to get something into her bloodstream to save her life," Mia replied. Daylor or Tilton must have looked confused.

"Thank you, Amelia," Alexius said.

Mia finished and showed Thali the empty bowl before rising and disappearing, Alexius now in Thali's view again. Alexius gently climbed onto the bed, and Thali could feel his weight press down next to her. He leaned over so she could see his face and took her hand in both of his, holding still as he closed his eyes, his face relaxing as he took a deep breath and exhaled. After another deep breath in and out, he lifted her hand and placed it on his forehead. He looked down as he slid her hand onto the top of his head. One breath later, Thali heard Alexius whisper something in a different language.

Suddenly, she surprisingly understood the words, "... of my own free will, I choose to serve this mortal, to protect her, her intentions, her will, and her heart, with all the skills and gifts that I have ..."

Thali's heart beat faster. This was something monumental, and she could feel the world shiver. Then, everything went still.

After another moment, Alexius slid her hand to his heart, looking her right in her now unfocused eyes. She knew he was looking for her. He wasn't in yet, but he was close. Eventually, he slid her hand down his forearm to his palm and kissed each knuckle before placing her hand gently back on the bed.

"Was that it? What now? She's still not moving, and she looks unfocused. I swear, Alexius, if you've tricked us in some way ..." Mia was babbling; her nerves were fraying.

"That was merely the first step," Alexius said.

Thali felt a breeze through the glass room in her mind as someone else arrived.

"Alexius. What did you do?!" Thali recognized Aexie's voice. She strode over to where Alexius now stood, right in Thali's line of sight. Aexie was her human self, and she wondered if her friends' jaws were on the floor. Even Thali was still stunned by how beautiful Aexie was.

And Aexie was furious. Her fists were balled as she glanced at Thali, then stared at her brother. "Alexius. How could you?" Aexie forced through clenched teeth. Her brow softened a touch when he replied.

"I'm sorry, sister, I had to." Alexius looked at the floor. Thali could see he was cowering before his sister's fury.

Aexie stood still. Both siblings stood almost unnaturally still as they stared into each other's eyes.

"Tell him I'm dead," Alexius said out loud.

Aexie's jaw tightened even more before she dropped her balled fists and disappeared from sight. Her disappearance cut through the tension she'd brought with her, and Alexius sat down on a creaky chair at the side of the bed.

"What do we do now?" Daylor asked from Thali's right.

"We wait," Alexius replied.

"And I suppose you're taking a quick nap," Mia muttered under her breath.

I'm here, Alexius's voice whispered in her mind, and Thali almost fainted in her own head. The whisper was as loud as a shout in her mind, and she had to take a moment to adjust.

How?

That was a blood oath. My life is now tied to yours.

Thali was quiet. She remembered Alexius telling her about dragon blood oaths. He'd just cut his immortal life short. He would die when she died. She was relieved to finally be able to communicate with someone, but as she thought of his sacrifice, she understood why Aexie was so angry with him.

Was there any other way?

This was the only way I could think of.

Why?

Thali, there is much I need to share with you. But right now, we have to save our strength for Xenon. He'll have noticed the shift of the blood oath and will return to check on you. When he does, I will be ready. Trust in me. I'll break your walls down from the inside.

Why did the blood oath open our communication?

The blood oath supersedes any other magic. Other than perhaps love itself, there is nothing stronger. And the blood oath is a kind of love. When I get you out of here, I will always be a weapon for you to wield.

I'm honored, Alexius. I will forever cherish this bond, and I will not misuse it. I am grateful to you.

Thali was saddened that she'd taken Alexius away from his family and his life. However, she couldn't think too long right now about what the blood oath really meant for him because she needed to be ready for Xenon. She was just wondering how Alexius would be able to take down the walls in her mind from the inside when she felt a fog appear in her mind. It enveloped her, and she had the distinct feeling that Alexius had sidled up closer to her.

Wrap yourself in your threads, Alexius whispered down their bonds.

Foolish dragonling. Xenon's voice surrounded them, echoing through her glass room.

I am here to fight on Lady Routhalia's behalf. Alexius's voice rang in her head.

How very noble of you. Does your brother approve? Xenon asked.

Alexius ignored the question. *It was wrong of you to hold her in here,* he said instead.

And yet I did it anyway, Xenon said.

Thali felt the distinct feeling of a sharp talon trailing along her arm. She froze, unable to see anything in the fog.

You cannot stop time and destiny from continuing, Alexius said.

Ahh ... so you are one of those. I knew someone very much like you once. You put all your faith in fate and destiny. Truth be told, you smell a little like him. But you know what I've learned in my centuries of life? Nothing is unstoppable. This will be for your own good too, you know. Magical creatures will be safe to roam freely as we should.

Lady Routhalia returns with me, Alexius said. Thali felt heat and flames burn the fog. It cleared for moment, and she saw Alexius out of the corner of her eye, now in dragon form, and across from them,

Xenon, now a golden dragon with black talons and black eyes leaning against a glass wall.

Xenon looked unlike the few dragons Thali had seen. He was much longer and thinner, more snakelike than pear-shaped. A long black mustache twitched independently. Strangely, he looked like a dragon from a drawing her mother had brought back from Cerisa. He was also clearly obsessed with his talons because he continued to stare at them, not sparing Thali or Alexius a glance.

Alexius didn't hesitate. His wing shot out to protect Thali as he whooshed blue-white fire from his mouth. As she peeked out from behind the wing, Thali watched it hit Xenon square in the chest. Yet he didn't even flinch. Alexius let out another shooting flame, this time aiming it at the wall behind Xenon, and the glass wall started to change color, developing a fog of its own where the heat hit it. But once the flames had stopped, though the glass wall had remained white in that one spot, it hadn't cracked.

My turn? Xenon bit down on one of his black talons and tapped the others on his bottom jaw, a satirically humanly gesture for a dragon. *Oh, what should I do? I have so many options.*

Thali felt herself thrown back against a wall as if a wave of water had launched her into the air. She saw Alexius also being thrown against the wall but fighting it. He flew slower and didn't lose his breath when he finally did hit the wall.

Enough, Xenon, a new voice said. The water disappeared.

Alexius was next to Thali immediately, his wings around her. As she watched, Alexius's brother, Xerus, walked through the glass wall Alexius had been trying to destroy, sparing them only a sad glance before walking right by them to Xenon.

Thali's gaze followed Xerus and saw Xenon's face still slack with surprise. *Xer, I haven't seen you since ...* Xenon popped back into human form, and Thali realized why they looked similar. They dressed from the same era, though Xenon was much flashier. But they still had the same long hair tied back into a ponytail, the same long coats with buttons, the same stockings and boots.

I know. Xerus smiled, putting a hand on Xenon's shoulder.

Alexius silently dragged Thali to where Xerus had walked through the glass wall.

Xenon put a hand on Xerus's shoulder and leaned in to kiss him. Alexius didn't wait to find out what happened. He jumped up and ran with Thali through the exact point Xerus had come through, stopping just on the other side of the glass wall.

A moment later, Aexie popped out of the glass wall in human form. As soon as she did, Alexius breathed out a stream of flames to heat the weak point in the glass wall.

"Thank you, Aexie," Alexius said.

"You owe me." Aexie disappeared and Alexius stood, focusing on the glass wall before him. As Thali watched, he shrank it until it was the size of a pea before crushing it between his claws.

Was he still in there ... ? Thali began. Her words reverberated in the chamber of her mind, and she realized she had to whisper.

No, he's too smart to have stayed. This was a separate chamber he created to disconnect you from your body. But we're back now.

So Aexie ...

Yes, Aexie can change into anything. Even into nothing or something or someone.

Thali nodded. How she could nod without being connected to her body wasn't something she could understand.

What now?

Now you have to fall asleep. And when you wake up, your body will wake up. It might take a day or two of sleep though, since you haven't slept at all, I assume.

Where will you ...

I'll be here when you wake up.

Thank you, Alexius. Thali yawned, unable to stop herself, mid-sentence.

Sleep, Lady Routhalia. You are safe now.

Thali had more questions for him, but her eyelids were incredibly heavy. Her vision grew smaller and smaller until the world fell away and she fell into a dreamless sleep.

Chapter Twenty-Nine
Eric

E LRIC FOUND HIMSELF WITH a free moment between meetings and needed to go check on Thali. He'd had a bad feeling from the moment she'd said goodbye, though he'd known she wouldn't stay behind and skip her exam for him. But since they'd brought her off the ship and he'd seen her laying there, unresponsive, he'd felt like half his heart had frozen in his chest. He was one of the most powerful people in the kingdom, and there was nothing he could do to rescue her. He'd never felt so helpless, never expected to.

When he reached Thali's rooms, he grabbed the doorknob only to find the door was locked. Panicked, he threw his shoulder into it before guards started to rush to the door to help him.

"One moment!" Mia shouted from the other side. In seconds, whatever was blocking the door was moved, and Elric opened the door to a packed room. Tilton and Daylor looked sheepish while Mia glared at him, and he was surprised to see even Alexius reclining in a chair. Elric was about to demand an answer for why they'd locked him out when Mia put her finger to her lips and pointed at Thali. Elric nodded then. Mia had his respect. She had been by Thali's side since childhood and even now, stayed at her bedside since Thali had been brought to the manor.

Alexius suddenly woke and stretched his arms. Then, he saw the prince. Rising, the dragon in human form walked over and whispered, "She's sleeping now. She'll wake in a day or two, back in her body."

"How did you ...?" Elric was at a loss for words. He blinked rapidly, looking from Alexius to Thali and back. "Thank you."

Alexius bowed his head and Elric nodded before hurrying over to Thali's bed, resuming his position next to her and holding her hand in two of his.

Thali

Two days later, Thali's eyelashes fluttered and she twitched. Elric jerked upright. Daylor, Tilton, Alexius, and Mia had stayed the whole two days and now leaned in, too. Thali's mother and father had even finally arrived. The room was crowded, but everyone's attention was suddenly focused on one face.

When Thali opened her eyes, she blinked several times, trying to adjust to the light. Elric's face filled her blurry vision first, and when she was finally able to squeeze his hand back, his eyes filled with tears as his smile broadened. Her heart thumped faster as she took in the faces of all the people around her. She smiled to see her mother and father and even a sheepish Daylor and Tilton further back. Then, she saw Alexius standing at the foot of the bed, looking relieved. Mia was next to Thali's head, and when she turned to look at her best friend, her neck cracked audibly, echoing through the room.

An old woman pushed between Elric and Mia. Thali recognized her as the healer who had been checking in on her and feeding her broth. The woman checked her pulse and looked into her eyes, then squeezed her mouth open to check inside.

"Thank you, Helen," Thali croaked in a whisper. The woman nodded at her and retreated from the room.

"So, you could hear and see everything when you ... when you were ill?" Daylor asked, poking his head closer.

Thali nodded. She was about to ask for something to drink when Mia reappeared by her head with a cup of warm tea. After Elric helped

Thali sit up, Mia brought the cup to Thali's lips. Thali swallowed the liquid, relishing the sweet honey coating her throat.

"Thank you. All of you." Thali looked around the room.

"Let's give the prince a few minutes, shall we?" Lord Ranulf cleared his throat and came over to Thali. He kissed her forehead, leaning in to touch her forehead with his own. "Don't you ever scare us like that again, understand?"

Thali nodded and let her mom squeeze her tightly before her mother and father stepped out of the room. Alexius nodded as he left, and Thali saw her parents corral him in the doorway on their way out. She felt a little bad for the questioning he would endure from her mother.

Let me know if you need saving, she whispered along the thread now solidly in her mind. Alexius scoffed in response.

A yowl interrupted Daylor and Tilton as they passed by the connecting door to the next room. Thali felt Indi, Ana, and Bardo impatiently waiting for someone to let them near her.

"You better open the door before they break through it," Elric said.

Tilton opened the door. He and Daylor quickly made their exit as the tiger and dog leaped into the room and onto the bed before piling on top of Thali. Indi began rubbing her chin all over Thali's head and chest, and Ana could not stop wiggling as she licked every available inch of Thali's skin she could find. Bardo kept to her feet and legs, circling her toes and slinking along the bottoms of her feet.

After a few minutes, Thali asked them to calm down. Indi tucked herself up along Thali's side, while Ana squeezed herself behind her back, and Bardo finally settled down on the edge of the bed's footboard.

Elric had never let go of Thali's hand.

"Are you really all right?" Elric searched Thali's eyes. His thumb circled her palm.

Thali nodded. Her own thumb circled the top of his hand, and she had a new appreciation for being able to return the affection. "You've been so dedicated. I ... I wanted to squeeze your hand back so badly when I was ... stuck."

"Who did this to you?" Elric asked.

"Another dragon. Someone who wanted me out of the way," she said.

Elric's jaw tightened.

Whispers of what Xenon had said to her floated back to her. "Are you all right, Elric?"

Elric's attention snapped back to Thali, and he smiled at her, taking her hand and gently putting his lips to the inside of her wrist. "Of course, I'm all right. I've been beside myself with worry for you. It felt like part of me was silenced this whole time."

"I've missed you, too." She squeezed his hand. She wouldn't tire of that anytime soon. "But I mean, your whole life, you've been preparing for your royal duties and then suddenly, magic comes back. Magical creatures, me, that's not what you've been preparing for. I'm not even sure there *is* a way to prepare for it."

Elric sank to his elbows onto the bed next to Thali, cradling her hand like it might disappear if he didn't pay it enough attention. "This is a pretty heavy topic for you having just woken up. I'm not sure Helen is going to be pleased I'm not letting you rest." Elric looked at his hands, looking deep in thought. He raised an eyebrow as he finally met her eyes, but Thali's face was set in concern and determination, so he continued. "Of course it's difficult. And I have no idea what I'm doing. But I never expected to have all the answers."

"You don't ... don't blame me?" Thali asked.

Elric froze, looking up at Thali, looking sincerely surprised. "Why would I blame you?"

"That exam in my first year, I think I'm the reason the gate opened. Someone used me to open it." Thali suddenly found the embroidered stitching on the bed sheets incredibly interesting.

Elric rose and sat on the bed, close to her. His fingers gently tilted her chin so she had to look into his eyes. She stared into the green eyes that made her love the color of sea kelp. "Routhalia, you are not to blame for that. Whoever manipulated you would have found a way to open those gates, with or without you. You have no way of knowing their true motivations. You cannot take responsibility for all the magic in the world. Understand?"

Thali nodded. She felt her heart beating faster and willed Elric's lips to come closer to hers. They did and she enjoyed a delicious moment of his soft lips on hers before he pulled back a few inches.

"I'm so happy you've come back to me safely."

"Me too." They smiled at each other, pressing their foreheads together.

A knock interrupted their moment, and Elric straightened as a royal messenger entered.

"Your Highness, you're needed in the study." The young boy looked nervous and turned red when he realized what he'd interrupted.

Elric sighed. "If Danroy is sending messengers, he must be drowning in problems. Now that I know you're all right, do you mind if I go handle some paperwork?"

Thali nodded. "No, please do. The kingdom won't run itself."

Elric grinned. He stood up, bent over for another quick peck, and left the room with the messenger. Her friends and family filed back into the room in small groups, and she was kept entertained all night. Thali spent most of it comforting them instead of the other way around though. They were all worried she'd disappear again. They even dined together in her room, and it was late in the night when everyone finally cleared out. Thali even finally sent Mia to her own room to sleep. She was grateful for her friend but needed a night alone for once.

Alexius stayed behind after the others had gone. He'd been quiet, standing by the window the entire afternoon and evening, staring out at nothing in particular. Thali's parents had been the last to leave; they were also staying in a guest room in the manor, and Thali was glad for once to have so many of her friends and family so close to her. She wondered what Tariq would think of her kidnapping. She decided to try and send him messages tomorrow morning.

Alexius sat in the chair by her window now.

Tell me more about this blood oath, Thali asked in her mind.

Alexius didn't move as he replied without looking at her. *You know everything you need to. We're connected until we die now.*

You mean until I die. You're immortal. Or you were. Thali looked down at her hands as she once again toyed with the embroidery on the edges of the sheets.

Humans feel emotions strongly. I've never ... well, it's been refreshing. And difficult. Please, do not feel so much guilt, Routhalia. I made my own choice freely.

But if I'd kept my mental shield up, you wouldn't have had to.

You underestimate Xenon. He's very old and very powerful. An Ancient. He would have found a way in. I'd been considering a blood oath with you for quite a while. That's why I'd distanced myself. This situation just ... made me decide sooner.

Why?

When you met me, I was tasked. I've always been a good soldier, an obedient son. But getting to know you brought me hope. That's not something I've really ever felt in a long time. My ... task, it put limitations on me. The blood oath frees me from them. I've chosen my side.

Side?

You've had a long day. I will explain more in time.

Alexius rose and headed swiftly for the door. *I will stay in the hall for the next ten minutes to ensure no one disturbs you.*

Thali was confused, but Alexius didn't offer an explanation as he left the room, closing the door gently behind him.

She started to test her body then, wondering how out of shape one could get with weeks of bedrest. She threw off her covers and wriggled her toes, then slowly went up her body, tensing and relaxing each set of muscles. A click made her snap her head in that direction. Garen was leaning against the wall next to her bed. She looked down at her tiger, dog, and snake, all thoroughly still asleep.

"So much for the warning system," Thali muttered as she looked back to the figure in the shadows.

A smile tugged at the corner of his lips as his eyes shone in a sliver of moonlight.

"I've always loved those toes," he said.

Thali felt heat rise to her cheeks, and she threw the covers back over her sickly-looking legs. But she couldn't take her eyes away from his face. A chasm opened in her chest, and she didn't know if it was good or bad.

"Thank you for getting the galinka," Thali said.

He nodded. Then swallowed. His arms were crossed, and she watched as he flexed his arms though his feet remained motionless. He was nervous. "You're pretty rusty if I made it all the way to this spot before you noticed me."

His voice was barely louder than a whisper, and a shiver traveled down Thali's spine at the sound. "I just woke up from weeks of being locked inside my own head. I think rusty is to be expected." She blinked to break the spell he had over her.

"I'm glad you're all right," Garen said.

"What ... why are you here, Garen?" Memories of the pain he'd caused her flooded back.

"Are you still going to get married?" Garen asked.

A loud whooshing rushed through her ears, and her eyes widened. "What day is it?"

"You're one week away," he said. His arms did not budge, nor did his body. It clearly took effort to stay as still as he was.

Panic rose in Thali for a moment. She was one week away from getting married. The words of the prophecy rang through her mind. "Yes." Her throat went dry. What choice did she really have?

"I'll always be there when you need me." He moved into the moonlight streaming through the window, opening its panels silently.

"Wait," Thali said.

Garen paused, the window open and a gloved hand on the edge of the sill.

"Where did you get it? The galinka?"

"Wanting to create more blood oaths, are you?"

"No, I just—"

"Joren helped me track it down. Then, he grew it and dried it out."

"Oh." Thali watched as Garen looked at her once more, their eyes connecting as Thali felt that chasm widening in her chest. He looked away as he disappeared into the night, closing the window behind him.

Thali was now blissfully alone in her room, the soft breathing of her sleeping animals a comfort. Suddenly, she couldn't stand to be in bed. She carefully got out of bed, testing her wobbly legs, and started exercising on the rug on the floor. Her animals ignored her, preferring to sleep. She didn't want to waste any more time. She had things to do.

CHAPTER THIRTY

T HALI WOKE TO SOMEONE yelling outside. Looking around, she realized she'd fallen asleep on the floor and blinked the sleep away as she felt a familiar twinge in her brain.

"NO ONE IS STOPPING ME FROM GETTING IN TO SEE HER!" Thali first thought it was King Shikji yelling. Then, she realized the familiar twinge in her head and the voice belonged to Tariq.

She heard some quiet murmuring outside her door as she scrambled to stand up. Her animals were gone from her bed, probably taken outside to relieve themselves.

"She needs to rest, and you're not going to help her rest if you keep yelling." Bree's musical voice floated through the doors, and Thali ran over to yank them open. Standing in the hallway right outside her room were Tariq and Bree. They looked out of place in the manor and here in Adanek.

"Lili, thank goodness you're all right." Tariq swept her up in a hug, lifting her clear off the floor.

"She won't recover if you squash her ribcage, either." Bree stood next to Tariq, looking completely beautiful as usual in a purple-and-gray dress.

Thali barrelled into Bree to hug her as soon as Tariq put her down. "I can't believe you're here."

Bree smiled, ushering them back inside Thali's room. Elric, hands on his hips, followed.

"Well, are you still getting married?" Bree asked.

Elric froze. "We haven't even—" Elric started.

But Thali nodded. "Of course we are."

"Really?" Elric looked at Thali. "I thought you'd want to regain your health first."

"The tailors are going to have to work around my body. But why delay? We have many guests coming. Wait, it's still a week away. Why are you two here early?"

"I knew something was wrong. We left early," Tariq said.

"And he made the crew on the ship work twice as hard." Bree rolled her eyes.

"I can't believe I didn't know. I hold you responsible, Elric," Tariq said as he turned to him.

"Whoa now." Thali stepped between the two princes. "Elric, why don't you find us some breakfast?" she suggested. Elric's eyes narrowed at Tariq, but he left the room.

Thali turned to Tariq. "He feels guilty enough without you adding more blame."

"Good. He should feel guilty. He should have told me."

"That's not how that came out."

"I'm leaving more guards with you."

"No."

"But it's a wedding present. Don't insult my country." Tariq pouted and lounged on a couch as Bree sat on the edge of a chair, always the elegant lady.

Thali rolled her eyes. "You're not seriously playing that card."

"I am."

Bree finally coughed to interrupt them. "Thali, why don't you dress, and we'll go for a short walk so you can show me the lovely gardens here. Tariq can pout in the corner by himself."

"Lovely idea." Thali gave Bree another kiss on the cheek before she disappeared behind a screen to change. It was early in the morning, and Thali was excited to get outside and get some fresh air.

In no time at all, she and Bree were walking in the garden behind the manor, her arm in Bree's. Tariq followed farther behind, still pouting.

"Thali, may I help you get ready for your wedding?" Bree asked as they toured the gardens that had been transformed to rival any botanical haven.

"Absolutely. I was hoping you would," Thali said.

Bree nodded. She had perfect poise, and Thali pressed her lips together as she tried not to laugh at all the eyes staring open-mouthed at her friend as they walked by. Thali found herself standing a little taller and becoming more aware of her own actions.

Elric had set up a breakfast for the four of them in the middle of a new garden, and as Thali sat down, she sensed Elric's need to talk to her. They hadn't yet had another moment alone.

"Tari, come here. I saw some flowers over there I think would be perfect for under my window at home. Come help me choose which Thali will give me as a gift." Bree said.

Tariq opened his mouth to protest when he saw Bree's face and quickly closed it before striding over to her and taking her arm.

Once the couple was out of earshot, Thali said, "I'm sorry we haven't had a chance to talk privately again." She looked at Elric sheepishly.

"You've just recovered. I don't blame you."

"So. Do *you* still want to get married next week?" Thali asked.

"Yes. I do. Being away from you, it was torture. I felt so helpless," Elric said.

"I know what you mean. I could see and feel everything. It was frustrating not to be able to do anything or say anything."

"Do you think you could handle an appointment with Cassandra this afternoon?"

"If by Cassandra, you mean Tayrone, then yes." Just imagining the woman with all the bright colors and fabrics made her dizzy. But the wedding was a week away. What other option did she have?

Elric nodded.

"Will you promise to be there with me?"

"Absolutely."

Thali reached for Elric's hand.

"Dinner will be with everyone tonight, I think," Elric said.

"That would be nice."

Elric smiled, and Thali felt like herself finally.

"Lady Ambrene, Your Highness, please come and join us." Elric stood and motioned to Bree and Tari.

Thali felt Tariq watching her. She knew he'd put her through an inquisition soon.

I'm okay, Tari. I promise. And I'll tell you everything later, after sparring in the afternoon?

He gave the smallest nod as he turned to Elric.

After their breakfast in the gardens, Elric had rushed off to see to more kingdom issues, and Bree had taken Tariq off to tour the school grounds to give Thali some space. After taking a moment to decide what she most wanted to do, Thali remembered that at this hour, her mother would be practicing her drills somewhere outdoors, so she changed to go practice with them. It'd be worth the soreness in her muscles to watch her mother spar.

When Thali turned the corner around the school to the open weapons field where she usually had classes, everyone turned and clapped. Besides her parents, Tariq and Bree, half the crew from her parents' ships, and a half dozen merchant students were still on campus.

Thali's cheeks warmed as she nodded, but she went to her parents and hugged them both before finding a staff and walking to the far edge and starting some of her forms and drills to assess her body. While her body was listening to her mind, she could feel it didn't have the strength or stamina she'd had before.

"It'll come back quickly, lass. Don't ya worry." Crab had come over to her, and she abandoned her staff to throw her arms around him.

"Good to see yer up and about," he said into her hair as he lifted her into a bear hug. He sounded emotional and Thali moved her head back to look at him.

"Are you all right, Crab?"

"I'm just so happy yer better. And I can't believe my wee little lass is gettin' married. And to the prince. Yer gonna be queen one day." He sniffed.

"Cousin! You've gone soft!" Master Aloysius strode up behind him. Crab put Thali back on the ground and swiped at his eyes as he turned around.

"Never." The cousins smiled brightly and grasped each other's forearms tightly as they looked each other over.

Master Aloysius and Crab then started to spar, and Thali used it as an excuse to take a break as she watched them test each other. She'd guessed Crab would be the better fighter as he'd trained with her mother all this time, but she was surprised when she saw Master Aloysius holding his own quite well.

"Want to do a little sparring of your own?"

Thali jumped and realized Alexius stood next to her. "Where did you ...?"

"I was walking through the forest." He motioned behind her. "I'll go easy on you."

As Thali and Alexius paired off, they settled into their comfortable routine, though he didn't take it easy on her as he'd promised. On top of the physical combat, he started to prod his way into her head, making her defend mentally and physically at the same time.

Elric has asked me to join your personal guard.

This surprised Thali, but she realized why. Alexius would be better able to defend her and be around her constantly if he had a good reason.

I told him I would be honored. Will you tell him of our blood oath?

Can I?

I am yours to command. You can do whatever you like with me.

Then yes. Maybe later though.

Alexius then swept her legs with the staff, and she used the opportunity to lay on the ground and rest for a minute.

You should get up before His Highness comes to beat me with his sword.

Thali rolled up into a sitting position. *Elric's here?*

The other prince.

You know, I think that might be a good sparring match to watch.

Alexius offered her a hand up and she took it.

Thali's knees buckled and Alexius caught her arm. "Maybe we overdid it," Alexius said.

"I feel a lot better though." Thali was drenched. She sat down on a nearby bench with Alexius and watched her mother with envy. She looked like flowing silk sparring with Tariq.

Daylor and Tilton made their way around the edge of the field to join her.

"Good to see you up and about." Daylor plunked down on the bench next to her.

"Thank you for all your help. I could see and hear and feel everything. But it was maddening to not move or say anything."

Tilton grinned and blushed. "We're glad you're back."

Thali noticed Daylor and Tilton holding back. She wondered how much Alexius had revealed to get them to participate in the oath. They weren't exactly avoiding her, but she could tell they had questions.

How much did you tell Daylor and Tilton?

I told them nothing of your abilities, only that you had abilities. That is for you to tell them. And I told them I knew of a way to try to bring you back, that my family has had healers for generations, so I had to perform the ritual. They suspect you haven't told them everything though.

"Are you walking back now?" Daylor asked Thali.

"Yes." The exhaustion suddenly hit her like a wave, and she took Daylor and Tilton's elbows and rose to go.

"I will stay," Alexius said, turning his attention to her mother's sparring match.

Thali waved to a few people as she walked with Daylor and Tilton back toward the manor. Or should she head for her rooms at school?

Tilton read her mind. "They closed the building you and Mia were living in for the summer months, so we moved all your things to the manor," Tilton said as they walked past her building.

Thali absentmindedly reached out to Indi and Ana, who bounded out of the woods toward them. They nuzzled her happily and fell in next to her. She smiled at how comfortable her friends were with her animals and thought back to how intimidated they'd been when they'd first met Indi three years ago. Tilton caught Bardo from falling off Indi, letting the snake slither along his shoulders. The group walked silently to the edge of the grounds where the forest path would lead them to the manor.

"Where are you ...?"

"We're staying at the manor too, for now," Tilton said.

"Oh! I'm glad," she said as they continued walking in silence. She trusted Daylor and Tilton. She wanted to tell them about her abilities and magic and all the things she'd been keeping from them, but she didn't know how to start. And she wasn't sure if they really wanted to hear it. Or how they would react to it.

They stopped at the foot of the stairs to the manor. "We're in the first-floor rooms down the hall." Tilton glanced up.

"Oh, those are nice." Thali found she was wringing her hands.

Daylor looked as awkward as she felt. Tilton suddenly wrapped her in a hug. "We're really happy you're all right, Thali. I know you have a lot on your mind, but if you ever need someone to talk to, we're here for you when you're ready." He pulled back and glanced at Indi and Ana. "About anything."

Thali nodded. They definitely had their suspicions. "I'll see you at supper?"

"Of course." Daylor started to bow and then thought better of it as he and Tilton turned and jogged up the stairs and into the manor. Thali slowly followed, praying someone had run a hot bath for her. She regretted not having told Daylor and Tilton everything right then, but she wasn't ready to lose them if it scared them away. Maybe her cowardice would melt away in the bathtub.

"How did you know something was wrong?" Thali tried to pry Tariq out of his pout. The two friends and Bree were enjoying tea in one of the manor's sitting rooms. Bree was inspecting the decor of the room: This one was all ivory and cream with bookcases, statues, and carvings of birds edged with gold. Thali was worried she'd get something dirty, but it was the only available room. She couldn't believe even the books had been rebound in various shades of white and ivory.

Tariq jumped up. "It was the strangest sensation. All of a sudden, I saw only blankness when I thought of you. After you left Bulstan, it was like you were too far away to be heard, but you were still there, like a slight draft. But this was different. It was like every time I thought of you, I was turned around or bounced back."

Thali had finished telling Tariq and Bree everything that had happened while she'd been locked away. She'd finished her tale with Alexius's blood oath.

Tariq's brows were furrowed. "Took him long enough."

"Tari! His life is tied to mine now. He gave up his immortality!" She hissed at him.

"I'm sorry, Lili, but whatever the future holds for us, that can only help," Tariq said.

Thali smiled. She liked that Tariq had used "us" not just "her."

"Have you told Elric?" Tariq asked.

"No. We haven't had much time alone together."

"He'll want to put him on your personal guard."

"He's already asked."

"Good to see he's capable of some smart decisions."

"Tari. That's enough. That's my future husband you're talking about," Thali said.

Tariq finally stopped pacing and sat down, his face softening.

"I'm sorry, Lili. He's a good man, a good prince. And he's treated you as you deserve. I'm just mad he didn't tell me."

Thali, sprawled on her couch opposite Tariq, nodded and turned to his fiancée. "Bree? Anything to add?"

"I'm not getting into this. Elric is a fine prince. I like him." Bree returned to sit with them and concentrated on some stitching.

A knock on the door preceded it opening to reveal a mound of floating fabric walking into the room.

"Mia?"

The fabric fell onto the nearest seat and Mia popped out from underneath it all. She looked a little flustered.

"Good. You're both here. Your Highness, try this on please." She dug through the pile of fabric and handed him a red-and-black jacket with long tails and a multitude of panels. As soon as Bree saw it, she put her stitching down and hurried over to take a closer look.

"Mia. This is beautiful. I love how you've combined the two fashions!" Bree turned to Mia. "Please tell me you will come and make my dress for our wedding!"

Mia laughed. "I do not do ships."

Bree actually looked scared for a moment. "No!"

"My apologies, Lady Ambrene. I would be more than happy to help you while you're here though," Mia said.

"Mia, call me Bree. We've known each other too long and share such deep friendship with Thali that I consider you as close a friend as I do her."

Mia blushed and nodded. She had been strangely more formal with Thali's friends lately, making Thali wonder why. She eyed her friend and made a mental note to ask her about it later.

CHAPTER THIRTY-ONE

T HE NEXT WEEK WENT by in a blur as Thali got caught up in last-minute wedding decisions and visits with family and friends. Her only relief was that since the palace was only a half a day's ride from the manor, the king, queen, and most of the royal court would travel to the wedding the day of. She hadn't even had the chance to ask Elric what had happened to the griffin in the basement. It felt like every time she went to do something for herself, someone was running up to tell her she was late for something else. And more than anything, she wanted to go see Rommy before her wedding, but there just hadn't been time.

Before she knew it, Thali opened her eyes to the sun dawning on the biggest day of her life. She carefully moved a tiger paw off her neck and tried to shift Ana over so Thali could free herself from the blankets. Today was the day she'd marry Elric. As Thali carefully extracted herself from her animals and got out of bed, she wondered how Elric would handle waking up with a giant tiger paw in his face. She smiled at the thought as Indi stretched to take up even more space on the bed. Ana curled up right in between Indi's legs and dozed off again. They'd wake soon enough to be bathed and attired themselves though. She'd let Mia decide what they would wear, so it was to be a surprise for Thali. And bless Elric, he'd agreed her animal friends could take part in their wedding. While Thali hadn't thought tempting Indi with a cart full of doves was a good idea, her tiger and dog would carry her train down the aisle for today's ceremony.

The door opened softly then as Mia snuck in with a tray, suddenly startling herself when the dishes rattled. Thali jumped up to help her and placed the tray on the little table beside her bed. There was enough food on the tray to feed four.

"Will you join me?" Thali asked.

"Just for a quick minute. I was going to wash them next." Mia's gaze slid to the bed.

Thali found a butter croissant, broke it in half, and smeared even more delicious butter on it. She looked up at Mia, seeing the look in her eyes that meant she was going over a list of what she had to do today.

"Are you sure this is what you want? To be my lady's maid? If you wanted to open your own dress shop, I'd be happy with that, too. I'd be your biggest patron. I'd even sponsor you if you like."

Mia shook her head and turned to Thali before sitting down and pouring each of them a cup of coffee. Thali was thrilled that being a princess meant she could have coffee every single morning. Then, grabbing a pastry herself, Mia threw her feet up and leaned back. It was so uniquely Mia to be able to change intentions quickly. "That might have been my dream once ... and I'll admit I struggled with the idea of being a lady's maid at first. But now? I'm going to set trends by creating all the things you wear, and I'll get to see my creations everywhere as everyone else scrambles to replicate them. It's like I get to clothe the kingdom but without all the work of making it all myself." Mia shrugged. "Besides, I want to be here. I want to be part of your life. And I like bossing you around, making all your clothing choices for you, and decorating your rooms. But more than anything else, I like helping the kingdom by taking care of you."

"But all the running around, taking care of my animals, bringing me coffee and tea and sweets? You don't have to serve me. I am capable of getting my own breakfast."

Mia stared into her coffee. "Thali, when you were stuck in your own mind, I thought you were dead. Now, all I want is to take care of my best friend. I want to make you fabulous dresses. Getting this stuff," she waved her hands at the breakfast tray, "is not a big deal. Once we're at the palace, I'll have less work." She paused to wink conspiratorially. "And the gossip is amazing."

"And what of you addressing Tari and Bree so formally?"

Mia sighed and put a hand on Thali's hand. "I'm not nobility. I know that. When we get to the palace, we'll all have to be a little more formal. I was practicing."

"But not with me, right?"

"When we're in your chambers privately, it'll be as you wish. But if there are other ladies or lords nearby, I'll have to address you formally."

"I hate it. You're my equal."

"I know you see it that way. And it makes me happy to be part of that. That's what makes you, you. That's why I love you so much. But this is one of the highest positions of honor I could attain without being noble. Trust me. I'm happy."

Thali's eyes narrowed. "Are you sure?"

"Yes." Mia smiled and put her cup down. "Plus, who else is going to handle Bardo, Indi, and Ana and the menagerie I'm sure you'll eventually collect?"

Thali smiled at that. Mia clapped her hands together and stood back up. Indi and Ana jumped up in the bed, sensing what was about to happen.

Thali asked her tiger and dog to go quietly and to hold still so Mia would have an easier time of it. She sent the images to them, and they followed Mia out of Thali's rooms, heads down but still following. Thali promised them their favorite foods tomorrow.

Thali rose with her coffee, taking another sip. She went over to pick up Bardo, who had moved to curl up in the sun. She took a soft cloth from her bathing chamber and wiped him down.

A soft knock interrupted her drifting thoughts as she finished up with Bardo. She was surprised Bree would be up already, but she supposed there was much she wanted to do to Thali's face and hair. "Come in," she said as she lay Bardo back down in his sunny spot. "So, what is your vision for my face today?" Thali folded the cloth she'd been using to wipe Bardo and hung it on the rack.

"A bridal one perhaps?"

Thali spun around and her eyes grew wide as saucers. "Rommy?"

Rommy stood by her bedroom wall. He looked better than he had in all her previous visits. She'd thought she'd have to accept his absence in her life after Alexius had said he wouldn't be able to bring her back to Etciel after the blood oath because his duty was now tied to her, not Xerus and the kingdom of Etciel.

Rommy had filled back out, his muscular form back, his jet-black hair shining again, and the gray eyes they shared twinkling with mirth as he strode over to his sister and swept her up in an embrace.

"Rommy. How? When?" Thali couldn't find the words.

"I couldn't miss your big day," Rommy said.

Thali held her brother even closer as she let the tears of happiness stream down her face. "I can't believe you're really here."

"I wouldn't miss this," Rommy said.

"But how?" Thali asked. She held him at arms' length, scanning his face.

A strangled cry made them both spin in the direction of the door. Lady Jinhua and Lord Ranulf stood in the open doorway, Thali's father the only thing keeping her mother from sinking to the floor.

"Romulus. Is that really you?" Thali's mother strode over, shock and purpose in her eyes. She reached out to grasp Rommy's face.

Thali's father let his wife hold their son first, going instead to Thali and holding her close. Thali saw the shock and amazement at seeing his son, alive and well, mirrored in her father's eyes as he neared. When Lady Jinhua finally backed away from Rommy to look at his face, he turned to his father, beaming, and held out his hand. Lord Ranulf walked right past his hand and embraced him.

"I've never been happier to be wrong," Lord Ranulf said.

"Father. It's good to see you," Rommy said.

As they pulled apart, Thali ignored the tension between her brother and father and watched her family coming back together. She couldn't stop the tears as they soaked her face.

A squawk came from behind Thali as Mia came back into the room, and an orange-and-black striped blur barrelled past her and right into Rommy. He was knocked down and covered in wet tiger fur by the time he managed to stand up. Ana trotted in much more calmly and kept her distance from Rommy, instead going to greet Lady Jinhua and Lord Ranulf warmly. She returned to Thali's side instead of greeting Romulus. She'd never been a huge fan of Thali's brother.

Mia stood frozen in the doorway, then slowly wiped her hands on the skirts of her dress before edging closer. "It's really you, Romulus," Mia said.

"Mia, why so formal now?" He went over to her and gave her a hug.

"I'm Thali's new lady-in-waiting." She gladly hugged him back before excusing herself and leaving the family to be together.

"Oh, thank the gods." Tariq's voice came from the space in the open doorway Mia had just vacated.

Rommy looked up. "I see they're letting just about anyone in here now."

They grinned at each other as Tariq strode over, and they shook hands vigorously. "I knew you'd be too tough to kill off." Tariq's grin reached all the way to his eyes.

Bree floated in after Tariq. "Romulus!"

"Lady Ambrene." He bowed low over her hand and kissed the back of it. Rommy and Bree had never really been as close as Thali and Bree.

"It's a shame Rania didn't come with us," Bree said.

"How is she?" Romulus stilled suddenly, waiting for the answer.

Tariq's face fell but brightened quickly. "She'll be much better once she knows you're alive and well."

Rommy paused, then nodded.

"But today should be about someone else!" Tariq turned his attention to Thali.

"Lili, I am here to officially offer you one last chance to escape." Tariq dipped into a grand bow.

Thali smiled but shook her head. She'd not left her brother's side and could not help but grab hold of his arm as if he might run away on her if she let go.

"No?" Tariq rose. He went to his best friend and took both her hands in his, kissing the tops of both. "Then, I will herd everyone else out and leave you with your ladies to get ready." He leaned down to hug her. "Truly though, if you want an escape route, pull your right ear. Anytime today. I'll make it happen." He winked at her as he stood up and started ushering her family out, including her brother. "Rommy, I believe you'd like to meet your future brother-in-law? Elric will have quite a shock seeing you today. And I believe he could use another scary big-brother speech, don't you, Uncle?" Tariq winked at Thali's father.

Mia squeezed through just as the door was closing, and Thali saw the quick surprise and recovery of her guards outside her room. She wondered how Rommy had gotten past her guards, but then, perhaps he'd come from a different kind of doorway.

Then, it was only Bree and Mia left with Thali. She noticed then the giant case Bree had brought with her. "What is all that?"

"Face paints."

"All of it?"

"This," Bree's finger circled her own face, "doesn't just happen."

"Not everyone can be as naturally gorgeous as you, Thali," Mia added as she helped Bree bring the case over to a low table.

Mia turned to Bree. "Hair first?"

"Definitely," Bree said. They each put a hand on Thali's shoulders and pushed her into the chair at her vanity. Bree unloaded all the things from the case, laying out pots and jars of varying sizes. Mia disappeared in the bathing room to come out with a basket filled with small cylinders.

"Actually, go bathe before we begin. We'll brush Indi and Ana while you do."

Thali couldn't resist a little fun. "What? Are you saying I stink?"

"Nope, but if they have to bathe, so do you." Bree said, crossing her arms and smiling as Mia escorted Thali to the bathing room, where Thali expected to see animal hair everywhere. But there was none to be seen.

"I took them to the bathing rooms in the staff area. I wasn't about to get your bathing rooms filthy today," Mia said as she went over to the steaming tub and lightly dipped a finger in.

"Perfect. Jump in. See you in a bit," Mia said, leaving Thali mercifully alone for a few minutes.

CHAPTER THIRTY-TWO

T HREE HOURS LATER, LADY Routhalia of Densria stood in front of a mirror, barely able to recognize herself. She started to giggle.

"Why are you laughing? Is there something wrong with your hair?" Bree checked one side her face and hair, then the other.

Mia, meeting Thali's eyes in the mirror, giggled too. "I think our flower here isn't used to being all painted and pretty."

"But you're always beautiful. We just made it more obvious." Bree smiled.

Thali tried to keep a straight face but couldn't help giggling some more. Bree's face turned stern as she narrowed her eyes at Thali. "I just never thought ..." Thali managed between fits of laughter as she tried to catch her breath, "... I mean, I feel like an impostor." She finally squeezed out.

"You're about to be a princess," Bree said.

That stopped Thali suddenly. She realized that technically, she already was a princess, a princess in a court of thieves.

"What's the matter?" Mia asked.

"Nothing. It's ... I'm nervous." Thali plastered on her best smile for her friends. They'd spent the last three hours working hard on her hair and her face, and she was their masterpiece. She owed them her gratitude not her doubt.

"You really do look beautiful, more beautiful than the queen did on her wedding day, I think," Mia said. "At least from what I've seen from the portraits in the castle."

Thali's eyes grew wide. "Mia, that's treason!"

Bree shrugged. "It's true."

There was a knock on the door, and Mia, Bree right behind her, went to open it. Stefan and Nasir, in their formal dress, entered. "My lady, if I may say so, you look beautiful." Stefan bowed deeply, the leather of his new uniform squeaking.

"That is very kind of you, Stefan. Thank you. Is it time?" Thali asked.

"We will stay with you until the ceremony so the other ladies may be dressed."

Bree and Mia gave her a hug and kiss, leaving the room as Amali, Khadija, and Derk stepped into the room to join Stefan and Nasir.

Thali looked at each of her guards. "You all look wonderful." Stefan had confessed when she'd returned to her body that they had been so ashamed that they hadn't protected her they hadn't been able to look her in the eye until she'd become herself again. Now, she felt a distance that hadn't been there before and hoped it would disappear over time.

"Aren't you on night shift, Nasir?" Thali asked.

"We're all on duty today, my lady." Nasir bowed his head and she nodded.

Thali had nothing to do then but stand and look out the window. Below her window, past the balcony, she could see all the guests gathering on the lawn in front of the manor. She smiled as she recognized so many people, people from all over the world. She was sad she hadn't had an opportunity to meet with any of them before today though she knew many were staying after the wedding in hopes of an audience with the new princess. This day reminded her of how much she missed just spending time with them all, relaxing and chatting and hearing about their lives.

Some of her childhood friends were present, and they looked so grown up and so much like their parents now. Thali smiled at the colorful mishmash of clothing from different cultures all brought together in this one spot on this one day.

Unable to sit for fear of wrinkling her dress, she looked sideways in the mirror again. Her eyes were lined in black from the ash sticks Bree had created, her skin was glowing, and her cheeks blushed from the red powder Bree had masterfully worked into them. Even her lips had been painted a bright berry color to make them stand out. However, that's where tradition ended. Instead of an only white dress, Mia had made Thali a white and red dress. It was her way of incorporating Thali's background. Red had always been her mother's favorite color because it was a lucky color in Cerisa. Mia had styled the dress in fine Adanek style, with an intricate lace neckline, a corseted bodice covered in diamonds and sparkling gems, and fitted sleeves that flared out at the wrists. The rest was a nod to Thali though. The skirts were multilayered and expanded outwards in a flow that reminded Thali of ocean waves, and the train was several feet long. But the most wondrous thing was that Mia had sewn a silver crystal dragon down the length of it, so it looked like a dragon stalked behind Thali. Now that Mia knew what Alexius really was, she had barraged him with a thousand questions about what dragons really looked like so she could get it right. She'd asked so many questions, he'd finally changed into his other form and let her poke and prod him until she was satisfied.

Unfortunately, Thali hadn't had a chance to add Alexius to her personal guard yet. She wished she had because she would have felt so much calmer having him close by. At least she would get to inspect her guards in their full armor before they escorted her on foot to the garden for the ceremony, where she would be able to select Alexius, Isaia, and two others to accompany her in the carriage and present her to her father to walk down the aisle.

Stefan cleared his throat and Thali turned, raising her eyebrows. He nodded. It was time. She took one last deep breath before making her way to the door. Mia had brilliantly folded up and pinned her train so it wouldn't be quite as troublesome to move in. She'd promised to be there to pull the pin out right before Thali walked down the aisle.

She sat carefully in the carriage, terrified of wrinkling the beautiful dress or stabbing her butt with the pin. The silver thread reflected the light in the carriage, and Stefan and Nasir moved their face shields in place to keep from being blinded as Thali stifled a laugh.

Thali had been talked through the ceremony of inspecting the guards and choosing her personal guards for the day, and she was glad only the king and queen would be there to witness any mistakes. Her five usual guards were already with her, but as the carriage came to a stop, she tried to remember all the things she'd been told. She would walk through a large open hall, where lines of royal guards would be waiting. She was to walk up and down the rows and select four more personal guards to make a complement of nine. Her actual team of royal guards would be much larger, but her choices today would rotate into her personal guard more often in the future.

Letting Stefan guide her to what must once have been a barn, she breathed in the horse and hay smells, taking comfort in them and the reminder of Arabelle; at least she'd get to ride her horse once at the palace. Indi and Ana sat flanking the hall entrance and fell in next to her as Thali stopped to take in the scene before her. Fifty guards filled the hall, lined up in neat rows on either side of a deep red carpet. There were so many more than she'd originally thought. The King and Queen Sat on a dais on the other end to observe. Thali reached up to her neck to pet Bardo and calm herself.

Though she knew she was to walk up and down the aisle, as she looked at all the royal guards, a moment of panic rose within her. They all looked exactly the same. How was she supposed to know which were Alexius and Isaia?

How are you feeling? Alexius asked in her mind.

Nervous. Which one are you? Thali looked down at her hands, absent-mindedly stroking Indi under the chin to buy her a moment.

I am the third one from your left in the first row. Isaia is two down from me. You'll want to pick the last one as well.

Thali took a deep breath and strolled to the carpet. As one, the guards unsheathed their swords and kneeled, leaning on their swords. It was symbolic of their weapons being hers to command. The effect of fifty armed guards kneeling at her presence was unnerving, but Thali gulped and stood taller. She walked up to the first guard on the left, and her five personal guards stayed back to allow her the freedom to choose.

Stopping at the third guard in that line, she reached over to Indi, who had four purple-and-silver ribbons laying over her jewel-encrusted coat. How Mia and Bree had managed to attach jewels to her dog and tiger were beyond her, but she did admire how they sparkled. She took one ribbon and tied it to the right wrist of the third guard. Thali carefully counted as she proceeded down the line and tied a ribbon to the fifth guard's wrist, realizing that even if Alexius hadn't told her which was Isaia, she'd have recognized him from the beautiful sword he carried. It was by far the most polished sword in the line up, and she smiled at her friend.

"Eyes up," Stefan said from the end of the hall. As one, the guards raised their chins. Thali saw the crinkle of a smile in Isaia's eyes and grinned back as she continued down the line. She didn't recognize many of the guards; most had come directly from the palace. She'd asked Stefan the other day if there were any he wanted her to pick, but he'd been too gracious to say.

Thali wished she could see their hands. She'd know who was best with a sword by looking at their hands. She continued down the line and recognized a guard with brown eyes she had seen practicing at the palace the last time she had been there. He was talented with his sword and bow if she remembered correctly and had even sparred with her once or twice. She remembered he was quick to learn the new steps she'd taught him and wasn't hot-headed like some of the others she'd often seen at the training grounds.

She reached for a ribbon and tied it to his wrist, then continued to drift as slowly as she could to the end of the line, wondering why Alexius had recommended she choose the last guard. As she approached the last kneeling figure, she felt heat crawl up her neck and cheeks and questioned why.

But the moment she stood before the last guard and saw his eyes, she stopped in her tracks. She'd recognize those dark-blue eyes and long brown lashes anywhere. How Garen had snuck in among the royal guards was beyond her comprehension, but there he was, mischief dancing in his eyes as he held her gaze. Indi nudged Thali's hand, reminding Thali to bend down and take the ribbon. Then, she reached out and slowly, carefully, tied the ribbon to Garen's right wrist, not breaking eye contact the entire time. Once she was done, her hands falling to her sides, the guards recited the ceremonial words. All she heard was *his* voice.

"I vow on my soul to serve and protect Princess Routhalia of Adanek. She may command me to do her bidding, and I will use all my skills to keep her safe and protect her interests above all else in this world. I will be her sword to wield as she sees fit."

They all rose then, and those guards who did not have a ribbon tied to their wrists stepped back. The four she'd chosen, and her own guards, surrounded her. They stopped for a nod from His and Her Majesty before the guards herded her to the carriage. Once outside, Thali blinked and shook her head to clear it. A lot of good it did her because when a guard offered his hand to assist her in ascending the stairs to the huge ceremonial carriage, she felt the heat bloom in her and knew it was Garen.

A short, silent ride later, she disembarked and followed her guards to the ceremony. They ascended a set of stairs, walking beneath silver canvas swathes, then descended a slope. She heard the gathered crowd in the garden, just beyond the final curve of the path, and saw the shadows of guards posted every fifteen feet along the outside of the covered canvas protecting her from sight and sun. She saw nothing but her personal guards' backs as they led her through the canvas cover before finally halting in formation just feet from the path's curve, where she'd make her wedding debut. Though her personal guards would stand behind her during the ceremony, for now, they shielded her from view.

When they finally parted, she saw her father, brother, Tariq, and Mia. Each of Thali's guards took a knee before her, bringing their forehead to the back of her outstretched hand before rising and backing away to take their position at the ceremony. She could hear the gathered crowd settle as the activity started.

Garen was the last to leave her, and he quickly kissed her hand before sweeping his brow to it. It was so subtle, she wouldn't have been sure it had even happened if she hadn't felt his lips linger on her gloved hand, just for a heartbeat. It was a challenge to not to watch him back away to join the others.

Mia came over and bustled around her, straightening and fixing this and that. Finally, she went and pulled the last pin to let the train out. It tumbled to the floor, and Mia unrolled the length of it, giving Ana one handle and Indi the other, both handles having been sewn into the fabric. Mia gently pulled Bardo from around Thali's neck and he slithered down to the miniature cart they'd created for him to pull. Somehow, Tariq had built it so the cart's floor would open and close slowly as the snake wriggled down the aisle. Mia had made the tiger and dog practice carrying the train and Bardo practice pulling his cart for the last few days. When all the animals were ready, Mia went and stood between the tiger and dog, also grabbing the train. She and Tariq would help carry Thali's train while Bardo slithered ahead of them and trailed silver petals along the aisle.

"How are you feeling, Lili?" Tariq asked. He placed his hands on her shoulders to steady her.

"Like this is all a dream," Thali said.

"Are you all right? Really?" Tariq asked. His eyes flicked to her right ear, and she grinned.

"Yes," she replied, holding her hands out steadily in front of her. He searched her face once more before taking up his position next to Mia, ready to drop even more flower petals as they walked behind Thali with her animals.

"I hope you don't mind, but we thought to walk you down the aisle together." Rommy said, anxiously glancing at their father.

"I'd love that." Thali looked at her brother, then her father, and linked her arms with theirs.

The music started. Thali and her entourage marched out of the covered tent into the sun and turned the corner. Rustles and gasps filled the summer air as the guests spied Thali and rose to their feet. Her dress sparkled like the sea, almost blinding the massive crowd as the sun hit the gems. The many faces she recognized from her past filled her with joy. Then, she saw Elric standing at the end of the aisle. His brilliant hers-only smile made her grin, and he was all she saw as her brother and father led her nearer to him one step at a time. The gasps continued as she walked down the aisle. She knew her little group looked impressive. It wasn't often you saw a snake slither down the aisle, followed by the bride with a tiger, a dog, a prince, and a genius dressmaker. Thali wished she could see how the silver dragon along her back shimmered and undulated as she strolled. At the end of the aisle, she embraced each of her family members, her mother included, before Thali's father finally took her hand and placed it in Elric's.

Elric's eyebrow raised in a silent question. Thali's smile just widened in response, and she cast her eyes downward to their joined hands as she felt heat flush her neck and cheeks.

"You're beautiful," Elric whispered.

Thali noticed the bright yellow before them when she dared look back up. Elric had turned the garden behind the officiant into a field of sunflowers, and her white and red dress and his shining silver-and-black dress coat stood out against it like jewels in a field of hay.

"Your Highness, as the future sovereign of Adanek, the responsibility of your people sits upon your shoulders. Have you chosen your queen with this in mind?" the officiant asked.

"I have." Elric beamed at her.

"And do you, as princess of Adanek, swear to put the people of the kingdom before your own wants, to be loyal, supportive, and faithful to your husband?" the officiant continued.

Thali thought of all the people of Adanek: the nobles, her friends, even those in the court of thieves. "I do swear it."

The rest went by in a blur, and before she knew it, Thali was walking back down the aisle, both guard contingents trailing her, only this time, she was a married woman.

That night, the king and queen of Adanek held a great feast in their honor, and Elric's family was quick to celebrate her brother's return. When Thali sat down to the banquet, she noticed an old wine bottle. It was out of place in the luxury and glamour of the evening.

"Remember when we stomped grapes last year?" Elric asked as he followed her stare.

A smile spread across Thali's lips. When she'd been miserable, Elric had arranged an entire day to cheer her up, and she remembered how he'd collected three bottles of the grape juice that day.

"I figured this was an occasion worthy of one of those precious bottles." Elric poured the wine into her goblet himself. She brought it to her lips and was surprised at just how sweet the wine was.

Thali was happy to watch her friends and family celebrate around them. She couldn't move much because of her dress, but people flowed continuously to her, so she didn't have to. The only time she found her eye wandering away from the guest in front of her was when one of the guards caught her eye and disappeared behind a column. She wondered how they would replace Garen's position as she assumed he wouldn't have left his position as prince of thieves for her personal guard.

"We look forward to our audience with you," the guest in front of her said, bringing Thali's attention back to the current conversation.

"As do I," Thali said and smiled. The older couple moved on, and the next person drifted over.

"THALI!" Daylor threw his arms around her, and Thali pressed her lips together to stop herself from laughing at how inebriated Daylor was. "Thali, did you know," Daylor got super serious as he slung his arm around her shoulder. "Did you know that you married a prince today? That makes you a princess now!"

"I'm sorry. He insisted on saying goodbye before agreeing to head to bed," Tilton explained.

"Thank you, my dear friend," Thali said as she hugged Daylor back. She pulled Tilton in too and held them for a minute before letting them go.

"Have a good time with the prince tonight, princess." Daylor whispered in her ear, then backed up and wiggled his eyebrows. Tilton's face paled.

"Get yourself to bed safely, Daylor." Thali giggled. She turned to Tilton. "Do you need help corralling him to bed?"

Tilton shook his head. "I'll manage. Sorry again. I'll see you in the morning." Thali nodded and Tilton dragged Daylor away.

When Elric and Thali finally left the celebration, the guests toasted their future children, and Thali flushed red enough to match her dress.

During the ceremony and celebration, palace staff had moved her chambers to adjoin Elric's, so that was their destination now. Their guards followed them as far as their common rooms, then stayed in the hall. The newly married couple closed the door softly behind them as Elric's eyes burned with flame. Thali drifted toward him like a moth.

CHAPTER THIRTY-THREE

T HALI WOKE UP IN Elric's arms in a delicious daze. She yawned and moved her legs back and forth, missing the weights that were usually her animals. She wondered for a moment where they were when she felt Elric's hand brush along her shoulder.

"Good morning, my beautiful wife."

Thali grinned, turning her head toward him. "Good morning, my handsome husband." She pulled the blankets up to cover her mouth.

Elric, smiling, tugged the sheet below her face. "Princesses don't hide behind anything." He kissed her forehead, sighing, as he pulled Thali against his chest and lay back into the pillows.

"What's the matter?" Thali asked, snuggling into her new favorite spot on his shoulder.

"I wish we could stay in bed all day."

"We can't?"

"We have a breakfast with all the foreign delegates and then we have meetings all day with each of the foreign guests."

"Like who?"

"Didn't you look at the schedule?" Elric asked.

"I have a schedule?" Thali asked, sitting up and feeling like she was already late. "I guess I better get dressed."

"Hmm ... maybe in five minutes." Elric pulled her back down, and they made the most of their last five quiet minutes.

Thali and Elric parted ways later to enter their closets and prepare for their first day as a royal married couple. Thali was amazed to find an entirely new wardrobe hanging in her closet, which she was also stunned to find was an entire room, one side dedicated to clothing and another dedicated to jewelry—jewelry she hadn't known she had. It even included a windowed alcove through another doorway where Mia now sat sewing with her machine.

"Mia, do you know where all this came from?" Thali asked as she took it all in.

"Well, I was responsible for all the dresses: I remade some, I commissioned others, and I made a few myself. Did you know I have a team of seamstresses at my disposal?" Mia put her work down and smiled as she stood and spun around the glorious closet.

"Really?" Thali asked. That meant Mia would be able to design her dresses as she saw fit, and her team could do most of the menial work. "That's fantastic! You get to be the boss!" She added with a laugh. She was happy for her friend even if Thali didn't quite understand how she'd been lucky enough to keep her close.

"And what about all this?" Thali motioned to the wall of jewels, picking up a simple pearl necklace.

"Ahh ... aren't they beautiful?" Mia sighed as she carefully ran a fingertip along the biggest bejeweled necklace Thali had ever seen. "Some are yours: the ones in these drawers here." Mia pointed at the lower drawers. "And the rest of the jewels in the drawers come from the royal stores. The queen chose them for you herself, so I suppose they're technically borrowed?" Finally, Mia waved at the upper half of the display wall. "And these ones here were gifts."

"Oh," Thali sighed.

Mia turned and pulled two dresses off their hangers: one lilac and one red. Thali shrugged. Mia narrowed her eyes as she glanced from one to the other then nodded at the red one. It was more subtle than Thali's wedding dress with its panels of black-and-silver piping, but she supposed it was quite reminiscent of Adanek's royal crest. Mia helped her dress, doing up the many stays and ties along her back.

"What about this?" Thali asked as she indicated a last, white velvet-lined section of the wall filled with jewels she'd never seen before.

Mia grinned. "From Tariq and Bree." Thali's eyes went wide. Her friends were officially insane.

It felt like an hour had gone by when she was finally appropriately dressed and polished and walked into the common rooms connecting her rooms and Elric's. He was sharply dressed in his usual princely gray pants and shirt with a red and charcoal coat; she noticed the piping along his coat matched her dress. As he took her hand and led her out of their rooms, Thali wondered how much staff this palace had. She'd already met two of her maids, and Mia had a team of seamstresses. She had a lot of questions to ask Elric later. Somehow, this hadn't been covered in her princess lessons.

They walked hand in hand down the hall, a complement of eight guards trailing them as they made their way to the banquet hall for breakfast. Thali smiled at Alexius, now wearing a uniform.

How are you settling in? Thali asked him.

Well. We should continue your lessons soon.

All right. Tomorrow. I plan to go to weapons practice, too.

Does your assistant know that?

I have an assistant?

You have a complete team. We all met and were briefed this morning.

Really? You're kidding.

Alexius nodded as Thali and Elric stopped at the big oak doors and waited to be announced. The doors opened, and the crowd quieted as the new royal couple walked in. Thali smiled when she recognized most of the foreign dignitaries gathered, and they all cheered and clapped as she and Elric approached the table. Elric's parents, the king and queen, had already arrived.

Thali wanted to go greet her friends—some she hadn't seen in a very long time—but she wasn't sure about the protocol now that she was a royal princess. So, she stayed at Elric's side, a step behind him, as he led her to the table. He helped her to her seat, where she hesitated a moment, wondering if she could still go around the table to greet her guests.

Elric looked from her to the chair, so Thali sat down. She sat to the left of the head of the table, next to Elric. As soon as Elric sat down, the first plate came out, and Thali was at least glad she had the chance to eat at this banquet, however princessly she had to do it.

As the meal wound down, conversation started to fill the room. Thali suppressed a grimace as she was seated next to the only guest she didn't know and made polite conversation with him as she waited for breakfast to finish.

Thankfully, Alexius stood nearby with all her guards.

Alexius, do you know the protocol for this? Can I go and visit with everyone?

Yes, you may. From what I understand, since breakfast is done, you need only excuse yourself to the dignitary to your left and rise to go speak with whomever you like. But I suggest you only spend a few minutes with each, including Prince Tariq.

Thali nodded ever so slightly and made her apologies to the foreign dignitary before she hesitantly stood up. She accidentally stepped on the hem of her dress and was forced to awkwardly lean forward and move the chair so she could step off her dress. Her cheeks blazed with heat, and she couldn't look up to see who had seen.

Alexius rushed over to help with the chair. The king and queen continued their conversation, though Elric's gaze followed her as he continued his own conversation across the table.

Relieved to be moving, and feeling a little freer, Thali went around the table greeting old family friends and asking about their countries and loved ones. As they spoke, she put together her own audience schedule in her head based on her friends' replies. Then, she thanked them and moved on to the next familiar face. Thali wondered who her secretary was and how they could have made an entire schedule without consulting her.

Finally, she reached Tariq, who took both her hands and kissed them before Bree held her hands and kissed her cheeks.

"How are you holding up?" Bree whispered in her ear.

"All right, I suppose. I have a schedule apparently. I feel like I need to catch up."

"We'll see you tomorrow, officially, but we'll be at weapons practice every morning. If you have need of us, send for us."

"When are you leaving?"

Bree winked. "We'll stay another week at most."

Thali nodded and thanked her but then couldn't help but hug her friends before she moved on. She sadly noticed her own family was not present. But she supposed if this was a breakfast specifically for important foreign guests, it made sense, even though her family would know most of the people here and they were also important guests. Thali hoped there was no other reason they weren't here.

As she made her way back to her seat, the king and queen rose, and everyone else followed suit. They nodded to Elric and Thali and left the banquet hall. Elric then presented his own arm to Thali, and they left the room with their own guards trailing behind them. The tension in Thali's shoulders didn't relax until they were back in their common rooms.

"You did really well endearing yourself to everyone at breakfast."

"I know most of those people. They've watched me grow up."

"Really?"

"Yes. Lord Anders has the most beautiful paintings."

"Oh? I believe that's what he gave us for our wedding: a painting."

"Where is it? Can I see it? Can we move it in here?" Thali was suddenly excited.

"Absolutely."

Thali froze. "Where are you getting all this information? I feel like I'm completely in the dark about everything."

There was a knock on the door to their sitting rooms and Elric mumbled, "Speak of the devil."

The doors opened and Thali was surprised when Tilton, Daylor, and a young woman with dark-brown hair twisted into a knot at the base of her neck and dressed in dark leggings, a tunic, and a formal overcoat walked in.

"Thali, I don't think you've had the pleasure of meeting my secretary, Avery."

Thali was stunned at the woman's beauty. She was ashamed of herself for assuming Avery had been a man, but the woman rushed over and bowed with a grandiose sweep.

"Your Highness, I'm ashamed it's taken me so long to meet you, but I feel as if I already know you. Since the moment Elric met you, he hasn't been able to stop talking about you!" She smiled brightly, but

Thali couldn't help noticing the usual smile crinkles around her eyes were absent.

"Yes, I'm surprised I haven't met you yet either," Thali said.

"I'm afraid it's my fault. I kept Avery here to help me hold down the fort while I was at the manor." Elric glanced from Avery to Thali. "You were asking me how I get my information, Thali. Avery here is the secret behind that."

Thali decided to shove away her thoughts of a beautiful woman being so close to Elric and embraced Avery. "I'm sure we'll make up for lost time and see lots of each other now." Thali smiled genuinely as she let Avery go.

The secretary bowed again, and Elric gave Thali a kiss on the forehead before turning to leave with Avery. "We have lunch with Lady and Lord Bellcamp. I'll meet you there," Elric said over his shoulder as he took the files Avery handed him. They ducked into his private office and closed the door.

Thali turned to Tilton and Daylor, finally getting over her shock at the woman's appearance, and squealed as she launched herself at her friends. "I can't believe you're here with me!"

"Us either. This is mind-blowing," Daylor said.

Thali took a step back. "So, you two are my secretaries?"

"For now, yes," Tilton said.

"Tilton, I think, is a little more suited for the job, but it's a lot of work, enough for two people for now. I think my job should be sending your messages. I wouldn't mind taking those where they need to go." Daylor scratched his head, looking like he was trying to remember if he was forgetting anything.

"So." Thali crossed her arms. "I hear I have a schedule."

Tilton blushed and said, "Yes, and I'm sorry I didn't send it along sooner, but I was trying to change some things. And I've had a bit of a crazy time figuring out how to do so."

Thali sat down on one plush couch and the men sat across from her. Daylor reached over the back of his couch to grab a stack of papers off the table, then handed them to Thali.

Thali looked at the papers. One day's schedule filled about ten pages.

"The first page is a general timeline of your day. The next pages include notes you might need for each of the meetings."

Thali scanned the pages. She knew most everything in the notes—and could have added to them herself. Suddenly, she flipped back to the first page.

"Tilton, I *need* combat practice. For my sanity. Please, Tilton," Thali begged.

"We're trying, Thali. Trust me, I know you need time for that, and probably time for Arabelle, Indi, Ana, and Bardo. But right now, there are a lot of people who have requested meetings with you, and they're only here for a short time." Tilton threw his hands up in his own defense.

"What are all these meetings for though?" Thali asked. "I don't have any power or responsibilities."

"You will though. For now, I think it's mostly just polite conversation. Plus, they'll be presenting you with gifts."

"Gifts?" Thali looked up, surprised. "Didn't they already do that at the wedding?"

Daylor plucked a grape from the plate of fruit on the table between them. "Oh yes. But those were for the newly married couple or the kingdom. These ones will be gifts specifically for you—to win your favor, of course." He reached over and grabbed two more grapes.

"And if they did their homework, and since they know you, they'll be beautiful gifts given you're a merchant's daughter and all."

Tilton glared at him disapprovingly.

"What? Thali doesn't mind us being who we are." Daylor shrugged.

"It's 'Her Highness.'" Tilton corrected, still glaring at Daylor.

"Please, both of you. I'd prefer you both still call me Thali. Please?" She turned her gaze to Tilton. His shoulders relaxed a bit, but he didn't help himself to the fruit.

As her friends led her from meeting to meeting, Thali realized Daylor and Tilton must have had some serious training. They clearly knew their way around the palace and shuttled her from one meeting to the other, only stopping to check a map once. By the fifth meeting, Thali was having trouble keeping the smile on her face. The meetings were all so formal and stuffy. Her guests would all bow when she walked into the room, try to reminisce about the last time they'd seen her—usually when she was a little girl—and then they'd present her with some extravagant gift. She'd examine it with feigned interest, her merchant eyes telling her exactly how lavish most of the gifts were, then say her goodbyes. Halfway through the day, she wondered what she was supposed to do with eight giant wheels of cheese.

Lunch with Elric had been more like another meeting, and she hadn't had the time to even speak more than a few words with him before they were back *on duty* and conversing with their guests.

By the time it was evening and Thali was getting ready for bed, she could only groan when she heard a knock on the common-room doors. At least the visitor would have to be familiar since her guards were standing on the other side.

"Come in!" Thali called. Refusing to put her tired feet back in her shoes, she resigned herself to knowing that whoever it was would just have to see her bare feet.

"Your Royal Highness," Rommy drawled in his best uppity voice as he bowed low with a sweep of his arm and a swish of his coattails.

"Rommy!" Thali couldn't help but grin. She moved a pillow and sat down on the couch, inviting Rommy to join her. When she glanced at the table, she was surprised to see steam coming from a teapot. Had that always been there? Had someone placed it there before she'd walked in?

"Tea?" Rommy bent over to pour them each a cup. "You look exhausted."

"Thank you, but I believe you're supposed to offer me compliments, not insults," Thali said.

"I'm your brother. I think it's my official duty to treat you as any older brother might treat their little sister." And to highlight his point, he let out a fart as he bent over to pour the tea.

"Eww, gross, Rommy!" Thali waved her hands frantically in front of her face to wave away the stink.

Rommy's hand hovered over the sugar as he grinned. "One spoon or two?"

"Two please."

"So, it was that kind of day?" Rommy handed her the teacup and sat down facing her on the couch.

"Rommy, I've never felt so useless and important all at the same time," Thali said.

"I noticed you didn't come to training today," Rommy said.

"It's not currently feasible with my schedule. Or so I'm told," Thali said.

Rommy took a sip of tea, carefully placing the cup back in its saucer before answering. "Rou, you are a royal princess now. Do you remember when we were in Bulstan and Tariq demanded five golden elephants to ride?"

Thali laughed at the thought. They'd been about eight years old, and Tariq had been going through a show-off phase. He'd demanded five golden elephants from the stables so they could ride into the forest and pick fruit from the tops of the trees.

"They had to paint five elephants to appease him." Thali laughed at the memory of how she'd been stunned to see five golden elephants waiting to take them for a ride the next morning after breakfast.

"If Tariq, at eight years old, can demand five golden elephants, surely the future queen of Adanek can participate in combat practice and have time with her animals." Rommy took one last sip of tea.

Thali saw his raised eyebrows over his cup and smiled. "I'm really glad you're here, Rommy." Thali smiled. She would do just that. She should get a say in her own life.

"I know you must be tired, Rou, so I'll leave you to sleep." He put his empty cup down on the table. "But I wanted to come and check on you. I know this must be quite an adjustment."

"Thank you." She too put her tea down on the table, then rested her hand over his.

"Oh now, come here." He swung his arm around her neck and pulled her head in as if to ruffle her hair. He kissed her on the top of her head instead before letting her go and rising. Then he winked at her and said, "We're on your schedule tomorrow morning. How about you meet us for combat then?"

Thali nodded. As Rommy strode toward the door, she asked, "Rommy, how long are you staying?"

He turned back. "As long as you need me, Rou Rou." He grinned before shutting the door behind himself.

Thali picked up her tea again and sat, slowly sipping the hot drink and letting it warm her body from the inside out. She sat back, letting the warmth wash over her like waves, taking with them the stresses of the day.

When Thali finished her tea, she sat up and sighed. Then, she stood and went to the window, staring out at the dark of night and realizing it must be later than she'd thought. And Elric still hadn't returned to their rooms.

She found Mia in her usual spot in Thali's personal rooms, sewing some beads onto a dress. Her lady in waiting sat at a little desk she must have commandeered for herself.

"How was your first day as princess?" Mia asked, not breaking her rhythm: needle, bead, fabric, needle, bead, fabric.

"Long. Thank you for setting out the tea."

"You're welcome. I knew you'd be busy. Tilton left tomorrow's schedule on the table there." Mia thrust her chin at a cute dressing table behind Thali.

Thali scanned the schedule, her shoulders drooping when she saw it was full of meetings again, though it pleased her to see her own family, and Tariq and Bree, on her schedule tomorrow.

"Mia, how are you settling in?" Thali asked as she turned, looking for a distraction.

"It's been a bit of a whirlwind, but people have been as kind and as helpful as they can be. Being personally selected has its perks." Mia stopped sewing to look up at Thali. "Would you like help with that?"

Mia put her sewing down and helped Thali out of the gown she'd worn to dinner.

"Do you have something less ... gown, more ... me? For tomorrow?" Thali looked around the fabric-filled room.

"No more princess dresses?"

"Well, something befitting a princess, but less ... well, restrictive. I didn't really feel like me all day."

Mia puckered her lips, staring at each garment. "I was hoping you'd say that," she said. "The policies for dressing you are pretty strict, but I've got lots of ideas, now that I know you're on board." Mia's eyes gleamed and Thali wondered if she'd made a mistake giving Mia full rein to dress her unconventionally.

"Wait, there are policies about how I dress?" Thali blinked, wondering if she'd heard Mia correctly. Mia nodded and Thali shook her head. "Well, I'll be meeting my family for combat practice, so where can I find those clothes ...?" Thali started to look around for pants.

"I had to hide those away when they moved all your clothes here. They're in that trunk under the table." Mia went over to the table where Thali's schedule had been and pulled the trunk out from under it. "Pants, vests, and all the manly clothes you love so much." Mia grinned.

Thali grinned back. "Manly clothes?"

"You should have seen your new maids' faces when they saw me putting them in there." Mia chuckled.

"Please, commission more shirts and vests please. And pants. The dresses are beautiful, but I can't wear those for the entire day. I'm going to need something to wear for training."

"There's my Thali." Mia smiled. "Wait here. I'll go make a note." Mia popped out of her alcove, leaving Thali to finish undressing, but after Thali had fumbled with the ties on the back of her dress for far too long and let out a loud groan, Mia reappeared and undid the ties enough so Thali could wiggle out of the corset. Then Mia opened the trunk and pulled out a soft cotton shirt and some leggings.

"Perfect." Thali took the clothes and dropped the shirt over her shoulders and pulled the leggings on.

"Well, that's it for tonight, I think. Good night, Thali," Mia said, picking up her sewing and heading out.

"Good night, Mia." Thali walked back to her bed to find there was still no sign of Elric. She tiptoed to the common rooms and peeked her head out the door. Stefan was standing guard in the hall and looked surprised to see her.

"Stefan, where are Indi, Bardo, and Ana?"

"In the stables. Would you like me to send for them?"

"Yes, please."

She wished they'd asked her if they could stable her animals. She'd have to make sure they could stay with her. They were family. And if she didn't have Elric tonight, then at least she would have her animals. Moments later, the door opened and Indi and Ana bounded toward her. She let them lick her to death before finally leading them back to her bedroom, where they leaped up onto the bed. Indi stretched out right away and let out a huge yawn. Ana made a few circles on the pillow before settling down, and Bardo slithered right to the headboard. Thali climbed in between them, stretched, and fell fast asleep.

CHAPTER THIRTY-FOUR

T HE NEXT MORNING WHEN Thali woke, she was pleased to find Elric sleeping next to her, Indi's back paws between their heads.
Looking out the windows, she realized it was still early—too early for
her schedule to have accounted for.

A thrill of excitement ran through her as she realized she had some
time to herself. She ran to her closets and was glad not to find Mia
there. She threw on a plain canvas tunic and vest and gently roused
her animals from the bed by touching on the mental threads that
connected them. Then the thought occurred to her she hadn't really
had a chance to train with Alexius lately.

Hello?

I'm here, Alexius answered.

Where's here?

Outside your door, actually.

Night shift?

Early-morning shift.

Can we go for a run and practice?

Absolutely.

Thali snuck out of her room into their common area, and when she
creaked the door open, she found three surprised guards and a smiling
Alexius.

"Good morning, Your Highness. Is there something the matter?" One of Elric's guards stepped forward.

"No, no problem. I woke early, so I'd like to go for a run."

"Very well, Your Highness." Nasir smiled, readjusting his uniform so he could move a little more freely.

As she opened the door wider, Indi and Ana walked through. Elric's guards took a step back, surprise on their faces. The tiger dipped into a stretch and yawned. Thali even saw a couple wide eyes as they stared at her teeth. Stifling a giggle, Thali strode purposefully through the hallways, letting Alexius lead her to the front courtyard.

"Shall we run to the training rings?" Alexius asked.

Thali grinned and broke into a jog. Alexius and Nasir brought up the rear. They'd exited out the front of the palace, so Alexius clearly planned to jog around the sprawling palace to the back to get to the practice field. Indi put them all to shame as she stretched out and ran a few steps before shortening and slowing her strides to match their pace. When they arrived at the training field, Thali was surprised to see a couple dozen people there already, mostly guards up early or finishing their shifts. They all froze as she walked up with Indi and Ana.

They all started to bow. Then, one man approached them. His almost white-blond hair gave his identity away. "Your Highness, may I introduce myself? I am Master Spencer Quinto. Is there anything I can assist you with?"

"Do you have a practice sword I may borrow for the hour?" Thali felt unnerved at all the eyes watching her.

"Yes, of course," Master Spencer replied. He waved, and another man brought a wooden sword to Master Spencer, who in turn presented it to Thali.

"Is there rhyme or reason to how you operate that I should know about? Or is there a space out of the way where we can spar?" Thali kept her voice sweet and unassuming, hoping there was enough authority in it not to invite questioning.

"Ahh ..." Master Spencer seemed at a loss for words when a familiar mop of light-blond hair jogged toward her.

Isaia bowed to her before nodding to Alexius and Nasir. "Your Highness, it would be my honor to practice with you. Over here, if it pleases you." Isaia led her and her entourage to a space on the side of the field.

Thali relaxed. "It's good to see you, Isaia."

"As it is you, Your Highness."

"Isaia, please, when it's only us, please address me as Thali."

"Of course, Thali. I assume you'd like to spar like we used to?"

Thali nodded. "Though I have to think I'm a little rusty after the weeks off."

Isaia nodded. Alexius and Nasir took up their protective positions, and Thali stretched and ran through a couple drills before she turned back to Isaia. Her body wasn't quite what it used to be, but already, she felt more herself than she had yesterday.

Thali ignored the crowd that had gathered to watch her and Isaia as they circled each other with their wooden swords. She was grateful Isaia had stepped up and she hadn't had to explain what she'd wanted to the surprised-looking Master Spencer.

"Spencer is my uncle," Isaia said as if in response to the question in her eyes.

"Ah."

"He's not used to seeing royalty behave so ... well, normally." Isaia tried to explain.

"Doesn't Elric come down here?"

"His Highness has private lessons with my uncle, usually in a private room or in the royal courtyard."

"Ah, so I'm an oddity." Thali nodded as she returned his blow with a twist and strike of her own.

"Not at all. A fresh breath of air is always welcome," Isaia said. Then he picked up the pace, and Thali was pleased she could keep up. He stepped it up again and disarmed Thali. A smothered gasp came from the gathered crowd. They must have expected Isaia to lose on purpose.

"Getting rusty, I see. Don't think this means you're off the hook later today." Tariq stepped through the crowd and picked up her wooden practice sword on his way to her.

"Thank you, Isaia. I'll see you again tomorrow morning." She nodded her head and Isaia bowed before leaving.

"Can we start our meeting now?" Tariq asked. At her nod, he handed her the practice sword and grabbed his own. "I'm not going to take it easy on you. Auntie wouldn't like it." He raised his eyebrow in challenge.

Thali smiled. "I wouldn't expect you to."

They exchanged blows until Thali knew she'd have bruises from the many flat blows Tariq had smacked her with. She was about to call it quits when she saw Daylor and Tilton at the edge of the gathered crowd. Wondering at first why she'd drawn such a crowd, she eventually decided they were probably all there to watch Tariq. His fighting style was much different from their own and always drew attention.

When she stopped to look up at them, the crowd started to applaud. Before Tilton or Daylor could say anything, Master Spencer stepped forward and bowed his head. "Your Highness, you are a great warrior. We would be honored any time you would like to hone your skills here."

Thali nodded, brushing the sweat from her brow. Tariq came over and put his arm on her shoulder, something that surprised Master Spencer even more.

Tilton finally coughed and Thali looked up. He tapped the sheet of paper in front of him, and she realized she was probably very late for something.

"See you later, Lili," Tariq said as he smacked her shoulder with his wooden blade on her way out. She waved at him while rushing off with Daylor and Tilton.

The next afternoon, Elric found Thali staring at the pink walls of one of their personal rooms. She had a rare few hours to herself.

"I know. There are a lot of rooms for just us." Elric threw his hands up.

"That's not what I was thinking, though you and I each have a closet and an office, and we have separate and common audience rooms, plus our bedroom. So you're right, it is a lot of rooms. But what is this room in particular for?"

"This is our private common room."

"I know, but what do we generally use it for?"

"We use it when we dine together or do something together but privately."

"Why wouldn't we just use our common audience room? There's no one there when we don't want them to be."

"I'm not sure exactly." Elric straightened his vest after buttoning it. He'd taken his vest off to relax while he enjoyed a rare quiet tea with Thali.

"Can I redecorate?" Thali looked up him hopefully.

"I would love that." Elric kissed her on the forehead before leaving Thali to stare again at the mostly bare pink walls.

She finally had a few hours to herself and summoned Tilton and Daylor, who arrived shortly after Elric had gone. They must have been nearby. "I'm going to need your help."

"Always at your service, Thali." Daylor winked.

They worked as quickly as they could, hauling heavy boxes into the room and dragging heavy furniture out.

Finally, the three sat on a trio of benches placed in a triangle in the middle of the room, admiring their work on the walls.

"Do you think His Highness was expecting this when he said you could redecorate?" Tilton looked around at all the gleaming metal.

"Well, he said I could do what I liked ... sort of," Thali replied.

Mia walked by the open doorway then, stopping and walking backward before turning around slowly. She stepped into the room and looked around, eyes wide.

"He said I could redecorate," Thali said, throwing her hands up in defense before Mia could say anything.

"Your Highness, we're all in here!" Mia called over her shoulder. She covered her mouth with her hand, obviously trying to hide a laugh. A moment later, Elric walked in.

His eyes grew wide too, and he spun around where he stood, only a few feet into the room.

Thali had hung her collection of weapons all over the pink walls of their private common room. She'd cleared the furniture but for a few chairs along the edges of the room and three benches in the middle.

"Did I get transported to the armory?" Elric's eyes were still wide as he took in all the shining metal that reflected his surprise back at him.

"You said I could redecorate. Plus, now we have a personal space to work on our combat skills."

"I thought you were going to change this room into a ...." his words disappeared as he looked around before finally shaking his head. His brilliant smile returned suddenly. "I should have known better. I don't even know what most of these are." Elric walked over to a pair of long, hooked swords. The tips curved back like a sharp cane handle, and on each hilt were raised crescent blades, protecting the wielder's hands. The only safe place to hold the sword was on the leather-wrapped grip beneath the crescent blades. And that wasn't all. The hilt of each sword tapered into long, pointy, talon-like daggers at the end.

"It's all sharp edges." He pointed to it, looking a little scared. "Who needs this many sharp edges? And what on earth is the hooked end for?"

"Those are tiger-head hooked blades. The back can be used like a sword or a dagger. The blades are for slashing and blocking, and the hook can grab an opponent's weapon. Plus, when you hook them together as one, you can extend your reach," Thali explained.

"Who are you trying to slice? You or your opponent?" Elric looked stunned. He walked over to another odd weapon barely larger than a throwing star that began with a small hilt and ended in a crescent again. Brilliantly honed dagger tips of varying sizes punctuated the short distance, top and bottom, between the hilt and the moon-shaped end. "And this?"

"That's a *mambele*."

"And what's it for?" Elric's face had relaxed some, but his brows were still raised high in amazement.

"It was a gift from a tribesman. It's for throwing or close combat. The curves are to help wrench a shield away from your opponent." Thali grinned, amused.

"I cut myself just putting it up there, Your Highness. I wouldn't suggest playing with it." Daylor looked balefully at his wrapped arm.

"Oh, I don't plan to touch any of those things." Elric looked at Daylor. "I'm sorry you cut your arm though. I assume a healer has seen to you?"

Daylor nodded, and the three friends took that as an excuse to leave. They said their good nights, bowed, and left the prince and princess alone.

"Are you mad?" Thali asked. She sat on the bench hugging her knees. This room made her feel more at home.

Elric smiled at her. "No. I'm not." He crossed the space between them and sat down next to her, pulling Thali into his lap. He kissed the top of her head as she curled up into him. "I am surprised though. But in a good way. I think it's all beautiful. They're as beautiful as paintings."

"I think so too."

"You have to be patient with me. I've had my life spelled out for me since I was born. Everyone always told me I'd grow up, marry a beautiful woman, make her my princess, have children, become king. No one ever told me I'd fall in love with the most unique, wonderful woman in the world and she'd surprise me constantly."

"I know I'm not what everyone expects. I like pretty dresses and some of the other princess things, but I can't just wear dresses forever. I think I'd go crazy." She felt his lips curl into a smile on her head.

"I know. I don't mind if you wear pants or vests or shirts or decorate our private common rooms like an armory. I chose you as my partner in this crazy life. I knew you'd shake things up a bit, but I think the kingdom needs it."

"Are you sure Lady Gabrielle wouldn't have made a better princess?"

Elric sighed and thought a moment before responding. "Lady Gabrielle is a fine lady. But she is *boring*, and I can't stand her nasally voice. Plus, she'd never have decorated this room as well as you have."

Thali smiled and squeezed Elric tightly.

Chapter Thirty-Five

T HE NEXT MORNING, THALI missed breakfast but did get to her first meeting on time. Her stomach grumbled, and she had a difficult time focusing and keeping her smile on her face as she greeted yet another foreign lord. Thankfully, recognizing Thali's arms would blossom into bruises after sparring with Tariq, Mia had dressed her in long shirt sleeves, a voluminous skirt, and a corset-style vest. It was still a gown, but it was a far cry from the fluffy princess dress she'd worn yesterday, so she felt more like herself.

The lord and lady from the far north seemed surprised to see her dressed as she was.

"Your Highness." Lord and Lady Duncan swept into a grand bow as the doors closed behind Thali. Lord Duncan was a corpulent man with a round belly and rosy cheeks, and his wife was shorter and rounder but had the warmest smile.

"Lord and Lady Duncan, how kind it was of you to travel all this way to celebrate my nuptials." Thali plastered on a smile and dipped her head.

Lord Duncan clasped his hands behind his back. "It is so kind of Your Highness to note our attendance. We were happy to represent our lands and witness your happy union. It has been five years since we last saw you?"

"Yes. That's a good memory you have there, my lord."

"I remember, when you were only a wee lass, we warned you to stay out of the moat around the castle for fear you would be eaten by the crocodiles. But then one day, I came out with your father for some air and just happened to look down and saw you giggling while you sat on one! You have always had such a way with animals, Your Highness."

Thali wondered if he suspected she had magic, but she couldn't sense any ill intention or suspicion, only genuine reminiscence. Again.

"Yes, my lord, crocodiles are often misunderstood. All carnivores are, really." Thali smiled, and the northern nobles didn't comment further. The nice thing about being a princess was no one really liked to argue with you.

Thali sat down, so the couple followed suit. Thali had always liked them and scolded herself inwardly for not being more generous with her thoughts. They had always been warm and friendly when her family went to trade with them.

Lord Duncan's smile grew as he rose suddenly again as if he'd forgotten something. Isaia took one step forward from his silent position at the door.

"Don't you worry yourself, laddie. I wouldn't harm your princess. She's one of my favorites, you know." He winked at Isaia, making Thali realize how few people she had met had even acknowledged her guards' presence.

Lady Duncan spoke up. "Dear, perhaps you should show her what we've brought."

"Yes, dear, thank you. I was just about to." He went over to a little table where a cloth was covering what Thali had long assumed was a gift for her.

"Rou—" Lord Duncan coughed. "Your Highness, I remember, when you were a wee little lassie, how much you enjoyed hearing about the many legends of our lands. And then when you were an older lass, you loved hearing the ballads our country is famous for. So, we've worked tirelessly and recorded all our known ballads and legends for you in these books." He pulled the cloth from the table, revealing a large pile of beautifully bound leather books. There were even small gems embedded in the leather. They were breathtaking.

Thali's eyes went wide, and she rose to go look at the books. Taking one gently in her hands, she opened it and saw a listing of the various ballads and stories. Some she recognized and some she didn't.

"Lord and Lady Duncan, this is a great honor. Thank you."

Lady Duncan's whole posture relaxed when she saw Thali's face. "We were worried it wouldn't be a fine enough gift for you, Your Highness."

"I assure you, Lady Duncan, these are wonderful, thoughtful, and very much appreciated. I'm grateful to you and your country for sharing your stories with us."

"All yer favorites, Your Highness, are in the purple book there." Lord Duncan pointed at it.

Thali picked up the purple book, shifting some of the others on the table to get to it. She opened it gently and saw that indeed, all her favorite legends and ballads were there.

"These will sit in my personal library. Thank you." She put the book down and nodded at Daylor, who hovered at the edge of the room. He moved forward to collect the books, looking a little perplexed.

Lady Duncan put a hand to her chest. "Your Highness, you honor us and our country. Thank you." She bowed her head.

"Come, Lady Duncan, what news do you have of your country?" Thali smiled kindly, for she was thrilled with her new books and truly wanted to hear all about their northern lands. She thought it funny, when she looked around, that Alexius was not here as he had claimed to be from that country when they had first met.

Lord Duncan answered in his wife's place. "Well, Your Highness, there has been a mess of hunting trouble lately."

Thali, who was used to only hearing of the good news in various countries, was a little surprised to hear the opposite.

"Dear, we shouldn't be worrying Her Highness with our little troubles." Lady Duncan looked sharply at her husband.

"Please, Lord Duncan, do tell me more. I've not heard of the troubles plaguing your country, and while I cannot promise assistance, I would at the very least like to hear of them. Especially if it concerns the animals of your country. They are some of my favorites." Thali smiled kindly. She wanted badly to hear of real news. So far, it had seemed to her that princesses only heard of the latest fashion trends and newest popular colors.

"Well, lassie, I mean, Your Highness," Lord Duncan looked nervously at his wife, but then to Thali. "It started a couple years ago, but there have been fewer animals to hunt. Hunters are coming up empty. At first, we thought it might be cyclic, that the animals just needed to replenish their populations, and maybe a round of bad luck. But then the hunters too started going missing, and those that do come back are saying it be eerily quiet in the forests."

"And what do the hunters think the cause might be?" Thali leaned in, but corrected her posture when she noticed what she was doing.

"The hunters think there is something new in the forests. Something bigger eating the others and scaring everyone else into silence." Lord Duncan looked at his hands, seemingly unable to look Thali in the eye. He shrunk into himself as if he expected a blow.

"And Lord Duncan, what do *you* think it is?" Thali prodded gently. She had seen enough magical creatures to know the hunters could be right.

"I've heard of some very strange beasts in the last few years, Your Highness, and I fear the hunters might be right. There is something bigger, something unusual, in our great forest that has yet to show itself," Lord Duncan said quietly.

A knock on the door made all three jump. Tilton poked his head into the room. "Excuse me, Your Highness, but your next meeting awaits you."

"Well, Lady and Lord Duncan, thank you for sharing this news with me. I will think on it and let you know if I discover anything important in relation to it. Please feel free to write me of any additional news and keep me updated. I look forward to seeing you again at supper tonight." Thali rose and nodded her head as Lord and Lady Duncan also rose, then bowed deeply.

"You honor us, Your Highness." Lord Duncan bowed lower than was necessary and Thali blushed at the honor.

CHAPTER THIRTY-SIX

THALI STOOD FIDGETING WITH her dress, smoothing the skirts for the hundredth time.

"You'll be great." Elric leaned over to whisper in her ear.

"So great that we can skip this?" Thali asked. She was hoping to avoid being presented to the court nobles as long as she could.

Elric patted her arm. "Don't you want to see our portraits? I promise, it'll be fun." Thali had almost forgotten about the portrait she'd had to sit for during last year's final exam when they'd landed in Kadaloona. Daylor had teased her for months after.

Thali narrowed her eyes. The only people who ever said court politics was fun were the prince or the king. It had never been fun for her, the outsider, the strange-looking one, the only one with dark, dark hair, gray eyes, and nonporcelain skin.

The doors opened suddenly, and Thali took a deep breath. She grasped his upper arm and walked a half step behind him as she followed him into the room, just as Sera had taught her. She didn't keep her gaze averted though; she brought her head up. If she was going to face a room of enemies, she would do so head on.

The room was filled with dashing men in tailcoats and ladies in pretty dresses. They were all younger than she expected, most close to her age or perhaps a bit older. As she and Elric walked along, the ladies nodded their heads and curtsied. The men bowed at the waist.

Elric pulled her to one side and began introducing Thali to this lord and that lady. Most were either freshly married or still single, and by the time they'd greeted the twentieth group, Thali had forgotten their names. Suddenly, a familiar voice to their left caught her attention. She turned and saw Bannick standing with Lady Gabrielle.

Elric followed Thali's gaze, and he smiled when he saw Ban. The prince waved him over, though Ban did not look at Thali as he made his way over to them.

Thali clenched her jaw. What was he doing here? Why was he wearing such fine clothes?

"Lord Bannick, I believe you've already met Princess Routhalia," Elric said. His eyes sparkled. "And Thali, you remember Lady Gabrielle? Lady Gabrielle is Lord Bannick's sister."

Thali's jaw was so tense she could get no words out. Elric didn't notice as he just laughed and grasped Ban's shoulder. "Ban here told me to keep his secret. He wanted to go learn about merchanting to better serve his seat on the trade council. I thought three years was a long time to learn about trade, but when this man wants to learn something, he dedicates himself to it." Elric clapped him on the back.

Thali's fist closed and twitched as the blood *whooshed* in her ears. She tucked her hands in her skirts. It was taking everything to restrain herself from punching Ban for deceiving her. Lords were supposed to be civil and gentlemanly, but his words back in their first year had been far from that. His attitude hadn't much improved since then, either. She'd once thought they were friends, but she couldn't have been more wrong.

Elric still hadn't noticed how she was feeling as he continued to converse with Ban. The poor blacksmith had just transformed in front of her eyes. He stood taller and prouder as he spoke with the prince. And arrogantly. He oozed arrogance. She certainly hadn't noticed that before.

"It seems you really enjoy surprises." Lady Gabrielle had wrapped Thali's arm around her own and was dragging her around the room as if they were the closest of friends. For her part, Thali was fighting the urge to punch everyone, so as soon as she neared the exit, she let go of Lady Gabrielle and ducked out, claiming she was going for some fresh air, and headed straight to her rooms. She didn't care that she hadn't even seen her portrait yet.

Freedom and relief rushed through Thali as she bustled out of the grand room. Just down the hall though, she ran into Tilton. He winked conspiratorially. "Feel like an adventure?" At her enthusiastic nod, he guided her up stairwells and down long hallways she was sure she hadn't even seen yet.

"Tilton, how do you know where you're going?" Thali finally asked.

"We were given a map and guided around once. I have a good memory for directions." Tilton led the way as Daylor appeared from a corridor and walked alongside Thali and her complement of guards that had hurried to trail them.

"So books, huh? I think I preferred the giant cheese wheel," Daylor commented as he kept pace with Thali.

"They wrote those books specifically for me. It's incredibly touching," Thali said as she grinned at Daylor and shoved him playfully.

They ascended another staircase, and Thali realized she needed to pay more attention to her physical fitness. She was a little out of breath as they reached the top.

"Where are we going?" Thali asked.

"To the roof," Tilton said.

He opened a heavy door, and the sun reflecting off the gray stones on the roof made her heart happy. Thali squinted and saw Tariq and Bree dressed in simple clothes.

"We're kidnapping you and going on an adventure." Bree ran up to her, linking arms with Thali.

"Thank goodness! Where are we going?" Thali asked with a smile. Her shoulders dropped as she exhaled, her body realizing it didn't have to deal with the formalities anymore.

"You'll see. I promise it's not far because we could only steal so much time, with Elric's help," Bree whispered in her ear.

"Elric knows?"

Bree nodded and smiled.

It warmed Thali's heart knowing Elric had foreseen how her presentation to the court would turn out and what she would need.

Tariq spoke with her guards, and she saw Isaia nod. Bree led Thali to the other side of the roof, then down a hidden staircase and into the forest. Not far in, a quiet clearing beheld a team of horses waiting. Obviously, her friends had planned this thoroughly, and her full complement of guards would be riding with them. A small part of Thali, though, wanted to jump on Arabelle and run away with her, away from all the watching eyes.

Instead, the trio rode off together, Tariq and Bree on either side of Thali, and her animals ran ahead. Thali was touched that someone had fetched Indi and Ana. The thundering of horse hooves behind her made her imagine she was being chased by bandits for a split second. Arabelle, sensing her moment of exhilaration then, increased her gait and pulled ahead of the other two horses.

Eventually, Thali pulled her horse to a stop as they arrived in a spacious, open meadow, where Ana and Indi had found a rock to sun themselves on. A picnic had been set up in the shade, and Thali grinned as she waited for Tari and Bree to catch up to her.

In moments they did, and after they'd dismounted, Bree pulled all the various food out of the basket as Tariq and Thali faced off in a little staff combat. The guards had set up a perimeter around the meadow, leaving them in relative privacy.

Bree had apparently packed a feast because Tariq and Thali made it through a couple rounds before the basket was completely emptied. "All right, you two, stop hitting each other with sticks and come and sit down," she teased.

They obliged and came to sit on the blanket. Thali was happy just to look around and feel completely at ease for the first time in a long time.

Can you hear me, Lili? a voice yelled in her brain.

"You don't have to yell," Thali said out loud to Tariq. She was feeling sorry for making Alexius deal with her yelling at him for the first few months she was learning how to converse telepathically.

"Was I yelling? How do I not yell?" Tariq asked before popping a grape in his mouth.

"I think of it like a feather touching the strand connecting us," Thali said. *Like this,* she said in her mind to Tariq.

How is this? Tariq tilted his head.

Much better.

"Interesting. I sent it to you like a teeny little breeze." Tariq beamed with pride at his accomplishment.

"Enough magic for now." Bree narrowed her eyes, looking from Thali to Tariq. "We're supposed to be giving Thali a break, not working her harder."

They shared the food between them and laughed and conversed like they used to when they didn't have so many titles weighing on them.

Bree and Thali packed up the leftovers of their picnic while Tariq played with Indi. Thali felt wonderfully refreshed from her time off and tried to push away the thought of her afternoon full of formal meetings.

"I wish Elric was here with us." Thali sighed as she realized how long it had been since she'd had a real conversation with her husband.

Bree finished putting the leftover fruit away, then folded her hands in her lap. "When you were ill, he didn't leave your side for quite a long time. And whenever he did leave, he was probably trying to find some way to help you. I'm sure he has a lot to catch up on."

"I know. And I know I'm whining, but I feel like everyone expects me to be someone I'm not."

"Thali, you're doing very well. Better than you probably realize. Just be careful of how many changes you put in place and how quickly." Bree looked up at Thali, all the while still folding the now empty cloths in her lap.

"What do you mean?" Thali glanced up too, but she had to stop wrapping the leftover breads.

Bree nodded at Thali. "The way you're dressed. The combat lessons. You're unlike most ladies, especially ones from court. The shock to them all will be too great if you change things too quickly. Try one thing at a time. You'll get less resistance."

"I don't know how you stand it, Bree. It's like they expected a whole other person when I showed up at the castle, like marriage would magically transform me into a typical princess." Thali caught sight of her hands and realized she was tearing a piece of bread to shreds.

"I grew up in it, Thali." Bree put a hand over her friend's. "I've had a lifetime to learn the rules and either find ways around them or discover what I can like about them."

"The ladies here aren't even as open as you are. And when I showed up for combat practice the first time, everyone looked at me like I had two heads." Thali slumped her shoulders.

Bree raised her eyebrows at her. "And yet, from what I hear, you earned their respect quite quickly."

"True, but those gowns, they're suffocating. I can't wear those all the time. I have to be comfortable in my own skin, don't I? And what if because I do that, Elric's family decides I'm not what they wanted after all?"

"Thali." Bree moved closer, taking both of Thali's hands in hers. "You are facing centuries of tradition. Of course it's all new and different to you. I didn't say don't change at all. I said only if you shock them all with too many changes at once, you'll only meet opposition. But I think you're good for them. They need change."

"And what if the royal family decides they don't want me? What if Elric decides he's made a mistake?" Thali's brows knit together.

Bree laughed. "Thali, Elric adores you. He will not cast you aside. Did you know you have so many foreign dignitaries here, the palace had to build a new wing for guests before your wedding? I don't think they've ever had this many visitors who wanted an audience with a royal family member. The king and queen have noticed your familiarity with so many dignitaries, and they admire it. I've seen it with my own two eyes."

"Wait. You mean to tell me I'm the only one with all these meetings with foreign dignitaries?"

Bree laughed again. "Yes, silly. Didn't you know?"

"No! I guess I never asked, either." Thali pouted. What had the king and queen been doing all this time? What had Elric been so busy with?

"Lili! Get over here. We have time for one more sparring match!" Tariq waved her over.

Thali looked at Bree with relief. "Thank you, Bree. I'm really grateful for your friendship."

Bree bowed her head. "And I am honored to be your friend." She patted Thali's hand, then looked at her fiancée and shook her head. "You better get out there before he hurts himself."

Thali grabbed her staff and ran across the meadow to spar with Tariq. She enjoyed sparring in such a large space as it allowed them to move around easier. Trading blows and dancing around each other, they found themselves on the other side of the meadow when suddenly a shriek from a large bird startled them. Before they could look up, a shadow descended over them, followed closely by a great winged beast with the head of a falcon. Its four-legged lizard body landed horizontally, its bulb-tipped, spiked tail swishing angrily over the grass, making it look an awful lot like a flail. Thali watched their guards split up, half running to her and Tariq and the other half creating an offensive formation in front of the giant lizard-bird.

"Can you see in its mind?" Tariq had positioned himself next to her.

Blinking furiously, she searched her mind, bolstering her defensive walls. She saw it appear in her mind as a yellow sparkling thread but could not touch upon it like she normally could with other creatures.

"I can't get in," Thali said as the sky filled with shrieks and shadows before dozens of smaller lizard-falcons the size of chickens came crashing to the ground.

"Bree, we have to get to Bree." Tariq looked panicked.

Thali nodded and shouted, "To Lady Ambrene!" as she and Tariq used their staffs to fight through the lizard-birds so they could get to Bree.

Thali was glad to have Tariq at her back as they sent the little lizard-birds flying. It was strange watching their forked tongues shoot out of their beaks. When the two made it halfway across the meadow, Isaia joined them, handing Thali his short sword as he wielded his longer one. Tariq had pulled his dagger out of his boot, and they began slashing their way to the other side of the meadow. Their offensive line grew as they collected more and more guards on their way. But they still couldn't move as quickly as they wanted to. There were just too many of the lizard-falcons in their way. The largest one remained still, watching the scene from afar.

Once they were surrounded by all the guards that had rushed to her and Tariq, Thali stepped behind Tariq. *I'm going to try to reach into his mind again*, Thali said in her mind. They could see Bree now, protected by only a half dozen guards as rows of lizard-falcons surrounded them.

He nodded and she grabbed the back of his belt as their guards surrounded them. Thali searched in her mind, found the brightest yellow sparkling strand, and pushed. She was banging on the door, trying to get in when she felt Tariq tense and quicken his pace. By the time Thali had begun reaching into the largest bird's mind, Tariq had slaughtered dozens of the little lizard-falcons. But as Thali opened her eyes, the ones separating her and Bree started to pile on top of each other to create a wall. Suddenly, they all melted into one bigger lizard-falcon about half the size of the first one.

Suddenly, the first giant creature shrieked, leaped forward, and dipped his head over the newest lizard-bird. It emerged with Bree in its beak. With a single flap of his wings, he was airborne.

"Bree!" Tariq shouted and threw his dagger into the creature's shoulder. It shrieked out in pain, dropping Bree as it turned away. She started to plummet to the ground, and in desperation, Thali grasped the sparkling yellow strand of the newly formed lizard-falcon in her mind and seized it. She willed the creature to fly up, catch Bree gently, then land and release her. Once it had fulfilled the task, Thali let go of the sparkly thread in her mind, and as she did, the creature melted back into little lizard-birds. The largest, wounded bird disappeared into the clouds, the smaller ones joining it in the air and amalgamating into a giant creature again. Thali rushed over to Bree, Tariq right behind her.

Tariq dropped to his knees. There was blood all over Bree, and it took them a moment to realize it was coming from her arm. A long gash stretched from her upper arm almost all the way down to her wrist. Thali untucked her shirt and started to rip it into strips.

Alexius, bring a healer, quickly. Lady Ambrene is injured. Thali hoped he would arrive quickly.

I'm coming.

Tariq cradled Bree's head in his lap and brushed her hair away from her face, carefully tucking it behind her ear as Thali quickly went to work wrapping bandages around her arm to keep the flesh together. A guard handed her strips of his own shirt when she ran out of what she could use of her own. The seeping blood was slowing when Thali heard hoofbeats. Alexius pushed through the circle of guards and looked from Thali to Tariq and Bree before furrowing his brow.

"The healer is on his way," Alexius said out loud. *I can help her, if you let me.* Tariq's eyes widened, and Thali knew he had heard Alexius too. Tariq nodded. Alexius put his hand over the bandages at Bree's wrist, and as Thali kept a reassuring hand on Bree's shoulder, she could feel the magic glowing over her friend's arm. After a few quiet moments, Alexius started pulling the bandages off as her old schoolmate, Jethro, arrived and broke through the circle of guards surrounding them. Thali looked at the newly exposed gash. While once it had reached from Bree's shoulder to her wrist, it was now half the size.

Jethro leaned over and poured a liquid from his bag all over the open wound. "This will prevent infection." He then took a salve and smeared it generously over the cut. Where the original cut would have been life threatening, this one was not nearly as dangerous. When he was done, he wiped his hands on a cloth and carefully took out some bandages. After pouring a clear liquid on them, he placed them on the cut before taking out another long, clean bandage and wrapping Bree's arm. "What happened?" Jethro asked. Thali was impressed with how calm he was.

A guard Thali didn't yet know explained what had happened.

Jethro nodded. "Lady Ambrene will be all right. We'll need to watch to make sure she has no internal injuries though. I will personally change the bandage twice a day, and she will need to rest for the next few days," he said, tucking in the end of the bandage and looking up at Tariq.

"Is she okay to be moved?" Tariq's eyes filled with concern.

"Yes, Your Highness. I sent a message for a carriage to come this way to help bring her back. It should be arriving shortly."

"Thank you." Tariq looked helplessly at Thali. She understood her best friend needed her to take charge. He was a natural leader and she usually followed his lead, but when it came to Bree, he was useless.

Thali rose and the ring of guards parted. The carriage Jethro had summoned was racing toward them from the south. She led Jethro out of the circle to give Tari and Bree a moment alone together. "Jethro. It's good to see you again. I didn't realize you worked at the palace now."

"I am only here temporarily, Your Highness." He bowed his head.

"Please, Jethro, we're old friends. Call me Thali."

He smiled as he gave her a sidelong glance. "That's very gracious of you. I'm here visiting my uncle, helping him while the palace is full of guests. As soon as it calms down, I'll be back on a ship bound for Cerisa, so I can learn more and gain more experience."

"I'm so glad you're here for now. If there's anything I can help you with, Jethro, please let me know. I'm immensely grateful to you for your skills."

Jethro took that as an opportunity to launch into an explanation about the liquids he'd used on Bree's wound and how he'd developed them during his travels over the last few years.

Thali nodded absentmindedly. She was happy for Jethro. In her first year, his skills had saved her then-captain, Isaia, the same Isaia who was now standing guard behind her. At the same time, she wondered if they'd had a chance to catch up.

When Jethro paused in his medical explanation, Thali bid him farewell and returned to Tariq to help him as he carried Bree to the carriage. The couple would have to travel back to the palace the long way now that they weren't on horseback. Tariq looked like a lost puppy, so though she'd been planning to ride Arabelle back to the palace, Thali decided to climb into carriage with them.

She turned to her guards and said, "We'll veer around the forest. Alexius, if you'll take our horses back and prepare the side entrance closest to their rooms for our arrival, we'll meet you there."

Alexius nodded and Jethro followed, helping him round up the horses. As she looked at Alexius's bright-red hair, she wondered how much faster he'd have traveled if he had taken his dragon form.

In the carriage, the friends rode in silence for a time.

Tariq finally spoke in hushed tones. "Thali, you controlled it, right? Made it catch Bree and set her gently on the ground?"

Thali nodded.

"Why couldn't you control the bigger one? And what did they want?"

"I ... I don't know." Thali had shoved the attack to the back of her mind, Bree's care being at the forefront of her thoughts. She looked up then and saw, for a brief moment, that Tariq blamed her. Anger flashed in his eyes, and he clenched his teeth. When he looked back down at Bree, Thali felt him biting down the words bubbling to the surface of his mind as he reeled with the shock of Bree's injury.

Tariq tenderly ran his fingers through Bree's hair and stroked her knee with the thumb of his other hand. She still hadn't woken up, though they could see her chest moving up and down.

Thali looked away, not wanting to intrude on the private moment—or risk seeing Tariq's anger at her again. Why hadn't she been able to get into the creature's head? She hadn't known what to do when she'd come up against that wall. It was clear she needed more training because she was useless to even protect her friends from those creatures.

Now, they'd harmed one of her best friends and she didn't even know why.

Thali got lost in her mind, drowning in the spiral of her thoughts. As soon as the carriage came to a stop, the door sprung open, and Tariq leaped down like a cat with Bree in his arms. His long legs took him quickly to the side door and he disappeared inside the palace. Thali sat in the carriage, hanging her head and feeling suddenly exhausted and very, very sad.

"Rou?" Thali looked up to see Rommy sticking his head into the carriage.

Thali tried to force a smile on her face. "Rommy." She stood up slowly and let her brother help her out of the carriage. Her guards had dismounted and stood waiting for her outside the carriage. Rommy, likely sensing her exhaustion as only a brother could, put an arm around her shoulders, gripping them tight and holding her up.

"Let's get you to your rooms, shall we?" Rommy quietly distracted her with stories about some of the people he'd been meeting at the palace as Thali fought to keep her face neutral. Suddenly, Rommy scooped her up and carried her to her rooms. The exhaustion took over so fast that she fell asleep on the couch the moment Rommy laid her down.

When she woke up, Elric was next to her, they lay in bed, and it was dark. His arm rested on her waist, and she realized she was in her nightclothes. The last thing she remembered was being in the carriage and walking with Rommy back to the palace.

Thali felt wide awake now. She blinked and knew she wouldn't be able to go back to sleep, so she carefully extracted herself from Elric's embrace, taking a moment to sweep his hair out of his eyes. She kissed his forehead and wiggled away from Indi and Ana, letting her toes reach for the fluffy carpet at the side of the bed. After grabbing an overcoat, Thali peeked into her closet. It must be late if even Mia had gone to bed. Tightening her overcoat, she tiptoed into the common room, surprised to see Rommy sleeping on the couch.

Thali tiptoed into the shared dining space and opened a few cabinets, hoping to find some remnants of something to eat. She must have missed supper and her stomach, now awake, had started to growl. Finally giving up, she stuck her head out of their rooms to find Nasir on duty. He looked startled but relieved to see her.

"Back on night duty?" Thali asked.

Nasir nodded. "It was Jaida's night off, so double duty for me."

Thali smiled. She had grown very fond of Nasir. He took everything in stride and was always smiling. His skills as a warrior were on par with Tariq's, so she was still trying to convince the guard to spar with her.

"Are you well? Do you need anything?" he asked.

"I'm all right, thank you, Nasir. I hate to trouble you, but is there any way I could get a cold plate of supper, or whatever they might have in the kitchen? Even hard tack. I'm famished." Her stomach growled fiercely as if punctuating her point.

Nasir smiled and chuckled. "I'll see what I can do." He nodded at another guard further down the hall, who peeled himself off the wall and quietly ducked into a doorway.

"Thanks, Nasir." She closed the door gently.

"You always did love food." Rommy sat up on the couch. His clothes were rumpled, and his hair stood up at odd angles.

Thali smiled and sat in the chair across from him. "I'm sorry I woke you."

Rommy waved her off. "I'm glad you did. This couch is awfully uncomfortable. I can already feel my neck complaining."

"Why are you sleeping here, anyway?"

"Checking up on my little sister, of course. Though Elric wasn't too pleased." Rommy rubbed the back of his neck, tilting his head to the side.

"What happened?" Thali asked.

"I think you were in shock. You practically fell asleep on your feet, so your guards filled us in on what happened." Rommy yawned.

It all came back to Thali then, and she looked down at her knees. "It's all my fault, Rommy."

"What is? Do you mean to tell me you sent for giant lizard-falcons to come attack your best friends?" Rommy sat back. "Because that is some extreme training."

Thali managed to crack a smile for a moment before she lost the will. "I've been doing all this training, yet I still can't do anything that matters. When it counted today, I was helpless, and I shouldn't have been."

The couch creaked as Rommy stood up and came to sit on the edge of the table in front of her upholstered chair. "Hey, little Rou, you can't put this much pressure on yourself." He grabbed at one of her little toes, shaking it gently. "In the last two weeks, you've become a royal princess, brought together countries and kingdoms that haven't even spoken to each other in years, and you just fought off two enormous lizard-falcons." Rommy raised a single eyebrow and continued. "I'd say you're accomplishing quite a bit."

Thali smiled, wiggling her toe free of Rommy's grasp. "But I could have saved Bree from getting hurt at all if I just could have gotten through to that lizard-falcon thing."

Rommy sighed, sitting up straight as he glanced at the door, his mouth pressed into a hard line.

"What? Rommy, tell me." Thali knew her brother well. She knew the look on his face meant he was holding something back, something he thought their parents might blame him for later.

"Please, Rommy, we're not children anymore. I can make my own decisions." Thali sat up and put her hand over her brother's.

He let out a deep breath. "There's a way for you to get the training you want."

Thali's eyes grew wide. That was the last thing she'd expected him to say. "How?"

"The reason your training is going so slowly is because you're not surrounded by magic. Most magic users are trained in the other world, Alexius's world. Training in Etciel strengthens you instead of weakens you. If you were to go there and train, say for a few months, you'd become a lot stronger a lot faster."

"A few months?" Thali looked toward her bedroom. She'd slid into a mountain of responsibility as princess, so how could she suddenly pack up and leave?

"I know, it's not convenient. Maybe you'd only need to be there a few weeks, in this world's time. I'm not sure how it works."

Thali's eyes narrowed. "How would we get there? Alexius said he couldn't go back. Otherwise, I would have come to visit you."

Rommy thought for a minute, staring at the books in the shelves behind Thali's chair. "There is one way. Aexie could get us through."

"But she's holding the ward protecting the castle."

"Alexius can stay and do that."

"But what about all the foreign dignitaries?"

"What about them? They'll wait a little longer for an audience with you."

"I should at least talk to Elric about it."

Rommy glanced at the door again. "Rou, Elric only wants what's best for you. Of course he'd want you to go train. Given how much you're dealing with as it is, he wouldn't begrudge you a few weeks."

"Wait, if Alexius is here, who will train me?"

"I'm sure Xerus would. He trained Alexius and Aexie." Rommy looked at the door a third time.

Thali raised her eyebrow. "Are you expecting someone?"

Rommy stood up, brushing his rumpled clothes with his hands. "You're expecting food." He smiled and moved to the bureau to grab paper and a quill.

"You want to leave now? Like right now?"

"We could wait a week, but what's the point? I know you, Rou. When you're determined to do something, you do it right away. You could write a letter to say what you need to, so why not leave now?"

Thali looked up at her brother. She thought of Tariq and winced. He was angry with her. Elric was busy anyway, and the other guests could wait. She thought of the suddenness of the attack that afternoon and felt a deep sense of urgency. Another attack could happen tomorrow, or tonight. She wanted to be trained properly so she could be useful as soon as possible.

Rommy came over to her, offering her the quill and paper.

She hadn't yet figured out exactly what was going on with her brother. She'd thought Xerus was perhaps keeping him hostage, but now her brother was here. Had Xerus let him come? She'd been surprised to see him at her wedding but still hadn't had the chance to ask how he had returned to her world. But this was her brother. She'd followed him around for the first sixteen years of her life and he'd always kept her safe, taught her, fought for her. Of all the people in the world, she trusted her brother completely. She nodded and took the quill and paper from him.

Elric,
I've gone to Alexius's world with Rommy to train magi-
cally. Alexius will keep the wards up to protect the castle.
Please take care of Indi, Bardo, and Ana. I want to
concentrate on this. I need to help you and the kingdom.
I'll be back in a few weeks.
Love always,
Thali

At the same time, Thali dove into her mind, wanting to check in with Alexius.

Alexius? she sent along their solid thread. But he didn't reply. She thought he must be asleep. Thali looked up then, startled to see Aexie standing on the other side of the room with Rommy.

Thali put the note on the table and walked over to Rommy and Aexie. "Should I change first?"

"We have clothes there," Rommy said. "Ready?"

Thali nodded. Aexie nodded a greeting, but her lips were pressed into a hard line, and her brows were knit together as she pointed a long purple nail at the wall and drew a small door. She pushed on the door and walked through without a sound. Rommy stepped through with one leg before offering Thali a hand. She put her hand in her brother's and turned around, looking at the common room she'd just started to call home. She would be useless to this kingdom if she wasn't trained.

She set her mouth in a determined line and took one step through Aexie's door. A knock on the main door made her turn her head, but Rommy pulled at her hand and she swallowed, turning back to follow him into the fog.

To keep up with my book news, sign up for my newsletter by clicking here or visiting: https://geni.us/CamillaTracynewsletter

A NOTE FROM THE AUTHOR

If you have read Soxkendi before this, or are re-reading this, please know that dragons can lie...Xenon can and does lie about certain elements of his past.

While Adanek's royal crest is black and red with a lion and dragon, Elric's family's crest is purple.

The creatures in this book were inspired by mythological creatures, with a heavy dash of my own imagination. I do have visual representations on my Instagram (@camilla_tracy), but please do send me your art!

Acknowledgements

Always first and foremost, thank YOU, dear reader, for picking up this book and taking the time to read. I hope you are entertained.

Thank you to my editor – Bobbi Beatty of Silver Scroll Services. There are so many things you do with my story, that I'm so incredibly grateful for, I could not express them all. But I am incredibly appreciative of your dedication, thoughts, ideas, and comments.

Thank you also to Lorna Stuber, not only for bringing attention to the details, but making me seriously think about commas and semi colons...

Thank you to the wonderful team at MiblArt who make the most beautiful covers. This cover was a concept for book two, but the moment I saw the dragon wrapped around her, I knew this was the cover for book three.

Thank you to my mom who has been a champion of my book and efforts, and has had her hand in the marketing too.

Thank you to my husband, Paul. This couldn't happen without your support in this crazy adventure.

Thank you to my friends and chosen family that continue to cheer me on.

Thank you to Thali and all my fictional characters. I can't wait for you to see where their adventures take them.

About the Author

Camilla is a lover of many mediums of storytelling. She loves to write strong heroines who can kick butt and find the love of their life. She always has projects on the go and loves to consume stories of all kinds—books, shows, movies, plays, amongst many others.

When she is not writing, Camilla is often found exploring animal behavior, crafting, drinking a hot beverage, and clicker training her animals.

Come visit her at CamillaTracy.com Or on instagram @camilla_tracy Or sign up for her newsletter by visiting: https://geni.us/CamillaTracynewsletter

Soxkendi

Cᴇɴᴛᴜʀɪᴇꜱ ʙᴇꜰᴏʀᴇ Aʟᴇxɪᴜꜱ ᴍᴇᴛ Thali...

It all started when my sister died. It broke my heart, and it set my family against me. I didn't exist to them for months because I reminded them of her ... and of what had happened. I was the salt in the wound that had cleaved all that was good and fun from their hearts.

Xerus, my eldest brother, tried his hardest not to ignore me, but the tension in his whole body when I was around was enough to tell me that I caused him more pain than anything else. My combat-training sessions with my next oldest brother, Jaxon, became rounds of silence punctuated only by grunts in response to my queries. Aexie, my next closest sibling, well, she left the room anytime I walked into one. So I laid low. I kept to myself and to my room, and that's when I discovered myself.

Did I mention I'm a dragon? I am the fifth born in my family. My father, Rixen, is the youngest son of the original twelve dragons. My mother, Elenex, is one of what we called "the wild ones." I spoke only to my parents for a hundred years after my sister's death. And then just when things were starting to look up—and my family was starting to include me again—life got worse than we ever could have imagined.

My father and mother were the only ones who didn't mind my presence, so I spent many a day with them in their throne room. There they would receive their guests, including the minor regional dragons. On this day, my training with Jaxon had taken longer than usual, so I strode in through a side door as my parents had already begun their public audience. I followed the flowing blues and pinks of the stone floor to the center, where the throne itself was outlined with a ribbon of gold. There were two seats: one for my father and one for my mother. My mother turned her head in my direction, and she nodded as I came up alongside her. I stayed standing as the next dragon came in. It was a caretaker of rare plants reporting that six of his dragonsbane plants had gone missing in the middle of the night.

"How many dragonsbane plants do you have?" my father, King Rixen, asked.

"I have only ten now. I had sixteen before. I have a license for each and a commission from the apothecary, Merwyn." The small brown dragon stayed low in his bow, obviously scared of repercussions.

"Do you know when they were stolen? Do you have any idea where they might be or who may have taken them?"

"No, Your Majesty. I know only that they went missing in the middle of the night, in the hours of pitchest black, for I was awake and watchful during the hours of light. I keep them locked in a separate greenhouse, one that is fortified and locked any time I am not inside. I have been applying for enchantments but have not yet received an answer."

"My apologies then." My father turned to me. "Alexius, go with this citizen forthwith and take note of the missing dragonsbane. Then please provide whatever enchantments are necessary—immediately," my father instructed.

I nodded and followed the little brown dragon out the main door and onto the rooftop courtyard.

"Brother," Xerus came around the corner as I exited the courtyard. "You may return. I will perform the enchantments."

My heart sank. I had been studying enchantments specifically for the last few years. However, I had to admit that Xerus was much better at them, so it made sense that he would do it if he was available, especially where dragonsbane was involved. I nodded and returned to the throne room. At my father's raised eyebrow, I leaned over to tell him Xerus had intercepted me and gone with the farmer.

He nodded and swished his tail, signaling we were ready for the next citizen.

A young purple dragon with yellow accents walked in with her head held high as if she was made of pure gumption. My heart stumbled and my breath hitched as she turned her attention to me. I stood a little taller next to my mother.

"Your Majesties, Your Highness." The dragon bowed and I couldn't take my eyes off her.

"What is your name, dragonling?" my mother, Queen Elenex, asked.

"My name is Brixelle. I've come today because my mother is sick, and we would ask for enchantments for our property so our labor could be eased."

Now it was my mother's turn to look at me. "Alexius, why don't you go with this young dragonette and provide her with the enchantments she needs?"

I only nodded because that was all I could manage while I told my feet to move one in front of the other as I followed Brixelle out.

"I am honored, Your Highness. Thank you," she said, dipping her head as she led the way out of the palace.

"The pleasure is all mine," I said. *Was that a stupid thing to say? I had been sent, after all. Did I sound creepy? Did I sound arrogant? Why did I care so much?* "Where do you live?"

"On the outskirts of The Gathering," she said. As we reached the edge of the rooftop courtyard, she looked over at me. "It'll be much quicker if we fly."

I only trusted myself to nod. Were her cheeks glowing? I motioned for her to go ahead first since there was only room for one dragon to take off at a time. She was so graceful when she took off, I stared a second longer to lift off than was probably appropriate.

I took a couple steps and stretched my wings out, soaring out over the balcony and quickly catching up with Brixelle. I flew alongside her and found my gaze sliding continuously to her, taking in how her purple scales shone in the light and how the golden scales bounced light onto the purple ones, making her purple glow so much brighter.

"It's not much farther," she said. "Just over the rise there."

I followed her gaze over the hillside to the last farm at the edge of the forest, then forced my gaze to remain off Brixelle long enough to appreciate the open farmlands. They were wide and hilly, beautiful with their green grass and large livestock herds.

We landed in the open grassiness, away from the livestock herds. "What enchantments would you like?" I asked.

"One to protect our livestock, some border alarms, and if you could, a weather detector would be wonderful." She smiled, raising her eyebrows.

I laughed. "I can't say I've ever heard of a weather-detection enchantment, but the others I can do. Can you show me your borders?"

"Of course, Your Highness." She lowered her eyes, and I thought my heart might leap out of my chest as my mind filled only with how beautiful those eyelashes were.

I coughed to refocus my attention. She took off again then, and I only needed to leap up and fly to follow her. We circled the edges of her land once. Her property was larger than I had assumed. No wonder she needed help. This was a lot of land to watch all by yourself.

"Would you object if I set wards up in sections? That way if someone or something triggers one, you'll know which section to attend to instead of having to search the entire property?"

"Handsome *and* smart," she said as she smiled at me.

My heart raced as I wondered whether she'd actually said what I'd heard. I felt the heat rise to the surface of my scales and knew I must be glowing. Shaking it off, I focused instead on the task at hand. "Do you have specific sections you'd like me to divide the property into?"

Brixelle nodded. "Follow me?"

Anywhere, my mind answered. I shook my head to focus again. "Lead the way. I'll start when we hit that rise there."

She nodded before pulling ahead of me.

I turned my attention inward and drew my light out, focusing on willing the light to be brighter than my surroundings. Then I molded the beam of magic into an alert enchantment as we approached the rise. With half my mind concentrating on following Brixelle, and the other half on the enchantment, I stretched the beam of magic along the path we flew until we finished one section. Then we did another and another. Making sections out of the larger piece of land took more time, but it would be more effective.

When we were finally done, the sun was starting its descent. "Would … would you like to come in for a meal? I'm sure it's not quite up to palace standards, but we have quality sheep," she said.

She scratched the dirt with her claws as if she was nervous, and this warmed my insides. "That would be lovely," I said before following her back to her home. It was a basic stone house with perhaps three to four rooms, from what I could tell from the outside. Little purple and white flowers surrounded it, and I thought it looked both cozy and beautiful.

We landed and she opened the tall wooden door. "I'll just be a minute if you want to make yourself comfortable," she said as she tried to fold blankets and tuck them into chests.

"If you'll point me in the right direction, I'd like to visit your mother." Perhaps I could give Brixelle a moment alone to ease her anxiety.

Brixelle looked stunned at first, so I continued. "You mentioned she was sick, so I'd like to see if my magic can help at all."

She glowed as she nodded and pointed down a wide hallway. I nodded my thanks and strode down the hallway to an open door. Brixelle's mother, a light-purple dragon the color of lavender, lay on a low bed.

"Your Highness?" She sat up suddenly, trying to quickly tidy the bed around her as I walked in.

"Madam, I'm pleased to make your acquaintance. Your daughter, Brixelle, came to my family to request enchantments for your vast property. I was lucky enough to be given the opportunity to oblige."

"I wish she'd told me before sending you in! I'm not dressed to receive royalty!"

"That is of no import to me. I'm sure Brixelle would agree that you spend your energy healing instead."

"Such a flatterer. And so kind! Please, please sit, Your Highness."

I pulled a stool over from the edge of the room and sat down. "May I?" I gestured for her fore claw.

"Ohh, of course." She glowed, though dully, and gave me her hand.

"I know a little healing magic, and with your permission, I'd like to investigate your illness."

She nodded, her glow brightening for a moment. It made me smile.

I closed my eyes as I was a little tired from my previous exertions, then let my light flow through my claw to the older dragon's. I put up a protective barrier at my own claw but let the light flow to her body, checking her lungs and heart, and found that infection had invaded the old dragon's respiratory system. It looked much like sludge was stuck to her organs, and I gathered it together, moving it upward through her system. "I'd like for you to cough. Do you have a receptacle nearby?"

She grabbed a bucket she must have used previously from the floor beside her, and as I nudged the sludge upward, she began coughing. Soon, a lump of brown goo landed in the bucket. I sent my light through her claw again and checked her body once more for infection, scraping more off as I found it and bringing it up the same way.

She coughed a few more times, releasing more brown goo. Then I took the bucket from her and aimed a fierce white-hot flame at it. When I was done, the bucket was empty.

"Thank you, Your Highness. That was so kind of you!" The older dragon grabbed both my claws and kissed them.

"You will be tired, so I want you to rest tonight and tomorrow. Understand? Stay in bed for a whole night and day before you get up."

She nodded vigorously, and the door creaked open. Brixelle stood in the doorway with some soup for her mother.

"I believe the prince has cured me!" mother sung cheerily to daughter.

"Oh?" Brixelle turned to me.

"I found infection in her lungs and brought it up with magic. She should be much better now, but I've asked her to rest for another night and day before she gets out of bed."

"I'm grateful, Your Highness," Brixelle said.

"Now get him out of here so an old dragon can eat her supper in peace!" the lavender dragon said. I noticed a glint of mischief in her eye and was about to say something when she shooed us away.

Brixelle led me back toward the kitchen, where we shared a whole roasted sheep. I was exhausted but also excited to talk with Brixelle.

After we had eaten, I finished the enchantments. For them to be complete, I had to set up a warning system inside her home. "These will light up depending on which section has been disturbed." I pointed to some candles I'd set up and included in the enchantment.

Brixelle came to me and kneeled. "Thank you." She grasped my claws and kissed them.

"No, no." I drew her up to stand again. "It is my pleasure to help. If you need anything, please send for me personally."

"Then thank you doubly." Brixelle was shorter than me by about a head, so with a soft flap of her wings, she floated up and kissed my cheek.

I glowed so bright that I lit up the room around us. Brixelle smiled and glowed to match my own luminosity. Flustered, I mumbled my goodbyes and flew home, thinking as I did that the land looked a little brighter than it had when I'd arrived.

Click here to buy now, or visit: https://geni.us/Soxkendi

Manufactured by Amazon.ca
Bolton, ON

36296043R00206